DAVID BICKFORD – as Under Secretary of State and Legal Director to the British Intelligence Agencies, MI5 and MI6, David has spent his working life diving into the cold, murky seas of terrorism, espionage and organised crime. At the forefront of the battle against international terrorism he was among the first to predict its onslaught. David is recognised, both in the Agencies where he was given the CB for his work and in the business he now runs, for his ground breaking solutions to defeat the terrorists and international organised criminals who threaten us.

The Face of Tomorrow

DAVID BICKFORD

Pretzel Publishing

The Face of Tomorrow
Published by Pretzel Publishing
18, Old Compton Street, London W1D 4JL
website: www.35mmpretzel.com

Represented by Elspeth Cochrane at
Elspeth Cochrane Personal Management

First published 2004
Copyright © David Bickford 2004
Ionism methods and processes patent pending

ISBN 0 9546990 0 9

Designed by Mercari and Typeset by SetSystems

To my brilliant wife Cary
with all my love for
everything she has done to make this possible

CHAPTER ONE

Abu Hamid scratched his left ear. He always did when he was puzzled. His training officer had told him it was a giveaway, but, however hard he tried, he couldn't stop his hand automatically straying to his ear when something didn't seem right.

His eyes switched to the harbour below him, indistinct in the starless night. The boat was still nosing its way in, leaving no wake, just a darker oblong in a dark sea.

He didn't know why he was puzzled by the boat. There was something about it. It wasn't the shape, although it was quite large. It could have been the speed or, rather, the lack of it. Then it struck him. There were no lights. Even though he was looking down at the port of Ireon from a steep angle, he would have seen the navigation lights if they had been lit.

Traffickers, he thought, nothing to do with him, anyway he was on holiday. Interesting to see how they operated, though. The scrubby hillside was littered with rocks, grey against the black bushes. He settled on one, shivering a little as the sweat from his climb dried in the cold air.

He wasn't even operational at the moment. He had come to the Greek island of Samos for some recreation after eight months in south east Turkey infiltrating the PKK, the terrorists fighting for the freedom of the Kurds and a homeland to be carved out of southern Turkey. He wiped his brow. He needed a rest from Kurdish terrorists and their constant bickering. He sometimes thought there was more danger of being caught out in the wrong PKK political camp than being caught as a spy, or, as his masters the G8 International Security Agency preferred to call him, a G8 agent. Certainly G8 looked after him a lot better than most of the PKK cell leaders he'd come across.

Without warning, the nose of the boat lifted. Abu Hamid watched intently as a huge wash surged from the stern, shoving the dark shape in a tight turn towards a bulky caique fishing smack lolling at anchor a hundred meters away.

A ripple of light outstripped the staccato noise of an Uzi sub machine gun. Others joined in, ripping up the silence, spraying the water around the caique, before being drowned out by the smashing, splintering noise of the boat mounting and splitting the caique in two as it raced through it.

Abu Hamid was on his feet, his hands clamped around his eyes, straining to focus on the boat as it streamed away, the prow high, the wake phosphorescent in its speed. Briefly, a searchlight stabbed out from its stern, roving over the wreckage of the caique. Just the tips of the high bow and cabin left now, before they too plunged to the seabed.

Then, as if in a final insult, the beam rested on the Turkish flag unfurling from the sternpost of the boat as it sheered away into the night.

CHAPTER TWO

John Hammond, Director General of the G8 International Security Agency, and Abu Hamid's ultimate boss, studied Hamid's message on the giant plasma screen in the G8 operations centre in Basingstoke, England.

Although he was the Director General, at thirtyfive Hammond was restlessly energetic and liked to be seen in the operations centre. His pale blue eyes flicking onto the huge screens ranged along the walls of the vast warehouse, which served as G8 Headquarters, and his sandy hair warning the operatives at their work desks of his approach with a question or word of encouragement.

He turned to the work desk behind him.

'Julia, this report from Abu Hamid about the Turkish attack on this Greek caique, he's not operational, is he?'

Julia Simmonds pushed a strand of chestnut hair away from her brown eyes and stood up. Hammond caught a faint drift of Picasso, the perfume she always wore.

'Hamid is holidaying on Samos at the moment. But he's the best agent we've got in the PKK so his report will be accurate.'

Hammond thought for a moment. Julia was his deputy, twentyeight and promoted personally by him so he had no concerns about her judgment. But if the message was genuine and accurate, it spelled trouble.

Turkey had given up trying to control the ten million Kurds who were pushing for an independent homeland in the south of the country. Instead the Turkish Government were pushing as many Kurds as they could out of Turkey into Greece. Along with the Kurds went other refugees from the Middle East and North Africa who had infiltrated through the porous borders into southern Turkey.

Relations between Greece and Turkey were a tinderbox as the Greeks rocked under the strain of trying in vain to stop the migration, with sealed borders, police, troops and the blunted, mind numbingly slow process of diplomacy.

Hamid's message was one of thousands of pieces of information that the G8 Agency's computers received, analysed and distributed every day. Information about every aspect of international terrorism and organised crime that the G8 Agency had been set up to fight and, like every other piece of information, this message now appeared on similar plasma screens in other G8 Agency Centres in Moscow, Washington and Tokyo.

'Better get Lev and Walt on line.'

Julia was used to Hammond's casual references to the Directors of the Moscow and Washington G8 Centres. 'Right. But here's Keithley for his meeting.'

Hammond followed her glance. A short, upright man walked briskly towards him behind a security guard, winding his way past the groups of operatives talking or bent over their computers at the workstations in the huge floor area of the warehouse. He was dressed in the full uniform of the Commissioner of the London Metropolitan Police.

'Hello, Lionel,' Hammond called. 'Come at the wrong time, as usual.'

Lionel Keithley smiled, his lean face crinkling at the edges. He'd known Hammond since the days they had been at Manchester University. Keithley had gone into the police and Hammond had specialised in information tracking, linking up with Michael Harris, the then Director of a tyre distribution firm who had later skated his way across the political ice rink to become Prime Minister. It was he who had appointed Hammond to his present job.

Keithley's smile turned into a laugh.

'Computers down, are they?'

Hammond laughed with him.

'For that you'll get the full tour, and like it,' he said. 'Come with me.'

Keithley wasn't prepared for what he saw. Although it had been set up a year ago in 2006, only a handful of people knew the extent of G8 work let alone about the targets G8 attacked. Even fewer were involved as G8 mounted their operations through Europe, America, Russia and the Far East, using massive computers to direct the activities of the G8 teams of operatives against the world's most threatening international terrorists and organised crime enterprises. Fighting against the destruction of terrorism and the degradation of narcotics trafficking, fraud, extortion, prostitution, alien smuggling, moneylaundering.

Keithley saw the huge plasma screens where the G8 Agency computers recorded the activities of the G8 targets as they crossed boundaries, as they moved their arms or drugs, or prostitutes, or money telegraphed from finance centre to finance centre across the world. He saw the computers coldly analysing the activities of both the innocent and the guilty, and the iciness of Hammond's Team Leaders as they planned their counter moves.

Shaken, he emerged into Hammond's office. 'We could never get away with half of that in the Met.' He gratefully accepted a glass of scotch.

Hammond sat down, leaving Keithley standing. 'Which is why the G8 Agency was set up. Fighting international crime and terrorism is a war. Policemen are trained for peace.'

Keithley slowly sipped his scotch, waved his hand in the direction of the operations room.

'No rules, then?'

It was always the same with policemen, Hammond thought. They always saw extremes; found it difficult to operate in the middle. It was their training. He had always admired the police. His father had been a policeman, until he had been killed one night by an armed robber. But his father had been the same. Things were either right or wrong, blurring at the edges was forbidden, no grey areas. An attitude that was perfect for dealing with street crime, theft and thuggery. But out there, in the wilderness of organised crime, among the deviousness and cunning of the scum of every race imaginable, it was different.

The scum were often lawyers, accountants, businessmen, bankers. Sophisticated, thinkers, planners with access to more money in their organisations than many member states of the United Nations. These people hid wrong under layers of right. And to get at wrong, G8 had to strip away the layers of right at a cost to right that was only bearable when the extent of the wrong was finally exposed. Hammond looked at Keithley. He wouldn't understand.

'Yes, there are rules. But . . .'

Julia's voice came through the desk computer.

'Lev and Walt are on line.'

Hammond stood up.

'Come and meet Lev and Walt. Perhaps they'll answer your question.'

'Are they here?'

'See for yourself.' Hammond turned and took Keithley down to the warehouse floor to the screen opposite Julia's workstation. Facing them on the screen were two men. A wiry African American and, almost hidden in a haze of smoke, a heavy set, greying man in the act of lighting one cigarette from another.

'Walt Sable, Lev Leviatski, meet Lionel Keithley, Metropolitan Police Commissioner.

Leviatski blew out a cloud of smoke. 'Good Morning, Commissioner.'

Walt laughed. 'Don't take no notice of him, Lionel. He's meaner than a bear in a hornets' nest today.'

Keithley smiled. 'He'd smoke them out quickly enough, I think.'

They all laughed.

'I see you have a friend, John,' Leviatski poked a finger towards Hammond, 'keep him.'

Hammond leaned forward. 'Have you seen Abu Hamid's news of this Turkish attack on Samos?'

'Not until just now.' Walt narrowed his eyes. 'How can we be sure it was the Turks? It was just a Greek caique sunk, wasn't it?'

'Hamid saw it all. Deliberate shooting and ramming by a boat flying the Turkish flag. The Turks showed it deliberately.' Lev tapped his desk to emphasise the point.

Walt looked thoughtful. 'Just some Turkish provocation, they've always claimed Samos. Why's it so important this time, Lev?'

'Because the caique was a Greek electronic surveillance vessel. It belonged to Greek Intelligence.'

'Targeted deliberately, then.' Hammond looked at Lev.

'Yes.' Lev brushed some ash off his desktop.

Walt jerked up his head. 'Could it have been a PKK attack?'

Lev shook his head. 'Abu was precise. It was a Turkish boat. Must have been Turkish Navy.'

'But it was at night. He was on holiday. He couldn't have seen much, might have been mistaken.'

Julia shook her head. 'The Turks shone a searchlight on the flag. Anyway Hamid is our best agent in the PKK. And if it was PKK he'd have heard something, the PKK are only carrying out sporadic bombings at the moment. An attack like this doesn't fit the pattern.'

Hammond broke the silence. 'I agree. It was the Turks and that spells trouble. The Greeks are wild that Turkey does nothing to stop the Kurdish migrants pouring across their border into Greece. The Turks claim that they could control their border if the Greeks gave them the islands near their coastline. We all know that's nonsense, it's just the Turks continuing their political fight to get more territory. What's more worrying is the Turks simply pushing the Kurds over the border to get rid of them. The Greek electronic surveillance was there to try and stop that.'

Walt shifted slightly in his chair. 'You think the Greeks will retaliate?'

Hammond and Lev nodded simultaneously. Walt grimaced.

'Damn Europeans. You're so . . . so . . . damn tribal.'

Hammond smiled.

'It's why we have our American and Russian friends to keep us in order. Can you,' he turned to Lev, 'and you Lev, speak to your Presidents. Get some pressure on the Greeks not to use force. Promise them another Draft Resolution in the UN. I'll speak to the Prime Minister, try and get something more going in Europe. We've got to break this deadlock, there's a powder keg out there.'

Lev drew in a breath, coughing as he caught the smoke from his cigarette end.

'Can you get Abu Hamid back on the case?'

Hammond nodded. 'Julia will fix that. And we'll get G8SUR to move off the PKK and concentrate on the Greek Turkey border.'

'Is that wise?' coughed Lev.

Hammond rubbed his forehead.

'We haven't the resources to have satellite surveillance on both the PKK and the border. The border's more important.'

'I agree,' said Walt. 'The PKK's been very quiet, the leadership's old, pretty ineffective.'

'Right,' said Hammond. 'Julia, will you re-correlate G8SUR as soon as possible.'

Julia nodded, switched off the plasma screen and started typing more commands into her computer.

Keithley watched her.

'Walt's right, you know. We are bloody tribal. Turf is all we care about.'

Hammond looked at Keithley. If he was talking about turf it meant G8 had something or someone Keithley wanted. Hammond studied him for a moment.

'Whatever it is you want, it had better be something you can actually use.'

Hammond's directness took Keithley by surprise. He answered without thinking.

'What I want is access to G8SUR.'

'What for?'

It wasn't the flat rejection Keithley had expected, but the answer wasn't promising. G8SUR was the G8 Satellite Surveillance, targeted on all G8 targets. The satellite tracked all their movements. The unique electrical impulses of their bodies were identified by the satellite and followed, wherever they were. The impulses could be detected in the dark, through cloud cover, in buildings, up to forty feet underground.

'Policemen are spending over sixty percent of their working days dealing with paperwork. Seventy percent of cases prosecuted with police evidence are lost, usually through that paperwork being faulty. I want to stop that.' Keithley paused.

Hammond said nothing.

Keithley frowned. 'I believe G8SUR could be modified to follow each policeman on the beat, interrogating suspects, in charge of police cells, at all times.' He drove on, knowing if he stopped he'd lost the initiative. 'The digital imaging would substitute for paperwork, it would be cast iron evidence. We can use G8SUR evidence in Court, no smart arsed defence could get round it. We could turn the percentages around overnight.'

Hammond leaned on the back of Julia's chair. 'I agree.'

Keithley was suspicious. G8SUR belonged to G8 and Hammond should be fighting to keep it. After all, turf was turf. Keithley decided to test the water: he didn't want to expose all his cards if, in the end, Hammond was going to say no.

'You haven't mentioned ownership, confidentiality,' he said cautiously.

Hammond stretched his back. 'There isn't any confidentiality. G8SUR has been exposed publicly by us in dozens of trials. The Courts have agreed to protect the technology from exposure, which is all we want.' He paused. 'As to ownership, we own it.'

It was as Keithley expected, Hammond was going to keep the damn thing. He leaned forward.

'The police will pay their way.'

'Plus twenty five percent for research and development?'

Keithley half closed his eyes. Hammond's name wasn't spoken in the government corridors of Whitehall, it was whispered. Whispers Keithley had heard. Hammond the strategist, who used his G8 super computers to sift and analyse information, who was brilliant, but, above all, who was ruthless. Hammond the friend and adviser of the Prime Minister. Twenty five percent of research and development was way over Keithley's budget and Hammond knew it. Keithley was sure now that Hammond would fight not to give him G8SUR.

'Fifteen percent,' he said desperately.

'Done.'

Keithley could hardly believe it. 'You mean you'll let me have it for that?'

Hammond touched Julia's shoulder. 'You hear that, Julia?'

Julia turned in her seat to look at Keithley, her brown eyes amused.

'You could have had it for free.'

Keithley swung around to Hammond.

'Free? What d'you mean free?'

Hammond nodded to Julia.

Her firm mouth broadened to a smile. 'You insisted we're tribal, should protect our turf.' She looked at Hammond. 'John never said so.'

'Bastard,' Keithley said, feelingly.

CHAPTER THREE

Melik Oren was excited. He had worked six months in the Camberwell bus depot and today was his last day. It was demeaning work cleaning the inside of Number 11 double decker buses. Dirty, low paid, long hours, cold and not only in the winter months. He shivered now in the cold June night air as he removed the seat from the front near side bench on the lower deck of the bus. He'd chosen to work the night shift. Less people around, easier to shift the bulky packages onto the bus.

He carefully unwrapped one. It resembled a cone, with a small cylinder at the base. He inched it under the seat. Took out a manual drill and painstakingly drilled the metal seat frame. Slowly, so slowly. The noise confined to the area he worked in. He was sweating now. Even though he had practised this a hundred times back in Diyarbakir in southern Turkey.

His mind drifted back. Diyarbakir had been idyllic. He had been working for the PKK as a mechanic with other PKK members, minding the cars and trucks, the bombers and close quarter killers used in their work. Celik, the PKK Leader, had been trying to reach a political settlement with the Turks, hoping to end the forced migration of the Kurds, through an endless series of meetings with the Turkish Government in Ankara. Work had been slack, only a couple of bombings or assassinations a month. Just enough, as Celik said, to keep the Turks at the negotiating table. So leave was easy to come by. Melik's short cropped black hair and high boned cheeks under lazy blue eyes had found plenty of girls. Particularly Tansu.

What had attracted him was her disinterest. She wasn't pretty, far from it, but she was often to be found in the cafes and bars around the harbour front. Sitting alone at the tables in front of the bright, wash painted buildings. He would sidle up to her. Would she like a drink? Some other time. Would she like to go fishing? Not today. Would she like a drive in the hills to Kazani? She didn't have all day. She became an obsession and he pursued her, nursing his ego through every rejection until, three weeks later, she'd asked him to go to church with her. He hadn't been in a church since his christening, but he went with all the ardour of a convert. She was dressed in white, her veil splashing snow on her long blue hair and he'd caught his breath as he sat down next to her. But she'd moved away, so he couldn't touch her. After the service, she'd asked him to tea at her home and smiled when he'd agreed.

When he'd arrived, he hadn't expected her mother to open the door or the gruff request to come in, or the four men who waited for him in the hall. Sweat had burst out of him.

'I didn't touch her. I swear. Please. I didn't.'

'Not much guts, have you,' the woman said. The men just watched him. He was shaking now, unable to talk.

*

They had taken him into another room and told him that they were a special PKK unit. They'd said the Kurds had to defend themselves and act before the Turks could mobilise and annihilate them. He had skills which were going to be needed and he had been chosen to help them. But it was to be done in secret, no one else was to know.

It was all so fast. The next day he was put to work in a hut in another part of Diyarbakir, constructing the cone shaped devices and practising placing them under the seats of a British double decker bus.

Two months later, Tansu came to see him. She gave him documents which identified him as a Turk who came from the Kurdish area of Diyarbakir, and told him to enter England as a refugee and take a job as a bus cleaner on the Number 11 buses in Camberwell, London. As he moved to kiss her she laughed and pushed him away. 'Wait until you come back,' she said.

*

That had been six months ago. Six months of boredom, filthy apartments and dull girls in Camberwell, England. He'd never seen

Tansu again. But what kept him going was the thought that when he returned to Turkey she would be there.

He turned to the third seat. Two more charges to go and he'd be finished. He'd already drilled the holes in the floor for the electric leads.

'Bloody 'ell, you don't need to take the bleedin' seat covers off.' A shadow moved along the aisle. 'You always do that?'

Oren jumped, cursing himself, his mind on Tansu and not the bloody foreman. He might have guessed that bastard would be snooping around. He was a Union man, constantly on the lookout for breaches of the regulations and a backhander for not reporting them. Oren knew he must agree, always agree, whatever he said.

'You no like this? I change it. Sorry.' He emphasised his accent.

'Well, it shows up the others, don't it? All the same, you bleedin' foreigners. Never stick to Union rules.' The Union man moved forward towards the seat, lifting his bald head to get a better view.

Oren started to sweat.

'Rules?' he mumbled.

'Yeah, you Turkish ape. Something you wouldn't know anything about.' The Union man started to push his way past him then stopped. 'What's this, then?' He patted Oren's pocket. Oren felt his mouth go dry.

'No answers, eh? I'll bloody see for myself then.'

He thrust his hand into Oren's pocket, took something out and peered at it. 'Fuck me, fuckin' brandy.'

He grasped Oren's chin and turned it towards him. 'So do I charge you or do I drink it?'

'Drink it,' Oren choked out.

'Fuckin right, you little Turkish shit.' He turned and lurched out of the bus, throwing a finger in the air as he went.

Oren tried to control his shaking hands. It took another half hour to finish his work. Finally he wrapped up the plastic covering, shoved it in his pocket and stepped off the bus.

'Finished?'

Oren whirled around. Esen came out of the shadows. Oren gulped. 'Fuck, Esen, where the hell did you come from?'

Esen ignored him. 'Electric leads into the cab? Detonator set?'

'Yes.' Oren kept his answer clipped. He didn't like Esen. He was a peasant from Artvin on the border with Georgia. They were untrustworthy bastards, never knew where their loyalties lay. Still, he was his partner, the bus driver, the guy who'd detonate the explosives. He had to get on with him.

Esen turned his mouth down. 'Are the leads hidden? I don't like the electric leads.'

'Well, you'll have to. I told you before, we can't use impulse detonation. Too much risk of interference down Whitehall.'

Esen put his finger to his lips. Oren found he was shouting. They were next to the automatic washing machine, the brushes flailing against the sides of one of the red buses. He nodded his head.

It was his last meaningful gesture. He felt himself swept off his feet. Hit by an ice cold wave of water. Blinded by spray. Coughing. Choking. Unable to cry out. Thrashing with his feet and hands. He couldn't wrench out of the giant hold gripping him. He felt the whip of plastic line. Gagged on another spume of water. Tried to scream as his arms became trapped in the gearing. Then mercifully crashed into unconsciousness as inexorably his body mashed through the mechanism.

Esen turned away, the first part of his job finished. He wasn't sorry: Oren was a moaner, always on about the cold and some bloody girl back home. He looked at his watch, three hours to go. Time for a shower and shave, bacon and eggs for breakfast. He'd grown quite fond of that in England over the last three months. He slipped out of the side door, as he heard the first shouts from the washing machine operator.

CHAPTER FOUR

She danced down the stairs.

'Mama, where are my shoes? My yellow shoes?'

She was seven years old and proud of her English. Her huge brown eyes and pageboy black hair were typically Turkish. And she was proud of that, too.

Ilke turned from the hallway mirror to glance up the stairs. Her diminutive daughter stood there. In her yellow dress. One hand hitching up her tights, which were a little too long.

'Don't do that, Leila. What would Mr Harris say if he saw you do that?'

The casual reference to the British Prime Minister struck no chord with Leila.

'He would be more shocked if they fell down,' she giggled.

'Leila.' Ilke tried to sound severe, but the effort dissolved into a gurgle of laughter, a mirror image of her daughter. She tried to look serious.

'We'll be late and Daddy will be furious. He specially arranged for you to meet the Prime Minister's daughter.' She used the word formally to impress the importance of the occasion. 'Now where are those shoes?' She climbed the wide, curling staircase. Took Leila's hand when they reached the broad landing.

'What will Daddy do when I'm with Susan?'

'He and the Prime Minister will talk business. Ambassadors do that, you know. It's not all parties and fun.' She added the last sentence for effect. They had been in London three years now, with all the trappings, favours and sycophancy that went with an Ambassadorship in a major city. That and the pleasure of a tight knit happy Turkish community had created a curious fantasy world. Ilke had her husband to pour the cold water of reality on

her existence when it became too comfortable. But it was difficult
to do that to Leila. Partly because she was very young, partly
because she skipped her way through life. And to take away that
happiness would be cruel. The brown eyes looked up at her.

'What does Turkish agg ... aggression on the Samos border
mean?'

Ilke was startled. 'Where did you hear that?' she replied in
Turkish.

'English, Mama. You said we must always speak English during
the day. I heard it on the radio just now. What does it mean?'

Ilke knew very well what it meant. Ever since Greece had joined
the EU they had grown economically stronger. Turkey had stayed
out. Squabbling among the Turkish political parties making conditions for entry into the EU impossible. The continual fight with
the Kurdish separatists and the terrorist PKK had drained the
country financially. Turkey was in a mess. And the only answer
was to remove as many Kurds as possible. The Greeks had done
nothing but complain and make trouble. Ilke's husband had told
her that yesterday's skirmish around the Greek island of Samos
had been Greek inspired. The Turks had gone nowhere near the
island. But no one had believed the Turks when they said so,
preferring to rely on history to point to the Turkish invaders of the
previous centuries.

Her husband had always said that relying on history was like
relying on astrology. It was a philosophy that had won him honours
at his university, the Turkish Ambassadorship to London at the age
of thirty four and the offer of the leadership of the Democratic Left
Party when he returned to Ankara in four months' time.

Today he would see Michael Harris, the British Prime Minister,
to try and persuade him that the Turks had no designs on Greek
territory, that all the intelligence pointed to the Greeks creating the
incident on Samos themselves. He had told her last night, in their
bed, that he had little hope of persuading Harris. All Harris was
interested in was supporting the Greeks and he'd asked that the
meeting be held in secret to downplay its importance. And the
press would be there to report a merely social occasion. The
Ambassador's wife and her daughter meeting the Prime Minister
and his family for the first time.

Ilke looked at her daughter. Remembered her husband's dejection as he left for work that morning. Remembered the caress he'd given Leila as he walked out of the door.

'Look, darling. There are the shoes, under your bed. Aren't they pretty.'

CHAPTER FIVE

The Prime Minister glanced at his watch.

'The Turkish Ambassador'll be here in fifteen minutes.' He glared at the woman in front of him. 'And I've got nothing to tell him.'

Mary Lifton, Head of South East Europe Department, British Foreign Office, shifted in her chair. Turkey had flagrantly sent a gunboat to the Greek island of Samos to sink a Greek surveillance vessel killing most of its crew. The Prime Minister knew damn well what to tell the Turkish Ambassador. Get off Greece's bloody patch.

She sighed inwardly. 'You might tell him that our sources confirm an attack by Turkey on Greek soil. And that hostilities by Turkey should cease.'

The PM smoothed a hand across his desk, his eyes following it. 'And the PKK?'

'PKK?'

His hand slapped the desk.

'Yes. The damn PKK. The Kurdish terrorists.'

'I know who they are, Prime Minister,' she said, coldly.

'Well, if you know who they are, why aren't you thinking of them and the fact that it might have been them.' He snapped.

She was used to nervous ministers, used to the job of watching their backs, dragging them away from pet issues, pet theories. Even the Prime Minister.

'They're not relevant, Prime Minister.' She held up her hand as he started to speak. 'I know they're Muslims. But they're not into the Muslim extremist thing. They're only interested in having a Kurdish homeland for themselves. Fighting the Turkish Government to give them southern Turkey and the ten million Kurds in

Turkey to live there. To create Kurdistan. They have no interest in attacking Greece.'

'You can't be sure of that. They're Muslims. And they're trying to get the Turkish Government by the balls.' He looked at her with raised eyebrows. The comment was sexist and he knew she was an equality warrior. 'Sorry. I mean they're on the ropes.' He started again. 'Can't contain them.'

She smiled patiently. 'That's the Turkish Government's problem. We've given them support to deal with the PKK terrorist threat.'

'Half an SAS squadron.'

'It's symbolic. We can't police the world.'

The Prime Minister picked up his pen. 'Have you ever thought of what would happen if the PKK did become the Muslim extremist thing, as you put it?'

She pursed her lips. 'Ever since Al Quaida and Saddam Hussein in 2003, our foreign policy has been dominated by a fear of the extreme Muslims. It's as if we're back in the Crusades. Only a few Muslims are extremist. The Muslims are not going to swamp us. I can't stress that enough. The Turks are kicking out some Kurds, for sure, but they're going to Germany and France. They're not our problem. And the PKK are under control. You don't have to appease the Turkish Ambassador. It's the Greeks we need to protect. If the Turks backlash into them, we'll spend years picking up the pieces.' She snapped her briefcase shut.

The PM dropped the pen. 'I need some room for manoeuvre.'

She smiled. Room for manoeuvre meant she'd won. Room for manoeuvre was what her job was all about.

'OK. Indicate, incursion, territorial waters and consider.'

The PM picked up his pen again.

'I'm sorry. What?'

'Amend what you're going to say to him to "Sources indicate an incursion by Turkey into Greek territorial waters. Perhaps Turkey should consider their position". The word "indicate" is loose, it allows for the possibility of mistake. An incursion could mean anything from a military aircraft straying to a drunk soldier losing his way. Letting them consider their position means they needn't do anything. But, at least, you've made your point.'

'Dictate that to me. Slowly.'

CHAPTER SIX

Esen drove the bus to his own timetable. The destination indicators on the Number 11 signalled that it was out of service. The conductor had been only too pleased to hop off when Esen had made the interior lights fail. Esen had told him to do some shopping or see a film before going back to the depot. He'd see to it the bus took a couple of hours to get back.

Traffic was heavy but Esen had plenty of time. It gave him a certain satisfaction to ignore the frantic waving of the bus queues, as he slowly drove past them until he spotted the Ambassador's limousine in Victoria Street. Where his PKK Intelligence controller told him it would be.

Traffic was backed up past Scotland Yard as usual. A haze of blue exhaust fumes slightly obscuring the Houses of Parliament and Big Ben in the June sunshine. He took time to glance around the pavements and linger on the girl tourists, scantily clothed in the hot weather. Every now and again he smiled at one. He knew he shouldn't as they might recognise him later but it was worth the risk when one or other of them smiled back.

The Ambassador's limousine crawled into Parliament Square and waited for the turn into Whitehall, opposite the Underground station, where he would run afterwards.

It was there that he caught his first glimpse inside the limousine of the bastard Turkish Ambassador. He leaned forward for a better look. Glimpsed the yellow dress. Leant lower. Saw the black pageboy hair. The brown eyes. The smile as she waved a small hand to him.

He jerked back. Ice cold down his spine. They hadn't told him about a girl. He couldn't kill a little girl. He edged the bus forward. Caught sight of Ilke. The mother. His heart was thumping.

Tearing into his throat. They hadn't told him this. They hadn't told him.

The lights went orange then green. The car inched forward. The girl was leaning over the back seat now. Waving. Laughing. The yellow dress moving this way and that. Esen took his foot off the accelerator. He couldn't do this, he couldn't kill her.

Suddenly a man bent over her. Looked back at Esen. Then deliberately turned her away. The bastard Ambassador. The bastard Turk.

Esen slammed his foot on the accelerator. Took the bus alongside. Thrust his hand under the dashboard. Pressed the switch.

The limousine took the full force of four charges. Lifting. Blazing. Spraying metal. Smashing. Heaped against the Foreign Office wall.

The front of the bus joined it. Torn away from the chassis by the blast of a fifth charge from under the driver's seat.

A yellow shoe on the pavement the only colour in the chaos of black.

CHAPTER SEVEN

The line of plumes swayed steadily down the aisle of Westminster Abbey. Beneath them, the breastplated Guard to the Members of the Honourable Order of the Bath, marched steadily towards the Chapel of King Henry the Seventh beyond the High Altar. Behind them, scarlet robed, walked the Members themselves, just as other Members had done, tall, proud, through centuries of strife, war and a few moments of peace.

John Hammond looked at the man he escorted. The startling success Lionel Keithley had achieved came rarely. Rarely enough to be made Commissioner of the Metropolitan Police at the age of thirty seven and to be made a Knight.

The procession moved slowly forward, past the lines of families and friends, past the Guards, brilliant in their scarlet uniforms. The organ majestic with Bach. Tall candles lit the Chancel steps, the Altar above and the magnificent banners which honoured the Knights and drew the Members' gaze as they moved towards the Chapel.

Keithley caught Hammond's eye.

'The lads at Scotland Yard'll be splitting their sides now,' he growled, hitching his scarlet cloak to climb the steps. 'Miserable bastards,' he added with a grin that ignored the sanctity of the place he was in.

Hammond caught the humour. Knew it was what pulled Keithley through fifteen years in the police and the political trench warfare of Whitehall. The choir started to sing Elgar's Spirit of England. A lone tenor joining them. Almost as if to show the isolation of leadership.

'You've only yourself to blame for that.'

Keithley caught his mood. 'You know one of my ancestors was

in the First Crusade in 1098.' He waved a hand towards the tomb of a medieval knight, carved in marble, protected by the pillared walls and vaulted ceiling of the Abbey. 'This place was being built then, and it saw my ancestors, Crusaders, walk down this aisle. Just as we are today.'

Ahead of them, Hammond glimpsed a plume wavering as a Guard trod unwarily in a crack in the aisle paving. He held his breath. But the Companion next to the Guard held his arm. And the plume settled into its steady sway.

'It may be a whim,' continued Keithley, 'but we're all Crusaders here, in a way. Fighting for right.'

'That's a bit deep for me,' smiled Hammond, 'I'll stick to G8, it's . . .'

The flat sharp report of the detonation cracked into the Abbey through the noise of the organ. Keithley gripped Hammond's arm.

'What the hell was that?'

'Bomb,' Hammond was short. 'I'll have to leave you to it. Sorry.'

Hammond strode down the steps and swiftly along the side aisle, past the tombs and over the paved tablets celebrating the pride of the nation. Past the lines of friends and family waiting in the nave, murmuring, tense, uncertain, unwilling to be the first to leave, to see what was happening, or to get away. The organist started to play a Bach Toccata.

Hammond stopped at the end of a line of chairs and leaned forward to a large, red faced man sitting next to a prettily dressed, pregnant girl in a short blue linen dress and hat.

'Stay here, Jack. The procession will return in a minute.'

Jack put a hand on the girl's knee. 'What's happened? I'm worried about Sue. The baby jumped all over the place with that noise.'

Hammond smiled at her. 'It's OK. You're safe here.'

Sue looked up at him. In that moment he looked older than his thirty six years. She'd caught the inflection in his voice. Usually charming and full of humour, it was now tense with a sense of urgency. She was worried for him. She'd known him since meeting Jack at university in London. Had heard all the stories of their time together since school in Midhurst, the footballing, their gap year hitchhiking to the Caspian Sea.

'I'll be fine,' she smiled, 'just don't forget you're going to be a godfather.'

But he'd gone.

*

The smell hit him as soon as he walked out of the Abbey side door. The stinging, smarting stink of burnt metal and rubber. Parliament Square was littered with fire engines and ambulances, their lights floating through the haze of black smoke, drifting down Victoria Street. Blown by the wind off the Thames. Some police were there, trying to clear the crowd of jostling, gawping people. Tourists holding their cameras high, hopeful of a picture of carnage. Newsmen, struggling to get to the scene, their television cameras working in the bright, handheld lights.

Hammond stopped as his mobile buzzed urgently. It was from Julia. A curt text message to meet her at the Prime Minister's office immediately.

Hammond turned his mind to the explosion. There hadn't been a bomb in London since the last of the Al Quaida suicide attacks in 2005, which had promoted the formation of the G8 Agency. The PM would think G8 had dropped its guard, but there was no intelligence, not even a rumour, to predict this attack. And Julia would have known if there had been. She was brilliant, quick, decisive and bright enough to frighten an Oxford don, not that that was so difficult these days.

'Sorry, Sir, no entry, Whitehall is closed.' The policeman blocked his way.

Hammond pulled out his ID card. No need to let the curious onlookers see an official pass. ID cards had all the information this police officer would need and since everyone had ID cards there was nothing unusual in the gesture. When the officer let him through there would be no indication of the reason either. He could be anyone from a cook to a Permanent Secretary.

The policeman took out his pocket computer and inserted the card. Checked the picture on the screen with Hammond's face. Took out a small plastic packet, removed a cotton wool pad and wiped the screen. The smell of alcohol seeped through the stench of the explosion.

'Taken to drink, Officer?' Hammond smiled, using the time honoured phrase which had appeared in an Evening Standard cartoon when the DNA procedure was first introduced.

'Just lick your finger and press it here, Sir.' The policeman stolidly offered him the screen. An old hand. As unperturbed by the jibe as he was by the debris and fumes surrounding him.

Hammond watched as the officer checked the DNA sample and background data on the screen. Not by a fraction did the officer's face change as he realised who he was dealing with. He slowly wiped the screen again, closed the computer, put it in his pocket, handed Hammond his card and stood to one side.

'Very well, Sir.'

Hammond skirted round the front of the Foreign Office. What remained of a double decker bus stood there. The lower front nearside half didn't exist, nor did the cab and front upper deck over it. Something else, some twisted, scattered, blackened metal lay against the Foreign Office wall. Smoke still plumed from what had been tyres. Among the wreckage half a dozen personnel in white suits were already shifting slowly, bending, putting items into plastic bags, stretching, adjusting their face masks and goggles. Opposite them stood the stone mass of the Cenotaph. Another figure in white. Yet again a silent witness to death.

The policeman waved Hammond through the cordon in Downing Street, watching after him as the door opened up to Number 10. He was ushered into the silent front hall, with its staircase to the upper floors. The walls papered in pale yellow Osborne and Little wallpaper, and hung with oil paintings of Prime Ministers over four centuries. Silent also, reassuring in their solemn, untroubled gaze.

Julia was waiting in the anteroom. Equally solemn and untroubled, her slim body moved easily out of the chair, her brown eyes seeking his. She started briefing him immediately.

'So far, we understand that a Number 11 bus was the delivery vehicle. Probably three or four explosive charges under the front nearside lower seats. Directed outwards. The target was the Turkish Ambassador,' she paused, 'the meeting between him and the Prime Minister had been well publicised beforehand as a social event. Victims were the Ambassador, his wife and daughter, and their driver.'

'Wife and daughter?' Hammond cut in. 'Bit unusual, visiting during the day.'

'Yes. That was published too.' Julia frowned. 'So it could be that the targeting was deliberate. The wife and daughter, I mean. To maximise the effect.'

Hammond sat down. 'Why was the front of the bus demolished?'

'Excuse me, Mr Hammond, would you like some coffee?' The PM's Assistant Private Secretary spoke quietly. His accent was Manchester, the same as the PM. Here to find out what he could and report to the PM before the meeting, Hammond thought. No APS would offer to get coffee unless there was something to gain.

'No, thanks.' Hammond gestured to Julia. 'Julia's OK as well.' He paused, looking meaningfully at the door.

The APS hesitated, looked at Julia. Deliberately, she crossed her arms, staring straight at him. Discomfort spread across his face as he almost ran for the door.

Hammond closed it and turned to Julia. 'He'll learn. Next time he won't fall for that trick. You'll have to think of something else.'

She smiled, smoothed her dress. 'I will. About the front of the bus. It's almost certain that a fourth or fifth detonation killed the driver.'

'Own goal?'

'Not necessarily. It doesn't appear to be a blowback from the main charges. It appears to have been a charge placed under his seat.'

Hammond studied the picture of Gordon of Khartoum, hanging over the empty stone fireplace, dying in a desperate attempt to save Sudan from tyranny. He thought of the Whirling Dervishes, throwing themselves at the British troops, overwhelming them in a series of hysterical, maniacal charges, stopping only when dead or when the last English soldier had been flayed alive.

'Suicide bombing?'

She moved towards the picture, thoughtfully holding the back of her short hair in one hand. 'I know what you mean.' She paused.

'There was an accident early this morning at the Number 11 bus Clerkenwell Depot.'

Hammond waited. Julia wouldn't have mentioned it if she hadn't thought it relevant. The trainers always hammered home that point. Time spent on irrelevancies is time given to the enemy. Irrelevancies were meant for the G8 computers. They could analyse them and spit them out in milliseconds.

'A man got caught in the bus automatic cleaning mechanism. Nothing left of him. His papers showed him to be a Turk. The bus driver was a Turk as well. That could mean they were Kurdish terrorists, PKK probably, a two man cell tasked to kill the Ambassador.' She spoke slowly. It was too soon after the event to have had any computer analysis of the information. She was analysing the data herself.

Hammond let her go on. It was always dangerous to analyse a conclusion on early data. All too often other information turned up to wreck the analysis. But he knew her, knew her lateral thinking, her innate caution about the apparent, her courage in reaching through the opaque, driving her mind to create form out of the droplets of fog.

Julia walked restlessly to a vase on a Regency half moon table in the corner of the room, absentmindedly took out a white daisy, began picking off the petals, dropping them on the floor. Hammond didn't move.

'The man killed in the cleaning mechanism was a cleaner, he cleaned the buses. That means he had access to the buses at night. He could have been the explosives engineer. Loading the charges under cover of the cleaning job.' She paused. 'When the bus exploded, there were no passengers and the driver had asked the conductor to get off. The only person on the bus when it exploded was the driver.' She picked another petal off the daisy. 'If the cleaner was the engineer, then he put an explosive charge under the driver's seat. He meant to kill him.'

Petals littered the carpet. Her fingers came away empty. She shook her head a little, raising a hand to smooth away a strand of hair falling across her mouth, stopped, looked at the daisy. No petals now, just the bright yellow centre. She motioned to Hammond to hold out his hand. Quietly he did so. She put the yellow centre of the daisy in it.

'I think that's the answer.'

He looked at it, hoping her analysis was wrong, because, if it was right, a deeper terror lay out there than he had imagined.

'Keeping the core intact,' he said.

She nodded, the look in her eyes confirming his worst fears.

He went on slowly. 'The cleaner, the engineer, was instructed to make sure the driver was killed. To ensure his silence.'

'Yes.'

'And the driver was instructed to kill the engineer to ensure his silence. He pushed him into the cleaning mechanism to make it look like an accident.'

'Yes.'

'So the outer petals are silenced. Only the core knows what happened?'

'Yes.'

'And the core cannot be reached.'

'No.'

He tossed the yellow centre on the floor.

'The PKK don't operate that way. They're not Quaida. They're not committed to death, to suicide. The PKK would never get volunteers if they thought they were going to be liquidated.'

She looked at him. He narrowed his eyes.

'We're looking somewhere else, aren't we?'

'I think so, yes.' She put her wrist in her other hand, turning it this way and that, as if she'd just had a hard session programming the computer. 'It's the fact that it's the Turkish Ambassador that worries me. That and the fact his family were targeted as well.'

'Greece.' He'd said it. He'd saved her from saying it, from telling the PM she'd said it, from the disbelief and anger of the PM.

She dropped her hands. 'I've got to feed it to the computer. There'll be extraneous information, of course.'

He looked at her, at her composure. He knew she was right. She'd check with the computer, of course, but it wouldn't do any good. It was Greece all right.

'It adds up,' she said quietly. 'The Turks attack Samos to take out Greek surveillance.' She paused. Hammond put her thoughts together.

'The Greeks are under international pressure not to retaliate. So they kill the Turkish Ambassador and make it look like the PKK did it to show the Turks can't control them. Putting the pressure back on the Turks.'

She nodded.

Hammond slowly shook his head.

'If it ever gets out that the Greeks did it, there'll be war. The Turks would be uncontrollable.'

A light reached her eyes. She never had to explain to Hammond, he was there as fast as she was.

'Yes.'

'Well, don't be so pleased with yourself. You've got to explain it to the PM now. And that APS you confused.'

Always the same, she thought. She always exposed herself to him for praise. Wanted his approval, even now, a year after he'd made her his first appointment in G8. She automatically smoothed her hair.

'That won't impress him either,' Hammond said dryly.

Ignoring him, she carefully outlined her strategy.

CHAPTER EIGHT

The APS came to usher them in to the Prime Minister. He carefully kept his eyes away from Julia. But, in the doorway, she slowly brushed past him, catching his startled glance with a brilliant smile then moving on into the room, as he lingered in the subtle scent of her perfume.

'Morning, John.' The Prime Minister was brisk. Using Hammond's Christian name to mark his long friendship with him and, Hammond thought with some relief, to show that this was to be a constructive meeting. Hammond had seen Julia's play with the APS. Perhaps her theory that the Greeks had killed the Ambassador would not be so difficult to fly, after all.

'I've asked the French and German Ambassadors to be here.' The PM raised his voice a little, 'Ronald, ask them to come in please.'

The APS started, reddening slightly. 'Yes, of course, Prime Minister.'

Hammond wasn't surprised that the French and German Ambassadors had been summoned. The huge Arab population of North Africa had been pouring illegally into France, out of control, for five years now and the French were using a harsh programme of repatriation and holding camps to stem the flow. The French had been pouring money into Greece to help stop the Kurdish illegals coming from Turkey.

Germany had also been funding the Greeks. Using them as a buffer to limit the Turkish population flooding Germany. The rightwing Neo Nazis were still under control, but shouts of "Auslander Raus" "Foreigners out" were heard more frequently now. Seven years after the millennium, illegal migration was top of the agenda for both Germany and France.

But the presence of the Ambassadors presented a problem. There could be no quick discussion with the PM to warn him how best to keep the Greek secret.

The PM rose from his desk. Walked away, past the fireplace, cold now in the summer months, skirted the richly upholstered chairs in front of his desk, brushed past a brilliant display of summer roses on a square table between the long, pale yellow, curtained windows, strode across the blue carpet and held out his hand.

'Frau Dahlem. Monsieur Flambert. Please meet John Hammond, Director General of G8. And his Deputy, Julia Simmonds.'

The men studied the faces. Quickly scanning the eyes and mouths for the signs of mood. Friendly, hostile, eager, bored. The women glanced at faces but absorbed clothes and hands. Well cut. Sloppy. Neat. Flashy. Strong. Thin. Fat. Weak. Information streaming through personal analysis, whilst the formal language was spoken.

Hammond took in Flambert's round face under the thin strands of smooth black hair. Middle aged, short and overweight, he'd started life as a banker, and was now a political appointee to London. Flesh puffed around the eyes, pushing them back. The lips were the same, so that his features were almost hidden, camouflaged. No truth to be found there, Hammond thought.

Julia found Dahlem's taste in clothes matched her own. Expensive, designer, cut to cover the figure but also to show it off. The total absence of vulgarity making her Nord Deutsch, a Berliner, in her forties, she was known for her razor edged mind. A career diplomat. Her hands were painfully thin, large knuckles and joint bones, no rings. A carefully controlled woman, but nervy, anxious her control might fail under stress.

They sat down, while the APS fussed around with coffee and tea, Dahlem asking for lime juice in water.

The PM addressed the Ambassadors. 'I've asked you to come this morning, urgently, because of two separate incidents in the last two days. The attack on Samos. And now, this morning, the assassination of the Turkish Ambassador and his family.'

'I did not know her well,' Dahlem murmured, 'but I am devastated. Her little girl as well. Those PKK murderers, they must be stopped.'

Julia moved forward in her seat, opened her mouth.

'Have you all the protection you need, Frau Dahlem?' Hammond cut across her.

'Thank you, Mr Hammond, yes.' Her fingers twitched as she linked them together in her lap. 'But whatever protection I have won't stop them if they are really determined.' She looked at Julia. 'Was that what you were going to say?'

The look Hammond had given her and his interruption had warned Julia off. Hammond didn't want her to talk until he let her know.

'I was going to say that I have a Turkish friend who spoke of the wife's hard work for their community here.'

Flambert raised his squat nose in her direction, sniffing out the lameness of Julia's reply. The burrowed eyes flicked to Hammond, trying to sense any communication to Julia, sieve out a meaning.

'You don't ask me about my protection.' He paused, the eyes fixed on Hammond. 'You are right, of course. France does not have the problem Germany has.' He paused again, sucked in a mouthful of coffee. 'And London has not been hit by the PKK for years.' He put down his coffee cup. Ignoring the spoon as it fell on the floor.

Hammond waited, staying silent, forcing Flambert to say more. It was an old diplomatic negotiating trick. Make the other side talk. Dahlem had missed the signals between himself and Julia, but Flambert had picked them up and was still trying to decipher them.

The PM kept quiet. Sensing that Hammond had good reason for his rude silence.

The room tensed, sensing an awkward, undiplomatic moment.

The APS bent to pick up Flambert's spoon and favoured Julia with a glance. 'G8 has done excellent work in keeping London safe, Ambassador Flambert. Ms Simmonds is responsible for that.'

Flambert snorted.

'Is that why my colleague the Turkish Ambassador and his family are spread over the Foreign Office wall?'

'I didn't . . .'

The Prime Minister cut across him. 'What Ronald means, Mr

Flambert, is that you are safe. I think you should be grateful for that.' The Manchester accent was harsh now. 'I think that we're grown up enough to think like Frau Dahlem. Terrorists will succeed if they are absolutely determined on a target.'

The PM hadn't lost any of his northern impatience with arrogance, Hammond thought. Hammond had seen it often enough. From the time he'd joined the PM when he was just Michael Harris, car tyre distributor, through his time as Home Secretary and then PM. Popular for his no nonsense yet warm Manchester personality. Popular too for applying business techniques to government and making them work.

Flambert went on as if the PM hadn't spoken. 'So who is responsible, Miss Simmonds?' He emphasised the Miss, as if painting her position in the infants' schoolroom.

Hammond settled back, nodded to Julia to show Flambert his full confidence in her.

She flicked her eyes over Flambert's face, then deliberately turned towards Dahlem. 'In December last year we received information from a source in Italy that someone was the target of an attack in Paris. The source was a waitress in Turin, her boyfriend was a car mechanic. He had been asked to make up some Paris number plates. He told his girl friend, but she hadn't thought much of it. He was into car theft, cheap Fiats mainly, into the Balkans. He produced the plates, but the people making the order came back to him, saying the expiry date was too early. They needed them to cover Quatorze Juillet.' She looked at the PM. 'Bastille Day.'

'I know what day it is, Ms Simmonds,' the PM murmured, looking at Flambert.

'Our source pricked her ears up at that. Bastille Day meant government celebrations. An attack on that day probably meant a government figure and that probably meant a terrorist attack. She reported to us. Because the Balkans were involved, we got the Moscow G8 Centre to put discreet surveillance on the boyfriend and the garage. Three weeks later they came up with a name. Kocik. He was a Serb, aged thirty, born in Sarajevo and worked there.'

'A Serb?' Dahlem sounded surprised. 'I thought all that was finished. With Milosevic.'

Julia drew her in. 'You are right. We were surprised too. A Serb planning an attack on the French Government indicated a revival of Serb nationalism. On both counts we became concerned. We decided to play it long.'

'What? And risk a French life? Did we know that?' Flambert poked a pudgy finger at her.

'The French are represented in G8, Ambassador. Some were on my Team.'

He glared at her. 'I'll look into that.'

Julia went on, ignoring him. 'Kocik was security conscious, using counter surveillance and keeping away from electronic communication. We followed him on G8SUR satellite surveillance. Gradually we built up a picture. The cell was five strong. It appeared to be receiving instructions from a Serb in Belgrade, a much older man. We discovered the target's identity,' she hesitated, 'I won't trouble you with his name.'

'Why not,' grunted Flambert. 'I should know such a thing if it's relevant.'

'It is relevant, Ambassador. But your own legislation prohibits me from mentioning it.'

Flambert pounced. 'Ah. He was in Intelligence.'

'As you wish.' Julia stretched the fingers of her right hand. Dahlem watched the gesture, a slight smile creeping onto her lips as she pictured her throttling him.

'By the eleventh of July we were no further forward with a motive. Then on the twelfth something happened which broke through the whole maze.' She paused, picked up her cup, took a sip, keeping her face straight as the cold coffee slid down her throat.

Flambert leaned forward, his eyes now intent on her face. The APS stood by the door, motionless, his lips slightly parted.

'The cell had a celebration. Out in the country, with the old man. G8SUR watched and recorded it. We sent the recording to the Paris Gendarme.'

'Gendarme,' ejaculated Flambert.

She ignored him. 'On Quatorze Juillet the target was liquidated by a car bomb in central Paris.'

Flambert jumped up. 'I remember, I remember. But it was a

street cleaner who was killed. A street cleaner. What are you telling me.' He was leaning over her now, his face red and blotched. The words thickened with his Marseilles accent.

The PM stirred. Hammond glanced at him, slightly shook his head. The APS saw the exchange, checked his movement towards Julia.

'The target had been with the French NATO peacekeeping force in the Balkans at the turn of the century. The five men were tobacco smugglers taking it to Albania for transportation into Europe. The target had collected the proceeds in Europe but had forgotten to pass them on. The older man was the gang leader.'

Flambert swung around to the Prime Minister. 'This is disgraceful,' he shouted. 'What has it to do with today's outrage. Nothing. Just a story to embarrass me. And in front of my German colleague.' He started towards the door. 'I protest. I strongly protest.'

The PM dropped the silver letter knife he had been holding. It clattered onto the silver inkstand. Bringing Flambert to a halt.

'Has it occurred to you, Mr Flambert, that today's attack on the Turkish Ambassador was personal? The family and that. Nothing to do with terrorism or,' he let the words hang, 'the PKK.'

Flambert turned to Hammond, his face livid, the folds of flesh trembling with rage. 'Is this what you're saying? Is this true? Some personal business? The Ambassador was corrupt? It was revenge?'

'I have every confidence in Ms Simmond's abilities, Ambassador.' Hammond looked at Dahlem.

'Having seen her, I too believe her. It is a personal attack, something bad in the Ambassador's life, not the PKK at all,' Dahlem said.

'Merde.' The word exploded into the silence.

The PM coughed. Picked up his letter knife. Turned a page of his brief with it. 'Shall we get to the essence of the meeting, now?' he enquired gently. 'I naturally wanted G8 to clear up any misunderstanding about the attack on the Turkish Ambassador before we addressed the other important matter.'

Hammond watched the PM with admiration. Without briefing, without knowing a thing about the Whitehall attack, the PM had followed Hammond's signals, had seen Hammond and Julia's exchange, had backed Julia's story about the Frenchman. Fortunately the story was true. Flambert would get confirmation of that, and when he did he would remember the PM's calm acceptance of the relevance of it to the Turkish Ambassador's death. So would Dahlem. To them the Turkish Ambassador had done something reprehensible, and those he had done it to had exacted revenge.

He listened as the PM continued.

'I am extremely worried by the Samos incident. I can see Greece and Turkey escalating their row until a full scale war. It's not more than a dozen years since the Balkans exploded and it's still touchy in Iraq. We just can't allow this to fester.'

'What are you suggesting, Prime Minister?' It was Dahlem who spoke first. The German who could see Germany in flames, with its huge Turkish population fighting the Greeks on its soil. The Foreign Ministry in Berlin had sent her an alarmed email just that morning. Intelligence out of the Turkish quarter revealed white heat at the Greek claims and Turkish agitators were demanding retribution.

'We need to go back to the idea of a European Union Army, to include some outsiders. Turkey being one of them. As long as Turkey remains outside the European Union we are going to have this tension. I have three years to go in this Government, and I don't intend to go through three years of this bloody nonsense between Greece and Turkey. If we can't get Turkey into the EU we can get them and Greece into an EU Army. That'll stop their quarrelling.' He threw the knife down on his papers.

'But that idea died five years ago, when your Government vetoed an EU Army. We've had time to think and a change of Government. We wouldn't accept the idea now,' Flambert said.

'Only because the French want to go their own way. The same as their attitude to NATO,' Dahlem flung at him.

Flambert was silent.

Hammond knew what to say next. But knew if he said it, Flambert would reject it on principle. He tried to catch the PM's eye, only to find Dahlem watching him. He had to take the moment, otherwise it would be too late. He passed his hand through his hair then rubbed his forefinger against his thumb. The slight smile that he'd seen on Dahlem's lips when she had watched Julia, returned. Her eyes moved towards Flambert.

'Mr Flambert, the difference this time is that you need Greece.

Without them, Turkey will keep the Kurdish migration sore running through Greece.'

It did not need the slightly harsh accent of her words to lift
Flambert's head. He was confused and angry. Angry with himself
for losing control. Angry with Hammond and G8. For years his
country had controlled its Intelligence agencies. Using them to
good effect in the political and economic interests of la Belle France.
Then G8 had come along, created by the G8 countries who feared
their Intelligence agencies were losing the fight against terrorism
and organised crime. Since then, Intelligence had come to the
French Foreign Ministry at the Quai d'Orsay in dribs and drabs.
The good stuff remaining with G8, shared only when the G8
Directors decided. And, worst of all, the French members of the G8
teams were completely loyal to their Agency. Try as they would,
the French Ministries had never succeeded in bribing, threatening
or blackmailing any of them to break faith.

He sat, smouldering. That little salope had fooled him, too. So
demure and sexy with that expensive perfume, as if she hadn't a
thought in her head. Then she'd taken him apart, piece by piece.
Shit, how the Germans would laugh. He could see the joke flying
round the emails in Berlin, the bloody French shafted by the Brits
again.

He stirred. He could retrieve something from the ashes. His
eyes narrowed until they were lost behind his brows.

'You're right, of course, Madame,' he said slowly. 'Things have
changed.' He looked at Hammond. 'We do need the Greeks. I am
relieved that this matter of the Turkish Ambassador does not
interfere with our decision on the Samos incident.' He swallowed.
'I apologise, if I seemed hasty.' His eyes emerged again as he
looked at Julia. 'To you too, M'mselle.'

'You will recommend the idea of an EU Army to include Turkey
to your Government then?' the PM stood up.

'Yes, Prime Minister. If you have not persuaded me, I must
listen to my German colleague.' He pushed his lips forward.
'Together Germany and France make the force in the EU, do we
not?'

The PM held his hand out to Dahlem.

'Thank you, Ambassador, for solving our problem. May I suggest a meeting of our three Governments within the next week to resolve a strategy for a new EU Army to include Turkey. We need not bother the other EU members until we have sketched out our wishes, I am sure.'

The Ambassadors nodded together. That was how EU business was done these days, the three players making the decisions first.

The APS ushered them out.

The PM looked up as his secretary came in.

'Fix us a drink, Belinda, will you please. And Hammond and Ms Simmonds too.' He walked over to the window overlooking Horse Guards parade, where the Grenadier Guards were practising for the Queen's Birthday parade. Their boots silent in the room as they hit the gravel courtyard, the officers looking like a mime as their shouted orders failed to penetrate the armour plate glass window.

'Bloody French,' the PM murmured, 'I'm not sure he's convinced about the EU Army.' He turned to Julia. 'But you had him fooled.' He took his drink. 'Now tell me what really happened to the Turkish Ambassador. And why you couldn't tell me.'

So while the white suited forensic officers worked outside on the wreckage where the Ambassador and his family had died, they told him the truth. The Greeks had killed him. They then explained why a lie which destroyed the image of an honourable man was necessary. Telling him that if the real truth about the Ambassador's death emerged from the painted and wallpapered confines of that room, the EU Army would never be born and there would be war between Greece and Turkey.

They left the APS dictating the Press Release that would blacken the Turkish Ambassador's name forever.

As she passed the bowl of daisies, Julia took one. 'He won't even have a decent burial,' she murmured.

'No,' Hammond replied. 'But you can put that on his grave, if you wish.'

CHAPTER NINE

The truck carrying Demir Sulan and Bora Hitay swayed and rattled along the road from Van on the Van Golu Lake in eastern Turkey towards Khoi and Tabriz in Iran. Nothing in their dress or their features or their truck showed them to be PKK terrorists of the eighth circle.

The PKK was like a complex target. The inner circle, the bull's eye, was Celik the Leader. The second circle, tight around the first, were the bodyguard, handpicked, known for years, through the hardships of climbing the ladder. The third circle, surrounding the bulls eye, contained the Leader's closest advisers. Rarely more than six to ten. A larger number introduced unacceptable risk. Risk of ambition, jealousy, greed, discontent, any of which could foment and suddenly boil into treason. The fourth circle held their wives, husbands, lovers, children. In the fifth and sixth circles lay the various terrorist cell leaders. Sometimes knowing each other, often not. Communicating with one or two of the advisers, never more, never knowing the whole. Sometimes meeting the Leader, but only when necessary. The seventh circle was occupied by the front line troops, the bombers, the close quarter killers, the triggers. Surrounding them in the eighth circle were the supporters. Those who supplied services, like safe houses, food, clothing, documents, money. Peopled by men and women living ordinary lives. Housewives, grocers, retailers, mechanics, lawyers, bankers. And, living not so ordinary lives, burglars, forgers, smugglers. The ninth circle encompassed their wives, husbands, lovers, children, whether knowing or not, all of them implicated, all of them vulnerable. Each circle getting larger and larger. Until the tenth circle. And the tenth circle was huge. Covering all those people, mainly Kurds, who came into contact with the other circles. Whether directly, as in conversation, or indirectly, as in hearing about them in the news. The tenth circle. As important as the first. Because in the tenth circle were all those people who might be persuaded, or swayed, or bribed, or threatened to enter into the ninth, eighth or seventh circles. And, once in, they increased the threat of the whole.

Demir and Bora were Kurds, but two years ago they had only been in the tenth circle. They had been working in a local garage in Van, repairing tractors mainly. Uninterested in Kurdish politics or the PKK, until the Turkish Army had put in a village guard as part of the Government policy of controlling terrorism. Van was a hotspot so the guard was put in. It hadn't taken long before some of the guard members began the extortion rackets common among the Turkish guards littering the Kurd countryside. Food or money or other favours, girls mainly, in exchange for not reporting anti government activity, whether the activity took place or not. Demir and Bora had come under the guards' spotlight early on. Mechanics were a valuable commodity around Van and the guards needed repairs to their trucks.

The first visit was friendly. The guards offered cigarettes, a joke or two and a polite request for help. The next visit was unfriendly. Two PKK members slid into the garage one evening. There were no cigarettes, no jokes, just the bald statement. If they helped the fucking Turkish guards once, they wouldn't help them twice. They'd be dead. The third visit had Demir's hand in a vice. The three guards had brought in an old Chevrolet truck for repair to the front axle. Demir had shrugged his shoulders, said there was too much work. The guards had simply taken him, hauled him up to the workbench and put his hand in the vice. Just turning the handle once had him screaming. Bora had shouted that they'd do it, mend the bloody truck, leave it with them, it would be ready tomorrow. The guards had taken Demir's hand out. He could flex it, bruised only. But as they left, the guards shouted that if the truck wasn't ready, Demir could expect three turns of the screw the next day.

That night Demir and Bora had skirted Van Golu lake on foot to where they knew the PKK had a patrol. When the patrol picked them up they begged for help. Four hours later three trucks drove up to their garage. All their tools and spares were loaded on board.

The guards' Chevrolet was hitched to the back of the third truck. As the trucks ground their way around Lake Van Golu and through the hills to the town Diyarbakir, Demir and Bora had watched the flames of their garage fan orange and yellow in the darkness. No one interfered, the guard never ventured out at night, they didn't want to die.

Since then Demir and Bora had stayed in Diyarbakir, a major PKK stronghold, working on trucks, tractors, bikes. Anything that helped the PKK move.

And now they were fully fledged PKK supporters in the eighth circle, with the sole intent of creating a Kurdish homeland separate from the bastard Turks who'd ruined their lives.

There was an air of excitement about them as they bounced around in the cab of their truck, fighting the heavy load it carried. They had driven past Van for the first time since they had watched their garage go up in flames. They hadn't stopped there, but they were exhilarated all the same.

The job they had to do was big. The biggest they had ever done.

CHAPTER TEN

A faint rustle first alerted Hammond. He stopped dead in the doorway. Gently closed the door behind him, listening intently to detect where the sound came from. The only reason for someone to hide in a meeting room of the European Union in Brussels would be to eavesdrop or sabotage. Although he was early, Hammond knew the maintenance staff would have finished their work much earlier. The immaculate floor length white cloth over the table with the various bottles of juice and mineral water confirmed this. The rustle seemed to come from a corner. A tall projection screen stood there. He started towards it. Quietly.

Suddenly, from his left, the tablecloth moved a fraction. Hammond held his breath. He wasn't operational. Never had been. He wasn't armed. The man under the table probably was.

Hammond spun on his left foot. Grabbed the white cloth. Pulled it and dived under the table. Scrabbling to cover the man with it. Bottles smashing to the floor. Glass splintering on the metal chair legs. Hammond felt a body. Ripped the cloth as he wound it round the man. Pulling. Struggling to get him wrapped in it. He kicked the table leg. Throwing the table off them.

'What the hell are you doing?'

The woman's yell pierced the room. Just as he saw the long blonde hair. And the long legs under the ruckled cream skirt.

'Get off me, you pig.'

The word "cochon" rolled out in high Parisienne French. Hammond felt the first seed of doubt. But he hung on.

She struggled again.

He strengthened his grip. 'Lie still. What are you doing?'

'Finding my contact lens, you imbecile.'

He climbed off her. Jerked the tablecloth so she rolled out. Her long, blonde hair flying around her face. The cut glass accent had decided him. No terrorist would use the word "imbecile", let alone with that accent.

'Finding your what?'

She angrily swept the hair out of her eyes, ice green with fury. The stream of French from her wide, full lipped mouth came straight from the slums of Montmartre. Hammond watched her with awe. Trained never to swear – while you're swearing the enemy's thinking – he listened in total admiration. Her delivery was immaculate, each syllable perfectly enunciated, emphasised by each hand as they straightened her skirt, her jacket, her scarf, her hair, in short, tiny movements, her flashing eyes never leaving his. Completely oblivious of the effect each small gesture had on him, allowing him to explore the beauty of her. She caught his eye and stopped, catching her breath.

He bent down. 'Here,' he said, offering her a slim, low heeled, cream shoe.

She opened her mouth. Shut it, took the shoe, wobbled on the other one as she put it on. He reached out a hand to steady her. She moved away.

'You haven't apologised,' she said.

'There's nothing . . .' He stopped, noticing a trickle of blood on her leg. He picked up an unbroken bottle of water, soaked a piece of tablecloth in it. 'I'm sorry I hurt you.' He dabbed the tablecloth on the cut. Looked at it. 'At least it's only a small nick.'

'So, you only apologise because you hurt me. Are you crazy?' she looked at her leg. 'Don't you apologise for attacking me?'

'We are about to have a high level meeting in this room. You had no business to be under the table.' He looked at the debris around her feet. 'How did your contact lens get there anyway?'

Her eyes swept over him, pale grey now, her temper still boiling, but under control. She took a breath.

'I know who you are.' She emphasised the fourth word. 'Hammond, the British delegate. You are just as I imagined.'

He didn't give her the satisfaction of asking what she meant.

'How did it get there? The lens.'

She shrugged. 'I put my briefcase down under the table. My hair must have caught it.'

'This?' he picked up a light brown leather folder with a square central brass lock, took it to the window and held it up to the light, tipping it gently this way and that. He stopped, narrowed his eyes, licked a finger and carefully pressed it on the leather. 'This it?' He held out his finger. A small shiny particle on the end of it.

She hesitated, relief conflicting with fury that he'd found it so easily.

'Yes.' She lifted it off.

He put the briefcase on the window ledge.

'There you are then. No need for all that rough and tumble after all. A little thought before you dived under that table and this room wouldn't have been wrecked.' He walked to the 'phone. 'We'd better get the place cleaned up before the others get here.' He looked at her. 'Can you see alright to get out of here?'

She had disliked Hammond the moment she read the French Intelligence Service brief on him. Quick. Farsighted. Lateral thinker. Devious. Manipulative. Untrustworthy. Heterosexual, but only short term relationships. The Intelligence Report was short and damning. Her Head of Department in the Foreign Ministry had warned her about him. The combination of his sandy hair, pale blue eyes and restless dynamism fatally attractive to women. Well, not this woman. She returned Hammond's look, satisfied that she disliked him even more now she'd met him. The pig. He had no manners, had insulted her beyond belief, had refused to apologise and was now ordering her out of the room. She felt an urge to crush him. She straightened her shoulders, drew herself up, narrowed her eyes.

'I am the French delegate to this meeting, Monsieur Hammond. I have every right to be in this room.'

Hammond watched the gesture, taking in her diminutive five and a half feet. His eyes creased slightly at the corners.

'M'mselle Dedain. I have known that from the moment you emerged from under your tablecloth. You are,' he paused slightly, 'unmistakeable.' He moved towards the door. 'Would you like me to guide you to a Restroom where you can replace that lens? Or can you find your own way?' His eyes went to the small disc on her finger, then back to her eyes watching them flare green again as she swept past him through the door.

He waited for a second, then walked quickly to the window, picked up her briefcase, tested the catch. It was open, unlocked just before she sat down and forgotten by her in the melee, in the heat of indignation at her treatment, in the need to storm out to show her contempt.

Her Foreign Ministry brief was only two pages long, written in the concise administrative language the French are so good at. Hammond had already digested the contents and replaced the briefcase on the windowsill when the cleaners came in to clear up the mess. He'd arrived at the meeting room ten minutes early, deliberately. The follow up meeting to the Prime Minister's proposal for an EU Army had no Chair. The UK, France and Germany considered each other equals and Hammond knew, from experience, that the EU bureaucrats here in Brussels would have arranged a round table so that no one was in a dominant position. But Hammond also knew that the meeting room had a long west facing window. The meeting was scheduled for seven o'clock in the evening and Hammond wanted to sit with his back to it so that the sinking June sun would face his French and German colleagues making them uncomfortable, squint, shade their eyes, lose concentration. So that he would naturally assume the dominant position, chairman in all but name.

The room was back to normal by the time the German delegation arrived. Hammond stood up, bowing slightly to a short, stubby, grey haired man.

'Herr Genscher, good to see you. Did you have a good trip? How's Berlin?'

Genscher, held out a thick fingered hand, resting his briefcase on the table with the other. He looked hot and wiped his grey moustache and spade beard with his fingers.

'Why can't these damn Belgians get their traffic system right,' he muttered. 'In Berlin we built the whole of the Mitte with hardly any traffic problems. Materials brought in by barge, then onto lorries and finally through tunnels to the building sites. Everything on time. The old wall demolished and a whole new city centre built in five years.' He wiped his face again. 'These people have had two hundred years to get it right and it's still a shambles. They couldn't even build a jam free route up here to these EU buildings. It took us half an hour from the railway station.' His German reeked of Ost Deutsch, Meissen, Dresden, somewhere near the Czech border.

'We're still waiting for our French colleague,' Hammond replied, his German slushing the endings to hide its lack of fluency. 'You're not late.'

Genscher turned, impatiently introduced a young, dark haired man, Major Stammler, his assistant in the German Defence Ministry, then plunged into the Belgian transport system again. Hammond mentally prepared himself for a lengthy meeting as he waited longer and longer for the verb at the end of Genscher's sentences.

The door opened and M'mselle Dedain came in, her hair combed, shining in the sunlight. Hammond saw the reddish streak in the fairness and inwardly smiled as he remembered her father's flaming red hair. He had seen that temper in her late father, too, when he'd met him at various meetings on terrorism in Paris and London.

She looked around the room. Hammond shook his head very slightly, moving his eyes to Genscher. She picked up the signal, acted as if nothing had happened.

'Herr Genscher, I'm sorry I'm a little late. 'Charmian Dedain.' She nodded at Hammond. 'Mr Hammond.'

She moved to get her briefcase from the windowsill, giving Hammond a questioning glance as she did so. His attention was focussed on Genscher. Satisfied, she picked it up and turned to introduce a tall, well groomed man behind her.

'I'd like you to meet Monsieur Roubel. Ministry of Defence.'

Genscher moved to the chair in front of the window.

'Sorry, that's taken,' said Hammond, pointing to his briefcase on it. 'Perhaps here, on my right.'

Genscher sat down, looked at Hammond.

'Are you by yourself?'

Hammond nodded. 'Good to see you all,' he began briskly. 'We're here to take forward the agreement between our Governments to form an EU Army to include Turkey.'

'Proposal,' interrupted Genscher undoing his case. 'Not agreement, proposal.' He looked at Dedain and smiled.

She smiled back, putting her hands on the table, the fingers quite short and strong. Hammond noticed a smudge of blue and yellow paint on the inside of her wrist.

'I think at this stage the French Government is happy with the word "agreement",' she said. 'Ambassador Flambert made that clear in London. We believe the British Prime Minister's idea has much merit, we must act to contain Turkey. An EU Army can do that if Turkey is included.'

Hammond smiled at both of them. What Dedain's Foreign Ministers brief had actually said was that the French should never participate in an EU Army. It would lose the French their control over their nuclear arsenal and their ability to deploy unilaterally in French West Africa and Guiana. But the French could not be seen to veto the British Prime Minister's idea, so Dedain had been instructed to support the strategic plan for an EU Army and then bog down the meeting in detail. Not obviously, but subtly, delay was her watchword.

Hammond could handle that. But he was puzzled by Genscher's response. In London the Germans had supported the idea of an Army, now Genscher had downgraded the idea to a proposal. That didn't make sense. The Germans needed all the support they could get to control the Turks. Hammond thought rapidly. The Germans' problem could be money, they could be looking for a deal to cut the cost of an EU Army. He spoke rapidly in German.

'I suggest we deal with manpower contributions first, they define the lines of command and,' looking directly at Stammler, he let the word hang, 'funding.'

Stammler jerked his head up, blinked in the sun, shading his eyes with a hand.

'Funding is the most important issue. Once we know how much each country is prepared to contribute we can work out,' he faltered, annoyed that he'd blurted out the importance of money, he'd meant to be more subtle, just talk about contributions, but the sun dazzle had confused him, 'manpower and administration,' he finished lamely.

Hammond knew for certain then that the German's problem was cash. Not surprising really. The cost of Germany's social programme was staggering. So the Germans had decided to trade agreement for the Army in return for reduced contributions to its cost. No wonder Genscher had tried to call the idea a proposal and not an agreement. Hammond had earlier discussed this possibility with the PM. "We need this bloody Army" the PM had slapped his hand on his desk. "Pay the bloody Germans. Pay anyone. But get the damn thing agreed". Then he'd looked at Hammond and grinned, "Don't tell the Treasury". Hammond's mind now raced. He needed time to get to the Germans and talk to them. With them in his pocket he could block the French delaying tactics. He turned to the Frenchman, Roubel.

'Any objections?' He almost spat out the words, in English.

Roubel was a cockerel. A Parisian career bureaucrat, egotistical, vain, arrogant, with all the baggage of the French grudge against the English. Dedain had no hope of stopping him, she could only watch as he exposed the French position.

'Yes. It's ridiculous to talk about manpower and financing. We should talk about line of command.' He squinted as the sun came out of a cloud. 'Where is France in that?'

Hammond turned to Dedain.

'Charmian, this will only delay things. We know line of command depends on manpower and financial contributions.' He paused, looking at the patches of colour on her wrist. 'Of course, if you want time to study your position further,' he trailed off, watching as she noticed the paint on her wrist.

'Thank you,' she said, motioning Roubel to get up.

Hammond watched her walk to the corner of the room by a coffee table, surreptitiously wetting a finger with her tongue and wiping the colour off her wrist. Roubel followed her.

Hammond raised his voice, speaking in French.

'Monsieur Roubel, if you are by the coffee machine would you be kind and pour us all some. I'm sure we could do with it.'

Stammler stifled a laugh.

'Herr Genscher,' Hammond leaned forward confidentially. Stammler leaned forward as well. Hammond stopped, looking at him.

Genscher raised his eyebrows at Stammler. He'd asked the Army to send him an experienced negotiator and they'd saddled him with this idiot, blurting out the German negotiating position like a tart on a street corner.

'Major Stammler, go and help Roubel with the coffee.'

Stammler's face reddened as he got up. He looked at Roubel huddled over the coffee machine with Dedain and awkwardly went to stand in the middle of the room.

Hammond caught Genscher's eye, flicked a glance toward Stammler and back to Genscher.

'Military,' he murmured. 'Always so readable.'

Genscher started to speak, but Hammond cut across him.

'The reason I want to start with manpower is that the UK is prepared to maximise its financial contribution.' He waited as Genscher digested this.

Hammond nodded as if Genscher had spoken.

'The size of financial contributions will be in ratio to manpower contributions. It must be so to get the waverers to agree. Belgium, Luxembourg, that lot.'

Genscher frowned. 'But Germany would be expected to contribute a large amount of manpower.'

'It's going to be Special Forces work, this Army,' Hammond replied, 'small elite units, not large lightly trained battalions. We'll need those, of course, but what we want are your Special Forces. Leave the fodder to the other countries. You will supply quality, but the numbers will be low. The guts of the Army will be German, French, British Special Forces supported by G8. The other EU countries will think they're involved but they'll be relegated to making up numbers, supply and administration. The British will make available enough manpower over and above our Special Forces to meet fifty percent of your costs. That's confidential between us. The French can pay for themselves, they'll want a large manpower contribution so they can have a strong line of command. But since the Special Forces have their own command, the general line of command will be irrelevant. That way the French look good and you and we get what we want.'

Genscher smiled, his moustache parting from his spade beard.

'I think we can shorten this meeting,' he said.

Twenty minutes afterwards the meeting broke up. Manpower and financial contributions had been sketched out and a line of command headed by the French was pencilled in. It remained for the deal to be sold to the other EU members. And Turkey.

Genscher and Stammler had gone. Roubel had left the room. Dedain came up to Hammond where he stood by the window.

'It was not polite of you to address me as Charmian, my first name. You did not do it to the others. Please don't do it again.' She turned to walk away.

'I only do it to people I admire,' Hammond said.

She stopped, curiosity overcoming dislike. 'Admire?' she questioned. 'How admire?' she spoke in English.

'Oh, anyone who can paint. You do paint, don't you?'

She moved towards the door. Opened it, her dislike returning in the look she gave him. 'I was right.' She walked through it. 'You are a pig.'

CHAPTER ELEVEN

Julia was puzzled. Bora and Demir, mechanics in the support staff of the PKK eighth circle hadn't left Diyarbakir for two years, since they had been forced out of Van. Yet on the plasma screen in front of her workstation at the G8 warehouse G8SUR showed them in an old Chevrolet truck lurching along the road from Van to Khoi towards the Iranian border.

She turned to Gunter, the tall, spare, lantern faced man who had called her to the screen.

'How long has G8SUR been following Bora and Demir?'

Gunter pursed his lips, narrowed his eyes. They were dark brown, like his short cropped hair.

'Since they left Van, about half an hour ago. I was about to switch the surveillance to the Greek Turkey border, but I thought it was strange, so I kept it on them.'

'So they came through Van from Diyarbakir?'

'Yes. That's why I didn't bother you earlier. G8SUR has had them as a target since they arrived in Diyarbakir two years ago, but they've never been outside the city. I thought they were going back to Van.'

He wasn't making an excuse. He was telling her the facts and his assessment of them. He was right, too. If she was called for every movement G8SUR picked up she'd never sleep, never get any other work done.

'Any idea what's in the back of the truck?' She watched as the surveillance zoomed in, showing a tarpaulin flapping wildly at one corner in the slipstream.

'The computer is checking it at the moment.'

'Any voice?'

'No. The truck's too noisy.'

'There may be some when they were loading, or we may get some when they get out.' She eased herself back in the chair.

Gunter noticed the movement. Very contained, simple. Only there was nothing simple about her. She wasn't thirty yet but she led their team, constantly expecting them to deliver as she did. Her mind restlessly probing, slotting pieces together, demanding more information. She always called it information. "Intelligence is for the intelligentsia" she'd say, toss her short chestnut hair and grin. "That's too slow for us" and demand another impossible deadline.

'Here's the data, when they loaded the truck in Diyarbakir,' he said, leaning forward slightly to look at the screen, hoping to catch a breath of the perfume she always wore. But he didn't. It was elusive, he thought, like her.

'What's that?' she asked, pointing the mouse at the back of the truck in a shadow.

Gunter took the mouse from her, manipulated it, typing in commands at the same time.

The shapes in the back of the truck sprang out in three dimensions. Tools. Spanners, screwdrivers, wrenches, torque tools, boxes of bolts, nuts. In one corner welding kit and in the middle, taking up most of the space, two massive hydraulic jacks. Demir and Bora were talking, the thick Kurdish dialect scratching through the console speakers. Gunter pressed a key. The speech appeared in typewritten English on the screen. Nothing but commonplace discussion about how to fit the tools in the space. Gunter ran the surveillance back and forth, to find some clue, some more information. There was none.

'What do you think?' she looked up at him. The straight eyebrows in a small frown.

He expected the question. She always asked Team Members their views. "Always say what's on your mind", she'd smile, "you wouldn't be here unless you were bright. So anything you say is worth listening to", then she'd pause, "even if it is rubbish". And they'd laugh. He laughed every time he heard it.

An archaeologist from Garmisch on the German Austrian border, Gunter still couldn't come to terms with being here in G8 as part of a Team fighting the PKK terrorists. He'd been here a year now. A year since he'd been disturbed in the church in Garmisch at an organ recital. He wasn't a churchgoer but he loved the organ. And he remembered sitting in those hard, straight shouldered pews as if it was yesterday. Always a struggle between enduring them or missing a concert. Every churchgoer in Garmisch must have gone straight to heaven for surviving those pews. The girl next to him had shifted uncomfortably throughout the first part of the programme. He'd looked at her. She'd smiled wryly at him, asked in whispered German whether there were any cushions. He'd smelled her perfume then, she'd told him later it was called Picasso, and when she left the pew in the interval he'd noticed her slim body moving easily under the summer dress, expensive, short, showing her brown legs. He went up to her, introduced himself. Somehow found himself missing the rest of the programme, found himself sitting at a café on the corner of the four crossway and glimpsing the mountains where she introduced herself as Julia Simmonds. She had been impressed that he was an archaeologist. She was a psychiatrist, graduated from London University, about to do a PhD with a friend who was a sociologist. They were going to Turkey, researching the Kurdish ethnic origins. Gunter began to talk about the Kurds and their countryside. He had done a number of digs there, specialising in Kurdish culture. He spoke Turkish and four Kurd dialects. The wine flowed, and he found himself agreeing to meet them both at the Geographical Society in London to discuss joining them in Turkey to add the archaeologist's view to their thesis.

A week later he'd arrived at the gloomy red brick Victorian building opposite Hyde Park in the pouring rain. Bored with Garmisch, he was looking forward to the excitement of the dig. And Julia was attractive.

The man who met him with Julia was a German who did almost all the talking. In that stark, brown walled, timber floored, narrow windowed room, he'd produced a file, slapped it on the dull wooden desk.

"Germany's under threat", he'd whispered so that Gunter had to strain forward to hear him. And in those next moments Gunter had been told of the PKK threat to Turkey, to Europe, to Germany. He'd also been told of his education, his degree, his digs in Turkey, his financial position. He hadn't been told of his women, of his experimenting with Es at University, of his continuous speeding tickets, but he knew they knew. He sat there, knowing there was nothing about him they didn't know. He flushed, nothing about him she didn't know.

Then they told him why he was there, what they did, at least, a teaser of what they did. He'd relaxed a little, sitting further back in his chair, ploughing his mind, turning up the furrows of boredom and frustration that lay there. Lack of funding in Germany, the difficulty of finding work in his field over the previous two years. Then he'd brought his mind back to what they were saying. The need for clear, calm, analysis, the need for lateral thinking, the need for calculating risk, the need for action to combat the terrorists, the international criminals, the moneylaunderers. It was like listening to an organ recital. And he'd turned his glance towards her, sensing a depth of understanding in her that was beyond his experience. Of course, he'd said yes and then galloped over the hurdles of their tests in what was known as the Grand National, finally holding on to his temper in a haze of exhaustion on the third day when he role played a manager dealing with a bloody minded, bull nosed customer.

Since then he'd found himself on the training course and, finally, in Basingstoke in this vast warehouse, where he was looking at the plasma screen and constructing his reply to Julia's question.

'There must be something important on. Those hydraulic jacks are heavy lifters and the welding equipment indicates heavy repairs. Also, it seems urgent. If it wasn't, they'd have sent out a recovery vehicle. Brought back whatever's in trouble for repairs at base. So there's something very heavy out there that they have to get going urgently. They don't have tanks, so it's almost certainly a lorry. Heavy load, so it's carrying goods, not people. If it was people they could walk. If it's goods it's almost certainly arms, possibly heavy weapons. My analysis is that they're shifting weapons and a transporter's broken down. Heavy lifting gear probably means an axle. Possibly a gearbox difficult to get to.'

Gunter had spoken without a pause.

She nodded straight away, looked at the screen again, brought up the satellite image. The truck was twenty kilometres nearer the Iranian border, now fifteen kilometres away. She got up.

'Keep an eye on them. They're going over the border, I'm sure of it. But they'll take a side track, they'll not sit on the main road, they'll probably go north over the mountains to Khoi. If it's weapons it may be something the PKK picked up in Iran and are going to run through the border to Turkey. But the weapons won't be on a main or secondary road. They'll be on a track somewhere. Get G8SUR to search.' She pressed a key on her console. 'I'm going to talk to Lev.'

The screen split suddenly to show Lev Leviatski peering at her through a pall of smoke. He was used to Hammond calling him at all hours, but Julia was different. If Julia called, it was necessary and urgent. He took another deep lungful of the Egyptian cigarette. He preferred Turkish but Hammond was always trying to cut his Turkish cigarettes down. Said they were too strong, always buying him these Egyptian things. He coughed. A wave of smoke rolling towards the personal computer screen in front of him. He waved his hand at it, thickset, like himself, the fingers stained with tobacco juice. He'd never had a filtered cigarette, couldn't stand them.

'Julia. What can I do for you? Is Basingstoke,' he pronounced it Buzzinstok, 'sunny now? Like Moscow?'

'Thank you, Lev. Yes.'

'Because you are there,' he laughed. Another cloud of smoke hurling at the screen.

She was used to his heavy flirting, brushed it aside as something he had to do, like smoking. But she never brushed his mind aside. She knew Hammond as the best analyst she'd ever met, ice cold, prepared to manipulate anyone and anything to reach an objective. But Lev was different. Underneath the analyst lay a cunning, an innate sense of how a criminal would act, or react and a remorseless stamina which ground down any opposition. Hammond was her alter ego, a companion. But Lev was her nemesis, a constant reminder of her failure ever to fully plumb the depths of evil. But none of this was in her mind as she laughed with him.

'Behave, Lev. I need your help.'

'Go ahead.' Ash spilled from his cigarette. He waved a hand over it, scattering it on to the floor.

She told him about Bora and Demir, told him about Gunter's assessment.

Lev's heavy, grey face only moved when she had finished.

'Hold on a minute. I'm bringing in Maxim.'

She waited. Maxim Byelov was her opposite number. Deputy to Lev, small, ginger haired with Lev's penchant for cigarettes. He was an expert in arms shipments, leader of the Team investigating the Moosar Group. Moosar for litter. A group which had started in St Petersburg, Russia, extorting money for the right to sift through the rubbish dumps. Paying the rubbish grubbers for their finds and deducting thirty per cent, beating up or killing those who tried to go on their own. The profits in Russia had extended the group to Novgorod then Pskov and other major cities. The enforcers were almost always former soldiers. Merciless. Through the military contact, had come access to illegal weapons. The rubbish business then rapidly expanded to an arms trafficking enterprise, which Byelov had been tracking for two years. Marking the leaders, traders, clients, tracing the assets, through bankers, accountants and lawyers. Moosar was ripe for plucking, but G8 let it run, preferring to wait, feeding off the stream of information about Moosar to crawl deeper into Moosar's clients which now included terrorist cells, drugs traffickers, extortion gangs, mercenaries. One by one these were taken out. Sometimes by a police swoop, acting on G8's information, sometimes by internal warfare engineered by G8 Teams, sometimes by secretly siphoning out funds from their bank accounts, plotted by G8 computer hackers.

Byelov's chunky frame pumped out energy, using all G8's ingenuity to keep the operation going, to take out as many Moosar clients as possible before the inevitable happened and Moosar became aware of what was happening. Then G8 would swoop, picking off the six heads of the group and the lawyers, accountants and other professionals who advised them. Just those. The rest, the enforcers, the loaders, packers, drivers, mechanics, would be left. Prosecuting them wasn't worth the time or money. Anyway, most of them would be under G8SUR surveillance and would lead G8 to other targets as they moved on.

Julia could almost feel Byelov's nervous energy as he appeared on her screen. A Russian cigarette between his fingers, the cardboard tube twisted in the peculiar double pinch that served, or didn't, as a filter. Byelov's accent was heavy, right in the back of his throat, rasping through the tobacco smoke. Julia spoke in fluent Russian.

'Hi, Maxim. Good to see you.' She knew Lev would have briefed him. 'Any ideas?'

He leaned forward. Julia winced at the red sweater violently clashing with his ginger hair.

'One of Moosar's planes went down last night. It's an Antonov 32. We picked up the pilot radioing Moosar in Chelkar, Kazakhstan, saying he'd engine failure and was putting down north of Marand in Iran.'

Julia hit the computer keys. In the left hand corner of her screen Marand appeared, about two hundred kilometres from the Turkish border. She waited to let Byelov finish.

He scratched his cheek, blinking as some smoke went into his eye.

'We don't know what's on board. But the Antonov 32 has got a rear loading ramp and a seven thousand kilos payload. I was very interested, so I sent a couple of our guys from Tabriz to take a look. I've got the plane coordinates if you want.'

By "a couple of our guys" Julia knew Byelov meant informants, agents, recruited for money, monitoring the Afghan, Iran, Turkey heroin route probably. She didn't waste time asking for details. This was going to be Byelov's operation, she didn't need to know who he'd sent. Instead she analysed the information. Bora and Demir were about to cross the border into Iran. The hydraulic jacks were for heavy lifting so they could be used on an aircraft. Moosar were in the arms business and one of their aircraft was down with a six ton payload capacity two hundred odd kilometers from Bora and Demir and in the direction they were headed.

'Hang on a minute,' she said as she punched the computer keyboard to bring up Bora and Demir's background. In the recess of her mind she had noticed Bora had spent two years in Melatya in central Turkey. She pointed the mouse at the name. The details sprang onto the screen. Bora had been employed in Melatya by Air Turkey as an engineer. He had left to return to Van to set up his garage business with Demir. She turned to her personal screen.

'You see that?' she said, knowing that on his identical plasma screen in Moscow the same information had appeared.

'Could be it,' he said. 'The airstrip is a drug transit, just a field. The Antonov 32's engine's are high and it has a long undercarriage. A rough landing with one engine out could mean undercarriage trouble.' He picked out another tube from a box in front of him, pinched it slowly between his fingers, lit it from his other cigarette. 'They'd need heavy jacks for that and an aircraft mechanic.'

Julia sat back and brushed the hair away from her eyes. Her fingernails were unvarnished. Out of the office she varnished them various shades of brown, with lipstick to match, showing off her eyes, but in the office she wore lip gloss, standard red and no nail polish. But her mind wasn't on that, it was on the Antonov, and the jacks. It was clear to her that any risk that the two were unconnected was small.

'Maxim, we've got to stop Bora and Demir getting to the Antonov. Can you contact those two agents you sent while they're on the road?'

'Yes. If you're thinking what I'm thinking, anyone trying to get to the Antonov will have to travel north up the track from the Khoi Marand main road. It's steep in parts. Our guys could arrange a landslide, push Bora and Demir over the edge. It doesn't matter if they survive as long as they don't get the jacks to the plane. A crash like that would almost certainly put the jacks out of action.'

'Yes. That's a possibility.' Julia swept the image through her mind. The two agents could work it, but it still left the aircraft with the cargo, whatever it was.

'Couldn't we destroy the arms? Set fire to the aircraft?' Gunter broke in.

Byelov looked at the end of his cigarette, narrowed his eyes, his mouth turning up at either side. He held the posture, the smoke from his cigarette slowly curling upwards towards his nose. Gunter jumped as Byelov suddenly gave a gigantic sneeze.

'Bloody Georgian tobacco.' Byelov viciously stubbed the cigarette out. 'It's good Gunter. Yes. We set fire to the damn plane. We don't want the arms anyway.' He paused, shuffling among his box

of cigarettes. 'But how to do it so they don't know? We mustn't let
them find out we have surveillance on Moosar.' He disappeared
behind the fog of the new cigarette.

Julia knew she could enter the debate again. Gunter had made
a good suggestion, now was the time for technical input. She spoke
into her desk microphone.

'Ron, is Torps with you?'

'Yes, but we're just about to drop him off on the Linton job.'

'Put him on from the van will you? Thanks.'

Torps was an ex torpedo Petty Officer. He played with tor-
pedoes like a swimmer with a dolphin. He could build them, run
them and demolish them. Burning a plane would be child's play.

Byelov coughed.

'Did I hear you asking for Torps?'

'Yes.'

'Then I won't get Alix out of bed.'

Julia feigned astonishment.

'Your engineer's in bed? At this hour? It's already after lunch in
Moscow?'

Byelov grinned.

'He had a hard night. He's getting married next week.'

'Oh.' She laughed. 'Stag night,' she said it in English.

'What?'

'Stag night,' she repeated, 'when the boys go on the town before
their wedding . . .' She stopped as she saw Byelov's blank look.
'Forget it,' she laughed again. 'Drinking.'

Byelov brightened up. 'Drinking. Yes, that's it. Drinking.' His
face became gloomy. 'But I missed it. Bloody Moosar. My life is
Moosar. Bloody Moosar. I wish . . .' He broke off as his screen
became alive with a new face, round and originally from Jamaica.

'Torps here. You want me?'

Julia nodded at Byelov. 'You do this, Maxim.'

Byelov broke into English.

'We think the PKK have an Antonov 32 in trouble on an airstrip
in Iran. Two hydraulic jacks are on their way, probably for an
undercarriage repair. We want to take out the aircraft and its cargo,
possibly heavy arms, without the PKK realising it's sabotage.'

They watched Torps hunched in the van, switching his mind

from the job he was going to, sitting quite still, focussing all his energy on the new problem. Suddenly he smiled.

'No use settin' fire to it,' his accent lilted out of the screen, 'what you needs is paint stripper.'

'Paint stripper?' Gunter jerked the word out.

Torps' smile burst into a chuckle. 'Yeah, man, let me tell you what to do.'

CHAPTER TWELVE

Waterloo International Railway Station was steamy in the hot June afternoon, and John Hammond attracted no attention as he caught the mood and patiently stood on the escalator taking him to the Eurostar departure gate. Just another businessman catching the 3 o'clock train for Paris for an evening's fun before a meeting the next day. Even the group of students sprawled in front of the ticket desks were subdued, slowly sipping Coke or dozing with their heads on their rucksacks. He had to look sharply at a skimpily dressed girl who suddenly stepped towards him from a stand advertising a hayfever cure. But her eyes were dull, bored and tired, so when he shook his head she listlessly fell back, dropping her hand with the leaflet in it.

Hammond looked at his watch, just enough time to buy a late paper before boarding. He walked more quickly now, feeding his ticket into the machine, moving through the security scanner, no baggage, no coins, no metal, nothing to attract notice. The security guards paid him no attention.

He swept round the corner to the newspaper stand. Collided with someone stooping over looking for something. Desperately tried to put his hand onto the counter to stop himself falling. Failed. Crashed in a heap. Sprawled over the idiot who was stupid enough to be bent down just around a blind corner.

'Merde, alors. Imbecile. Qu'est ce que vous . . .'

The tirade stopped. Hammond found himself transfixed by two blazing green eyes.

'You.' The word was venomous.

He half sat, gently rubbing his elbow. 'Lost another contact lens?'

Her full lips parted. She took in a breath, followed his eyes and quickly arranged her skirt over her legs.

'Let me help you look.' He glanced up at the newsagent who was bent over his counter, gazing at her with his mouth open.

'Got a torch, Sam?'

'I don't need a bloody torch.' She crouched onto her knees.

'Always good for finding contacts.' Hammond was standing now, looking down at her, laughter in his eyes.

'I haven't lost my bloody contact, you idiot.'

'What on earth are you doing down there, then? You seem to have a habit of burrowing around on the floor.' He stopped.

'Oh! Is this it?' He picked up a train ticket, went to pick up her briefcase.

She pounced on it, dragging the leather case towards her. Took hold of a chair, pulled herself up, hobbling on one foot as she found a loose shoe with the other.

'I'll have my ticket too, please,' the words ground out, her hand stretched in front of her. Rigid.

He gave it to her. 'No word of thanks, Charmian?'

She tossed her hair, a blonde strand floating back over her nose. She blew it away. Turned, gripping her case and ticket, walked into the crowd, stiff and uncompromising. People stared after her as she barged through them, her case ploughing a furrow which she followed.

Hammond pushed his way back to the ticket desk, shoved into the front of the queue.

'Sorry. Urgent,' he smiled, 'Father's just telephoned. Mother's in hospital.'

There were murmurs of sympathy. The queue held back. He pushed his ticket over the desk.

'Change this seat to Carriage 1 Seat 46, please.'

'I thought your mother was ill.' The ticket clerk glared at him, her cheeks pouting under the bottle blonde swept up hair.

He winked at her, the pale blue of his eyes switching to inviting humour.

'I'd do the same for you.'

She looked at the short sandy hair, took in the firm chin, the charm in his voice. Gave an audible sigh.

She reached down, pulled out another ticket, wrote across it, pushed it through the window slot.

He took it, saw she'd written her phone number in the corner.

'You could be reported for that.'

She laughed. 'By you? That'd be nice. I've never been reported before.'

He laughed in turn, waved the ticket, looked at his watch, started pushing his way back through the crowds. Heard the loudspeaker announce the departure of the Paris train in three minutes. He shoved in earnest then, only hesitating to apologise to an old lady as he held her to one side. He climbed into Carriage One just before the doors closed.

'Hello, Charmian,' he said, 'I didn't know you were on this train.'

She started, colour flooding her cheeks, half stood, looking around the carriage.

His mouth turned down. 'No. It's full, I'm afraid.'

She sat down again, dropped a hand to rub her knee.

'Did you get hurt again? I'm sorry,' he sounded genuinely sympathetic.

She glared at him.

'You seem to spend all your time jumping on girls.'

The couple opposite exchanged glances. The woman leaning forward a little, her bright red nails clamped onto her plastic coffee cup.

Hammond noticed it.

'Lets go and eat,' he said.

'You think I would eat with you?' She shook the pages of her newspaper. 'After that?'

The red nails squeezed the cup, the coffee swirling up alarmingly near the rim.

'With you crouched down like that, how could I help it?'

The coffee erupted out of the cup. Swimming across the tabletop.

Charmian jumped up.

'Scheisse.'

'You speak German?' Hammond gave her an appreciative look.

She was dabbing her handkerchief at a drop of coffee on her dress. Pale orange and cream, simply cut, with a halter neck, a long, gold Russian chain her only jewellery

'I speak Russian and Spanish, as well,' she hissed. 'Now get out of my way. I want to clean my dress.' She gave a withering look at the woman now cowering in her corner.

He gave way as Charmian moved out of the seat. 'Russian and Spanish, as well? I'd call that very talented.'

When she returned, his seat was empty. The woman opposite silently pointed to a card on the table. It was an invitation to meet the Greek Cultural Delegation at the Cluny Museum in Paris that evening. Scrawled across the bottom he'd written "How's your Greek?"

CHAPTER THIRTEEN

The Curator of the Cluny Museum, or to be exact the Musee National du Moyen Age in the Sixth Arrondissement of Paris, saw the flash of the silver cigarette case. He sighed heavily, knowing this sort of thing would happen. Diplomats these days were not what they were, no respect for the truly beautiful things in life. He had not wanted the Reception here. In this room housing these precious fifteenth century Lady and the Unicorn Tapestries, the beautiful wife of the French crusading knight looking down from the walls, each of her senses portrayed in the taste of fruit, the sound of a lyre, the smell of a flower. But the Minister of Culture had insisted. The Foreign Minister was entertaining the Greek delegation to the International Forum on Looted Art and he wanted to emphasise the Frenchness of the tapestries. The Curator apologetically pushed his way through the chattering officials, between the Minister for Defence and his ultimate boss the Minister for Culture.

'Excuse moi, Monsieur, pas de fumee.' He motioned towards the walls of the room.

The hand of the man he addressed froze on the silver case, carefully nursed the flat Turkish cigarette back to nestle among the others, snapped the case shut, sliding it into the pocket of his dark blue Favourbrook suit. He looked at a large, gold and onyx signet ring as his hand came away from the pocket.

'I am so sorry, Monsieur Thibault, I should know better. This ring was worn by my ancestors, when these tapestries were being stitched by the ladies for the merchant de la Viste. I know their value.'

The Curator was impressed by the man's historical knowledge and lineage and by the personal use of his name.

'You are kind to understand, Monsieur,' he made a slight bow, 'and to remember my name.'

'The kindness is yours Mr Thibault. You gave a private tour of your Museum to my wife, Madame Dedain. She loves this room. She asked if I would commission tapestries to be made for her, as de la Viste had these made for his wife, Lady Claude.' His eyes swept the room and returned to rest on Thibault. 'I told her that it had cost de la Viste the equivalent of five million francs.'

Thibault's face went scarlet as he remembered the tall, graceful Madame Dedain, widow of General Dedain, the last of the Dedain family, tracing its routes to the Revolution and Napoleon. Her visit to the Museum had been some months after the death of her husband. Thibault had thought that she was using the private visit as an excuse to start going out into the world again and the five million franc donation she made, whilst she'd sipped wine in his vaulted, sixteenth century oak furnished office, reinforced this view, particularly as, in the time honoured way, she had insisted that he should accept a trifle as his commission for work well done. He clearly remembered escorting her down the ancient monastery stone stairs and into her chauffeured Jaguar in the cobbled courtyard before opening his envelope, dropping down in surprise onto a rare fourteenth century stool, staring at his cheque for half a million francs.

The man was speaking again. 'When she came home she told me what a delightful afternoon she had had. How excellent you were at your job,' he paused, 'and how you deserved her thanks.'

Thibault's eyes widened, the impact of the words numbing him. She must have already been married to this man when she had visited. A large commission from a widow was one thing, from a businessman, and this man looked every inch a businessman, it was another. The possibility for pressure, for obtaining illegal artefacts was obvious. Thibault started to sweat. There had been a series of high profile trials recently, of civil servants caught accepting commissions. Nasty stuff, ignoring the unwritten code that had eased the administration of French government for centuries.

'My dear Mr Thibault,' the man was smiling now, 'you will be sorry to know that museums are not my interest. If they were, I would have accompanied my wife. You can be sure you will not catch me trying to smoke here again.'

Thibault devoured the words, almost hugged the man, almost gasped for air as the noise in the room and the heat of the bodies rushed back into his senses. He'd been foolish to worry, stupid to think that everyone was on the make. He clenched his hands, steadied himself.

'Please give my regards to your wife, Monsieur. And tell her that even the gift of these tapestries would be poor reward for her graciousness.'

'If you are talking of Monsieur Albert's wife, then you are right.' The tall, austere, iron grey haired Minister of Defence looked down at Thibault.

His eyes moved on. 'Albert, how is she? Not here tonight?'

Thibault quietly moved away as Albert lifted his large head to look up at the Minister. 'Ah, Gilbert, good to see you. Francesca is at home. Charlie is with me tonight, unless she's already gone.' He turned. 'Charlie, oh, you are here, I thought you might have left for that awful Ionist exhibition.'

Charmian Dedain laughed. 'Hello Minister, take no notice of Albert. You would think he would have learned some taste since he married my mother.'

'Tell me Charlie,' The Minister of Defence raised a plucked eyebrow, 'what is this Ionist exhibition?'

'Post modernism ended with the twentieth century, Minister,' a voice cut in, 'now, after seven years in the wilderness, the avant garde have discovered Ionism.'

Charmian swung round, slopping her drink over the Minister's jacket.

Hammond took a handkerchief from his pocket and dabbed at the wet patch. 'Ionism, relates to the Ion belt in space, electrically charged particles. As art it depicts our future, confounding the old ideal that art reveals our present or past.'

He stepped back, handkerchief poised, looking at Charmian. 'No harm done, Charlie. Primary colours are sprayed on to small metal filings of all shapes and sizes. When dry the filings are mixed together. Spread over the floor. The canvas is then daubed with thick plaster, thrown on or spread by hand. The canvas with the wet plaster is then suspended horizontally over the filings. The artists then take two strong electric magnets and manoeuvres them around the back of the canvas. The particles are attracted randomly towards them and onto the plaster.' Hammond stopped, taking in the Minister's astonished face. 'That is Ionism.'

The Minister shrugged his thin shoulders. 'Did you know this, Albert?'

'My dear Gilbert, Charlie lives in Montmartre. When she is not at the Quai d'Orsay working for our friend the Foreign Minister, she is there, supporting every starving artist in the village. And painting furiously herself.' He stopped a waiter. Took a glass of white wine off the tray. 'Yes, I think painting furiously is the right expression. I know all about Ionism, I can assure you. In fact I have a room full of Ionist paintings.' He paused to take a small sip of the wine, making a show of it, savouring it, sliding it over his tongue. 'Well,' he added, 'a garage full, actually.'

Gilbert gave a shout of laughter and patted Hammond on the shoulder. 'Albert, how did Paris survive before you came to join us? Do you know John Hammond?'

'No, but if he knows about Charlie's art he can escort her to this exhibition and I can have a quiet evening with Francesca.' He held out his hand. 'I'm Charlie's stepfather and,' he held out her hand, 'this is Charlie.'

Charlie snatched her hand away. 'I already know Mr Hammond. I have no need of an escort.'

Albert looked at Hammond, his eyes just flickering under their heavy lids. 'Yes, but I need a quiet evening. Monsieur Hammond?'

'I'll be delighted to go with Charlie. From previous experience I'm sure it will be very exciting.'

*

'He has some force I think,' murmured Albert as he watched them go.

'Yes,' replied Gilbert, 'he holds some interest for me too.' He sipped his drink. 'Is there anything to this new bond the Mauritius market is offering?'

Albert frowned slightly at the change of subject. 'Are you asking my advice as a private banker in Paris or as a businessman with interests in Mauritius?'

Gilbert thought about the question. Albert was the Director and

sole shareholder of the Banque Matin. Established in Paris four
years earlier, the bank had rapidly attracted large sums of knowing
money, but only money from families or businesses that had been
traditionally wealthy. No firm or private person with wealth of less
than twenty years standing got through the elegant wrought iron
doors in Rue de Rivoli. Albert had spurned the financial centre of
the City and gone for an old fashioned, tall windowed, balconied,
ornate office building in an elegant shopping area, relying on
electronic communication to conduct his business. No client came
near his bank. The private and personal encoding chip provided by
Albert guaranteed to keep all communications completely secret,
safe from the prying eyes of all, even the French Intelligence
Services.

And Gilbert had used Ministry of Defence Intelligence to dig
around into Albert's past before he had decided to use him as his
banker. Intelligence had told him that Albert was Lebanese. His
parents had been killed by the French in World War Two for
supporting Lebanese independence. Little was known of his early
life, until he emerged as a gold trader in Beirut, later switching his
operation to Vienna where he bought into Grazprivatbank and, as
a private banker, took over Dempsey's Bank. Dempsey's was
shrouded in mystery, some people claiming it had been owned
illegally by a prominent British politician. But the takeover had
been declared legal and a year later Albert had moved his whole
operation to Paris. He had married the widow of General Dedain.
Like his forebears since Napoleon, Dedain had been a vital part of
French society and government. Albert had also taken the widow's
daughter, Charmian, into the family, rapidly becoming her friend
and calling her Charlie as only her intimates were allowed to do.

Since knowing him and using his bank, Gilbert had found
Albert witty, popular and kind. No large French charity went
without a Banque Matin donation. Above all, he was shrewd.

'Advise me as a banker,' Gilbert replied, 'I don't know your
reputation as a Mauritian businessman.'

Albert smiled. 'Banque Matin established Banque Onde in
Mauritius three years ago, investing in the Indian subcontinent.
Mauritius has always had close links there, but I felt they were
underdeveloped.' He stopped as a short woman with cropped

black hair over arched black eyebrows and black eyes put a hand on Gilbert's arm.

'Minister, so elegant, so enchanting. This room. These tapestries are so, so,' she paused, as if searching for a superlative, 'French,' she smirked.

Gilbert turned to Albert.

'May I introduce you to Madame Simitis, the leader of the Greek Cultural Delegation.'

Albert held her hand and smiled into her eyes. 'Yes, the tapestries bear little comparison to your sculptures and temples, Madame.'

She recognised the faintly foreign accented French, sensed an ally in him. A day spent enduring French cultural superiority had been wearing and the wine had been temptingly good.

'I am forced to agree with you, Monsieur. After all it is not surprising, Greek democracy was supporting the arts when tribal warfare still raged in what is now France.'

Albert remained silent, letting Gilbert speak.

'A situation that is reversed today, Madame, I think.'

She snatched her hand away from Albert.

'That is a matter for the Turks, Minister. Excuse me, please.' She swung round and bumped a way through the crowd.

'Bloody Greeks,' Gilbert said. 'Always so damned culturally superior. Thank you, Albert.' A thin smile spread on his lips. 'Most adroit to lead her on like that.'

'Greek art is so cold, I think. All that marble and stone.' Albert looked up at the huge tapestry hanging by itself between the entrances to the room. He flicked his fingers towards it. 'The Lady and the Unicorn,' he said, 'look at her. Vibrant, rich, beautiful, serene. That is French art. That is France.'

They went quiet as they studied her, dominating the tapestry, her veil held in worship by a lion and unicorn.

Albert broke the silence. 'As a banker, my sources tell me the risk attached to the Mauritius bond is higher than normal. A good return, but a risky venture. But my sources may not be right.' Albert paused sliding his hand into his jacket pocket, wishing he could light one of his Turkish cigarettes. 'As a Mauritius business-man, I would highly recommend it. The bond is for the purpose of updating the Indian internal bus transport system. The Indians are good at running buses.'

Gilbert lowered his voice. 'If by "banking risk" your sources mean war between India and Pakistan, my sources assess that risk as very low.' His voice dropped to a whisper. 'And my sources are impeccable.'

Albert bent his head towards the tapestry and looked at the treasure chest held in the Lady's hand. 'Then I have no doubt the bond is a very good investment indeed.'

CHAPTER FOURTEEN

Hammond waited until the taxi reached Pont St Michel before he spoke.

'Do you always do as Albert says?'

It was not a good opening. Charlie simply shrugged and continued to look out of the window.

They passed the massive, gloomy grey stones of the Palais de Justice in silence.

He tried again as they crossed the Pont au Change.

'Paris makes me speechless too, particularly driving over the Seine on a June night with a pretty girl.'

She turned at that.

'I'm not a "pretty girl" as you put it, I am a senior member of the French Foreign Ministry,' she paused, 'in case you have forgotten.'

'How could I forget, I have the bruises to show for it.'

The taxi lurched to one side throwing Charlie against him. For a moment he felt the softness of her, before she pulled herself away.

'There you are,' he murmured, 'more bruises.'

She laughed. 'You are impossible, what about my bruises and the cut on my leg.'

He bent down to look at it. 'How is it?'

She moved her legs away, smoothing her short yellow skirt with her hands.

'Keep your eyes to yourself.'

'For an artist living in Montmartre you're very modest, not the way Albert described your painting at all.'

'Albert knows nothing about me,' she flashed,' my values are those of the Dedain family.'

He met her eyes. 'Then why do you do as Albert asks?'

She shook her head slightly and turned to look out of the window again, jerkily pushing her blonde hair to one side.

The traffic had eased in the Boulevard de Strasbourg and Hammond watched the boutiques and cafes and their soft lights stream past as they turned into Boulevard de Magenta. Paris was alive with people eating their evening meal at small pavement cafes, or just sauntering in the sultriness of the night. He let the images drift through his mind until the taxi turned into the Square Willette, just below the Sacre Coeur Cathedral and stopped sharply.

'We're here,' Charlie muttered.

She opened the door and the inside of the taxi was invaded by the madness of Henri Quinze, the electronic bass literally thrumming up Hammond's arm as he put his hand on the door to get out. He felt his other arm grabbed by a girl in an electric blue bodysuit who put a pair of shoes into his hands.

'What are these for?' he asked.

She shook her head, pointed to his feet and then the floor of the open fronted art gallery behind her. It was glass. As people shuffled over it, thousands of brightly lit particles shimmered underneath, moving and scattering with their footsteps.

He took Charlie's hand and put his mouth to her ear.

'We must have a truce,' he yelled, 'we need each other if we're going to survive this.'

Her wide mouth broke into a smile which reached her eyes.

'Okay. But this is my world now. Put on your shoes.'

He bent down, helped put her shoes on and then slid into his.

As he walked across the floor the coloured chips under the glass flew and floated under the glass forming fantastic patterns that flashed and glowed in the lights.

Charlie laughed and pointed. 'Look, you're painting pictures.' She turned. 'Like those over there.' She pointed to some canvasses on the wall, primary coloured backgrounds with swirls of metal chips streaked across them in a maelstrom of brilliance. 'You are an Ionist.'

'It's fantastic,' he shouted, 'how does it work?'

She pointed to his shoes. 'The soles are magnets and the chips under the glass floor are iron filings. As you walk, the magnets attract the coloured iron filings. That is Ionism. They don't just use plaster on canvas, you know.'

'And the music?' He pointed to his ears. 'Are they using iron filings in that, too?'

Her eyes sparkled. 'Yes. Sound waves are pushed through under the floor. As the iron filings move around they alter them. The sound is then reproduced on computer and sent out on those speakers.' She pointed to some small silver boxes at intervals in the ceiling. 'So you are making your own music as well.' She put her head on one side to look at him, her hair falling onto her bare shoulder. 'It's better than just being a bureaucrat, I think.'

He opened his mouth to reply but she had moved on, pulling him behind her, nodding to people as she went, waving her long arms delightedly as she spied a particular friend, her low pitched laugh greeting them as she hugged them and introduced Hammond.

He watched her, the short yellow skirt with its blue sash and matching top blending with the vivid colours worn by the crowd around her and realised now why she wore her bright clothes, in contrast to the other French civil servants, and why her gracefulness here changed to awkwardness, even clumsiness, in her work. Charmian Dedain was a front, a building erected by her parents in the cold design and style of eternal and honourable service to France the Dedain way. But the building was empty, the real Charmian existed here, as Charlie, in a welter of brilliance and excitement.

Deep down Hammond knew that it was here that Charlie reached for the future, just as he reached for the future with the plasma screens in the warehouse in Basingstoke. They had that restless search for knowledge in common. It was something he could build on.

He felt easier now. Getting to know Charmian Dedain, gaining her confidence, earning her friendship was essential. It was a sure path to the information he needed about what the French were up to and also a vital track into the enigma that was Albert. Albert the moneylaunderer and confidante of Gilbert, the French Minister of Defence.

But, as Hammond relaxed, he also issued himself a caution. Charmian Dedain could easily be dealt with at arms length. Charlie was a different matter. He would need to steer well clear of her.

CHAPTER FIFTEEN

Bora and Demir stopped their truck at the roadside café just outside
Marand in Iran. A dozen or so other gaily painted trucks and an
assortment of cars were parked on the sandy strip alongside. The
wooden structure of the café was faded and it was held together
here and there by rusting metal, an old Coca Cola sign nailed
diagonally across one end clung to the bleached, split timbers. They
parked the truck at the far end, away from the café, climbed out
and walked slowly across the heat hazed sand. Bora opened the
café door and they went inside, ordering mint tea and taking
advantage, with everyone else, of whatever cool air the inevitable
creaking ceiling fan could provide. No one stirred in the blazing
outdoor sun.

Except Byelov's G8 agents Abu Hamid and Mahmud. They
were crawling through the brush on an approach to the truck.
Gently pushing aside the mixed myrtle and pistachio bushes.
Stopping every few seconds. Before resuming the slow rhythmic
movement of their limbs. Like swimmers in treacle.

Abu Hamid gently came to the edge of the sand strip, ten yards
from the truck. Carefully he lifted the bottom branch of a grimy
smoke bush, biting his lip as yet again he cursed the luck that had
made G8 cut short his leave on Samos and bring him here.

'Perimeter clear.' G8SUR picked up his whisper, relaying it to
Byelov who was watching the operation on his plasma screen in
the Moscow Centre. Byelov studied the surrounding area shown
on the screen. There was no movement.

'Confirmed.' He said.

Abu Hamid waved Mahmud forward. He came in a gliding,
oiled movement. Slithering under the smoke bush. Across the
sand, climbing almost snakelike over the truck's tailgate under the

tarpaulin where it wasn't fixed to the side. In his hand a small canister.

The noise of a motor hummed onto the screen. G8SUR zoomed out, the road a shimmering ribbon. A bus wavered in the heat as the driver ground down through the gears, saving his brakes, if he had any. He was going to stop.

Byelov leaned into his microphone. 'Hold on both of you. Bus approaching.'

He saw the bus was an old Bedford. A relic of Iran's imperial past and trade with Britain. The bodywork was covered in bright, green, yellow and blue paint. Brilliant lines and dots and curves. Blue smoke gushed from the exhaust and a spume of steam gushed from the radiator. It fussed noisily into the space by the truck.

Byelov tensed for any sign of movement from Mahmud. The truck remained still, the tarpaulin undisturbed.

The door of the bus opened, sounding like a tin of loose bolts. Two women slowly climbed out. Their black burkhas covering their faces and bodies. They were followed by a man in western clothes, a baseball cap slanting across his head. He jumped down the steps beating the dust off his clothes. Finally the driver stepped down, hitching his djellabah as they walked over to the building. The door slammed. Leaving the lorry park in silence. The only sound a slight hiss from the bus radiator.

Abu Hamid started to move the smokebush branch again.

'Hold it.' Byelov's voice was sharp. G8SUR zoomed in on the bus. Crawled along its length. Suddenly stopped. Zoomed in further. On the man in the back seat. Crouching down.

Byelov spoke again. 'Don't move. Hostile in bus.'

The man was dressed in a black djellabah, making it difficult to see him in the darkness of the bus interior. He started moving. Backwards. On his knees. He reached under a seat. Dragged a reed basket towards him. Rummaged through it. Took out a magazine. Flipped through the pages. Byelov almost felt he could hear the buzzing of the fly hovering around his eyebrow. The man shuffled backwards again. Byelov could see the sweat dribbling down the man's oval face, catching in his beard. This time he found a cardboard box. Opened up the flaps. A trickle of flour spilled onto his lap. Carefully he pushed his fingers into it. Feeling around.

Mahmud was clenching his fists under the tarpaulin. Pouring sweat in the humidity. He had been there eight minutes so far. He was feeling suffocated. Desperate to search for air. But he knew that any movement would shift the truck body. Or the tarpaulin. If the man on the bus was an ordinary thief he would keep clear. Keep quiet. But if he was secret police he could be on him like a hyena. Mahmud bit his lip to stop his lungs from heaving.

The only thing to break the silence was the man scrabbling the box back under the seat. And a blowing noise as he scattered the flour particles.

In Moscow, Byelov jumped as metal hit metal. The tarpaulin on the truck bulging.

The man in the black djellabah jerked up his head. Turning violently to look behind him. Turned back. Rapidly crawled to the back seat. Slid onto it. Pulled his scarf over his face and fell still.

Byelov shivered as the cold sweat rolled down his back.

'It's OK. Clear to work. Clear.'

Straining to be calm, Mahmud lifted the tarpaulin and gulped in the hot, dry air. Filling his lungs. Trying to slow his heartbeat. He opened the canister and crawled to the hydraulic jacks. Careful to avoid bumping the tarpaulin. Using both his hands he spread the paint stripper over the rubber pressure pipes on the jacks. Liberally splashing the stuff as it rapidly evaporated on them. The smell was overpowering. His head began to swim as the fumes took out the oxygen in the confined space. Almost sobbing, he emptied the last of the canister onto the pipes.

Mahmud almost fell out of the truck. Crawling painfully across the sand. Clutching the cylinder. Abu Hamid leant forward. Pulled him the last few feet. The bush closing over them.

Byelov watched the screen as they went. Abu Hamid coaxing Mahmud through the myrtle, sage and thyme. Then up and stumbling towards their own truck. Byelov knew that Mahmud would have stayed to apply enough of the paint stripper to perish the rubber. Torps had insisted that it must be applied in the heat, so that it would dry and remain unnoticed. Byelov hoped that Bora and Demir wouldn't stay too long in the café. Torps had said that the paintstripper had to be applied in time for it to weaken the rubber but not obviously perish it.

Byelov nervously rubbed his eyes. Torps was brilliant at demolition, but Alix, his own engineer, knew the Antonov 32 inside out. Byelov wondered if he should have checked with his own engineer before okaying such a risky operation.

CHAPTER SIXTEEN

Gilbert Armand sat listening to the President of France, in the President's private office. The high ceilinged ornate room was otherwise silent, separated from the buzzing Paris traffic by the cobbled courtyard in front of the building and by the bombproof glass in the windows, carefully disguised to retain its eighteenth century architecture.

At least, Gilbert looked as though he was listening. He didn't care to be bawled out in front of the Foreign Minister. As Minister of Defence he had a dignity and a war record to protect. His stint as a Colonel in KFOR, the Kosovo peacekeeping force, had won him a Croix de Guerre for negotiating calm out of a dozen manic incidents where Albanians and Kosovans were working themselves into a killing frenzy and only he and his men lay between a peaceful night or mindless slaughter. During that time, his President had been delicately negotiating his way up the political ladder. A favour here, a fix there, comme il faut, no stench of open drains, of unburied bodies, of hours of covert, motionless surveillance.

The President glared at him. 'Why did you send that spineless civil servant, Roubel, to a meeting about the EU Army? He was demolished by Hammond, and that bloody German.'

Gilbert remained motionless, his arms resting on the long Louis Quinze dining table that served as the PM's conference table, his eyes fixed on the railings beyond the window across the courtyard.

'I told you that I wanted delay.' The President's voice rose. 'Delay. What have I got? Bloody near agreement for the bloody army. Your bloody useless Monsieur Roubel sat there while Hammond sorted out the bloody EU Army with Genscher. A package they can easily sell to the other bloody useless EU members. Didn't you brief Roubel to watch out for the bloody English offering to pay for it all?' The President leant forward across the table, his puffy cheeks inflamed, his eyes wide, slightly popped.

Gilbert didn't move. His mind was back in the Cluny Museum, from where he'd just been summoned: he was thinking about Ionism and Charlie. Extraordinary these artists, always thinking up something new, something startling. Perhaps he should get in on the ground floor. Albert might help him, it was just the sort of thing to make a lot of francs in a short time. Invest in a couple of artists, invest in Albert's daughter. His mind began to take a different turn. Investing in Charlie could produce more than a financial return. The long blonde hair, the green eyes, and he remembered her legs, those legs.

'Gilbert.'

Gilbert blinked, catching the smirk on the Foreign Minister's face.

He pointed to him. 'Your comments should be addressed to Claud, here, Monsieur President.'

Claud's face changed, cautious, wary.

'Why Claud?' The President put his hands together, a defensive gesture, his friend Claud Benoit under attack.

'Why Claud? Because the Foreign Ministry led the delegation with M'mselle Dedain. No doubt you have her report. My man Roubel was in no position to challenge her conduct of the meeting.' He sat back. Pity about picking on Charlie, but, following his earlier train of thought, he could always console her later.

The Foreign Minister put his hand on the table, started to speak. But the President interrupted him. He had no wish to see his friend Claud put down by Gilbert. Gilbert was a hero. In a France which had lost every war in distant memory, Gilbert had come back from Kosovo in a blaze of publicity. He had been on CNN constantly, filmed chatting to Albanians and Kosovans alike. Patiently accepting their insults, turning the conversation to football, art, films, music, anything to defuse the passions of either side. Surprisingly his culture had found a chord in those he spoke to and they raised their standards to his. His men never struck anyone or shouted abuse. They were good humoured and acted with restraint. He knew how to win hearts and minds. So his election as a politician was a foregone conclusion on his return to France. And his appointment as Minister of Defence was a publicity coup that no new President could afford to miss.

'Well, I just want to record my disappointment with,' the President caught Gilbert's eye, 'the outcome,' he faltered. 'I'm not interested in blame. Only results.'

He stood up, more assured now. 'I called you together today because we need to stop this drive for the EU Army right away. We have one more meeting at most with the English and Germans before the plan is put to the EU members as a whole. After that we will have great difficulty in stopping it.' He paused, his eyes wandering over the gilt edged murals and ceiling paintings of his room, trying to seek some comfort in what he was about to do and some reassurance that these two men in front of him would agree, or at least not disagree to the extent they would undermine him. His eyes dropped to his desk and his phone. He picked it up.

'Send them in.'

Gilbert and Claud looked at each other, wondering what the twist was.

The two men who came in were almost identical. Short cropped, greying hair, round heads on square shoulders, brown jackets over grey trousers and black shoes. One of them wore round, steel rimmed spectacles. He adjusted them with his right hand in a sort of salute.

'Monsieur President,' he said, ignoring the other two Ministers there.

The President looked at Gilbert and Claud.

'You know the Director and Deputy of the President's Intelligence Unit.' Then he turned back. 'Are the arrangements ready?'

'Yes, Sir.' The thin spectacles of the Director reflected the blue, green and white of the mural behind the President's desk.

'Run through them, please.'

The man glanced at the two Ministers then turned back to the President. The spectacles rose slightly as his nose wrinkled.

The President raised a pudgy, white finger. He didn't like these Intelligence types. Always out of control, trying to run the bloody country themselves, full of innuendo, weaving half truth into fact. A nudge here, a wink there, throwing out marbles. No Minister was safe with them. Any Minister who thought or planned otherwise was a fool. He smiled inwardly, relishing the thought that Gilbert was about to find that out. He caught Claud composing his face, lips a little pursed, eyes fixed on the papers in front of him, breathing deliberately slowed, prepared for anything, his mind ready to grapple with any insinuation. Bland phrases jostled to the front of the memory, on call to be plucked out at a second's notice, delivered without pause, plausible, defensible. But then Claud was an old hand. No former Mayor of Marseilles would have lasted two minutes without a dictionary of impenetrable answers to awkward questions. The President was pretty sure he could count on his old friend Claud. Gilbert might need a little whipping in though. The President flicked his finger at the thin, glinting spectacles.

'Get on with it.'

'All of it?'

'Yes.' The peremptory command gave him Presidential stature.

'Very well.' The man pulled off his spectacles, stared vacantly at the blue panelled double door at the far end of the room. 'Three weeks ago the Greeks staged an assault on their island of Samos. They immediately accused the Turks.'

'The Greeks?' exclaimed Gilbert. 'Are you sure? Our Military Intelligence reports confirmed it was the Turks.'

The President settled back. As he had thought, this was going to be enjoyable.

'Your Military Intelligence reports, Minister.' The spectacles were swept in a dismissive arc. 'We let them go. It was not in our interests then to contradict them.'

Gilbert dug deeper.

'How do you know your reports are correct?'

The spectacles were replaced, each lens carefully arranged either side of the nose, the sidepieces lifted and placed over each ear. The eyes refocused to settle on Gilbert's face, the lips twitching momentarily downwards.

'The next day the Turkish Ambassador was assassinated in London,' the eyes flicked towards the President then resettled on Gilbert, 'by the Greeks.'

Gilbert looked up at the Foreign Minister. 'This is absurd. Claud, you got your reports. It's absurd, isn't it?'

Claud agreed wholeheartedly with Gilbert. He had read the Foreign Ministry reports. Turkish attack on Samos, revenge assassination of the Turkish Ambassador.

'I thought you knew already, Gilbert,' he replied suavely. His hands and eyebrows rose at the same time. 'My sources are different to yours.'

Gilbert fell silent. He was sure that all this was just as much news to Claud as it was to him. But he'd just given Claud the perfect opportunity to hint that it wasn't. And at the same time he'd shown his own military intelligence to be slack if this story about the Greeks was true.

The President waited to see if Gilbert would dig himself further into the pit. He needed him to be uncertain so as to make the proposal that was coming more palatable. The silence went on a little longer, then the President nodded to the spectacles, which had remained steadily watching his Defence Minister. They glinted in response.

'The Greek activities were designed to make the EU think that Turkey was out of control and to stir up the EU to support Greece in a planned military strike against the Turkish isthmus north of Istanbul. The Greeks have been itching to get the Turks off the mainland of Europe for years. They have assessed that we will think the strike is in French interests as it will create a barrier to Kurdish migration from Turkey and warn Muslims in North Africa that strong measures will be taken against further migration from there into the European mainland. Their assessment is, in our view, correct.'

Claud listened to this theory of French foreign policy without a murmur. To his mind, the thought of relying on the Greeks for anything was laughable. He'd knocked about with them during his days as a seaman out of Marseilles. Always good in a fight, they were hopeless in any organised work. But to contradict this man in his spectacles would be extremely foolish, because he and his colleagues were the ultimate determinors of power. Claud had come across them before, when his activities as Mayor of Marseilles had required its use of a couple of banks in Monaco. Nothing really criminal, just a little sheltering of some cash for a rainy day. The colleagues of the man in spectacles had been polite, charming even, but they had produced copies of all his secret accounts, photographs of all the people who had donated to them and had quietly and briefly told him that his future lay in government. The Mayor of Marseilles was too small a job for him. They even told him which Ministries he would preside over, in the order he would inherit them. To date they had been right. So, as far as he was concerned, the Greeks were the most reliable of allies. And anything France could do to assist them was farsighted and sound foreign policy.

Gilbert laughed out loud, dismissively waving his hand at the spectacles. 'Your assessment? What does that count for?' He swept his hand towards the President. Knocked an ashtray into an uncontrolled slide across the polished tabletop where it flipped over an open orange juice bottle.

'Merde.' The President jumped up, grabbed his handkerchief. 'Here. Stop it going on the carpet.'

Gilbert sat still. 'Fuck the carpet. Are you listening to this idiot? Saying it's in our interests to support a Greek attack on Turkey. Did you hear that?'

The President struggled to reach the spreading pool of juice. His handkerchief spread out as he glanced at Claud.

'Claud tell him.'

Claud kept his eyes on his papers and instantly selected the correct phrase for the moment.

'This assessment has your approval, Monsieur President.' Claud hadn't a clue why. Only that the President had selected him to answer the question and that the man in the stupid spectacles had given him the answer. To join with Gilbert now and question the reasoning of the assessment would be political suicide. But to give the assessment his own personal blessing would be to burn his boats if things went wrong. A simple statement confirming the President's thinking kept him on the tightrope. Claud was tempted to look at Gilbert, but he resisted, deliberately kept himself still, detached, avoiding engagement.

'But is it your assessment, Claud?' Gilbert emphasised his concern. 'It can't be.'

Claud didn't move.

'This is madness.' Gilbert pushed his chair back, flung his hand through his hair. 'Stop mopping up that bloody orange juice and answer me.' He bent over, thumping his fist on the table at the President.

'Sit down Gilbert. You're making a fool of yourself.' The President was icy. 'I'm not having my carpet spoiled because you're too naïve to accept political reality.' He raised his hand as Gilbert started to speak. 'Face facts. We can only just control the rioting on our streets against this wave of migrants coming from Turkey and Africa. If we lose control, there will be anarchy. The bloody British don't have our problem. Ever since they secured their borders with the agreement in 2005 there have been no illegals going through the Tunnel. And only a handful get through by boat each year. The English are only interested in an EU Army to corral the Greeks and Turks. If France goes up in smoke they couldn't care less. They'll walk away as they've always done. They did it to my father at Dunkirk and they'll do it to me.'

'They didn't walk away in Kosovo,' Gilbert cut in. 'If we back them on the EU Army, they'll help us with the migrants.'

'On their terms,' the President snapped. 'Hearts and minds, civil rights, appeals in the Courts. That doesn't work, we've seen it. The system's clogged up and still the bastards come, our ports and border towns are choked with them. The Turks pile them into Greece. We keep pouring cash into Greece to try and stop it. It's bleeding us dry. They can only stop thirty percent of the migrants, the rest come on in, most ending up here or in Germany. We've got camps overflowing with them. Every time we send a boatload back there's a fight at the docks here and in Africa. We can't get them back to Turkey.' The President stopped. He was breathing heavily, drops of sweat trickled from his thick greying hair down over the podgy cheeks into the crevices around his mouth.

'We've got months, at most, before we're lost.' He muttered the words, slumped into his chair, his eyes fixed on the papers in front of him. 'We don't want a bloody EU Army and anyway it won't stop the bloody Turks. If we support the Greeks we can secure their eastern border.

Gilbert pre empted him. 'The situation's not as bad as that. My reports from the camps and navy ship movements don't support you. There are difficulties, yes, but anarchy? Rubbish.'

'Your reports?' The spectacles reflected the tabletop as they turned to him. 'Your reports failed to register the Greek attack on Samos.'

Claud now knew which way to jump. It was the perfect moment with Gilbert on the back foot. He shuffled his papers together.

'It is obvious we must support the Greeks.'

The President smiled, Claud was playing the right notes at just the right tempo.

Gilbert saw the smile, stood up.

'I've had enough of this. I'm not going to be a party to madness.' He pushed his chair away.

'You will want to hear this Gilbert.'

There was something in the President's voice which made Gilbert turn around. He hadn't traded with Serbs and Croats without sensing the slightest inflection in a voice and instantly analysing its meaning. The President was warning him. About his career? Perhaps, but that was politics. He could survive an open row on this issue, possibly come out of it even stronger. But it might be useful to stay and see what the threat was. Identifying it early in this fight would help later on. He sat down again.

The President looked at the spectacles. 'Tell the Ministers about Operation Albert.'

The spectacles were adjusted again, the minutest twitch, conveying the weight of a policy already decided.

'Albert is the owner and sole shareholder of Banque Matin here in Paris and Banque Onde in Mauritius. He is Lebanese. He was a gold trader and linked in with German, Polish and Russian organised crime in his early teens, becoming the moneylaunderer and fixer for seven mafiyas throughout the 80s and 90s. He established a high rolling gambling casino in Vienna and links with Grazprivatbank to assist in those activities.'

Gilbert felt himself go cold. In all his experience as a soldier he had never felt the real ice cold of fear. He desperately wanted to shout that this man was talking nonsense. That he'd had Albert checked out, that he was clean. But he daren't. Any intervention in

Albert's favour, any hostility would bring suspicion. And suspicion would bring questions. Awkward questions about confidential information and the timing of certain investments.

Gilbert kept his eyes focussed on the spectacles, forced his hands to relax on the tabletop.

The spectacles were taken off and slowly polished on the brown tie. 'What is not known, except by my service, is that Albert is the banker for the PKK. He handles all their finance and launders their cash to hide it for their operations and their investments.'

'But he's a Lebanese Christian, the PKK would never trust him.' The words were out of Gilbert's mouth before he could control them.

The light from a wall lamp flickered onto the spectacles as they turned towards him.

'At this moment, an arms shipment is travelling on an Antonov aircraft from Chelkar, Kazakhstan, to Van in Turkey. It was arranged by Moosar in Russia and the arms are bound for the PKK. Albert financed the deal.' The spectacles returned to face the President. 'Or, to be exact, we did.'

Gilbert was too stunned to speak. This bastard was financing arms to the PKK, was paying for terrorism. And the President knew it, approved it.

Claud shifted in his chair. 'I presume there is a good reason for this.'

The spectacles didn't move. The President cleared his throat, put his hands on the table.

'Albert has been an asset of my,' he coughed, 'the President's Intelligence Unit for two years now. He has assisted us in a number of cases when we have taken out organised criminals, including some of the alien smugglers. He has agreed, in return for irrevocable banking licences in France and Mauritius, to finance and direct an attack by the PKK on the Greek island of Limnos. The arms shipment is for that specific purpose.'

'I don't understand,' Claud muttered.

The President gave a small sigh. 'Gilbert has a point. The British and some other EU members will never support a unilateral Greek attack on Turkey, but if Limnos is attacked in force by the Turks they will have no option but to support Greek retaliation.'

Claud frowned. 'But it will be the PKK which will attack Limnos, not Turkey. There is no reason for the Greeks to retaliate.'

The spectacles looked up at the ceiling. 'The PKK will be in Turkish Army uniform. Equipment, codes, rations. The Greeks won't wait a moment. They'll be over the border and piling into Istanbul before the Turks have had time to blink.'

Claud shook his head. 'The Greeks will never be able to drive beyond Istanbul. The Turkish Government will still control middle eastern Turkey.'

The President smiled, stretched. 'Albert is ambitious. He sees the PKK creating an independent Kurdish homeland in southern Turkey, Kurdistan. While the Turks are busy fighting the Greeks, the PKK will launch a coup against the Turkish Government. With the Greeks on one side and the PKK on the other, the Turks will be forced to give the PKK what they want. Once the Kurds have their own country in Kurdistan Albert will stop the mass migration.'

'How can Albert control that?'

'Because, my dear Claud, Albert is set to become the new President of Kurdistan when the PKK take over.'

Claud ploughed on. 'How? How can that be assured?'

The President shook his head. 'Money, Claud, money. The PKK need it. We have it. Albert is the banker. He will be President of Kurdistan for five years. That's all we need. After that, who cares?'

Gilbert's mouth formed a tight, angry line.

'Bloody brilliant. And these PKK Muslims are going to have a Christian President?' He spat out the words. 'It's not an operation. It's a farce.'

For the first time he saw the eyes behind the spectacles. Darkest black, like twin tunnels, endless. The mouth below them worked, slowly, etching out each word.

'But you will not say so outside this room unless you want a microscope on your affairs with Albert.'

Anger surged through Gilbert, tinging his face red.

'I'll see you in hell first.'

But as he turned and walked through the tall mahogany door he knew in his soul that he wouldn't.

CHAPTER SEVENTEEN

At 3.00 am the next morning, the hydraulic jacks under the Moosar Antonov failed. Bringing the port wing smashing to the ground. Pulping Demir and Bora. Charcoaling their bodies. As the wing tank ruptured. And the aviation gas exploded. Burning the plane and the PKK weapons to molten metal.

*

Byelov reported Abu Hamid's and Mahmud's success to Julia. It didn't take long for them to decide that the destruction of the weapons shipment had dealt a massive blow to the PKK and that it was safe enough to follow Hammond's orders and turn G8SUR's attention away from them to watch the Turkish Greek borders.

Torps was delighted when he learnt that a tin of paint stripper was to be placed in G8's black museum.

CHAPTER EIGHTEEN

'Why did the pilots of the Antonov crash? Where are they now?'

Tansu recoiled slightly. She had come to Strasbourg to ask Albert for more money for another arms shipment to cover those lost in the Antonov. He was the PKK banker, it wasn't his job to ask questions about the accident. That was her job as the PKK Chief of Operations.

She studied him in the dim light of the private upstairs dining room in the Coq d'Or. His hooded eyes didn't waver from her face, the only movement he made was with the little finger of his left hand, the onyx ring glinting in the candlelight.

'You think I have no business to enquire?' His voice was flat, emotionless, intimidating.

She decided to slap him down. Celik, the PKK Leader, had personally asked to see her after the accident. She had been worried that he would blame her, but he had dismissed her apology. Accidents happen, he'd said, but it was vital to get another arms shipment in quickly, the PKK needed arms to defend itself if Turkey and Greece went to war. She tightened her lips.

'Yes. You have no business to enquire. That is a matter for Celik. You are just the moneyman.'

Albert took in the thin line of her lips, the scrawny angular body, the short cropped dark hair with the fringe that reached her eyes, black now in the shadow. He knew about Tansu. He knew about her Kurdish mother, tortured by Turkish Intelligence for sixteen days before dying, her body lost forever in some lime pit in the middle of Turkey. He knew about Tansu's vow, made when she was fourteen, to fight the Turks whenever and wherever and not to stop until Kurdistan was her independent homeland. He slowly selected a cigarette from his case and lit it with his gold

Dunhill lighter. His mother too had been killed for a cause. But he
had watched.

'Celik is a fool,' he said, deliberately.

She flung down her knife and fork, the sauce on her plate
splattering across the white linen tablecloth.

'I'll not stay here and listen to this.' She made to get up.

'You'll listen and like it,' snapped Albert. 'You have carried out
two major operations without Celik's knowledge.' He counted them
off on his fingers. 'The attack on Limnos and the execution of the
Turkish Ambassador in London. As Leader of the PKK he'd kill
you if he found out.'

Her eyes narrowed. 'Why would he find out? You wouldn't tell
him, we agreed we needed to get the Greeks at the Turks' throats
without him knowing.'

Albert leaned forward, his face close to hers, his finger tapping
on the table to emphasise his words. 'Tansu, we're not working
together. You're working for me. Until I came on the scene the PKK
was spent, Celik nothing more than a negotiator and the idea of a
free Kurdistan nothing more than a fantasy. He wouldn't have
agreed to what we're doing. But we have to do it. We have to get
the Greeks to attack Turkey. We needed weapons to do that. You've
lost them. If you're to blame then I'll find someone else to do your
job. Do you understand?' He leaned back, his hand reaching for his
glass of Riesling.

'Now, why did the pilots crash and where are they?'

Tansu opened her mouth to reply. Shut it. Gripped her fingers
together. Albert made a small movement with his glass, the wine
eddying into a little whirlpool. He watched it, wordlessly.

Suddenly Tansu shrugged. 'An engine failed and they damaged
an undercarriage strut when they landed.'

'And?'

'The crew are being looked after by us in Van. We are working
out how to get them back to Moosar.'

'Kill them.' The words were spoken so quietly she hardly heard
them.

'What?'

'Kill them.' Albert tapped his knife on the table. 'Do you want
me to spell it out?'

She raised both her hands.

'But they're Moosar, they belong to Moosar. If we kill them that's the end of the arms shipments.' She angrily pushed her plate away. 'They'll come for us too, kill some of us, for revenge.'

Albert turned the knife, catching the candlelight, throwing silver flashes around the room, onto the red painted walls, gilded chairs and heavy ornate curtains.

'Did Celik tell you that?' He raised a hand. 'No don't deny it. It's just how he thinks. Like this room, old fashioned, out of date.' He narrowed his eyes, leant forward on his arms. 'My dear child, I was dealing with the Moosars of this world before you were born. What did they send you?' He paused, drawing his lips back. 'I'll tell you. A broken down aircraft and a crew who couldn't fly it. Did you check the arms? Do you know what condition they were in?'

'We didn't . . .'

'No, of course, you didn't. You didn't get the chance because the aircraft went up in smoke before you could inspect them.'

Tansu felt her knees weaken. She had been so caught up in the blame for the jacks failing and sending the aircraft up in a fireball that she hadn't given the arms or the crash any real thought at all. She looked up at Albert, his face half hidden in the shadows, the flickering candles just picking out his eyes and the wet lips. This little Lebanese Christian shit was right. The blame lay with Moosar. And Celik hadn't noticed. She turned her mind to other things that she suddenly realised Celik hadn't noticed. Why had both the jacks failed? Why had Abu Hamid suddenly returned from his holiday in Greece? And there were other things, other operations, things she had dismissed as bad luck. They came crowding in on her.

Albert poured some Riesling into her glass.

'Yes, there are other things, aren't there? More difficult to accept now.' He leant away from the table to put the wine in the ice bucket, the rattle breaking the silence, jerking her head up.

'Celik is my leader. He has led us for two years now. I will not have him criticised.'

'I was criticising Moosar at this moment,' Albert said gently. He stretched out his hand, the stubby fingers finding hers. 'Of course, you must defend Celik. You are young, idealistic, and Celik is a hero. An old hero, perhaps, but that has an attraction as well.'

She had left her hand under his, not knowing quite why. He was everything she hated in a man: short, stocky, heavy eyed and with a total contempt for the world. But through his fingers she felt a magnetism, a power, a force that seemed to sweep into her. She shook her head suddenly and drew back her fingers, keeping her eyes locked onto her wine glass. She picked it up, her hand trembling slightly.

'Why kill the crew?' she asked.

He turned his hand palm upwards.

'To show Moosar that we will not tolerate second rate work or shoddy goods.'

'But they will retaliate.'

He drew in some smoke from the flat Turkish cigarette. 'They need our money and they need our business. If Celik had let me deal with them direct instead of insisting on doing it himself they would have known my intentions beforehand,' the rest of the smoke trickled out through his lips, 'and we would not have had all this unpleasantness.' Albert looked into her eyes and saw that she understood him. He waited.

Tansu bent her head, slowly tracing the inlay on the tablecloth with her finger.

'So we have to teach Moosar a lesson. It is necessary.'

Albert didn't move.

She slowly drew her hand across her forehead, still looking at the tablecloth. Her eyes barely moved.

'Celik will not approve.'

'No.' The simple negative was just whispered across the table.

'I will have to think about that,' she murmured.

He took her hand again. 'Yes,' he said, simply.

She let her hand rest there. For sixteen years she had been fighting the Turks. First, as a courier, then keeping safe houses, moving on to plant bombs before becoming the Deputy Chief of Operations. She had lost count of the number of Turks she had killed or caused to be killed. And her Kurdish homeland was still as far away as it had been at the beginning. She knew, deep in her heart, that there was something lacking in the leadership. It wasn't the will to terrorise, to maim, to kill. It was something else. Until she had met this man tonight she hadn't recognised it. But now she knew. It was the ability to have foresight and be ruthless in exploiting it.

This man sitting in front of her had that quality in abundance. And he had something else. He had the magnetic ability to win people over. And she had already carried out two operations at Albert's command without telling Celik.

He was speaking again, reading her thoughts.

'You, too, have the same qualities, foresight and strength.' He paused, drawing her hand towards him. 'And you are no longer a child.'

Later, Albert let her quietly out of the side door. She had submitted just as he'd known she would from the first few moments of meeting her. She needed a mother figure. Someone to show her the obvious and then soothe her and flatter her into doing something about it. What he'd done with her on the baroque sofa in the dim corner of that faded dining room was to reveal his maleness, to counter the mother image and become necessary for her other needs.

He picked up his mobile phone and keyed in the number of the Director of the French President's Intelligence Unit.

'Albert here. Tansu is under control now. She's quite convinced that Celik did a bad deal with Moosar and has made other mistakes as well. She believes he's no longer effective.' He paused. 'She is near to being convinced that she is good enough to take over from him.'

He idly pushed a wine glass to one side.

'Yes. I think Celik will be gone within days. The Turks had a woman Prime Minister, you know, there's no reason why the PKK shouldn't have a woman as their leader.'

He smiled, listening again.

'Yes. I can arrange a new shipment with Moosar within a few days.'

He listened again.

'No, the pilots will have to be killed, I'm afraid. Tansu will be much more confident after that, confident enough to take out Celik. At least, she will be after I've had another word with her.'

CHAPTER NINETEEN

Gilbert was in his shower when the phone call came from Military Intelligence to tell him about the destruction of the Antonov. He didn't return to the shower but instead carefully dressed, mentally steeling himself for the phone call he knew would come next. When he had stormed out of the President's office he had felt, deep down, that he would have no alternative but to support the President's plan to help the Greeks. But since then he'd had time to think. The French people were against war. They had shown that when they had walked away from Iraq, so they certainly wouldn't want to get involved in an adventure between Greece and Turkey. All he had to do was to go public with the President's plan and people would flock to support him. With his peacekeeping record in Kosovo he might well be swept into power. Become the new President for peace.

The real danger lay in the threat that his investment dealings with Albert would be exposed. But he'd thought about that too. The President's Intelligence Unit would be desperate to prevent any revelation that Albert was one of their assets, one of their informants. They would not only lose a valuable tool within the PKK but also amongst Albert's private clients who were powerful members of the French elite, an elite the President relied on. They expected the Government at least to keep their lives discreet. Having thought it through, Gilbert was confident that he could oppose the President's plan and win.

So when the next phone call came ten minutes later he was able to agree the meeting with the President's Intelligence Unit with a degree of self-assurance that surprised the Director.

A little later that morning, in the slight chill of a June river mist, Gilbert had his own surprise when he saw the venue of the meeting. The twin hundred horsepower outboards were already rumbling on the twenty five foot high prowed, high cabined river cruiser. She was tied up to a grid on the Seine just below the Parc Andre Citroen, facing up river. Gilbert looked down and saw the figures of three men aboard. He immediately recognised the two Intelligence men who had been at the meeting with the President. The Deputy was at the wheel, the other was the Director, this time his spectacles were slightly fogged with fine rain as they peered up at him. With a shock he saw that the third man was Albert.

Gilbert let his driver go and, thinking rapidly, clambered down the ladder let into the stone wall and grasped the cabin housing to jump into the stern well. He ignored the Intelligence men and held out his hand to Albert.

*

'Good to see you, Albert. How's my investment in the Mauritius bond doing?'

Albert smiled and gave a little shrug. 'I told you, the Indians are very good at running buses.'

Gilbert turned to look directly into the misted spectacles.

'Good. I want to make a very good turn on that investment.'

He staggered nearly losing his footing as the Deputy shoved the twin throttles forward and shot the boat away from the grid. 'Why the hell are we on this boat anyway? Why couldn't we meet in a civilised place?' he had to shout above the roar and crackle of the engines.

'Because G8SUR can't pick up your voice over the noise of these engines,' the spectacles had been taken off now and were being polished on a brown, gold striped tie, 'that is, if you don't shout so loud.'

'G8SUR? Why would G8SUR be listening in?'

The spectacles were waved at Albert. 'They might be interested in him. We don't know, but they might have learned about him.'

Albert smiled again and gave a small bow.

'I think not, but I'm flattered by your attention. Shall we get down to business, I have a plane to catch at,' he looked at his watch, 'twelve o'clock.'

Gilbert leaned forward to catch Albert's words. Out of the

corner of his eye he saw the spectacles being replaced on the nose and ears, trembling slightly in the vibration as the two hundred horsepower met the strong down river current. They turned towards him.

'Minister, I require you to meet your contact in the Kazakhstan Government to arrange documentation to cover a weapons shipment to the PKK.'

Gilbert struggled to check his surprise.

'What are you talking about?'

'PKK operations failed to secure the last shipment. They made too many mistakes. I want to be in complete control of this one.' Albert put out a hand to steady himself.

Gilbert wiped a fine spray of drizzle from his brow. 'The Kazakhstan Government will never sell arms to the PKK.'

The spectacles shifted slightly.

'Who said they were going to?'

'You did.'

'I said you were to arrange the documentation for a shipment from the Kazakhs, not the shipment itself.'

Gilbert stared at him.

'You want me to persuade my Kazakh contact to forge documentation for an arms shipment that the Kazakhs aren't actually making?'

The nose screwed up, lifting the spectacles with the movement.

'I don't understand why I am not making myself clear.' They turned to Albert. 'I am making myself clear, aren't I?'

Albert nodded, his eyes fixed on Gilbert's face.

'I don't think that's Gilbert's problem,' he looked over Gilbert's shoulder, into the mist, 'Gilbert doesn't understand where the arms will actually come from and how he is to persuade his Kazakh friend to obtain documentation.'

The spectacles made an upward movement.

'Tell him.'

Albert sat down on the side bench, slowly removed his silver case and took out a cigarette.

'The weapons will be bought by me from Moosar, an organisation with outlets in Kazakhstan. The Kazakh Government documentation will get my weapons unnoticed into Turkey.'

'Unnoticed?'

'Yes. They will be designated as agricultural spares. A Kazakh Government authorisation will get them across the border without any problems.' Albert turned his cigarette over and studied it. 'You will give your Kazakh contact one hundred thousand US dollars to secure the documentation. We could have made it less, but we want to be sure.' He flipped the cigarette into the water.

'I won't do it,' Gilbert's voice was flat.

The spectacles were taken off. 'You won't do it through your contact? Or you won't do it at all?'

'I won't do it at all. The whole plan is outrageous. I'll not be party to France stirring up war between Turkey and Greece.'

'The President . . .'

'Don't "President" me, don't threaten me. I'll go public, spread the whole thing across the press.'

The sudden silence let in the howl of the motors. The only tangible thing in the swirling mist. Gilbert had no idea where they were. He couldn't see either bank. They may have passed under some bridges but he hadn't noticed. Some hazy lights to starboard suddenly loomed into view but disappeared just as quickly. He caught the sheen on the spectacles as they moved.

'That is very foolish. I think you know that we have a full dossier on your activities with Albert here. The information you have given him,' a pause, 'confidential information, information of a secret nature.'

'You won't expose Albert.' Gilbert leaned forward, his forefinger poking the air, 'you won't risk the PKK finding out about him,' the finger stabbed at the spectacles, 'or you.'

Albert's eyes narrowed, his lips a tight line.

'Why will I be exposed?'

Gilbert put his hand out, touching Albert's arm. 'You won't, my friend. To damage me they,' he jerked his head at the spectacles, 'will have to show that I'm corrupt. The only way they can do that is to reveal my investment dealings with you in the Banque Matin and Banque Onde. I would retaliate by revealing your role as their asset. They'll never do it. You are the PKK banker. They need you or they lose their window into the PKK.' He gripped Albert's arm, smiling at him.

Albert removed Gilbert's hand. 'What about Kosovo?'

Gilbert's head shot up.

'Kosovo?'

'Yes. Kosovo. The information you gave me when I was working for Milosevic, for the Serbs.'

Gilbert's heart began pounding, he felt sick.

'What information? I never met you in Kosovo. You never worked for the Serbs.'

Albert's eyes focussed on the engines, still snarling at the stern.

'But that is what I will say. Your investments with me have nothing to do with it. The only thing I will make public is the fact that you fed me with information which helped the Serbs kill the Croats and the Kosovans. "Ethnic Cleansing", I think they called it.' He turned to look at Gilbert. 'Information which was secret to the French.'

Gilbert was white, his hands clenched.

'No one will believe you. My record,' he stopped, checking himself, 'read about it.'

The spectacles inched forward.

'You were a hero because the Serbs listened to you, did as you asked.' He let the words sink in. 'When Albert tells his story, tells about the help you gave him, the secrets, people will understand why.'

Albert tapped a fresh cigarette on his Dunhill lighter.

Gilbert stared blindly into the grey void. He knew it wasn't his own reputation they were talking about. In Kosovo he had represented France. His actions, publicised throughout the world, had won back for France the honour she had lost in two world wars and the lost battles for her colonies. After Kosovo, French people spoke with pride about France the peacemaker. If his reputation was wrecked, France would go down with him. He opened his hands and stared at them. The fingers trembled slightly. He had never seen that before. It had always seemed so easy. His personal life had never been in the equation. It had been other peoples' personal lives that had given him the key to unlock their differences. National pride, greed, guilt, distress. For the first time, it hit him that his success was due almost entirely to his ability to discern the weaknesses in others. And he had been so confident that it was due to his ability to inspire this, so confident in the adulation of the world press that he had failed to spot his own weaknesses. Had opened himself up to Albert and now to this bastard, who was lounging against the rail, his spectacles completely misted, so confident that he did not need to use his eyes to emphasise that it was useless to fight him further.

The river mist cleared slightly and Gilbert stared out of the boat at the nearest bank. They were exactly opposite the Parc Andre Citroen. They hadn't moved at all. The Deputy at the helm had simply shoved the boat into the stream and kept it there, using the engines to fight the current. A simple deception. Just like the one proposed by Albert. And just as effective. There was nowhere to go. Gilbert felt drained.

There was nothing else to say. 'When do you want me to start?'

The spectacles leaned forward followed by a hand clutching an envelope.

'Your plane tickets and the cash. The meeting's already been arranged. He's expecting you in Almaty tomorrow afternoon. The Kazakh Government's been told that this is a private, exploratory meeting to discuss the future supply of arms by the French Government.

'You were that certain,' Gilbert said bleakly.

Albert didn't move as the boat bumped gently against the ladder on the grids.

'Gilbert, you are a patriot, one of the few.'

Gilbert turned before gripping the ladder.

'You can cancel my investments. Send the money to this bastard,' he pointed at the spectacles.

They jerked off the nose a little as the boat ground against the grid.

'What's changed, Minister? It's yours. You keep it.'

CHAPTER TWENTY

'Hello, John.' Charlie held out her hand in formal welcome. Hammond inspected it, carefully holding it up to the evening sunlight.

'No paint,' he said, solemnly.

She pulled her hand away, looking quickly around her.

'Don't be ridiculous, this is business.'

'I thought it might be,' he replied, glancing around at the other people there: politicians, diplomats, bankers, their wives and partners, some jostling to get near their host, the Minister of Finance, others spread around the large open square in front of the Ministry of Finance building on the Rue de Bercy. Waiters weaved in and out of the guests carrying trays of drinks and canapés. Lights had been set up around the perimeter and they slowly became brighter as the sun set over the Seine. Hammond looked up at the enormous Finance Ministry block buildings, bleaker than the square, sandwiched between the Gare de Lyon and the River Seine.

'Only the Ministry of Finance would hire an architect who could design such a desolate square in such a delicate city,' he paused, 'just like their fiscal policy. Do you really think they can be persuaded to pay France's share of the EU Army?' His eyes dropped down to hers.

For a moment he saw them widen, then the lids lowered, hiding the light green. 'Of course, haven't we already agreed that?'

'I thought this Reception the Minister of Finance is holding might be to tell us that the money isn't there,' he kicked at a loose pebble on the paving, 'you know, delay things somehow.'

This time her eyes stayed wide open.

'You did read my papers.'

'What on earth d'you mean?'

'When we first met at the meeting in Brussels, when I was looking for my contact lens, when you took my briefcase.'

He was incredulous. 'Are you really telling me the Finance Ministry is going to delay? You mean that's the French brief, to delay things? I can't believe it.' He gestured towards the crowd milling around the Minister. 'I was only joking about him, all Finance Ministries try everything not to pay for anything.'

Her face was pale, an odd, confused look on it.

He put a hand on her arm. 'I never looked in your briefcase.'

She was chalk white now. 'Oh God.'

'What's the matter, Charlie? Is this man bullying you?' Gilbert came up and stood in front of Hammond, swaying slightly. 'He's known to bully people.' He flung an arm around her. 'All Intelligence men do, you know.'

'No, I wasn't bullying her, Gilbert, I was telling her about the Turkish Ambassador's death, about his little girl actually. Or, to be more precise, about the shoe we found, the only part of her that existed. But that's something you'd be used to after your Kosovo experiences.'

Gilbert slowly took his arm away from Charlie, inched himself to his full height, his face red around the thin cheekbones.

'I resent that, Mr Hammond. I resent that very much. I could never get used to that barbarity.'

'Different to some of your colleagues, then.'

Gilbert froze. 'If you are referring to that shit who was involved in that tobacco smuggling racket, I know about that and I can assure you that it was the only incident of its kind.'

'That's not what I heard.'

'You bastard, you are dishonouring France, you . . .'

Charlie cut in. 'For heaven's sake Gilbert, keep quiet, people are looking.'

Gilbert was breathing heavily. 'I won't have these things said, they attack France, they attack me.'

'That's a nationalistic attitude,' Hammond said dismissively,' it seems to accord with your policy not to join in the EU Army.'

'There are two sorts of nationalism, Mr Hammond. One protects the homeland at all costs, like the Americans, the other protects the homeland whilst respecting its obligations to the int . . . inter-

national community.' He swayed, shook himself slightly. 'I personally believe in respecting our obligations, joining the EU Army.'

'Meaning others in your Government don't?'

Anger clouded Gilbert's eyes again.

'Shit. You . . .'

'Gilbert,' Charlie tried to cut in.

'Shut up, Charlie. You and I know.' He threw a hand at
Hammond. 'He's right. There are people here,' his hand described
an arc around the square, 'people here, our own Government
people, who only want their snouts in the trough,' his voice rose,
'they don't care about the rest of us, the rest of the world . . .'

'Gilbert,' Charlie was tugging at his arm now.

He stopped, looked at her, startled. He then looked at the empty
glass in his hand. 'I need a drink,' he said and abruptly left them,
staggering a little as he moved around a couple in front of him.

Charlie turned to follow him.

'That was a rotten thing to do to him,' she flung over her
shoulder.

Hammond watched her go, the blonde head quivering with
angry indignation. Then, slowly, he threaded his way through the
guests, nodding to one, shaking hands with another before stopping to speak to Francesca Dedain. It took him only a few moments
before he realised where Charlie's deep green eyes and elegance
came from. Francesca was old France, witty, intelligent and
enchanting in a light green sheath dress that matched her daughter's for indefinable Parisian chic.

Whilst Hammond was entertained by her mother, Charlie had
caught up with Gilbert. His head was tilted back as he poured a
brandy down his throat.

'What d'you want?' he almost snarled as he put the empty glass
in front of a waiter and motioned for another.

For the second time that evening Charlie looked around her.

'I need to talk to you, Gilbert.' She hesitated. 'Alone.'

'Alone? That's good. I've been wanting to talk to you alone ever
since I met you.' Gilbert's words slurred a little as he took her arm
and steered her away from the remaining hard core diplomatic
reception drinkers around the bar. 'Not that we're alone,' he flung
his hand towards the Quai de la Rapee where the traffic thundered

along, cutting the square off completely from the river. 'We're . . .' he stopped as he caught sight of Hammond talking to Francesca.

'Bastard,' he muttered, 'talking to me like that. Bloody English, always so bloody superior.' He swallowed a mouthful of brandy.

'He's not like that.' Charlie regretted the words as soon as she had spoken them. 'What I mean is,' she stumbled, searching for the right phrase, 'he provoked you, deliberately. I thought you would have seen that. I tried to tell you.'

Gilbert looked down at her, the lines below his cheeks etched deeper as he turned his mouth down. 'I made a fool of myself, didn't I?'

Her bottom lip briefly moved against the other. 'You told him that the Government's split over the EU Army. You told him . . .'

'What are you going to say about it?' He shifted his eyes to look over her head, out of focus, unmoving, as he waited for her reply.

'To John?'

The eyes flicked to hers, suddenly intelligent. 'John? So it's John, is it?'

'If you hadn't drunk so much I'd resent that. You know I mean Hammond. It's common in the Foreign Service to use colleagues' first names.'

'Not when you say it like that, it isn't.'

Her body tensed under the dress.

He raised his hand, smiling. 'No. Don't reply, come and work with me, instead.'

She was caught off balance.

'Work with you?'

'In my Ministry. I can get you promotion, I want a foreign policy adviser I can trust.'

'Why this all of a sudden?'

He looked into his glass. 'I like you, you tried to take care of me this evening. I pay back my debts.' He hesitated, tipping his glass from side to side. 'Also I need a friend.'

She laughed, her hair falling across her face as she shook her head.

'You have more friends than any other man in the country, even the President.'

He looked at her swiftly. 'Not in the Cabinet, I haven't. You know them, are intimate with them. Your father was their friend, your mother entertains them.'

Charlie slowly brushed the hair from her eyes, taking in Gilbert's tall, angular frame, the thin almost ascetic face, the attractive honesty of him. He was nearly drunk, his words edging on indistinct. She had never seen him like this. He was always correct, controlled, adding a spice of humour to any situation. In a surge of sympathy, she imagined him ranged alongside his cabinet colleagues. Her own Minister, a street politician from Marseilles, working both ends towards the middle. The middle being the President, who kept his other Ministers on the sidelines, as he manoeuvred them against each other, using whatever titbits his personal Intelligence Unit could dig up. And she knew immediately that Gilbert was in trouble. Something had happened to make him behave so out of character. Something serious enough to actually undermine a man of his moral strength.

'What's happened?' she said, softly.

'They're going to . . .' he stopped, his eyes fixing on a lorry as it ground past beyond the square. 'Your stepfather . . .' He stopped again, looked blindly at her. 'I can't do this, Charlie, I can't do this to you.' He took a step forward, his hand feeling around her for the small of her back. 'I just need you, I just . . .'

'There you are Charlie, I've been looking for you.' Francesca Dedain marched up behind them and took Charlie's arm. 'Mr Hammond here is ready to take you to dinner.'

Charlie turned, flushing.

'I don't think . . .'

Francesca tucked her hand into Gilbert's arm. 'Did you forget the time darling? I'm sure Gilbert will excuse you. And I haven't seen him for an age.' She edged Gilbert away.

Hammond watched them go, Francesca almost as tall and certainly as elegant as Gilbert, holding him tight to keep his footsteps in line. He turned to Charlie.

'Your mother could teach you a thing or two on how to manage drunks,' he observed.

'You're always so perfect,' she flashed at him. 'Well, perfect is not my ideal, it's too cold, too precise, too . . . too English. Gilbert was right, you are bloody superior.' She turned on her heel.

'I wouldn't go without me. Gilbert will see you and be after you in a second. Even your mother won't hold him.'

Charlie slowly turned back.

'You think of everything, don't you? Well, not this time. I'll leave with you but I won't have dinner with you.'

'That's all right,' Hammond said cheerfully, 'I'll take you to the Gare de Lyon and put you in a cab. A quiet night or are you Ionising?'

She was forced to laugh.

'I do not Ionise, I am an Ionist, an artist.'

'An artist first, I think.'

She looked up at the Ministry block.

'I keep telling you, I am a member of the Foreign Service.'

He put out his arm to stop her crossing the road as a motorcycle flashed by hooting its horn, the car behind swerving. 'You don't concentrate enough for that,' he said.

She shrugged him off, striding across the road, catching her long strapped handbag as it fell off her shoulder.

'You might have provoked Gilbert, but I am immune,' she threw at him.

'Well, I can see you know all about provoking Gilbert,' he snapped.

She had reached the sidewalk. Surprised she turned to look at him, her mouth parted a little, her eyes shading a lighter green.

He joined her. 'Well, d'you want this cab?'

She shook her head slightly. 'No. I want a drink, please.'

He looked at the men swarming around the café, laughing loudly, swearing, an English football crowd, out for the evening.

'In this hole?'

'No. Let's go to L'Imbecile in Montmartre. I'm feeling more stupid than usual this evening.'

The cab journey passed in silence. Each occupied with their thoughts. Only made aware of each other's presence when the cab hit patches of cobbles, jerking them to one side or the other, touching lightly or bumping heavily, depending on the cab's speed. On each occasion the sensation increased the awkwardness of the atmosphere. Each of them trying to define the feeling in the sense of something to be borne rather than welcomed. It was a relief when the cab finally swung into the kerb in a small road behind the main post office. L'Imbecile was in darkness. Not a light shone, not a person lingered near it.

Hammond looked at it out of the window. 'It's shut. I might have known.'

But he was talking to himself. Charlie was already out of the cab, opening the door and going in.

Hammond jumped out, handed some change to the driver and followed her. The interior was as dark as the exterior, except for a faint phosphorescence around the walls. As his eyes became accustomed, he discerned tables ranged round a small room with couples sitting opposite each other, drinking from tall, black glasses, their faces barely visible in the faint glow. They were all engaged in low, earnest conversation. The odd laugh punctuated the near silence, but that was all.

Hammond saw Charlie sit down at one of the tables. He took the chair opposite hers. It was surprisingly comfortable, padded black leather on a supple black aluminium frame. The tabletop was black glass, with subtle silver flecks which reflected the light in a series of shifting patterns.

'What is this place?' he asked.

'It's where we,' she hesitated, 'where the Ionists come to think. No more than two people are allowed at each table. They talk to each other,' again the hesitation, 'about anything, their ideas, their art, their worries,' she traced a pattern with her finger, 'their future.'

'But why's it so dark? I can only just see you.'

'Because it helps people say what they feel. They can say things in the dark which they would never dream of saying in the light.' She looked around, the faint radiance catching the fairest streaks in her hair as she turned. 'It's why it's called L'Imbecile.'

Hammond stayed silent, sensing that to say anything would offend her somehow. Once again he was in her world. This time, a complete opposite to the mad evening spent at the art gallery. This was the other side of her. Hidden, deep, half understood but as vital as the emotions that lay in her art.

'When my father died, I spent a lot of time here,' she murmured, 'I thought I would understand,' she lifted her hand and let it drop on the tabletop. 'But I never did,' she said simply.

He didn't grasp what she was saying. 'You didn't understand what?'

'Why I loved him but could not find anyone else to love as much.' She smiled at him and made a small tilting gesture with her head and shoulder.

'What about Gilbert?' he asked.

'Gilbert!' she exclaimed.

'You were deep in his confidence just now. I thought it was more than,' he paused, 'business.'

Her eyes glinted. 'Gilbert is a friend, he's in trouble, that's all. And he was upset by what you said to him. You were very rude, you know.'

'Gilbert wouldn't have been upset if he hadn't already been in trouble. And he wouldn't have told me that your Government is split on the EU Army, is probably against the whole notion.'

Her head dropped. 'You wouldn't have known that if I hadn't told you.'

He eased his hand across the table and put it on hers. 'Charlie, you're not to blame. This is your world,' he nodded around the room, 'it's not the world of half truths and lies. I don't think it's Gilbert's world either. He's too honest. Is that what he was talking about?'

'I don't know, John. He's seriously worried and it's about the Government, but he didn't tell me why. I hope, I wish . . .'

'Charlie, this conversation never took place, I would never willingly put you in the position of confidante. I didn't mean to earlier this evening. It just happened. I hope you'll believe that.'

She nodded, quiet now.

He smiled. 'Well, if we can get hold of a waiter in this gloom and get a drink, I think I can help you out of your other problem.'

Her eyes darted to his. 'Other problem?'

'After we've got that drink,' he promised.

CHAPTER TWENTY-ONE

Rosie hurried into the kitchen as soon as she heard the crash.

'I told you I'd make the coffee, Mr Hammond. Now look what you've gone and done.' She bustled about picking up the pieces of bright purple and orange coffee mug, muttering, 'broken my Christmas present to you.' She looked gloomily at the broken bits in her hand. 'And you can't get these mugs in France. I got it special from Alf Green's.'

Hammond bit his lip. Alf Green's was Rosie's treasure trove, where she found the most hideous bric a brac that even favourite aunts could find no home for. It was hidden in the dingiest corner of Dalston in East London where Rosie was born. Ever since Hammond had hired Rosie as his housekeeper twelve years earlier, after she'd retired as a cleaner from MI6, she had proudly presented him with ever more ghastly trophies of anniversaries or holidays. He remembered, with a shudder, that orange sun hat she'd once given him. He hadn't deliberately dropped the mug, but, biting his lip even harder, he found it very difficult not to give a cheer over its demise.

'It's not like you to go breaking things,' she said, 'just like my old man, God rest him. His mother said the only time he broke things was when he was courting me.' A thoughtful look crossed her crinkled face. 'You're not courting, are you?'

'Don't be ridiculous, Rosie. Of course, I'm not.'

She sniffed disbelievingly. 'Come to think about it, you've been smelling of April and May all morning. What's she like? Not like that Russian girl, I hope. I don't hold with foreigners anymore, letting you down like that.' She stopped, her eyebrows rising under her dust cap. 'She's not a Frog, is she?'

This time Hammond laughed out loud. 'Honestly, Rosie, you're in Paris, you just can't go around saying things like that, you'll land us both in jail. I don't know why you come here, if you don't like them.'

She put her hands on her hips, emphasising her stoutness.

'Don't you frown at me like that, Mr Hammond. You know very well why I come here. If it wasn't for me you'd have to rely on these Frenchies to look after you. All that red wine and garlic. It's not proper. And as for cleaning,' she looked around the gleaming kitchen, 'well I've never seen one of 'em with as much as a mop in their hands. No I'll come over here each week until we go back to your London apartment,' she said in a resigned, saintly way.

He laughed again. 'You're incorrigible, Rosie.'

'I know what I am, Mr Hammond, and I know what I'm not.' She tipped the pieces of mug into the garbage bin with a crash. 'And I'm not living in Frogland. I never trusted Catholics,' she added inconsequentially, 'nor Communists, neither. Heathens the lot of 'em.' She started to untie her apron. 'I'll live in Dalston, it's civilised there and it's only a hop to Waterloo and the Eurostar.'

Hammond was left speechless, as he often was with Rosie. Dalston was the crime capital of London, every slacker, hacker and whacker had at one time or another lived or visited there. Rosie's husband had been one of the slickest key men in British Intelligence, sliding in and out of buildings like oil through a pipeline, and he hadn't learnt his trade at training school.

'Did you water the tomatoes?' he asked.

'Yes. Lovely they are. And don't tell me them Frenchies would have thought of a vegetable garden on the roof, because they wouldn't. Good English seeds, too. I've put in some beans,' she added as an afterthought.

'Now, your food's in the freezer and there's clean sheets on the bed. I'll be back next Thursday as usual.' She bent to pick up a shopping bag and packed her apron into it. 'I'll be off now.'

As she walked towards the kitchen door she stopped in front of a mirror, put a felt hat on her head, seized the brim either side with her hands and gave it a sharp downward tug.

'No use you turning the conversation like that, Mr Hammond.' She rammed an old fashioned hatpin into the felt. 'You're courting and she's a Frenchy.' In the hall she moved his tennis rackets out of the way. Opened the door. 'I can read you like a book.' Triumphantly, she shut it behind her with a snap.

Hammond sighed and reached for another cup. He slowly poured the scalding coffee into it and thoughtfully blew across the surface. He didn't allow his mind to go where Rosie had trodden but instead dwelt on Gilbert and the reason why he was under such pressure. He had believed Charlie when she'd said she didn't know. He felt she could find out, he'd seen Gilbert's pass at her. But he wasn't sure he wanted to push her down that route. She might get suspicious.

Making up his mind, he walked into the sitting room, glancing, as he often did, at Wolf Kahn's Corkscrew Swamp. The painting reminded him of the work in G8, with its bright blue and purple suspending the maze of pastel rushes in the foreground.

On the other side of the waxed maple floored room, hung, in complete contrast, Trees Against a Magenta Background, the slashing yellow and dawn rose crashing through the early spring trees to flood the simply furnished room with blinding colour. A close friend had suggested he should replace it with Encroaching Fog Bank, but, as Hammond said, one reminder of his work was enough. Besides, he wanted at least one of Kahn's works that revealed his genius with bright light. He walked between the large sofas and the clean lined sycamore wood desk

Just beyond the desk, hidden behind a shutter of the tall French windows overlooking the Rue Bonaparte opposite the School of Fine Arts, was a small panel. He licked his forefinger and put it on the glass. The tall plasma television unit slid open to reveal a small cabin with a workstation, chair and large plasma screen. He eased himself inside, sat on the chair and closed the unit behind him. The safe room was impenetrable. No hostile could see him, hear him or intercept his messages.

He typed a command into the computer. The screen showed Julia at her workstation, her short chestnut hair moving back as she lifted her eyes to her screen.

'Hello, John. Good to see you.'

Hammond panned his screen out to cover the other workstations, picking out casually dressed G8 operatives typing or leaning over their screens or talking in small groups. He could see some of the huge plasma screens on the walls of the Basingstoke warehouse and the information flashing across them.

'Got the troops under control I see.'

She smiled. 'Never know when you're going to drop in. I've got Lev and Walt online as you asked.'

Hammond watched his screen split as Lev appeared, emerging from his usual cloud of smoke, trying to stifle a chesty cough.

'Thanks for such a good job on the Antonov, Lev.' Hammond leaned forward. 'Abu Hamid and Mahmud did very well. Are they OK?'

'G8SUR picked up a query about Hamid. A female voice speaking to Celik on his mobile. We haven't identified her yet. Celik told her that Hamid was solid. She didn't sound convinced, though. We're keeping an eye on him. There's no problem with Mahmud, he still can't believe that paint stripper worked,' Lev laughed gutturally, before coughing again. He thumped his chest. 'Cough,' he said.

'Too much smoking, more like,' said Julia. She turned her head as the screen split again to reveal Walt. 'Hello, Walt, I hope you realise American Tobacco have a lot to answer for.'

'I don't touch that trash,' gasped Lev, 'only pure Turkish, or those disgusting Egyptian ones Hammond sends me.'

'There's nothing pure about Turkey,' Walt said, dryly.

Hammond smiled. 'That's what I want to talk about. The plan to bring them into an EU Army with Greece.'

'I thought that was approved and going ahead.' Walt's southern drawl became more pronounced.

Hammond read the signal heralding a bout of impatience.

'Except the French,' he interjected.

The storm was spectacular. Even Lev, who was used to Walt's tirades, looked awed. Four years after the French had shafted the Americans in the UN over Iraq, the merest hint of French politicking still lit up Walt's touch paper.

Hammond waited patiently. It was Lev who seized the advantage when Walt paused for breath.

'The French generally or the French in particular?' he asked.

Hammond smiled again. Lev always dealt in the personal, his

knowledge of human nature and his calm acceptance of the extremes of human behaviour lending him a benign contempt for the computer driven analysis G8 relied on.

'I believe there is a split in the French Government that is more dangerous to the EU Army concept than just delaying it.' Hammond paused. 'The French Minister of Defence, Gilbert Armand, is under a great deal of stress at the moment.'

'What sort of stress?' Walt grunted.

Hammond told them about Gilbert's behaviour at the Ministry of Finance Reception, careful to leave out any reference to Charlie.

'It's bizarre all right.' Walt rubbed his ear. 'I knew Gilbert when I was in Naval Intelligence. Never lost his cool, never drank much, strong under pressure, honest.'

'Honourable, you mean.' Lev's eyes screwed up against the curl of smoke trickling up from his ashtray.

'Honourable?' Julia repeated.

'Lev's right,' Hammond said, slowly. 'The word is honourable.'

'But just because Gilbert's got problems, that does not mean the French Government has.' Walt began looking for a way out.

Hammond pushed his shoulders back, looking directly at the screen. 'I read their brief.'

There was a silence.

'You didn't tell us this before, John.' Lev studied his lighter.

'The Brussels meeting met all our needs. It was irrelevant.' Hammond glanced at Julia.

She took his lead. 'What's important is to learn more about the French split, what they're going to do.'

'Ah, Julia,' Lev smiled, 'always managing us.'

They laughed.

Walt leaned forward. 'Now's the time to attack the French President's Office.'

'We've been through that before, Walt,' Lev said. 'It's political suicide for G8 to eavesdrop on any President let alone the French.'

'Who'd know?' Walt persisted.

'The French operatives in G8.' Hammond replied. 'They keep everything from French Intelligence but they wouldn't keep that from them. Would you if we bugged the White House?'

'Damn French,' Walt muttered. 'I just see a blur when they're mentioned.'

'That's why we have, Lev.' Hammond laughed. 'Any ideas from Moscow?'

Lev's hand moved from his chin and stayed suspended, the fingers stretching a little. 'Gilbert knows something,' he said, slowly, 'so Gilbert's the target.' He drew on his cigarette, his eyes looking beyond his screen, beyond his audience. 'And Gilbert is an honourable man,' he put his hand on his desk top, 'which makes him an easy target.'

'Easy?' Julia repeated Lev's words for the second time. 'I would have thought it would make it more difficult.'

Lev looked at her under his eyelids.

'Your only fault, Julia, is that you can comprehend ultimate goodness but you cannot accept that the capacity to do harm is limitless.'

She looked away, knowing he was right. She dealt every day with the dwellers of the deepest sewers but could never see the next deepest level until it came face to face with her.

'That's a strength, not a fault,' Hammond said, quickly, 'we need someone apart from the lawyers to keep a perspective.'

Lev's eyes rested on Julia. 'I didn't say it was a bad fault,' he hesitated, 'but it can be a magnet for pain,' he said, softly.

Hammond and Walt looked at Lev, knowing what he meant and knowing that one day, like them, she would pass through that barrier, with all that it entailed.

Walt broke the silence. 'So where's Gilbert's weakness? Women?'

'That's so out of date, Walt.' Julia laughed, as she punched the keys on her computer. They waited until she had finished.

Their screens suddenly split again to show some text in the top right hand corner.

Walt flicked his hand dismissively. 'So Gilbert's a close associate of Albert, Chairman of Banque Matin, Paris.'

Julia didn't reply as she typed in another command. More text appeared.

'That's no help either,' Walt said.

Lev leaned forward. 'Not so fast, my friend.' He read the text aloud. 'Banque Matin associated with Banque Onde, Mauritius.' Again he squinted faintly at some object above his screen. 'Is that all there is, about his relationship with this Albert, I mean?'

Julia worked at the keyboard again.

'He meets with him regularly at receptions, dinners, that sort of thing. There's nothing sinister in that,' she said.

Hammond opened his mouth to mention Gilbert's relationship with Albert's stepdaughter when Lev cut across him.

'There doesn't need to be,' Lev said decisively.

Hammond covered himself. 'What d'you mean, Lev?'

'Gilbert meets the banker, Albert, in public. People see them, they are obviously close. Banque Matin is linked to Banque Onde.'

'And?' queried Walt.

Lev waved his cigarette at his screen.

'Banque Onde is in Mauritius. Mauritius is a tax haven. Bank secrecy. Launders the cash for many of the Asian gangs, Japanese Yakuza, Chinese Tongs.'

It became very quiet.

Then Julia shook her head. 'We can't do that.'

'Why not?' Walt interjected. 'We've got the means. And this damn French Government is about to jerk us around. I say we do it. Take Gilbert to the cleaners and tell him we'll leak it to the press unless he tells us what the hell's going on.'

Julia's hand clenched. 'But he won't give in to blackmail. Lev said it, Gilbert's an honourable man. Men like that can't be bought.'

'No, Lev's right, Julia,' Hammond murmured. 'We open an account in Banque Onde in his name, or a nominee account traceable to him, and make a pattern of laundered payments into it, traceable back to an Asian gang or one of the Tongs or Yakuza. That would finish him if it was made public, worse it would finish his image.'

'But what motive would he have? What reason would he have for links in the Far East?' she shot back.

Walt slapped his hand on his desktop. 'Hell, Julia, he's the French Minister of Defence. They're selling arms everywhere. Everyone knows the Asian gangs and such have their fingers in that pie.'

'The only question that remains,' said Lev, 'is how much?'

'Anything less than ten million dollars might not create enough pressure,' said Hammond.

'Make it fifteen,' spat Walt, 'cheap at the price.'

'We'll get it back, anyway.' Lev raised his bushy eyebrows. 'Just transfer it to us after he's broken. One way or the other,' he added.

'OK,' said Hammond, 'Julia, set up investment companies in Nauru, charter a sea container from Bombay to carry ten million dollars split into boxes, destination Nauru. Mark them "computer equipment" for the investment companies. Do the same for five million from Madras, make the destination two insurance companies you will set up in the Cook Islands. Issue bearer shares from the investment companies and single premium insurance policies in Gilbert's name from the insurance companies. Open an account in Banque Onde in the name of a private accountancy firm you'll establish in Calcutta. Push a couple of million dollars into it via Singapore, through the Comoros Islands. Create instructions from Gilbert to the accountants to support their appointment as his nominees and to authorise opening the account and depositing the documents. Backdate the appointment three or four months.'

'Authority for funds for the administration costs of all this?' she queried, crisply.

'Agreed?' asked Hammond to his screen. Lev and Walt nodded.

'When do you move on Gilbert,' asked Walt.

'Soon,' replied Hammond, 'we don't have much time.'

Lev held up his hand, the nicotine on his fingers plainly visible on their screens. 'If you approach Gilbert with this, John, he'll know it's G8.'

'Quite,' replied Hammond, 'that's why Julia will do it. He doesn't know her. She'll approach him using cover as a Turkish Intelligence agent who wants to know what's going on.'

Julia shifted uncomfortably as Lev and Walt scrutinised her.

'I speak Turkish,' she said, defensively.

'And Russian,' added Lev. 'It's an excellent idea. In fact,' he said, brightly, 'we could have gone along with Walt's original idea, without all this complicated finance thing.'

Julia said something in Russian.

Walt blinked. 'I didn't know that was possible,' he said.

CHAPTER TWENTY-TWO

The sugarcane weaved and flowed in the updraft breeze of the gentle slope, flickering silver, gold, green, black as the leaves twisted this way or that. In the distance the tall, upright peaks of the Rapilles shone like chocolate fingers on a birthday cake.

Albert mentally shook himself as the comparison crossed his mind. He was becoming far too soft on Mauritius. Ever since his first visit with Francesca on their honeymoon, he had felt swept away by the magic of the place. There it was again, he thought. Magic. What a stupid, childish word. He'd never had a childhood, so how could he think of such a fantasy? Abruptly he turned away from the wooden railing and looked across the wide veranda which went the whole way around the single storey, wash painted, old French colonial plantation house. The apricot paint was faded, the white shutters peeling here and there. A clutter of wicker chairs bore signs of long use, the once bright cushion covers now softened by the strong sunlight.

'Sit down, while we wait,' he pointed out one of the chairs to Tansu, 'the old girl always takes her time.'

He watched Tansu as she sat down, her thin legs poking out of a baggy pair of shorts and her narrow chest lost in a loose, buttoned up shirt.

'We'll go shopping this afternoon,' he said.

She squinted against the sunlight as she looked up at him. 'Why?' she sounded impatient. 'We won't have time, we need to prepare for Celik. He'll be here this evening.'

'The only preparation we need for Celik is to show him that you are becoming sophisticated.'

'What do you mean, sophisticated?'

'You're still a child to him. When did you start with the PKK?

Fourteen? Fifteen? You were a puppy. He still thinks of you as a puppy. I know better.'

She flushed. When Albert had told her he wanted her to come with him to meet Celik in Mauritius she had literally felt her stomach turn over. She had never experienced that before. She had never taken much notice of men. And they hadn't taken much notice of her. She knew she was unattractive, and, after a frustrating couple of years in her late teens, she had learned to use her thin, anomalous features to her advantage. She was able to pass through Turkish security with hardly a glance. Essential when carrying a bomb or a weapon. And vital afterwards when the hunt for the face that caused the carnage was at its most terrifying. It had been years since she had thought of a man as anything other than a tool to inflict violence with or an animal to evade. Albert was over forty years older than her, an old man, yet in Strasbourg she had given herself to him as if he'd been the idol of her teenage dreams. And however many times she asked herself why, she had not been able to explain it.

Albert was talking again. 'You are Celik's Chief of Operations but you have no say in political decisions. It's time you did.'

She folded her skinny arms. 'I'm not very good at the political stuff. Who needs it anyway? It's violence that wins. Makes people take notice, is the only effective way.'

'Where's violence got you? The PKK was nearly wiped out by the Turks at the end of the century. Even now you are only riding on the gains of the Iraq war. You have no real say in Turkish Government. Until you understand politics, practice politics, the Kurds will remain under the heel of Turkey.'

'That's not what Celik thinks.'

Albert picked up a jug of lemonade and poured some into a glass. 'I've told you, Celik is a fool.'

Tansu took the glass. 'You said this before,' she sipped some of the tart liquid, 'in Strasbourg.'

He nodded, his tongue moistening his lips.

The gesture fascinated her. 'I can't . . .'

He put his hands on the arm of the chair and leant over her, his voice harsh. 'Celik is losing. Either you lose with him or you take over.'

'Who'll follow me? Have you thought of that?'

'The operational people will follow you.' Albert's eyes bored into hers. 'The bombers, killers. They'll follow you anywhere, you know that.' He straightened. 'But that's not all. When the PKK leadership know I'm supporting you they'll have no option but to follow you. I own the money. I told you. Only I know where it is.'

Her eyes were slits. 'Celik will kill you.' She pushed herself up from the chair. 'After he's fucked you up so much that you'll tell him anything,' she hissed.

He stood aside as she pushed past him. 'And you,' he said evenly.

She stopped. 'Me?'

'If he's as good as you say, he'll find out about you and me. He won't trust you after that.' He paused. 'You know what that means.'

The sound of crickets was the only thing to break the silence. Albert stretched out his hand and roughly took her arm. 'If you want a homeland for the Kurds you are going to have to take over from Celik. I know you admire him. It will be difficult. But it's got to be done.'

She shrugged him off. 'The killing's easy,' she said, 'it's the other, the politics that's difficult. I'm not sure I want it.'

Albert leaned back on the railings. 'I will teach you,' he said, softly. He looked her up and down. 'You will enjoy it.'

'Believe me nothing that Albert teaches is in any way to be enjoyed.'

They looked around, startled. In the dim light of the doorway stood a diminutive figure, cascading Indian silk shawls embroidered in shimmering tinsel and beads, her pale blue eyes mesmeric in a face almost hidden under the huge brim of a local palm plait hat. 'So don't go to him for lessons, my dear. I'm Nina Dedain, Albert's aunt-in-law. A suitably complicated relationship for a complex man.' She turned to Albert. 'Isn't that so?'

Albert paid no attention. 'Tansu, this is Mademoiselle Nina Dedain.' He emphasised Mademoiselle. 'Your hostess.'

Nina smiled. 'You see what I mean, my dear. Only Albert would lead you to believe there was some significance in my being unmarried by using the word "hostess". Perhaps you now think I am a retired Paris tart living on her earnings in a former French colony.'

Tansu forced a smile in return. 'I think nothing of the sort, M'mselle. I am sure Albert meant no such thing.' She hesitated, looking at him. 'It is very good of you to have me at such short notice,' she said quickly.

Nina ignored her as she caught at a loose scarf as she turned. 'Pandit, bring the tea.' She turned again to look Tansu up and down, taking in the thin, scrawny figure, the tight, rather cruel face, 'and bring those honey cakes, as well.'

She sat down, throwing her hat on the wooden floor. 'There, that's better. What brings you here, Albert? This young lady doesn't look like one of your usual clients.' She laughed. 'She's certainly not a fat cat.'

'You're wrong, Nina,' Albert replied smoothly, easing himself into a chair beside her. 'Tansu has extensive holdings, her father has just died.'

Nina leaned over to put her hand on Tansu's arm, but she caught herself, something stopping her. 'I'm so sorry, my dear, forgive an old lady's curiosity. Albert usually has such,' she paused, patting her faded red hair with her crinkled fingers, 'such elegant clients,' her blue eyes widened, piercing against the sun-light, 'not that you . . . well, yes to be candid you're not, you need taking in hand. We have marvellous boutiques here. We'll go to Port Louis this afternoon.'

'But I . . .'

'A good idea, Tansu.' The heavy lids drooped over Albert's eyes. 'I can then be here to meet our other guest.'

'Other guest?' Nina's head jerked around. 'What other guest?'

'You've met him before, Nina. You remember Celik, you rather like him.'

'I can't stand him,' she said, picking up her hat. 'Are you coming, my dear?'

Tansu looked surprised.

'Shopping.' Nina smiled patiently. 'We're going shopping.'

The middle of Tansu's lip lifted slightly. 'I really don't have the time. I have no interest in shopping. Anyway, what about tea?'

Nina pushed one scarf end under another, the indigo clashing violently with the orange as she stood up. 'Tea? Shopping is always more important than tea, my dear.' She pulled a stick from the wicker umbrella stand and started down the veranda steps. 'Pandit, the car,' she shouted over her shoulder.

Albert pushed Tansu after her. 'Go,' he said, between his teeth. 'Get some decent clothes.'

He loathed the stupid old woman, but he was careful to treat her politely. As the late General Dedain's sister she carried weight in Mauritius, despite her increasing eccentricity. As Charlie's aunt, he grimaced at the thought, there was a bond between the two that was forged in their mutual nonconformity and expression of it in art. Charlie had often sought solace with Nina when the General's heavy orthodoxy had threatened to crush his daughter. And Albert was careful to foster that relationship even though the man was dead. He wanted Charlie to be his friend, his confidante. He might be an asset to the French President's Intelligence Unit, but every scrap of information he could get to safeguard that position was vital, and Charlie was not only senior in the Foreign Service she was also close to Gilbert, where the real power could lie.

Albert's thoughts were disturbed by a servant, a Chinese, white faced in a black tunic. He didn't remember seeing him before.

'A guest, Sir.'

Celik walked onto the veranda. Short, wiry, his hair so dark it had to be dyed, his face creased from brow to chin, deep crevices that changed shape when he spoke.

'Albert,' he said, briefly.

'Celik,' replied Albert. 'A drink?' he gestured towards the servant.

'Whisky, ice, no water.' Celik watched Albert dismiss the servant. 'Aren't you drinking?' He pulled one of the cane chairs towards him and sat heavily against the cushions pressing the fingers of one hand against his forehead. 'No, of course, you only drink Riesling. Too bland for my taste.' He drummed his fingers on the arm of the chair. 'Where's Tansu?'

'Out.'

'Out where?'

'With Nina, sightseeing.'

Celik looked annoyed. 'We've got work to do.'

Albert took out his silver cigarette case, carefully opened the lid, offered it to Celik.

'It's policy, we don't need her for that.'

Celik studied the case, watched it glinting in the bright glare.

'True. All she can think about is her next kill. She has absolutely no emotions, only a killer's instinct. She'll never make a politician.' He took out a flat Turkish cigarette. 'Odd. She's so naïve, so unworldly, yet she can plan an operation like no other.'

Albert took out his lighter, lit the Turkish, waiting until the end glowed.

'Yes. Until she meets someone else who is more talented.'

Celik glanced at him sharply. 'What do you mean?'

'Nothing.'

'No. Tell me. You think there's a problem with Tansu?'

'Alright. The last operation was a mess. She was completely outclassed by Moosar. They ran rings round her. Sold her a broken down aircraft with no arms aboard. But she blames you for it.'

The chair creaked as Celik shifted his weight.

'Blames me?'

'She says you made the deal with Moosar.'

'But she was the operational planner. Why should she blame me?'

'As you said, Tansu is the most feared killer you've got.'

The chair creaked again.

'How do you know all this, about the aircraft, about Moosar?'

Albert studied his Riesling, holding it up to the setting sun, throwing pink and yellow beams across the veranda behind Celik's head.

'I set up their worldwide laundering corridors, acted for them for twenty years.'

'Who else has she told that I'm to blame?'

Albert shrugged.

The crevices around Celik's mouth shifted as his voice hardened.

'You're saying that she dared to openly question my authority?'

Albert put his wine glass down on the cane table with a snap.

'This is not my business. How you control, discipline your people is not my affair. You came to talk about your negotiations with the Turks. How are they going?'

*

Later that evening, after dinner, Tansu checked the corridor outside her bedroom. It was quiet, no footsteps on the wooden floor, the low lamplight adding to the sense of stillness. She crossed over to Albert's door, opened it and slipped in.

Albert was sitting by a shuttered window, a lamp behind his back shining on some papers on the low table in front of him. He began to wave her to a chair when his hand stopped in mid air.

'Your hair,' he said, 'it's different.'

She grimaced. 'Clipped close to my neck. They said it gave me,' she narrowed her eyes as she looked at him, 'presence.'

'I noticed it immediately,' he replied. 'The dress too. Although I think dark brown is a little,' he paused, 'stark, shall I say?'

'I'm going into politics, not prostitution,' she replied, sharply. 'I need to be stark. I need to be like you.'

He shrugged. 'There's more,' he said, slowly studying her.

'Eye make up, lipstick,' her chin lifted, 'it's gunk, but apparently I need it. Got any objections?'

He drew on his cigarette, carefully tapping the ash into a copper bowl on the table.

'I approve. It all makes you someone who will be noticed. You're not attractive, but when you say something you attract attention. That is the first requirement in politics. Getting yourself heard.'

He smiled, thinly. 'The second is getting into bed with the people who matter.'

Later, as she lay beside him, she frowned. 'Celik was very formal tonight.'

Without a word, Albert got out of bed and went to his dressing table. He picked up a small digital recorder and went back to sit beside her. 'You need to listen to this.'

'What is it?'

'A recording of a conversation Celik had earlier this evening on his mobile. At least it's a recording of Celik's end of it. I wasn't equipped to record both ends.

'You recorded his mobile? How?'

Albert lifted up his head. 'For someone who is the operational planner for the PKK, that is a foolish question. Listen.'

His face remained immobile as he watched her listen to Celik's part of the conversation he'd had with him that afternoon while Tansu was fantasising in the Port Louis boutiques. She didn't speak until the end.

'The bastard,' she spat out, 'he believes it. He believes I blamed him, told people. Whoever it was on the end of that mobile he believes them.' She sat up, the sheets ruckling around her. 'They're dead,' her voice was ice. 'I'll make sure of it, they're dead.'

'You don't know who they are.' Albert lifted up the top of the sheet to cover her. 'You only know what Celik believes.'

She looked at him, the dark eyes flat, emotionless.

'I know what he'll do to me.'

'Yes.' Albert didn't bother to clarify.

Her eyes shifted. 'He won't do it here. He didn't bring his minders and I've got my Chinese guard.'

'So that's who he is,' murmured Albert.

She ignored him. 'Celik'll do it when I get back to Turkey.'

'Yes,' said Albert again.

She picked up the digital recorder.

'Why?' she asked, 'why would they do it?'

Albert took her hand. 'You're a woman in a Muslim world. You have got too powerful. After the Antonov arms shipment went wrong your enemies expected Celik to complain, do something. But he didn't because he knew it was an accident. Something that could happen to the best planner. So they have decided to take you out. Using him.' He paused. 'Emphasise their male superiority, show that women are alright for the day to day jobs but can't be leaders.'

Her body was rigid under the sheet. 'You were right. Right all along.'

Albert bent his head quickly to her hand, his eyes hidden as he kissed it.

*

It was late on the following afternoon that Nina was roused from her nap on the veranda by a sweating Pandit. At first, she couldn't understand what he was saying, but she was brought wide awake by Tansu's Chinese servant, wild eyed and gabbling, who rushed through the door. She instinctively threw her arm up in front of her face. And it wasn't until Pandit had forced a large brandy between her lips that she began to understand.

The Chinese had found someone. Someone who had been lying in one of the sugarcane fields when he had gone for a walk. He sobbed and jabbered. He had looked. The eyes were staring. The head was split. The blood streamed.

She stopped him then. Her mind quite clear. Ready to meet the catastrophe. She wished that Albert was there. But he was in Port Louis. She hadn't seen Tansu, but that thin, wasted girl would be useless in a crisis like this.

She took Pandit with her. The Chinese was quiet now. Just shaking every now and again as the shock hit him.

They turned down the brown, stony track past the house, past the small banana plantation, the broad, split leaves rustling in the breeze. Pandit held some bougainvillea fronds to one side as she passed between the dry stone walls where the track narrowed. She didn't notice the orange and pink blossoms glistening in the late sun. Nor did she notice the tall frangipani trees in the meadow on her left, the red petals screaming to the blue sky.

She knew she was near when the track met another running across it, bordering the tall cane, too tall to see over and leafed to the ground.

A little further on she found the body. The head had been caved in. The dark hair, shaved at the neck, matted in blood. Half hidden by the cane leaves.

Wordlessly, she gestured to Pandit to turn the body over.

It was Celik.

CHAPTER TWENTY-THREE

'Keep it brief. Stay dominant. They'll fall in.'

Tansu nodded. Albert's tone was quite different to the one he'd used after Celik's body had been discovered.

She glanced out of the window. Mardin in southern Turkey was certainly different to Mauritius. All she could see across the plateau below her and into the distance was a sweltering heat haze, shimmering over the last lowlands of Turkey and the Syrian plain beyond. The heat inside the isolated sandstone house was unbearable. There was no air conditioning and the arched windows were open, seeming to emphasise the oppressive atmosphere by failing to attract even a faint breeze.

But she didn't complain. She'd arranged the meet here because she'd had other meetings here, planning meetings with her active service units, her bombers and assassins, and she felt secure. She needed to feel secure. The row she'd had with Albert in Mauritius had left her furious, yet feeling exposed. She had known fury before, but a sense of exposure was new to her. And she didn't like it.

The tunnels of extremism had let in no light on her immature teenage years. The passions normal to that time had been directed to hatred and disciplined to obedience. Keeping to the shadows allowed her to live. By avoiding relationships she escaped the need to trust, reduced the risk of betrayal. And the lessons of adolescence had continued into adulthood. It became second nature to remain plain and sexless, to concentrate every fibre on killing and maiming the enemy, the Turks.

Until Albert had made her focus on what she had really become. Not a close quarter killer, not a bomber, not a quartermaster, not an adjutant, but a leader. When Albert opened that door and she had put on the clothes, the make up, the hairstyle she suddenly realised she was no longer fourteen but a woman of thirty, who had wasted sixteen years blindly supporting a cause that had failed. A cause that had failed for want of true leadership. And when she looked into the mirror of Albert's opinion, she knew he was right, she could acquire the position for herself. She was able to add personality and image to her recognised skill for creating violence.

Putting on the mask of make up and stepping into the world of chic had surprised her. She had felt a surge of power as she watched the reactions of Albert and Nina and others. The sudden interest in what she was saying. A noticeable air of deference.

Which was why she had killed Celik in such a public way and why she had had her first stinging, raging row with Albert.

She had told him that her public execution of Celik by her obvious murder of him would cow any opposition in the PKK to her takeover. He had been icy with rage, questioning with his eyes narrowed to slits, what the rest of the world would make of Celik's murder on a plantation linked directly to him and his banks in Paris and Port Louis. She had tried to persuade him that no one would care, that the important thing was that Celik, the PKK Leader, was dead.

But he had icily showed her the politics beyond that. The need for him to be shielded from any taint of PKK collusion, the need to keep the French as allies, the need to continue with the plan to attack Limnos, to take advantage of the chaos caused by the inevitable war between Greece and Turkey. Albert's anger had made her feel exposed. She had always exercised power through violence. Now, lashing her with his tongue, he insisted that her killing of Celik should remain secret. She had spent much of the journey back to Turkey arguing within herself whether she wanted the job of leader at all.

Today she and Albert were here in Mardin, in this stone floored, stone walled, precipiced house overlooking the baking Syrian plain, waiting for the PKK's three senior advisers to come and investigate what had happened that late afternoon in Mauritius when Celik had died. And Albert expected her to persuade them that she should take over. Take over as their leader. This was her first real test in politics, he had said.

She shifted slightly as the advisers' bodyguards came in. Two of them only, because they knew Tansu and knew she and Albert were unaccompanied. The guards, dressed in loose khaki, patted them for weapons.

The advisers were dressed traditionally and observed the tradition of small talk over sugared coffee before murmuring, discreetly, that they were sad to learn of the death of Celik and would Tansu and their honoured banker, Albert, tell them what they knew.

Albert gently sipped his sweet, thick coffee. Watched Tansu as she told the story.

Celik had decided to visit Le Paradis, the remote, well known Mauritius resort hotel on miles of white beach beneath the Morne Mountain. She delicately stirred her coffee as she told them that she did not know why he had insisted on going alone. Tansu watched from under her brows as they exchanged knowing looks and nodded at her tact. She told them that Celik's body had been washed ashore two miles up the beach. He had head injuries consistent with being hit by a boat propeller. The authorities had been informed. There had been an inquest and the Coroner had pronounced accidental death due to a boating accident.

The advisers looked at Albert who nodded, but said nothing.

One of the advisers coughed quietly and asked if anyone else had been involved. Tansu looked at the table top in front of her and murmured that Celik had been seen to enter the water by himself. His business partner, she had lifted her eyes to look at a spot on the wall behind the advisers, had already left, she had added.

The advisers exchanged more glances and spoke among themselves, softly, sipping their coffee.

'The matter is closed,' one said, looking at Tansu. 'We accept there was nothing you could do. You handled an awkward situation very well.' He paused. 'I am authorised to tell you that Birol Ereha,' he nodded at the man on his left, 'is our next leader. It is the wish of the three of us.'

Tansu drew in a breath. 'Without a debate? Without discussing it with me, your Chief of Operations?'

Birol looked at her, his rheumy eyes flickering slightly. 'I am the eldest. It is right I should now lead.' He paused. 'Anyway, you may be our operations chief and you may not wear the chador but you are a woman. And women do not interfere in our politics.'

Tansu glared at him. 'I do not agree.' The two guards stepped towards her. Birol held up his hand to stop them. 'What are you saying?'

'You should know that I executed Celik,' she spat, 'he was old and out of touch. As you are old and out of touch.' She looked at Birol. 'And you will not be our leader.'

She waited as her words sank in.

Birol's mouth tightened. Wordlessly he nodded to the guards and jerked his head towards Tansu.

The three shots were muffled by the silencers. There was hardly a sound as the bodies of the three advisers slumped on the chairs. Birol's eyes glazed wide with disbelief as his corpse slid onto the floor.

She turned to Albert, her nose pinched white with anger.

'Try and keep this private.'

Albert leaned back in his chair. 'What are you so angry for?'

'Because you were wrong. You can't talk to people like that.' She gestured towards the three bodies.

'Of course not,' he replied calmly. 'I expected you to kill them.'

She narrowed her eyes at that. 'You told me to talk to them, persuade them.'

'I told you to persuade the leadership. You've done that. You've shown them that their guards are your own people. After today you'll have no trouble persuading the rest of the leadership to support you.'

'I could have done that by making Celik's execution public,' she snapped.

'Yes, my dear. But I could have been publicly involved in that. Who is going to publicly involve me in this?'

'You selfish bastard.'

He smiled. 'Another necessary quality in politics.' He paused, looking at the bodies. 'What are you going to do next?'

'Next? Get on with the next weapons shipment and sort out the attack on Limnos, of course.'

Albert watched the guards pick up Birol's body and roll it into a red patterned carpet. 'I think you should consolidate.'

'Consolidate? You've just said the leadership and the rest of the PKK will support me. What's there to consolidate?'

Albert looked at the door as the carpet thumped into the lorry backed up to the opening.

'You have to look outside,' he murmured. 'Politics is about pressure when and where it's least wanted.'

She gestured impatiently. 'That's Limnos. The Greeks won't expect the attack and the sooner we stop playing games and get on with it, the sooner we'll win.'

He stood up. 'The Limnos attack is at least four weeks away. We've got to get the weapons and the men into place. Four weeks is a long time for the leadership to sit around. They will talk, then they will plot. They will pressure you just when you want to concentrate on Limnos.'

She looked up at him, slowly brushing her hand against her fringe. 'You mean take out more of the leadership?'

'No,' he almost shouted. 'I mean you stir up the outer circles, the supporters, let them see you can lead, can achieve something for them, and that you need them,' he added.

She started to pace the stone floor, skirting the remaining bodies and the three pools of blood, scarlet in the sun blazing through the door.

'Stir them up? Riots you mean? In Istanbul, Ankara.'

He tapped a cigarette on the table. 'Riots in Istanbul or Ankara don't get publicity,' he said.

'Where then?'

He snapped his lighter and put the flame to the cigarette between his lips. 'Paris.'

CHAPTER TWENTY-FOUR

Gilbert walked slowly across Panfilov Park, the broad expanse of grass and trees failing to hide the massive wooden structure of Almaty's Zenkov Cathedral. He had often wondered at the creative genius of his French ancestors who had chiselled and carved and then hoisted stone on stone to create the Notre Dame Cathedral in the dim medieval past, but he was left marvelling at the sheer artistry of the Kazakh carpenters who in the same period of history had sawn and planed and jointed the trees to form the Zenkov without a single nail so as to remind the faithful of the reality of the Resurrection.

He felt that the Cathedral was a testament to the Kazakh spirit, resurrected again after years of oppression, to create the dynamism that was pushing Kazakhstan so fast into economic prosperity. And it added to his reluctance, his sense of personal diminishment, that he was here in Almaty with a hundred thousand dollars to bribe an old friend to help with a weapons shipment. Not that bribery wasn't the norm in Kazakh business, but in 2007 the Kazakhs could and should have passed beyond that simple stage in their democratic development. Then he almost laughed out loud. Who were the bribers? The great French democracy, the President of which had no qualms about creating a war between Greece and Turkey to preserve its sovereign independence.

He looked once more at the great Cathedral before turning towards the Arasan baths, the place he was to meet Engels Sarsenov, not his opposite number in the Kazakh Government, but a close adviser and friend.

A grizzled man in a loose shirt and baggy trousers leaned towards him, some birch tree branches in his hand.

Gilbert stopped, uncertain. He had no wish to punish his body with the whippy twigs, but Engels would expect it, would indulge himself in the Russian sauna and probably make free with his birch branches, particularly if he was off the wagon. Gilbert knew Engels well. He had periodic tussles with teetotalism before crashing into a rollicking spree with his beloved vodka which could last for months until officialdom finally couldn't cope any more and another final warning was issued. Then the bottles were traded for lemon tea and a foul temper. The man with the spectacles in the President's Intelligence Unit hadn't bothered to find out which stage Engels was in so, reluctantly, Gilbert pulled out some change and held it out, not feeling in the least like exchanging grins with the old man as it went into his pocket and he handed over what seemed like a tree top.

He collected his towel from the pretty girl at reception (all the girls were pretty in Almaty), changed and walked into the sauna. The hot steam glistened and wreathed on the white marble, drifting to obscure Gilbert's vision. He hitched up his towel and walked towards a heavy, damp paunch, folded over a white towel, darkened with sweat. A pudgy hand worked its way to a dish piled high with thin cut salami. Alongside it were two thick shot glasses and a bottle, quarter full, of vodka. The fingers closed around the bottle and brought it to a pair of thick lips. At least, Gilbert thought, he'd done the right thing buying the birch twigs. Mentally steeling himself, he walked over, took the bottle away and poured out a shot of vodka, drinking it straight.

'What the hell?' The paunch wobbled as its owner sat bolt upright, the Russian lightly slurred with alcohol and its Kazakh origins. 'Shit, it's you, Gilbert,' the French was also lightly slurred with alcohol but it came out as though it had been through a mangle. The pudgy hand appeared again, this time to grab Gilbert's and pump it up and down.

'Shit, Gilbert, I can't thank you enough for coming. Two whole days away from that hellhole Astana, it's paradise, my friend, paradise.'

'Is Astana still as bad as that?' Gilbert laughed, sitting down beside the plate of salami, catching a whiff of its pungent aroma as the steam heated it up.

'As bad? It can never be anything else. The idiot who took the capital away from here and plunged it into that dust bowl should be shot,' he paused, 'well not shot,' he added, as he remembered the patriarch President whose decision it was. 'But what good did it do when all the government officials are finding excuses to come back here?' He burped. 'And the girls, there are no girls in Astana, well, not what you'd call girls.' He plucked a slice of salami from the dish with his thumb and forefinger. 'I mean they're all here. What pretty girl would go and live in a desert when she can dwell in an oasis,' he said, poetically. He swallowed another mouthful of vodka, his cheeks bulging as he drained the bottle. 'Here,' he shouted to a sweating attendant in the corner, 'bring another bottle.' He looked at the heaped plate of salami. 'And another cold plate of this, it's hot, disgusting.'

His eyes darted to Gilbert's. 'D'you know how much it costs me to have a life?' The eyes disappeared as his brows folded over them, heralding a wheezy chuckle. 'A fucking fortune.' The brows popped up abruptly. 'So I hope you've come to replenish my bank balance.'

Gilbert looked round, uneasily.

Engels' chuckle wheezed again. 'Don't worry so much, they can't speak French,' he took the fresh vodka bottle from the waiter and waggled it, splashing liquid onto the floor. 'They can hardly speak at all,' the wheezing turned into a belly laugh, exploded into a coughing fit.

Gilbert waited, feeling the sweat ooze down his backbone as the steam bit into him. Engels gasped and took the shot glass Gilbert handed him, tipping the vodka to the back of his throat.

'So what do you want? Let's get the business over and then we can have some fun. Get out of this place and go down to the Platinum bar.'

Gilbert toyed with his glass.

'I need some help.'

Engels' fingers scratched at a spot on a roll of fat behind one of his kidneys.

'How much help?'

'Fifty thousand US.'

'That'll last me a week.' Engels' stomach rumbled. 'Less.'

'It's a small job.'

'Fifty thousand'll buy you a ticket to the toilet.'

Gilbert put his shot glass down, picked up the bottle and deliberately tossed it onto the floor. It hit the marble and shattered. Glass skittering in flashes like lightning.

'You clear up your own mess,' Gilbert said as he climbed to his feet.

The attendant pushed himself away from the wall.

Engels' fleshy hand stopped him, then grabbed Gilbert's arm.

'You didn't used to be so fucking touchy. What happened?'

Gilbert stopped, shrugged.

'It's not just Astana that's a dung heap, you know.'

Engels' tiny eyes caught the light.

'Paris? You don't mean Paris! I don't believe it.'

'Politics,' Gilbert began.

'Oh, shit, politics,' Engels let go Gilbert's arm, 'that's what money's for, Gilbert, to help you forget.' He scratched again. 'Although fifty thousand won't help much.'

Gilbert retied his towel.

'And a hundred?'

'That's a good night out.' Engel took a deep breath, shifted his bulk to the edge of the seat and braced his legs, the flab wobbling with the effort. 'We need the cold pool,' he gasped, 'I can't think here.' He reached for another bottle and waddled past the attendant.

It took a few minutes for Engels to make his way to the cold pool and carefully ease into it. He shook himself suddenly as the temperature change grabbed him. Waves of water splurged out and slapped against the sides, racing back to break against his mass. Gilbert stepped into the maelstrom, the freezing water snapping his jaw shut and grinding his teeth together. He tensed, waiting for the waves to subside, concentrating on the domed ceiling above as he counted slowly to ten for his body to acclimatise.

Engels ducked down, his bald head disappearing under the water as his left hand held up the half empty vodka bottle, like King Arthur's sword. Gilbert watched the bottle wavering in the air. Without warning he was drenched as Engels lurched upwards, his body almost weightless in the water. A short, thin man on the far side was submerged.

'Bastard,' the man shouted, as the water sucked away from him, only to return and leave him choking as his mouth opened to hurl another yell of protest.

'Who are you calling a bastard,' Engels roared, starting to wade across the chop.

'Engels,' yelled Gilbert, 'the vodka.'

Engels halted, lifted his hand from under the water, staring, dismayed, at the bottle, now full.

'Now look what you've done,' he bawled at the thin man, pushing his weight against the water towards him. The thin man started shouting for the attendant.

'Oh hell,' muttered Gilbert, pushing himself off from the side, shoving the water away as he waded towards Engels' vast body.

By the time he reached Engels the thin man had scrambled out of the pool and was slithering and slipping his way to the exit.

'That's right,' screamed Engels, 'fuck off.' He threw the bottle at him, 'and stay fucked off.'

He spotted the attendant as he rushed into the pool room.

'Clear up that fucking mess and bring me another bottle.'

The attendant disappeared back through the door.

Engels gathered water with his massive arms and rubbed it over his belly. 'Fucking Russian barbarians,' he grunted as Gilbert reached him, 'they just don't know how to behave.'

He caught the expression on Gilbert's face.

'Oh, you haven't had much fun recently have you, my friend. Well, we must alter all that.' He came to rest at the side of the pool breathing heavily. 'Now what do you want?'

'It's simple,' Gilbert said.

Engels squinted at him.

'What I want,' Gilbert murmured, looking around, 'is an agricultural machinery export licence.'

'Where to?'

Gilbert bit back a laugh at Engels' reply. "Where to," he'd asked, not "what for". The licence could have covered enriched uranium for all Engels cared. A licence was a licence and a hundred

thousand dollars would buy it, as long as he knew the destination
so the form could be filled in.

'Erzurum,' Gilbert said.

Engels' brows rolled up his forehead. 'Erzurum? That's Turkey.
Is it going by air?'

'No. Rail. There'll be a lot of it.'

'Shit that means it will have to go through Georgia, Azerbaijan
as well possibly. They'll want a cut for sure.' His eyes disappeared
as he contemplated losing a slice of his cash.

Gilbert said it quickly. 'No they won't. It's going to be a
government to government consignment.'

Engels' eyes flew open. 'For a hundred thousand? No it fucking
isn't.'

Gilbert picked up the vodka bottle the waiter had quietly put
beside them on the side of the pool before retreating behind the
door again.

'You know what happened when you tried my patience before,
Engels.'

'Yes, you gave me another fifty thousand,' Engels replied,
unperturbed.

'For everything.' Gilbert poured out two shot glasses, handed
one to Engels. 'So don't try my patience again.'

'Shit, someone has kicked you in the balls,' muttered Engels.
'For fuck's sake, don't you enjoy bargaining any more? Hell, in
Kosovo you were a byword for it. You even stopped me shipping
in arms. Me.' He shifted his eyes sideways, watching Gilbert's face.
'You know the reason why? Yes, the cash helped. But it was you. It
was fun. We had a laugh, tossed it around, saw which way it all
fell. Drank some vodka, took out some girls.' He let his eyes slide
away to look across the pool. 'Now you're as tight as that little
bastard I chased out just now.'

Gilbert suddenly felt tired. Overwhelmingly tired. He was losing Engels and he couldn't do a thing about it. Engels thought of
only one commodity. Himself. And if it didn't work for him, it
didn't work at all. Gilbert had known that Engels would balk at a
government to government consignment. He was too close to the
Kazakh Ministers. If the deal went sour, the Turks would lunge for
their necks. Politically, it was suicide.

'You're right,' Gilbert muttered, 'I shouldn't have asked you if I couldn't take a joke.' He started to move away.

For the second time that evening Engels grabbed Gilbert's arm.

'You know the other reason I helped in Kosovo?' he asked, his mouth a little blue in the icy temperature.

Gilbert shook his head, his eyes hooked on Engels' face.

'Because you became a friend.' He held up his hand as Gilbert started to speak. 'Some bastard's got you in a wringer, I know it. Just as you should know that I'm here to help you get out of it. Whatever you want, it's yours.' The rolls of blubber quivered as Engels shook Gilbert's arm. 'Don't forget that. An enemy of yours is an enemy of mine.' He paused to shoot down a generous helping of vodka, his body sending out more waves as it spasmed to the raw liquid.

'Now, this fucking consignment. You'll get documentation covering agricultural machinery from the Government of Kazakhstan to the Government of Turkey for, let's see,' he thought for a moment, 'tobacco cultivation, part of the mutual co-operation to eradicate poppy cultivation.' He beamed. 'That sounds good doesn't it. Weapons, is it?'

Gilbert jerked his head up.

'Of course, it is,' smiled Engels.

Gilbert looked down at the water, at his white, shrivelled palms. 'You don't have to do this, Engels.'

'Shit, Gilbert, this is fun.'

'It's trouble and I can't thank . . .'

'Oh shut the fuck up.' Engels poured another shot down his throat. 'Now where are those fucking birch twigs.' He grinned, his eyes disappearing again, 'I must punish myself.'

CHAPTER TWENTY-FIVE

Hammond waited in the French Ministry of Interior conference room. He showed no impatience at the delay. The concealed cameras would pick that up and put him at a disadvantage when the French decided to turn up. He turned sharply as he heard Genscher's grating German.

'My taxi driver took me up the Rue du Cinque, the idiot, it was jammed. I told him to take Avenue Matignon but he wouldn't.'

Hammond gritted his teeth as he forced a smile. He wondered if Genscher ever opened a conversation without talking about the traffic.

'And why,' continued Genscher, his Ost Deutsch quickening, 'are we meeting here at the Interior Ministry. What's the EU Army got to do with them? More delay, that's what it is.'

'I am sorry to say that you are right, Herr Genscher.' Charlie walked into the small, white walled meeting room, the long windows half hidden by the tall, grey shutters. 'The Ministry of Interior have some problems.' She smiled at him, her pale lipstick matching the open neck shirt under the well cut black suit.

'Your life seems full of problems.' Hammond looked amused as he held out his hand to her in greeting.

Her eyes flared for a moment. 'I said the Interior Ministry had problems, not me.'

Hammond pulled out a cheap, dark wood chair from under the dark wood table and studied them.

'Is that why our meeting has been downgraded?'

'It was the only room available at such short notice, I'm afraid. Good morning, I'm Jean Tricot, Permanent Secretary here. Mr Hammond?'

Hammond turned to shake hands with the man who'd spoken,

taking in the dark, curly hair and long eyelashes over Tricot's watery brown eyes and fat cheeks.

'I hope that means this meeting will be short as well.' He glanced at Genscher. 'I see Major Stammler isn't here, that should shorten it.'

Genscher's mouth pinched inwards. 'Major Stammler is on a course,' he said shortly.

'Learning diplomacy, is he?' Hammond laughed.

Genscher sat down, ignoring Tricot. 'Let's get on with it.' He began opening his briefcase.

Tricot glanced at Charlie, his eyes questioning. Imperceptibly she shook her head.

Hammond caught the exchange.

'Is Mr Roubel on a course as well?' he asked, innocently.

'He has other more important things to do,' Charlie said curtly. 'We are all here, so Mr Tricot will fill you in.'

Tricot put a fat blue file on the table in front of him, unbuttoned his jacket and sat down, his hands hugging the folder.

'M'mselle Dedain has just told you that unfortunately we have a delay on putting the proposal for the EU Army to our other colleagues in the European Union.'

'The proposal is clear, it was tied up at our last meeting in Brussels.' Genscher cut in. 'The other EU members have a right to know what's going on. There are rumours already. I have had both my Belgian and Czeck opposite numbers 'phoning me asking me if I know anything about negotiations for an Anglo Franco German Army.'

Tricot put his fingers together, flexing them.

'We have an internal problem that must be overcome before we can make the proposal public.' He opened the folder carefully, wetting a finger before leafing through the papers. 'Now let me see.'

Genscher shifted impatiently in his chair.

'Yes, here we are.' Tricot's finger stopped as it ran down a page. 'Places of vulnerability within France.'

'Café L'Imbecile,' murmured Hammond.

Charlie reddened and bit her lip.

Tricot lifted his head from his papers. 'Where was that?'

Genscher looked at his watch. 'I'm on the fifteen twenty out of Charles de Gaulle.'

Tricot bent his head to his papers again, his curly hair bobbing with the movement.

'The EU Army will be a defensive force for the whole of the EU territory. That means that it will defend our vulnerable points, nuclear and oil installations, gas and electricity distribution, rail concentration, airports.'

Tricot looked up for confirmation.

Hammond and Genscher remained motionless, waiting for the question before committing themselves.

Tricot gave a little shrug, went back to his papers, his wet fingertip flipping them over like a bank teller counting notes.

'We don't want Czecks, Poles, Maltese nosing around those installations.'

'What about Greeks?' Hammond put in.

Tricot ignored him. 'The Poles and that lot will have the right to enter and guard our sensitive areas.' He sat back, wiping his finger on his jacket lapel. 'We won't accept that.'

'What have you got you don't want us to see?' Genscher said, rudely.

'That's not the point,' Charlie began.

Tricot put up a hand to stop her, his head shifting from side to side as though searching for something.

'What's that noise?' he said.

They listened. A dull, rumbling sound came in through the windows.

'That's very loud,' Tricot sounded surprised. 'The window's armoured glass.' He got up and went to the tall window overlooking the Place Beauvau. He drew back the shutters. 'What the hell?'

Genscher pushed his chair back and ran to the window.

'Scheisse, there are hundreds of them.'

Hammond put out his hand to stop Charlie and walked to where Genscher stood, open mouthed. Marching, running, shouting and waving placards were hundreds of people coming down the Rue du Faubourg and the Avenue de Marigny towards the Interior Ministry. Hammond could see that more were pouring out of side streets to join the mob on the main roads.

He turned and walked back towards his seat, looking at Charlie. 'It's only a demonstration,' he said curtly. He nodded towards Tricot. 'Looks like he's got another problem.'

She choked, her eyes brimming with laughter.

'It's no joking matter.' Tricot puffed out his cheeks, walked to the table, sat down dusting an imaginary speck off his jacket. 'These bloody migrants. They don't know when they're well off.'

'They're Kurds,' said Genscher over his shoulder.

'That's unusual,' said Tricot getting up again and going back to the window. 'You're right. Look at the banners. "Free Kurdistan", "Stop the Concentration Camps".' He looked at Genscher. 'What bloody concentration camps?'

Genscher stepped back. 'What are you asking me for?'

Tricot put his hand out. 'I'm sorry, I didn't mean . . . wasn't implying . . .'

'Well, don't,' snapped Genscher. He looked out of the window again. 'Where are the police. There aren't any police.'

Tricot peered up and down the streets. 'You're right. Shit.' He crossed over to a low cabinet along the wall and picked up a phone.

'Maurice? What the hell's going on out there? Where are the police?'

'What?' Tricot's fingers dragged through his wavy hair.

'Shit.' He banged the phone down. Looked at Charlie.

'The police weren't expecting them. They just materialised from the side streets. No warning.'

'How the hell am I going to catch my flight?' Genscher grumbled. 'Look at that lot. It'll take hours to shift them.'

'They're just protesters,' said Tricot.' You only need to walk through them for two or three blocks and you can find a taxi.'

Hammond slapped his hand on Tricot's file. 'So the quicker we get this meeting over, the quicker you can go.' He sat down and began leafing through the papers. 'Now, these vulnerable points, where are they?'

Tricot waddled back and snatched the papers out of Hammond's hands.

'This is a confidential file, Mr Hammond.'

Hammond leaned back. 'And so are your instructions Tricot. Delay, delay, delay. Isn't that right?'

Tricot avoided Hammond's eyes. 'We cannot have foreigners guarding our installations,' he said, sullenly.

Hammond's mouth tightened.

'You won't. The idea is to stop the Turks and Greeks fighting and get them together. If there's any defending to do, it will be on the EU borders. If the borders of France are breached we will be happy to let you defend your own installations.' He paused. 'Like you did in 1914 and 1939.'

There was a shocked silence.

'My God,' breathed Charlie. 'You don't have to be that rude, John.'

'Grow up, Charlie,' Hammond snapped. 'The Greeks are just seeking an excuse for war. If we don't tie them up in this EU Army we'll be swamped with people like those Kurds out there, it will just get worse,' he pointed to the window.

'And what if they don't want to have your bloody EU Army?' Tricot blustered.

'They won't have any choice,' Hammond said, calmly. 'Once we announce the concept, the Americans and Russians will pile the pressure on both Greece and Turkey. Stability in that region is essential for both of them, particularly Russia.'

The mulish expression on Tricot's face suddenly froze as the building shook to a rending, splintering crash.

'Bomb,' yelled Genscher, diving under the table.

'No,' shouted Hammond. He swung round to grab Charlie as she ran for the door. 'Stay still. It's not a bomb.'

'What . . .'

'Shut up.' Hammond slapped his hand over Charlie's mouth. 'Listen.'

They waited, Genscher holding on to the table, Tricot with his mouth half open, their eyes staring at the window.

Beneath them, they heard a low growling sound, rising and falling, then rising louder.

'They're inside.' Hammond let go of Charlie and went to the window. 'They've rammed a JCB into one of the downstairs windows. They're climbing in.'

Genscher staggered to the window. 'Scheisse, that's the digger that held up my taxi.' His face whitened as he caught sight of the crowd milling and shoving around it, their mouths open in muffled screams. Men in T-shirts, women in chadors, heaving and fighting to get through the rubble made by the digger.

A sharp crackle bit through the faint din. There was a sudden silence. Then the sound of screaming yells exploded into the room as the mob broke through. Stamping feet, shattered glass, split doors. They howled as they crashed through the hall into the main offices.

Tricot was ashen. 'The guards,' he mumbled, 'the guards.'

'They're no good to us now,' said Hammond sharply. 'We can't get out. Where can we hide?'

Tricot picked up his file, holding it to his chest. 'How could they get in? How could . . .'

Genscher grabbed his arm. Began shaking it. 'Where do we hide. Shit, get a hold of yourself.' He swiped the file out of Tricot's hands. 'Where the hell do we go?'

Tricot shook his head. 'Go? Go? Yes, of course.' He jerked his head up as feet clattered on the stair below. 'The safe room, the documents safe room.' He began to run for the door.

Hammond grabbed Charlie's arm, bent down, scooped up the file, pushed her after Tricot.

Tricot pulled open the door, smashed into a heavy bearded man racing down the corridor.

'Bastard,' the man yelled, his face contorted. 'Bastard.' He began beating Tricot with a wooden placard holder.

Charlie stopped, then pushed on towards them. 'Stop it, stop it,' she shouted.

Hammond jerked her back, holding her with one hand, pushing Genscher into Tricot with the other. Tripping him. Sending the three men sprawling.

'The safe room,' he shouted at her, 'where's the safe room?'

'But Tricot, we can't leave him,' she yelled, fighting to free herself. He shook her. Pointed to the stairwell. 'Do you want to die?'

She looked over the stairs. Streaming up, screaming, barging, flailing placards, contorted faces turned up towards her, came the vanguard which had smashed through the downstairs window.

Shocked tears poured down her face, as she turned, ran down

the corridor, her hand dragging along the wall to steady her. She raced around a corner, staggered to a fist smashing her shoulder. Jarring her hip. Bringing her to the floor.

The fist lashed out at Hammond. Caught his chest. He fell back. Heard the screams behind him. Feet scrambling. Sliding. Shoving along the corridor.

A shaven headed man appeared behind the fist. Spit dribbling from his mouth. He drew his arm back, Hammond ducked. A black shawled woman raced, shrilling around the corner. Tripped over Charlie. Slammed into the man. Shoved him over Hammond's back. Arms flailing. Mouthing curses. Hammond pushed against his legs. Hard. Straightened. The man hit the banister rail. Suspended. Eyes wide. In terror. Rolled, tumbled, plunged. The scream cut off. Abrupt. Two floors down. On the marble floor.

The scene froze. Eyes on the blood pooling across the white, glistening stone. Voices choked in horror.

Hammond grabbed Charlie by the shoulders. Hauled her to her feet. Blindly she pushed past the silent, chadored woman. Swung left into a space let into the wall. Turned to find Hammond.

He shoved her forward into the room. She fell heavily over a floor plate, the bottom sill of a half open, foot thick steel door. Hammond pulled at the door to close it behind them. Gasped at the weight. The cords on his neck stood out with the strain.

Suddenly the silence was shattered by a wail of grief. A shriek now echoing along the corridor. Followed by a manic howl as the mob surged to life again.

Hammond slid through the gap into the room. He started to pull the door shut. His feet against the sill. His back arched. The door began to swing. A hand pushed through. Grabbed the edge. Sought a hold. Scrabbling.

Hammond shoved every ounce against the sill. Grunted. His whole weight heaved. The door grated. Charlie turned the central wheel. The lock closed. A trickle of blood oozed down the door edge. Where the fingers had been. Glistening almost black against the grey metal.

Hammond slid to the floor. Chest heaving. Sweat streaming. He closed his eyes.

Charlie inched her way around the room, along the shelves of files and papers. Blood trickling down her legs. The sleeve of her jacket hanging down. Her feet bare, the toes already blackening. Shaking, she slumped into a desk chair, folded her head in her hands.

There were no sounds outside. The document safe room was solid steel. Its only other occupants orderly banks of papers. Some scattered when the staff ran out instead of shutting themselves in.

Hammond opened his eyes and looked at Charlie. 'You're alright now.'

She lifted her head, dark smudges under the green of her eyes.

'And Tricot? Genscher?'

Hammond winced as he stood up.

'Don't go guilty on me. Would you prefer to be out there?'

Numbly, she shook her head.

CHAPTER TWENTY-SIX

Gilbert sat down in the waterfront café of the Istanbul Golden Horn Hotel and winced as the sun caught the small waves in the harbour and streaked a flash of light into his eyes. He groped for his Polaroids and shakily put them on. Through the fog of his hangover he dimly saw a white stone domed mosque. Its two soaring minarets seemed to compete with the giant twin towers of the bridge arching the waters of the Golden Horn. Immediately below the small, umbrella'd café where he was sitting, dowdy, rubber tyre lined cargo boats, sleek pleasure craft, streamlined runabouts plied or skimmed their way to and from the Bosphorus. Istanbul was still a strange mix of archaic and avant garde.

His hand shook as he lifted his coffee cup to his lips. He sipped the bitter sweet, thick liquid and thought again how sensible he had been to break his journey from Almaty. The previous night was just a haze. He had a vague recollection of Engels being thrown out of the women's section of the Almaty baths. Something about his birch twigs. Then there was a lurching taxi drive to the Platinum Bar, which lived up to its name. Built the previous year, it was retro chrome and coloured neon lights and retro Almaty girls, dressed in skimpy bright leather when they were dressed at all.

After that, Gilbert's memory became a dark tunnel until he woke late that morning in his hotel room, alone, with the concierge banging on the door, shouting that he would miss his flight to Paris. The very thought of Paris and the Director with the spectacles and the President and Claud made him reach for the phone, cancel the flight and book an indirect route back with a night in Istanbul. He tried to contact Engels but he couldn't be found. Gilbert abandoned him to whatever new excess he'd found in Almaty and had followed a shaky path to Istanbul.

He took out a handkerchief and mopped his forehead. There was a breeze but last night's vodka was still pouring out of him. He was glad the café was almost empty. He needed some peace. Also, he thought, as he sat at the table by the waters' edge, he needed time to think.

He looked across the Golden Horn to the hills and the sweep of buildings following the contours in the distance and wondered if his political career was what he really wanted.

Before he had gone to Kosovo his existence as a soldier had been ordered and predictable. The odd muddle in training programmes were the only glitches in the smooth, amusing fraternity of the officers' mess. His air of detachment and ability to organise had helped him up the promotional ladder to the rank of Colonel. As for his personal life, women had never caused him concern. He wasn't willing to commit himself to the give and take of a long term relationship. Those that he had known were attracted to his sense of honour and were intrigued by an indefinable, well hidden, sensitivity. But none could pierce his reserve beyond a mutual interest in culture. And they had drifted away, remaining friends but nothing more.

Then had come his tour in Kosovo. For the first time Gilbert had observed man in the extremes of fanaticism. Nothing in his elegant schooling and military training had prepared him for the tribal savagery so casually meted out between men and women who had learned to hate. On his first patrol he had found a Serb gun commander casually firing on a small village in the hills. He had marched straight up to the commander and shouted at him to stop. Within seconds the French troops had been surrounded and faced the gunners' kalashnikovs and the commander's unblinking stare. Humiliated, Gilbert had taken his men back to the French base. He'd spent a night lying in his bunk, sweating as he relived the half heard, muttered contempt of his patrol. Next morning he'd left his officers behind and taken two sergeants with him to where the commander was still bombarding the village. Gilbert didn't say a word but sat down with his sergeants and opened the brandy and cigarettes they had brought with them. The bombardment didn't stop but, curious, the commander had strolled over to him with his interpreter. Gilbert avoided any discussion of the commander's activities but instead had asked him about his family, his men and the villages they came from. Intermittently, over the next three days, they'd met and talked while the bombardment continued. Finally, satisfied he'd destroyed the village, the commander had pulled out.

Gilbert swirled the coffee in his cup and smiled to himself as he remembered. He had been totally ineffective. But he had ordered his officers to adopt the same tactics and learn about the men and women who hated each other so much. Little by little small results started to trickle in. A shooting stopped here, a house saved from destruction there. And gradually his reputation had grown. He was a man who looked underneath the violence and tried to understand the causes, tried to understand the tribal and religious differences. He became a peacemaker.

After Kosovo, he had come to believe that what he had achieved on the killing ground of Kosovo he could also achieve on the political ground of France. At the next election he was carried on the tide of his popular vote. During the early days, he had found politics to be easy. Defence issues in France were limited to keeping the nuclear deterrent and sniping at the Americans. It was rather like being back in the officers' mess, power without much responsibility and most of it faintly amusing. There was no role for peacemaking, except to support France's refusal to become a belligerent in the Iraq War.

Then had come the flood of refugees from North Africa and through Turkey. For three years now France had tried to contain it. The defence forces had been drawn in bit by bit. Patrolling the coastline here, manning observation posts there. Work that should have been done by civilians. He had protested, but the Cabinet had overruled him. When the President had ordered him to use troops to put down riots in Marseilles he had resisted, but the Cabinet had overruled him again. And again.

Now he was sitting in a café in Istanbul having set up the cover for an illicit weapons shipment to the PKK to start a war. A war to stop immigrants from Turkey getting into Greece and the European mainland. The whole thing was fantastic, unbelievable if he hadn't heard it from the President's lips.

As he watched the evening shadows lengthen across the water, his mind drifted through the fog of alcohol back to that night in Kosovo. Reliving those faint murmurings of his men, he had learnt that they blamed his arrogant behaviour with the subcommander for their humiliation. And he knew they were right. From then on, understanding and patience were his watchwords. But, as he brought his mind back to the present, to this café in Istanbul, to his deal with Engels, he suddenly realised that understanding and patience in politics were useless without arrogance. He had submitted to every political demand made of him. He had become a poodle. What was good for the Party, for the Government, was good for him.

He gazed at the lights beginning to emerge on the distant hills and realised that he had gone too far. The ruin of war between Greece and Turkey could never compensate for closing a migrant gateway into Europe.

He looked at his empty cup and glanced around the café to find the waiter. The place was now littered with the usual quota of men. There was a light sprinkling of women, most of them tourists, all of them dressed in the common uniform of smart jeans and crop tops. He caught a waiter's eye and beckoned him over.

'Yes Sir.' The waiter flapped the cloth he was carrying at a fly.

'Another coffee, please.'

'And for the lady?' The waiter glanced over his shoulder.

Startled, Gilbert followed the waiter's glance. Sitting down at his table was a woman with short brown hair wearing a white cotton shirt over a multi coloured skirt. Gilbert caught the faint essence of her perfume, saw her eyes flick from his to the waiter.

'Coffee for me too, please,' she said in Turkish.

'Wait a minute,' Gilbert called, but the waiter had gone. He turned to her. 'I'm sorry,' he said in English, 'but the waiter's made a mistake. I didn't ask for company.'

Julia switched to French. 'But I'm interested in your company.' She slid a copy bearer share certificate across the table.

Gilbert frowned. 'I don't want to buy anything.' He glanced at the certificate. 'Certainly not bearer shares in the,' he studied the certificate, 'Stalchek Investment Corporation.' He pushed the certificate back across the table.

Julia's wide mouth lifted in a half smile.

'But you have already bought them.'

He laughed. 'I might not remember much about last night but I'd remember buying a load of dud bearer shares.'

Julia stared at him.

He looked amused. 'Don't tell me Engels did something stupid.'

'You bought these five months ago,' she said, pulling out a sheaf of statements and studying them.

'Give me those,' he snatched them out of her hand. Read the figures on the receipts for payments to Stalchek Investments and other investment companies.

He laughed again. 'Ten million dollars? I paid ten million dollars? How?'

'I'll come to that.' She looked into her bag and pulled out two other documents. 'What about these?'

Gilbert found himself staring at two single premium insurance policies in his name from two Cook Island companies. Suddenly he knew this woman, whoever she was, was serious, was trouble. He shook his head, trying to clear away the mists left by the alcohol.

'You had a hard night,' she said, 'I would have talked to you yesterday, but I thought you were too far gone.' She paused. 'Anyway it suits me better that you feel grim.'

'You were there last night?'

Julia nodded.

'Who the hell are you?'

'That doesn't matter. What matters is that you own fifteen million dollars in bearer shares and insurance policies. You haven't earned fifteen million dollars. So where did the money come from?'

'You're with that bastard Albert, aren't you? Got nervous about exposing his supposed dealings with me in Kosovo, has he? I might have known it. Well,' he flicked the documents across the table, 'this doesn't impress me either.'

'Excuse me, Sir.' The waiter leaned over, swept his tray to one side and in one easy movement put down a coffee in front of Julia. 'Anything else,' he said to Gilbert.

Gilbert leaned over and took Julia's cup. 'Yes. You can ask this tart to leave. She's bothering me.'

The waiter bent down, took the cup out of Gilbert's hand and put it in front of Julia, the black liquid shivering but not spilling.

'We do not have such women here,' he said loudly and untruth-
fully as he flapped his napkin at another fly settling on a table
behind him. He straightened his shoulders and minced away,
satisfied he'd earned the fifty dollars she'd given him.

'If that didn't put you in your place,' Julia smiled, 'what about
this?' She handed over a copy of his instructions to Sanjay Vijay,
Accountants, Calcutta.

His eyes went straight to his signature. He knew he hadn't
written it but he instantly recognised it as his. He felt the vodka
rise to his throat as he read the instructions. The purchase of the
bearer shares. The acquisition of the insurance policies. And,
finally, the payment of two million dollars into the accountants'
name in Banque Onde, Mauritius.

He swallowed, groping to give his mind time to think
coherently.

'None of this means anything to me. Anyway I've done what
they wanted. So tell Albert to go to hell.' He pushed his chair back
and started to his feet.

Her brown eyes were almost black. 'You can tell Albert what
you like, but what do I tell my employers?'

For the second time he felt the bile in his throat. He stopped,
half leaning on the table. Stupidly thinking that her eyes were
liquid, like the coffee in front of her.

'Your employers?'

'Turkish Defence Intelligence Agency.'

He felt punched. She hadn't looked Turkish. But now, as he let
his eyes drift over her, he saw the darkness of her hair, realised
why her eyes had caught his attention, the slimness of her, the crop
top, the designer jeans. How could he have thought she was
French? And she had spoken Turkish when she'd ordered coffee.
Gripping the table he slowly sat down.

'I don't talk to Turkish Intelligence Officers.'

'Then these,' she pointed to the documents, 'don't matter to
you.'

'No.'

She gathered up the documents, stuffing them into her bag.

'Well, then, goodbye.'

Confused, he watched her stand up, her bag bumping against her narrow hips as she put the strap over her shoulder.

'Is that all?'

'For me, yes.'

He felt compelled to go on.

'And your employers?'

'That's up to them.'

He knew the answer but forced her to give it.

'They'll use it, won't they?'

She returned his look, her eyes blank, hard, not a spark in them.

He suddenly realised that in his stupor he hadn't asked the girl where the money had come from. But as soon as the thought crossed his mind, he dismissed it, Turkish Intelligence would have created a source. Bribes for defence contracts, most likely. He knew if he did not co-operate with Turkish Intelligence they would publish the documents. And if the documents were published he would be shown to have fifteen million dollars he couldn't account for. There was no way out. The thing with Albert was different. It was political. This was personal and the mud would stick.

'Will some Raki help?' She didn't smile.

He nodded. 'But make it brandy.'

She signalled to the waiter.

'Two brandies,' she said in Turkish. 'And make his very large.'

His moustache twitched. 'Triple?'

'At least,' she replied. 'And have one for yourself.'

His bushy eyebrows rose as his head bobbed sideways to give Gilbert a furtive glance.

'Are you sure you want him drunk? He'll pay well. It's not worth rolling him, he'll cause a stink. I know his sort.'

'Have two drinks,' she said.

'Alright. Have it your own way. But don't say I didn't warn you.' He stalked off, his back arched.

Gilbert sat silent until he'd taken a mouthful of brandy, rolled it around his mouth and swallowed it.

'What do you want to know,' he said.

She leaned forward, her perfume drifting across the table.

'We have heard rumours that your country, Germany and the

UK have had secret meetings.' She paused. 'Secret meetings about forming an Army to protect Europe.'

Gilbert said nothing.

She put her hands on the table, the brown varnished nails inching further towards him.

'If this Army is formed will it include Greece? Will it threaten us, the Turks?'

Gilbert felt a sudden release of tension, felt his whole body relax. He knew now how to respond. The years of repression in the cabinet, submitting to the President, the humiliation on the boat when he was mentally beaten into surrendering to Albert, the degradation of his meeting with Engels forced on him by that bastard in the spectacles, all of it rose in his throat like the acid of his overhung vodka. At last he could act on his own, act according to his conscience, act out his will. He pushed aside his brandy glass, leaned forward, breathing in her perfume, the attraction of her.

'You may tell your employers,' he murmured, 'that they shouldn't send young girls to do a man's job.'

He watched her go. And with her went his political career. But he didn't care. He had acted as he should. As an officer should. France came above all. Even if he didn't agree with her policies.

Looking up he saw the minarets bathed in light, reaching up the glinting stone into the sky. In the arc made by the lamps floated the white streaks of seagulls, silently circling. He had regained what he'd lost since Kosovo. His self respect. His honour.

The waiter dropped the bill in front of him.

'You're paying, she said.'

CHAPTER TWENTY-SEVEN

Lev was in a playful mood. His heavy features creased as he smiled at Hammond out of the plasma screen in the G8 Basingstoke conference room.

'What were you doing in the document safe room with that, what's her name, Charlie?'

Hammond sighed inwardly. Lev had to have his fun.

'Trying to get my hands on some of the documents there.'

Lev looked slyly across at Walt, who was looking amused out of his section of the plasma screen.

'For three hours? What did you find?'

Hammond straightened his back.

'Nothing. Well, nothing except Tricot's file on the French sensitive areas and we knew all those, anyway.'

Walt joined in. 'Nothing's not good, John. Not for three hours.'

'That's how long it took to get the Kurds out of the building.' Hammond snapped.

Lev made a pretence of studying his cigarette end.

'I heard they had to telephone you to get you to open the door.'

Julia appeared on the screen, sitting next to Hammond, her mouth a tight line.

'Shouldn't we get on?'

Lev looked at Walt from under his eyebrows, one of them lifting faintly.

'The meeting's brought to order.'

Walt laughed openly.

'OK Julia, we'll leave it 'til our next visit to Basingstoke. So tell us about Celik. How did he die? Who's taken over the PKK?'

Julia looked at Hammond. He nodded. 'We'll get to Gilbert afterwards,' he said.

She leaned on the conference table, looking at the plasma screen on the wall in front of her, concentrating on Lev before switching her eyes to Walt, so that she held them for a few seconds, emphasising that Hammond had given her control.

'Celik visited Mauritius four days ago. He stayed at the Paradis. The day after he arrived, he went swimming and was hit by a boat propeller. His body was washed up on the beach shortly after.'

Walt took a sip of coffee from the mug on his desktop. 'This didn't come from G8SUR otherwise you'd have told us about the boat owner.'

'No. G8SUR wasn't operating against Celik at the time. We've concentrated the Turkish arc on boat movements towards Greece. The information comes from the inquest held in Mauritius.'

'What was Celik doing in Mauritius?' Lev asked.

'We have no idea,' she replied.

'Has someone gone to find out?'

'No. We've downgraded the PKK to be able to increase our targeting of the Turkish and Greek Governments.'

Lev tapped some ash into the tray on his desk.

'Any results?'

'Nothing out of the ordinary. The Greeks are still taking diplomatic action about the Turkish gunboat attack on Samos. But it's not heated. It hasn't suited the Greeks that the Turks think their Ambassador in London was killed in some personal vendetta. But there's nothing the Greeks can do about that except tell the Turks. And they're not about to do that. So things are pretty quiet.' She paused. 'At the moment.'

Walt frowned. 'Do we know who's taken over in the PKK?'

Julia looked at Lev.

'Abu Hamid has been keeping his head down after the Antonov sabotage. So we don't know for certain. However, it's likely to be one of Celik's three advisers and most likely to be Birol.'

'Birol's the eldest,' Lev put in, 'the most experienced. That makes sense.'

'That's good,' added Walt. 'He won't give a lot of trouble. He's one of the old guard who got their fingers burnt in the 90s.'

Lev slowly lit one cigarette from the other, sucking to get the tobacco to burn, rivulets of dark smoke coming from his nostrils. They waited, knowing the sign when he was thinking.

'Why didn't Celik have a bodyguard?' he murmured. 'Why a boat propeller? Whose boat?' He rubbed his lips against his forefinger. 'I think we should know these things.'

'But if Birol's in charge, does it matter,' Walt said impatiently. 'After we intercepted the Antonov weapons shipment the PKK doesn't pose a real threat. Celik was past it. So's Birol. The Turks can put up with a few killings and bombings. We don't want to switch time and money allocated to keeping Greece and Turkey from each other's throats to the PKK.'

Julia waited, watching Lev. If Lev was uneasy, she wanted to know why. The G8 computers supported Walt's analysis. She had already run the data through them. That was why she hadn't followed up Celik's death with a check in Mauritius. But Lev was delving below the norms of behaviour, digging into the pit of his experience.

Lev looked up, his eyes so desolate that Julia mentally recoiled from learning how deep his thoughts had gone.

'I think,' said Lev, 'that a people dedicated to a homeland never stop until their dream becomes reality. The purge of the PKK in the 80s and 90s won the Turkish Government time, that was all.' He stopped, drawing on his cigarette. 'How many Kurds are the Turks pushing over the Greek border? So many that we are desperate to form an EU Army and Turkey to join it to prevent war.' He ran his hand over his thick greying hair. 'If we are that desperate, how desperate are the Kurds? We are driven to fury by the French delaying tactics. John told us of his anger with Tricot at the meeting in the Ministry of Interior.' He paused, his hand making a deliberate sweeping gesture across his desktop. 'Celik achieved nothing. So how angry are the Kurds? Angry enough to kill him? Change leadership?'

'Wait a minute,' interrupted Walt. 'That doesn't add up. Birol is even less effective than Celik.'

'Who said Birol has actually taken over.' Lev replied quietly.

'Come on Lev. That's speculation without any information at all.' Walt looked at Julia. 'Did you run Celik's death through the computer?'

She nodded.

Walt lifted his hand.

'And?'

'The computer supports you,' she said simply.

'There you are then.' Walt slapped his hand on his desk. 'You can't beat the computer.'

Lev leaned forward. 'I know human nature. I learned about it in the Lubianka, I watched it in the Gulags. I tell you, Celik's death needs questioning.' He sat back again. 'I agree, the computer has the logical answer, but desperate people aren't logical, terrorists never forget the advantage of surprise.'

Hammond spoke for the first time, his pale eyes focussed on Julia.

'I think Lev has something. We should investigate more fully. I suggest we alert Abu Hamid, ask him who's taken over the PKK leadership. I also suggest we send someone to Mauritius. But keep it low key. The important thing at the moment is Greece Turkey.'

There was a silence as they looked at Walt. He sat, studying his coffee cup, the edges of his mouth turned down. Finally, he spoke.

'In that case I'll volunteer to go to Mauritius.'

They laughed, the tension eased, Hammond put up his hand.

'Before we decide, I want you to hear Julia's report on her contact with Gilbert.'

Walt stopped laughing.

'Gilbert? The French Defence Minister Julia was setting up? This should be interesting. What did he say the French were up to?'

Julia stiffened, then pushed herself away from the table a little. Lev watched her. 'Not much, it seems,' he laughed.

She pushed her hands forward on the tabletop, no nail varnish now, just red lipgloss.

'That's where you're wrong, Lev.'

Walt looked surprised. 'You mean Gilbert actually talked? Told you the French policy?'

'You expected him to?' she countered.

'Well, we created a helluva lot of pressure. Most would have buckled under that. So he did, did he?'

'No,' she said.

'Hell, Julia,' Walt exploded, 'stop playing games. Either he told you or he didn't.'

'He didn't tell me about the split in the French Government. But he did tell me that he thought Albert had got nervous about exposing his supposed dealings with him in Kosovo.'

'What the hell does that mean?' said Walt, tartly.

Julia put her hands in her lap, almost primly. Hammond recognised the gesture as a warning that she'd reached the end of her patience. But he said nothing. She was perfectly capable of handling Walt and Lev.

'Would you like the computer printout or me to tell it?' she replied.

Walt's eyes lit up. 'If you're going to be that icy, I'll have the printout.'

Lev exploded in a cloud of smoke, waving his hand to clear it and peer into his screen.

'Come and work in Moscow, Julia. You're wasted in England. You're a Russian.'

'That's a nice compliment, Lev.' She turned back to Walt. 'Gilbert also said that he'd done what they wanted and that I should tell Albert to go to hell.'

Lev's face became still. 'You mean you let him think you were working for Albert?'

'He assumed I was from the moment I showed him the bearer bonds.'

'So Albert's blackmailing him,' Walt murmured.

'Gilbert said "they".' Lev put in. 'He said "he'd done what they wanted". That means Albert's working with other people.'

Walt nodded. 'Is that something to do with Kosovo? Gilbert said something about his dealings with Albert in Kosovo.'

'Supposed dealings,' Julia corrected.

Lev twirled his ashtray in the silence, then looked up.

'Gilbert's saying he didn't have dealings with Albert in Kosovo. So Albert made them up. Why should that bother Gilbert? That's no leverage in blackmailing him.'

Julia glanced at Walt. 'We had no leverage either, we made up the bearer bonds, the insurance policies, the fifteen million dollars.

He wasn't frightened by that.' She paused. 'He told me my employers shouldn't send young girls to do men's work.'

Walt remained impassive. 'Did he still think Albert was your
employer?'

'No. I'd declared myself as Turkish Intelligence by then.'

'I can't make sense of that,' said Walt. He reached for his coffee
mug.

'The computer analysis is interesting,' said Julia.

'It always is,' said Lev dryly.

She ignored him.

'The computer confirms that Albert is not alone in blackmailing
Gilbert. It also confirms that Gilbert caved in. Did whatever it was
they wanted. But at first the computer couldn't figure out why he
would cave in to their blackmail and not to ours.'

'At first?' queried Lev. 'You mean it found an answer?'

'No,' said Hammond. 'Julia found the answer. I'm telling you
that because she wouldn't.'

'What was it,' Lev went on, curious now.

'I fed into the computer the word "honour",' she said.

'Honour?' Walt looked puzzled.

'Gilbert is an honourable man. That's what Lev said when we
discussed this operation. Remember?' she replied.

'Go on,' urged Lev.

'The computer analysed that there are two sides to Gilbert. His
personal honour, his standing in the community.'

'Yes, yes, of course,' Lev cut in. 'And his public honour, the
honour of France, la gloire de la Republique.' He slapped his
forehead. 'I should have seen it.' His eyes switched to Julia. 'You
are Russian,' he said. 'No Englishman could have thought of that.
They don't understand the French.'

'Woman.' She smiled. 'The computer understood though. Whatever Albert concocted to blackmail Gilbert, it attacked his public
honour. He wasn't prepared to have France embarrassed.' She
paused. 'We attacked his personal honour and he was quite prepared to throw that away for the good of France.'

'My God,' said Walt, slowly. 'He really is an honourable man. I
can't believe it. So we go to Kosovo to find out what it's all about.'

'No,' countered Julia. 'We go to Mauritius. That is where Albert has his secrets. In his bank. Banque Onde. If we can find out what it was Albert had to blackmail Gilbert with, we can use it as well. And Gilbert will cave in to us.'

'Two birds with one stone,' said Walt. 'The answers to Celik and Gilbert. Both in Mauritius.'

Hammond shook his head. 'There's one question remaining, and that is why Gilbert met with Engels in Almaty.'

'Engels? The Kazakh Government fixer?' asked Walt.

'Yes,' nodded Julia. 'Gilbert thought I'd been following him in Almaty the previous night. He told me he'd been with Engels.'

'Almost certainly a defence contract,' said Walt dismissively. 'Nothing to bother about.'

'Let's concentrate on Mauritius.' Lev stood up. 'Is that it for today?'

Hammond nodded. The plasma screen went blank.

Julia stretched. Her long arms lifting towards the low grey sound proof tiles that formed the ceiling. Hammond caught the movement. Unaccountably he thought of Charlie and was immediately annoyed with himself. Charlie was a target.

Julia glanced around, saw Hammond watching her and dropped her arms. 'Thinking of Charlie?' she said.

'No I'm bloody not,' snapped Hammond.

Julia stooped and signed off the plasma screen computer. She'd never heard Hammond swear before.

CHAPTER TWENTY-EIGHT

Abu Hamid pushed past the market stalls, brushing away the Diyarbakir street vendors in the same way that he brushed aside the flies that buzzed from the piles of melons and fruit into his eyes and nostrils. Now and again the pungent aroma of spice overcame the dark stench of the littered alleyway. The black basalt walls on one side seemed to absorb all the air and in return blast out waves of heat. The cars and vans poured their exhausts into the fetid atmosphere as they hooted their way through the bustle, literally nudging the slow or old out of their way. Abu Hamid hated this part of Diyarbakir but it was essential to pass through it before any meeting with Tansu. Usually she only met the various terrorist cell leaders, fifth circle PKK, and only met them after they had cleared themselves of any surveillance by dodging through the narrow lanes of the fruit market until they were sure they were not followed.

Abu Hamid had gone into the market wearing a yellow shirt and dark blue jeans. After ducking into a plastic sheeted shelter behind a stack of date boxes, he'd come out of the back wearing a djellabah, followed a moment later by a man wearing a yellow shirt and jeans. They'd gone separate ways. It was simple, but usually effective. And various stallholders in the Market Square and tenants in the crumbling buildings surrounding it, watched for anything suspicious, any movement which meant Turkish Intelligence was mounting surveillance. They were the supporters, the eighth circle, not knowing Abu Hamid's name, or even why they were watching, only remembering his number to dial on their mobile to alert him if they saw danger. The number changed every time and often there were three or four people to watch out for, three or four numbers to remember, and that stretched the older members of the eighth circle. But they were proud, and desperate to fight the Turks, so they lay awake at night and repeated the numbers over and over.

Abu Hamid's mobile did not vibrate in his pocket before he reached the dark, arched doorway let into the flat roofed stone building in the narrow alley bordering on the gold market. He didn't glance over his shoulder as he slipped inside. That would have looked suspicious. Instead he turned left through a crack left open by a heavy studded door which was immediately shut behind him and locked. Above his head was a television screen. It showed the alley and the space in front of the door. Both were empty.

He nodded to the woman by the door and walked up the stone steps alongside the wall. They curved round until they reached a black wood floor in a small windowless room. Two men stood there. Each held a Glock machine pistol pointed at Abu Hamid's head then his stomach as he mounted the stairs and stood in front of them. He raised his arms and let one of them search him. They took away his mobile and a roll of dinars, all he ever carried on him when he was called to a meeting with Tansu, all anyone was allowed to carry when meeting her.

He didn't speak to the men. On duty, Tansu's bodyguard spoke to nobody but each other and her so he would have to wait for her to tell him who the new Leader was. He'd been surprised when G8 had asked him to find out, he thought they would have known. His handler hadn't explained much, just told him to remember that he might be under suspicion for the Antonov sabotage and to be careful.

One of the guards flicked open a concealed panel, pressed the palm of his hand against a glass plate. The door behind him slid open.

Abu Hamid hardly contained his surprise. Sitting at an oblong table in another windowless room were a dozen or so men and women. He immediately recognised two of them. They were PKK cell leaders, like himself. Other faces were familiar. Faces he had seen on his G8 handler's laptop during briefings, faces of cell leaders he had not met. He schooled his features, recognised nobody and walked to an empty chair halfway along the table.

There was an air of nervous anticipation. Everyone sitting at the table guessed that all the cell leaders were present and knew that such a meeting had never happed before. Nobody spoke, maintaining the discipline instilled by Celik and his predecessors. Communication between cell leaders was only made with the Leader's permission, unless in emergency.

The room was bare of furniture except the table and chairs. There was no air conditioning, no air vents. There were no ceiling or wall lights. Just portable fans and bare bulbs on standards connected to portable generators.

Abu Hamid made a quick assessment for his report to G8. There was no possibility of listening devices being planted there. The portable generators, and the lights and fans they supplied were almost certainly inspected by eighth circle electricians and mechanics immediately before any meeting. He noticed the exhaust was passed by a pipe through the wall to the room outside where the guards stood. The generators were muffled, but speaking in a whisper was impossible. Abu Hamid made a mental note that this side effect prohibited any discreet exchange of information or comment. The cell leaders were on their own.

There was a stir as Birol's two bodyguards came in. Abu Hamid looked around. It was clear that, like him, no one had expected Birol to be present. The summons for the meeting had come from Tansu. So there were going to be no surprises. Birol had taken over and kept Tansu as his Chief of Operations. He settled back, watching the other cell leaders do the same.

One guard walked to stand behind the head of the table, his Glock held across his waist, his eyes restless. The other guard waited by the door.

Tansu came next, flanked by her personal guards, striding towards the head of the table. Abu Hamid involuntarily joined in the startled murmurs around the table. Tansu was different. She was not wearing a chador, she was dressed in a black, linen trouser suit and low black leather shoes. And she was showing her hair for the first time, cut short at the nape of the neck. As she passed him, Abu Hamid noticed she was wearing eye shadow and lipstick. He was amazed. Tansu had been fanatical about wearing the chador. He had never seen her in makeup. He wondered what Birol would say when he saw her.

The door shut. With a shock Abu Hamid realised the guard had slammed it. Making sure everyone heard. And everyone looked. To see that Birol wasn't there.

'Birol will not be coming. I executed him and the other two advisers yesterday afternoon.'

Stunned, the cell leaders swung round to face Tansu.

She stood at the head of the table, upright, her thin features accentuated by the bare light bulbs.

'If anyone objects to my taking over the leadership, say so now.'

She looked around the table, her mouth pursed in a tight arrogant line.

No one spoke. They just sat, staggered by the bombshell she'd dropped. Abu Hamid's mind was racing. The worst thing for Turkey, for G8, was Tansu. She was ruthless, worse, she was successful. As an operational planner she was brilliant. Only luck had prevented the Antonov arms shipment reaching the PKK. Once she had control of the cell leaders she would direct all PKK activities. She would light up Turkey, destroy the work the Turks had done since the 1980s to keep the PKK in check. He knew that now was the time to act, to play on the cell leaders' loyalty to Birol, to demand an election. On the other hand, the moment he stood up to make the demand he would become the centre of attention. Nothing could be more dangerous to his role as a G8 agent. Once the spotlight was on him it would remain. Making his work almost impossible. And his handler had warned him to be careful. Challenging Tansu wasn't being careful.

He flicked his eyes around the table, taking in the frozen faces, hearing only the hum of the generators.

He jumped up.

'Tansu,' he shouted, 'I support you. Our cause is blessed. We shall . . .'

The rest of his words were lost as the cell leaders leapt to their feet, shouting for her, thumping the table with their fists, their faces alight with hope.

As he shouted with them, Abu Hamid knew he'd taken the right decision. Tansu was dangerous, but far less dangerous when he could report on her plans and movements to G8. They would know what to do, how to eliminate her and when. He bowed as

Tansu caught his eye and nodded, smiling for the first time he could remember. At that moment he understood why she had abandoned the chador, why she was made up. She was going to lead from the front, in public, make the political case for the Kurds.

Abu Hamid had no political sympathy for the Turks, he was a well paid G8 agent who worked for money. But, as he smiled back at Tansu, he felt a flutter of fear. She would be hard to break, and until she was dead, the Turks would feel pain they never knew existed. Then another thought occurred to him which made his smile even warmer. With Tansu as his main target he could increase his G8 pay by at least half. He waved his hands in the air, cheering for her.

CHAPTER TWENTY-NINE

The home of the Mauritius Coroner was in the old trading quarter of Port Louis, lying uneasily next to the modern docks and financial centre. The building was white stucco, with tall blue shutters guarding the narrow paned white painted windows glinting in the sun. A wrought iron balcony ran around the first floor, standing on tall iron pillars with graceful arches spreading away to hold its weight. It was painted washed blue to match the shutters.

Hammond saw Lionel Keithley's wry smile and laughed.

'I told you I'd need you here. The Commissioner of the Metropolitan Police will prise open an old fashioned bureaucrat far quicker than the Director General of G8 he's never heard of.'

Keithley took another look at the front of the building. Squinting in the glare.

'If he's this old fashioned I'll need a crowbar to open him up.'

'Tell him you're a Knight of the Bath. He won't be able to resist that. The French love our Royal Orders.'

Keithley looked surprised. 'He's not French, he's Mauritian.'

'French descent. They're French first. Mauritian second. Like the French Canadians.'

Keithley shook his head. 'You're such a cynical bastard. Well, lead the way to our Coroner.'

They climbed a short, iron balustraded, flight of steps. Hammond pulled the bell stop. They waited, watching their taxi pull away up the narrow street, its reflection flickering in the small square windowpanes of the French colonial trading houses.

The door was opened by a Chinese servant who ushered them into the cool interior. Pale Chinese rugs were spread over the wooden floor and Hammond and Keithley were able to admire them because the only furniture was a low, long ebony coffee table surrounded by four ebony and cane latticed sofas. The ebony was made even more stark by the blue wash on the walls.

'Yes, they are Dutch, made from local ebony over three hundred years ago.'

Hammond and Keithley turned to face a short, wiry man with a shock of white hair which matched his white linen suit. Hanging from the top pocket were the folds of a blue silk handkerchief, the same colour blue as his neat bow tie.

'Henri Montigny, Coroner for the Morne Brabant District.'

Keithley took the Coroner's outstretched hand. 'Thank you for seeing me.'

The Coroner shook his head. 'I'd be foolish not to see Britain's most senior police officer. Anyway, your visit intrigues me. Tea? Coffee?' He sat on one of the sofas, ignoring Hammond.

'Tea, please,' said Keithley to the Chinese servant, now waiting patiently in the shadows at the far side of the room.

The Coroner looked at Keithley again. 'Your man can go with my servant, if he likes. Have some refreshment in the kitchen.'

Keithley's smile wasn't purely formal. 'I'd like to keep him with me if I may. Take notes and so on.'

The Coroner waved Hammond to a sofa.

'Very well, but there won't be many notes to take. Celik's death was straightforward. An accident. I can't say it was a regrettable accident. The man was a terrorist, the world's better off without him.'

Keithley's cane sofa creaked as he sat on it.

'Celik wasn't just a terrorist. He led the PKK.'

The Coroner's narrow chin creased as his mouth turned down.

'That means nothing to me, Sir Lionel. Mauritius has no terrorism. We live here as Christians, Chinese, Hindus, Buddhists, Muslims without fear or hatred. We live in peace, we trade in peace and we offer our financial services in peace. What is the PKK to us?'

Keithley waited as the Chinese servant put a tray on the table and poured out tea, putting a slice of lemon into each cup and handing them around. There was no milk.

Hammond had to control himself as Keithley stared at his cup. Keithley had drunk builder's tea all his life. Dark, milky, thick and sweet. For a moment Hammond thought Keithley was going to break, then suddenly Keithley brought the cup to his mouth and gulped. For a second his eyes bulged, then he swallowed.

'Very nice,' he said.

'It's local,' the Coroner replied. 'I can recommend where you can get it.'

Keithley's eyes bulged again. 'Very kind. There was some talk that Celik wasn't alone at Le Paradis.'

The Coroner shrugged. 'Was there? I suppose it would be unusual for someone to be alone at Le Paradis. But it is respectable. Expensive. Exclusive.' He sipped his tea. A delicate movement.

Keithley pressed on. 'The boat owner?'

'Boat owner?' repeated the Coroner, slowly.

'Yes,' said Keithley, 'the one that hit Celik.'

'Oh. I see what you mean. The boat owner. Yes. Well, there wasn't one. Couldn't be found. There are always dozens of boats around there. And Celik's body wasn't discovered until some hours afterwards.'

Keithley's cup rattled as he put it down on the tray.

'The autopsy report. It was very brief. Just the head wound. Nothing about the lungs, sea water, that sort of thing.'

The Coroner pinched his trouser leg between thumb and finger and gently hitched it up, showing a glimpse of a pale blue silk sock.

'Why spend valuable resources on something that's obvious? A boat propeller hitting a skull . . .' his voice trailed away.

Keithley leaned forward. 'I don't wish to sound impertinent but a full autopsy would be helpful to us. Perhaps I could arrange . . .'

The Coroner uncrossed his legs. 'But the body's been cremated. Didn't you know?'

*

As they walked up the street, leaving the Coroner's black ebony and white stucco behind them, Keithley nodded at the picturesque, painted trading houses and then towards the tall, glass, steel and concrete structures of the finance centre.

'He might be old fashioned but he's in the twenty first century all right. He got that inquest and cremation sewn up with no fuss

at all. The PKK'll not bother Mauritius. The old bastard made sure
of that.'

'The French took over Mauritius when the Dutch left, so they've
had three hundred years to practice self interest,' said Hammond.
'That's what the ebony furniture was there to tell us.'

'Bastard,' repeated Keithley, feelingly. He walked on a few
paces. 'There's nothing more to be found here. Have you got any
more sources?'

'One in Turkey,' replied Hammond. 'But he hasn't reported in
yet.'

'Well I hope he's more forthcoming than that old buzzard
Coroner.' Keithley laughed. 'We'll complain to the President when
we see him at tonight's reception.'

*

Hammond couldn't complain to the President that night, when he
and Keithley visited Le Reduit, the President's great double fronted,
colonnaded mansion, for the simple reason that only Keithley was
allowed into the magic circle.

The Reception was held outside, the gardens lit by dozens of
lights on tall standards, which filtered onto the flame trees and
hibiscus bushes. Hammond followed a path to the bar and ordered
a scotch on the rocks. He looked around at the crowd on the lawns.
So different to the crowd that would have graced the lawns when
the house was built. Then the only economy was sugar. Now
Mauritius was the offshore finance hub for South Africa, India,
Singapore and China. And the guests at the President's Reception
were a true reflection of the huge wealth generated by the billions
of dollars that rocketed through the banks, insurance companies
and mutual funds in Port Louis. Gold was the guests' common
demoninator. Gold watches, gold chains, gold bracelets, gold saris,
gold teeth winking and gleaming as they caught the shafts of light
from the tall standards.

Somewhere in the crowd, Hammond heard a woman laugh. It
was so distinctive he automatically lifted his head and for an
instant looked for Charlie. He was annoyed to feel a twinge of
disappointment. Charlie was a target. Nothing more. Suddenly, he

heard the laughter again and caught a flash of blonde hair. If Charlie wasn't there, he thought, he could make do with second best. He crossed the lawn to the group where he'd heard the laughter. There were two men in dark suits. Standing between them with her back turned, was a faded red haired woman enveloped in silk shawls, the gold braid twinkling in the lights. Behind her, Hammond caught another glimpse of blonde hair.

He touched one of the silk shawls gently.

'Excuse me, ma'am.'

The shawls flared out as the woman abruptly turned. Hammond found himself facing a pair of electric blue eyes and a red mouth turned up at the corners in amusement.

'It's not me you want to excuse, young man, I'm sure. These two gentlemen have already disappointed me by denying it, so what are you going to say?'

'I was going to say that I wanted to talk to your sister.' Hammond said, solemnly.

'When you're bored with her you can come back to me,' she said laughing. 'Anyone who can flatter an eighty year old with such grace by telling her that her young niece is her sister, is a treasure indeed.' She turned her head. 'Charlie, I've found you a husband.'

Hammond looked sharply over her shoulder. Charlie turned, an odd, arrested look on her face.

'John. What . . . what . . .'

'Charlie. What are you doing here?' said Hammond, stupidly.

The woman glanced from one to the other.

'Well, Charlie,' she breathed, 'you never told me about him.' She emphasised the last word.

Charlie burst into laughter, her eyes bright.

'Nina, he's a work colleague.' She held out her hand to Hammond. 'I'm sorry. I never expected to see you here. Meet Nina Dedain, my only and favourite aunt.'

Hammond took her hand.

'If you look like your aunt at eighty, I will marry you,' he smiled. 'But what are you doing here?'

'I asked her to come and rest after that nasty riot,' Nina said.

'But it wasn't . . .' Hammond started.

'The office gave me leave,' cut in Charlie. 'They said I needed some time off.'

He saw Nina look at his hand, which was still holding Charlie's. He dropped it.

'How are you, anyway?'

'I'm fine.' Charlie hesitated. 'Thanks.'

'It was nothing,' he murmured.

'I didn't mean thanks for saving me,' she flashed, 'I saved you. If I hadn't found the safe room . . .'

'If you hadn't . . . that's rich . . .'

'Come now, children.' Nina threw one of her gold shawls over her shoulder. 'If you want to quarrel, let's do it at home like civilised people.' She turned to go. 'Come on. Where's Pandit.' She looked around. 'Pandit,' she shouted. 'Come on, John, whatever your name is, find Pandit for me. What are you hanging back for Charlie. Neither of those two gentlemen are any good for you.' She raised the white parasol she was carrying. Prodded a waiter. 'Get Pandit for me, Raj, there's a good fellow.' She turned to Hammond. 'A good servant, Raj. Trained him myself. I was sorry to see him go. But the President offered me such a good transfer fee.'

Hammond raised his eyebrows. 'Transfer fee? Isn't that slavery?'

Her eyes met his. 'No. It's good sense. Like your football transfers. And Raj gets three times what I could pay him. Ah. There you are Pandit. Where were you? Skulking around smoking, I'm sure. No don't deny it. Just get us home.'

*

The main highway out of Port Louis passed in a blur as Pandit made sure he overtook everything in front of him. He never swore or gesticulated. Leaning back in the leather of the vintage Jaguar, he simply tailgated until the driver in front had had enough. And if that took too long, a nudge or two on the fender ensured success. The turn off onto the secondary roads leading into the sugar cane was accomplished in a smooth slide on and off the sandy side path. The headlights served no purpose as Pandit drove over the narrow asphalt by memory, the sugar cane flashing by either side in a haze of green and yellow, whipping down and up in the frantic back-draft. The odd bicycle or oncoming car were negotiated with a touch of brake or accelerator that never seemed to alter the pace. Pandit never used the horn. The only sign that he was actually awake was a slight smile, which never altered however dire the emergency.

When they arrived at the house, Pandit helped Nina out of the car. She stood by the bonnet for a moment, breathing in. She turned to Hammond.

'I love the smell of a car that's been driven fast. Of course, it's no longer so crisp, the burnt rubber and benzine of the really old cars. But,' she looked lovingly at the ancient Jaguar, 'this is as good as it gets. And,' she put a hand on Pandit's arm. 'Pandit passed out top in the police driver's test.'

Hammond felt bewildered. 'How do you get a police driver?'

'Part of Raj's transfer fee.' She smiled. 'I gave up driving a couple of years ago. Well,' she corrected, 'it gave me up really. A tourist bus I wasn't expecting. No one hurt but there was some complaint made and my insurer got to know my age.' She sighed. 'So inconvenient. Still, Pandit's the next best thing. Come on in.'

Hammond followed her and Charlie across the gravel driveway, up the wide steps, across the veranda and into the reception room. There was no ceiling, just beams and the wooden battens under the roof tiles. The flat white paint that covered the walls and roof made it cool, the shuttered French windows open onto the veranda. The furniture was old and worn. A scattering of rugs lay on the tiled floor and odd chairs and a large sofa sat haphazardly alongside an assortment of tables covered with photographs in coloured frames and books everywhere. There was no furniture alongside the walls. They were covered with oil paintings.

Hammond saw they were all portraits. Painted in strong, stark lines, using layers of primary colours. Against the white walls, the sitters leapt out and seemed to join him in the room.

He glanced at Charlie.

'So you're not just an Ionist, after all.'

'They're Nina's,' she said. 'She taught me to paint.'

'Strong,' he murmured. 'Vital. I could shake hands with them. Why haven't I seen her work in London, Paris . . .'

'She never sells her work.' She paused. 'That is something else she taught me.'

'Would you sell one of your paintings to me?'

She looked at the floor as if embarrassed. Shook her head.

'Certainly not.'

'What about Gilbert?'

Her head came up, green eyes blazing.

'You told me in L'Imbecile that you wouldn't ask me about Gilbert.'

'That was before I found out what sort of trouble he is in.'

'What do you mean? You are always hinting something bad about Gilbert. It is . . . it is sans pitie.'

'You should know. It's your stepfather Albert who's black mailing him.'

She gasped, brought her hand round, slapped his face, her ring leaving a red wheal on his cheek.

He didn't move.

'That was stupid, Charlie, childish. And it won't make the truth go away. If you know about Albert, you'll do better to tell me than to try and help Gilbert.'

'Get out,' she hissed. 'Get out.'

'Not another quarrel, darling,' Nina murmured, as she swept in, trailing yet another silk scarf behind her. 'It's so unsettling for the servants. Now, John, can I get you a drink?' She looked around. 'John? John?'

'He's gone,' Charlie said, flatly.

Nina sat down in one of the faded rose chairs. 'Really, darling, I do wish you wouldn't keep losing your men.' She sipped her martini. 'And he was such a nice one too. Just right for you.'

'Salaud.'

'Charlie. I don't know where you pick up your language.'

'You taught me.' Charlie knelt down and put her arms around Nina's waist. 'Oh God, Nina, what a bastard he is.'

CHAPTER THIRTY

Abu Hamid felt exhilarated. The meeting room was silent now as he stood next toTansu. After the shouting and yells of support for her leadership had died down, she had asked him to join her at the head of the table.

He stood there, blinking in the bright light from the electric bulbs. There was a hush, so full of expectancy that it seemed to drown out the drone of the generators. Tansu let it continue, let it dominate, let it dwell on Abu Hamid by her side, so that they both seemed to grow in stature.

She put her hand on his shoulder.

'My brother Abu Hamid was the first to support my leadership, I am the first to support him as my Deputy.' She put out her hand into the silence. 'He is younger than you,' she said. 'But he is wise and he acts on his own initiative. He is the future I want.' There was a murmur from the table, movement as the cell leaders shifted their bodies to listen more closely.

Tansu removed one of her diamond earrings and put it on the table in front of her.

'This is a symbol of the future. It is sophisticated, tougher than any metal or stone,' she paused, 'and it draws attention. That is to be our watchword. The old days of hit and run, a bomb here, a killing there, are over. From now on we are going to be in the eye of the public. I am going to be the policy maker, speaking by satellite link to the press and television. My Deputy will protect me, arrange my movements.'

She looked around the table.

'My policy is to have a Kurdish homeland within twelve months.'

There were murmurs, then shouts of disbelief.

She picked up the diamond earring and held it up, the facets radiating out yellow and blue flame.

'We are going to be as hard as this. We have already shown our teeth with the riot in Paris. We killed no one, which showed the French and the world that the Kurds can be organised and disciplined.' She put up her hand to still the questions. 'I have spoken with Moosar in Kazakhstan and have agreed to meet to arrange another weapons shipment in two weeks' time.' She ran her hand slowly down the nape of her neck drawing their eyes away from the ring. 'These weapons will be used by you,' her hand circled the table, 'to attack the Greek island of Limnos.'

This time, she couldn't stop the babble of voices. The guards brought their fingers off the trigger guards.

'Listen to me,' she shouted. 'Listen.' She motioned the guards to stand back.

The cell leaders watched her gesture, gradually falling silent, some of them leaning heavily on the table, ready to shout their dissent again.

'The French Government is supporting us. They want to stop the Turks pushing us Kurds over the border into Greece. They want us to attack Greece in the guise of Turkish troops so that Greece will retaliate and clear the Turks off mainland Europe. While they are fighting, we will take over the Turkish Government.'

The cell leaders sat speechless, gaping at her in sheer disbelief.

'Who will take over the Turkish Government?' one of them called out.

'You will,' she said. 'All of you. With me as your Prime Minister.'

'And the President?' called out another.

'Our banker,' she replied, 'Albert.'

'But he's a Christian.'

She leaned on the table, her mouth a tight line.

'Albert is a powerful force. He's one of us,' she said between her teeth. 'Anyone who forgets that will regret it.'

'You mean he knows where the money is,' muttered someone, but his words were lost in the throb of the generators.

Tansu stood away from the table. 'In three weeks we attack Limnos. I want all cell leaders to report to my Deputy for instruc-

tions. We will split into two groups.' She looked at the two men
standing opposite her. 'Sulan and Yener will attack Limnos with
their troops. The rest of you will take over key points in Ankara to
carry out the coup.'

'How will we hold Ankara, the Turkish countryside?' asked
Sulan.

'Once we have taken over, we will sue for peace with Greece.
They will negotiate with a Government that has thrown out the
Turkish aggressors. And we negotiate with Turks who want to
form a new Government for Turkey which recognises a Kurdish
homeland.'

'And the Turkish Army? Will they be asleep while we take over
their Government?' Sulan pressed.

'They will be too busy fighting the Greeks. What can they do?'

Sulan slowly nodded. 'I believe you are right. We will have our
homeland in twelve months.'

The murmur of assent grew around the table.

'There is one other thing,' said Tansu.

They looked up at her, now completely held by whatever she
said.

'We need to soften up the Greeks so that they are on the very
edge when we attack Limnos. We must be sure that they declare
war on the Turks. They must be wound up tight as a clock.'

Abu Hamid could hardly contain himself as Tansu outlined the
operation. His previous assessment of her was abandoned. For the
first time, he realised that she had no safety net. Her ability to plan
tragedy was limitless, no barrier existed in her conscience beyond
which her mind would not go. He was sure G8 had never had a
target so utterly devoid of humanity.

He suddenly realised she had stopped speaking and was looking at him.

'Are you ready for the tasks ahead?'

Numbly, he nodded.

'Wait for me,' she murmured, 'we need a planning meeting.'

He watched as she moved with her guards to usher out the cell
leaders. Each of them to leave the sprawling building by a separate
exit.

He watched as the electricians took away the fans and all the electric lights except the one nearest him, ready for his meeting with their new Leader. He felt a glow of satisfaction as they treated him with deference, making sure he wasn't disturbed by their shifting of generators and coiling of cables.

Suddenly the light went out.

'Hey,' he shouted, 'not that one.'

There was no reply. Just the scraping sound of a generator being moved.

'Hey,' he shouted again.

The silence was broken by the sound of the great steel door closing.

'Hey,' he yelled, rushing towards it. 'I'm here. Wait.'

He crashed over a chair. Sprawled onto the floor. He scrabbled to his feet. Blindly staggered against the table. Felt his way down. Hitting another chair. Throwing it against the wall. Fighting the panic welling inside him. He slammed against the wall. The breath driven from his body. Sobbing he desperately clawed at the door. It was shut. He moved his hand to find the handle. Couldn't find it. Moaning now, he ran both his hands all over the door. The handle wasn't there. Just a blank sheet of steel.

As he slid to the floor he clearly heard the voice of his handler warning him to be careful.

CHAPTER THIRTY-ONE

Nina was sitting on the veranda sketching when Charlie came down for breakfast. A strong breeze bent the sugar cane towards the house, lifting the corner of her sketchbook. In the distance, the tops of the Rapilles peaks were hidden in a stream of cloud.

Nina brought her charcoal down the page in a forceful curve.

'You'll need your raincoat today, Charlie.'

'Yes.' Charlie leaned over her shoulder and studied the sketch. 'That's John. What are you drawing him for?'

'I draw all my guests.' Nina's hands shaded around Hammond's mouth. 'I like his eyes. He's honest.'

'Honest? He wouldn't know the truth if it was hung from a banner between the Rapilles.'

Nina looked out across the cane fields.

'I suppose he wouldn't, dear,' she laughed, 'in all that cloud.'

Charlie stood up straight and stiffly walked to the balustrade.

'Do you know what his job is?'

'No, darling, but I'm sure you're going to tell me.'

'He's the Director General of G8.'

'Oh. G8.' Nina blew away some charcoal. 'I see.'

'Aunt, you can be maddening sometimes.'

Nina lifted her head away from the paper, thought for a moment, then leaned forward, flicked a small crease at the edge of Hammond's left eye.

'Yes, that's it, it's that trick he has of quizzing people, the laughter behind his beautiful eyes.' She sat back. 'When you call me "aunt" I know you are hiding something.'

'I'm certainly not. It's just that John Hammond is ruthless, but he hides it behind layers of charm and you've fallen for it.'

Nina very deliberately put her charcoal down, rubbed her

fingers on a paint blotched shawl draped around her shoulders, pushed her huge straw hat back from her eyes, looked directly at Charlie.

'And you've fallen for him.'

Charlie walked over to the breakfast table, picked up a piece of cinnamon toast and carefully spread some honey over it.

'You wouldn't say that if you'd heard him last night.'

Nina picked up a tin of fixer and shook it vigorously.

'Nonsense. I always quarrel with my men. It spices up life.'

'You mean you're still quarrelling at your age?' Charlie exclaimed through a mouthful of toast.

Nina experimentally squirted some fixer on a corner of the sketch.

'Of course.' She sighed as she drew the can back and sprayed a fine mist over Hammond's face. 'And if I were your age I'd enjoy quarrelling with him.'

Charlie put the toast down on the plate, poured out some coffee.

'He accused Albert of blackmail.'

Nina's hand continued its smooth sideways movement with the can. 'That doesn't surprise me.'

'Nina, Albert's my stepfather.'

'And not fit to be in the same room as your father.' Nina said, shaking the can again. 'Not that he ever was,' she added inconsistently.

'You're wrong. Albert's been great to me, you know that. Helped me with my art, paid for exhibitions, even bought my friends' paintings, and he hates Ionism.' Charlie hesitated. 'Anyway, you always said my father was too hard on me.'

Nina put the top on the can and placed it beside the box of charcoal.

'He was, darling, but that's not the point. The point is that your father had a code of honour and Albert has not. The fact that your father bullied you with it as a child and pushed you into the Foreign Service when you were an adult is neither here nor there. It's in the past. Albert is the present and I don't like him. If John Hammond says he's a blackmailer, I believe him.'

Charlie pushed a chair away from the table and sat on it.

'But why? What proof have you? Except you don't like him? You're being unfair.'

Nina shut the charcoal box with a snap. 'I'm surprised to hear you say that, Charlie. I thought I'd taught you by now that life isn't fair.' She drew the scarf away from her neck and began folding it. 'If you want to know why I don't trust Albert I'll tell you. But you will not tell your mother. I don't want her worried.'

Charlie nodded wordlessly.

Nina pushed herself to her feet.

'Give me your arm. We'll go into the garden.'

They walked down the veranda steps onto the lawn, the thick stemmed grass cut evenly to sweep into borders of red, orange, white and pink hibiscus, frangipani, and bougainvillea, a riot of colour flickering in the sun trying to shine through the low cloud.

'Do you like my new tea garden,' Nina asked, adjusting her hat and pointing to a large square of dark green bushes topped with delicate yellow leaves. 'I love the colour of tea bushes just before they're plucked. Such a cool contrast to the hot colours of the shrubs.'

'It's beautiful,' said Charlie, going over to feel the texture of the leaves. 'It would make a brilliant painting.'

'Ionist?' smiled Nina.

'Yes, I think so,' nodded Charlie, 'a first layer of different dark green filings, then glue and a litter of yellow green. Some silver, perhaps, to get the reflection.'

Nina put her head on one side, the sun creeping in under the brim of her hat to catch the blue of her eyes.

'You should have kept to your art, Charlie. You're not a bureaucrat, however clever you are. You're not hard enough, worldly enough.'

Charlie walked back to her.

'Are you preparing me for what you have to say about Albert?'

Nina took her arm, walked on to the gravel path leading to a row of tall royal palms, the leaves waving and rustling in the stiff breeze.

'I suppose so. I don't want to do it, you know.' She bent to pick up a broken palm branch and push it to the side of the path.

'Albert's bank, Banque Onde, does not have a good reputation in banking circles here.'

'The old banking people don't understand offshore finance, Nina. They disapprove; say it's tax evasion. Albert is one of the most respected offshore tax specialists in Paris. He acts for the most respectable families and corporations.'

'They say he launders money for the Russians, East Europeans,' said Nina, stubbornly.

'Launders?' Charlie laughed. 'Nina, what do you know about laundering?'

'Enough to have hidden your mother's money from him.'

Charlie came to an abrupt stop. 'You've hidden her money? How? She stills spends it like water.'

Nina prodded a weed with her parasol. 'Only the interest. She's never had a clue about money. He'll never find the capital.' She laughed. 'Nor will she.'

Charlie put a hand on her arm. 'Darling, you can't do that. What happens if . . . if . . .'

'I die? It's taken care of.' Her eyes took on a flat look, mulish.

Charlie stared at her.

The sun suddenly disappeared behind a scud of black cloud. A drop of rain splashed between them onto the path. Nina looked at it. 'We'd better go in.' She turned then stopped. 'There was a man killed here last week.'

Charlie's eyes widened. She opened her mouth. 'Who was killed?'

Nina took her hand and gripped it.

'Albert made me promise not to tell anyone. He . . . he was threatening . . . no . . . no . . . he didn't threaten me exactly . . . he was . . . It was in the sugar fields. The man had been hacked to death with a panga by one of the cane cutters. Albert said there'd be a scandal. I'd have to leave Mauritius if it was found out.' She bit her lip. 'I couldn't do that.'

Charlie shook her head. 'It doesn't make sense. What scandal?'

Nina took her hand away, steadied herself. 'The man was staying here. I didn't know until he arrived. Albert had invited him. The inquest said he'd died in a boating accident. Propeller.'

'Propeller?'

The rain was falling in large drops now. Pattering on the huge palm leaves high above them. Nina put up her parasol, clicking it open.

'I'm sorry, darling. I shouldn't have told you. Wouldn't, if you hadn't been so stubborn about Albert.'

Charlie stood stock still. 'Was the man's name Celik?'

'Yes, darling. How did you know?'

'I was briefed in the Ministry,' she said shortly. 'Celik was the PKK Leader. He died in a boating accident here. The Inquest said so.'

Nina nodded her head. 'Yes. Of course it would. That's what the Coroner was told.'

Charlie brushed the rain out of her hair. Quick. Angry.

'And you've made up this fantastic story to get at Albert? The laundering, mother's money. And now this. What's happened to you, for God's sake?'

Nina stood in the rain, trying to ignore the pain in her chest as she watched Charlie push past her and run up the path to the house. She didn't know how long she stood there before she heard the Jaguar race down the drive.

*

'Albert's bank is firewalled. The best I've come across. We can't attack his personal records.' Hammond grimaced. He waved his hand at the plain white walls of the Mauritius Airport VIP lounge. 'Banque Onde is just like this place. Nothing to show what's going on.'

Keithley looked around him, taking in the simple red sofas around the room, the vases of lilies on the desk at the far end with the solemn police officer sitting there, waiting for the incident that would never happen.

'The bank's firewalled its computers?'

'Yes. One set to receive instructions. Another set to send them. Personal records on a third set. No linkage between any of the computers. A separate one for each client. You can't hack into any central database. Albert has one time security keys and locks for each client as well. The encryption is changed every twelve hours. Well over a thousand k.'

Keithley whistled under his breath. 'A thousand k?'

Hammond frowned. 'That depth of encryption will have our computer working overtime. The whole attack on Banque Onde was a flop. We've got nothing out of it. And it'll take months to get anything.'

Keithley watched the policeman swat a fly with a small drinks mat. 'The girl? Charlie?'

Hammond stood up. 'Nothing. She's hooked on Gilbert. She's not talking.'

Keithley looked sideways at Hammond for a moment.

'So we've got bugger all to show for our visit then.' He paused. 'Still, it's not all been wasted.'

Hammond's chin came up. 'Oh?'

Keithley smiled. 'I think I'll come back. Bring the wife. It's beautiful here.'

'Time to go,' snapped Hammond.

They didn't speak as they walked to the aircraft. The rain battered on the roof of the open passageway leading to the parking apron, bounced off the tarmac, splashing their shoes. A dripping stewardess stood at the end of the walkway, her mouth in a fixed smile as she picked up umbrellas from a pile and opened them in a shower of water, thrusting the handles out.

'A bientot,' she smiled, 'come again soon.'

Hammond grunted, ran up the stairway to the aircraft door, ducked his head, nodded curtly to the steward, turned, tripped and crashed to the floor.

'Merde. Imbecile. My cabin case.'

Hammond shook his head. Sat up to look at Charlie. She shook the case at him. 'See this? My mirror, it's . . .' She stopped. Her eyes narrowed. 'You.'

Hammond reached for the seat back and pulled himself up.

'You have a distressing habit of repeating yourself, Charlie. Now if you'd move, you're in my seat.'

Two bright spots of colour appeared on her cheeks.

'This is my seat.'

Keithley leaned over her shoulder.

'Quite right, John. I swapped seats with her. Knew you'd like to be together.' He walked further up the aisle.

Charlie clenched her teeth.

'Steward. Steward.'

He came bustling up. His blonde quiff falling over one eye. He swept it away. 'Do you have that trouble, luv?' he asked. 'Hair always falling about.' He glanced behind him. 'The Purser's always complaining I'm untidy. But I tell him there's nothing I can do. I was born like this, darling, I tell him. Now what can I do for you, luvvie?'

'I want to change my seat.'

He looked at Hammond. 'I don't blame you, luv, nasty looking brute he is. I wouldn't want to sit next to him.' He stopped, looking Hammond up and down. 'On the other hand . . .'

Charlie's voice rose. 'Now.'

'I'm sorry, darling, the flight's full. I'll see what I can do later. When we've taken off.' He looked at Hammond again, deliberately shivered, then walked up the aisle after Keithley, taking his briefcase and putting it in the overhead locker.

'Sorry Charlie,' muttered Hammond as he squeezed past her into the window seat. 'But you'll have one consolation. It'll be as bad for me as it is for you.'

They sat, side by side, in silence. Ordering their pre flight drinks in short, almost inaudible sentences. The engines started one by one. The aircraft trembled. The onboard music competing with the noise outside.

Charlie clenched her hands on the armrests. The engines whined and the aircraft lurched as the brakes were released. Her knuckles went white. The flaps grated as they wound down. The wing dipped in a trough, the white port wing light bouncing up and down. Charlie swallowed. Fixed her eyes on the magazine in the seat rack in front of her. The blue taxiway lights rippled by like sea water. The undercarriage jarred into another dip. Beads of perspiration started on Charlie's brow. She brought her teeth down on her lower lip, swallowing again.

The aircraft lurched to a stop, swaying. She moved her hands, the fingers clawing into the leather. The engines revved, throwing out a roar as the thrust heaved the huge weight forward. Charlie quickly brushed away a trickle of sweat from her cheek. Her breathing rapid now. Trying to suck in air. The wing rocked and plunged as it gained speed. The runway lights blurring past in a white ribbon. The wheels bucked and rumbled as they hit the concrete dividers. Suddenly a flash lit up outside, crashing into the cabin.

Charlie flung herself across Hammond, her head buried into his chest. He held her. 'It's all right Charlie, it's all right. Just lightning, thunder.'

CHAPTER THIRTY-TWO

'This is the Kazakh export licence.' Albert carefully picked a document out of the inner pocket of his dark grey suit. For a moment, as the piece of paper stuck, the green silk lining glowed in the low light. 'Issued by the Ministry of Agriculture.' He opened it. 'It authorises the export of agricultural machinery for the production of tobacco in the south west region of Turkey.' Albert passed over the papers. 'You'll see the manifest is in order, as well. Tractors, trailers, ploughs, that sort of thing.'

Romin Ablysov, the young and respectable Deputy Manager in a leading Kazakh agricultural machinery chain but in fact Moosar's chief weapons salesman, scratched his shaved head, rubbed his fingers together, then took the documents. He sniffed, wrinkled his nose and peered at them, tweaking the pages to open them up as he ran his eyes down the columns.

He had another scratch then put the papers on the table.

'They're very good,' he said. 'Had them done in Paris, did you?'

Albert pushed his shirt cuff back and looked at his watch.

'No. They're genuine.'

'Genuine?' Romin picked them up again. 'Must have cost a fortune. I could have saved you plenty if you'd asked me for them.'

Albert smoothed his cuff. 'I have a very good reason for them not to be questioned.'

'The service in this place is shit.' Romin banged his glass on the table, glared at Tansu, sitting next to Albert. 'Why can't you sort out some drinks?'

'I think you should know Tansu has taken over,' Albert said quietly.

Romin frowned. 'Taken over?'

'From Celik,' Albert replied.

'From Celik? Shit, that makes her . . .'

'Exactly,' said Albert.

Romin glanced at Tansu and swallowed.

'Right. So we've got the export licence. How's it to be done?'

Tansu moved her coffee cup to one side.

'Ship them by rail through Azerbaijan to Baku then through Armenia to Kirovakan for the border crossing to Turkey. We'll take it from there.'

'Why not fly it?'

Tansu's top lip curled onto her teeth.

'After last time?'

Romin shrugged. 'That was an accident. Could've happened to anyone. Anyway, you finished it off. Shit, those mechanics of yours . . .'

'It wasn't our mechanics.'

'Well, the fucking plane didn't catch fire by itself.'

Tansu clenched her hands. 'I think it was sabotaged by one of ours.'

Romin lifted his head, blinked. 'One of yours? PKK?'

She nodded, tight lipped.

He scratched his nose. 'You think? You don't know?'

She nodded again. 'We soon shall. We've got him and he's thinking about it.'

Romin took his finger from his nose, looked at Albert.

'Thinking? She says he's thinking? Shit, it's Moosar, us, me that bastard is thinking about. And who's he told? Shit, he could've told the whole fucking world by now.'

'No,' said Tansu, sharply. 'He came back too soon after the aircraft caught fire to have spoken to anyone.'

'And what about before?'

Albert took out his silver cigarette case. 'If he was responsible then of course he knew about it before. There's nothing we can do about that. That operation was blown. But I'm not blown.' He looked at Tansu. 'Nor is she.'

'How d'you know?'

Albert selected a cigarette. 'French Intelligence would have told me.'

Romin put his hand out and took Albert's cigarette from his fingers.

'You can be sure of them, can you?'

Albert flicked his lighter, the flame mirrored in his eyes.

'No. But it doesn't matter. The same as it doesn't matter whether Abu Hamid talks or not.'

Romin put his cigarette to the flame, his head on one side. 'Abu Hamid? That's his name?'

Tansu shook her head. 'It doesn't matter. He's where he can't do any harm. That's what matters.'

Romin looked at his empty glass, caught Albert's expression.

'I agree. Kill him now. Be safe.'

'I want it to be slow,' Tansu said flatly. 'I want the other cell leaders to know he died of thirst, heat exhaustion, in the meeting room they last saw him in. I want them remembering that, every time we meet there in the future.' She paused. 'There's another reason, as well.'

Romin dropped his eyes from hers.

'OK. So why aren't you worried about French Intelligence?'

Albert slowly lit his cigarette. 'We only need them for another two weeks. A month at most. By that time we will have your arms shipped through Baku into Turkey and we will have attacked Limnos. After that, we play our own game and French Intelligence will have no relevance.'

Romin moved his glass in a small circle, then reversed it.

'What about me? Moosar?'

'You'll be safe. French Intelligence will be far too busy fanning the war between Greece and Turkey to have time for you.'

'Can you guarantee that?'

'Yes,' replied Albert, simply.

Romin let go of the glass.

'Shit.'

'So we don't need any more mistakes on this arms shipment,' Tansu's voice was harsh.

Albert put his hand inside his jacket pocket again, pulled out some more papers. Romin squinted at them, trying to read the print in the half light. Albert pushed them nearer him.

'There's a shipping container in the Cook Island's Entrepot. These are the documents of release. You can fill in the destination and consignee.'

Romin stubbed his cigarette out in his glass, pulled the papers towards him.

'Why?'

Albert briefly lifted his fingers from the table.

'Payment.'

Romin glanced at Tansu.

'But she's already paid us. Is this a bonus or something?'

'No. It's twenty million dollars for a duplicate arms shipment.'

Romin's fingers went to his nose again.

'Duplicate?'

Albert leaned forward.

'I want another shipment exactly the same quantity and type of arms as the shipment going by rail. But the second shipment will go by air direct to a strip near Bandirma, northern Turkey. The aircraft will take off ten hours after the rail shipment departs Baku.'

Romin's finger kept scratching his nose.

'Shit.'

Albert gripped Romin's wrist.

'Is that clear?'

Romin nodded.

'Except I don't want cash.'

Albert moved his hand to the documents.

'Just release the container to the Aftam Bank and they'll give you a draft or arrange a property or bearer share purchase. Anything you want.'

'Aftam Bank? Where's that?'

'The Cook Islands. You won't even have to ship the container.'

Romin squinted at the papers again.

'Why a second shipment the same as the first?'

Albert looked at Tansu.

'Insurance.'

Romin sucked his teeth.

'It's a helluva premium. Not that I'm complaining,' he added.

'Security comes at a price,' murmured Albert. He turned to Tansu. 'Shall we go?'

She got up. Romin was startled to see she was wearing a slim black sheath set off with a fine diamond studded belt.

'Shit,' he breathed, 'you've changed.'

She leaned over him, her thin lips next to his ear. 'So have the PKK. Don't forget it.'

She turned away to follow Albert, startling Romin again as she took Albert's arm and pressed against him as they walked out of the Hyperion bar into the sultry Almaty night.

CHAPTER THIRTY-THREE

Charlie loved the sun streaming through the high, arched bow window of her studio on the top floor of her apartment in Montmartre. The first of the summer rays crept through mid morning and kept the room warm and bright until late afternoon. Visitors often commented that there was no north light. Charlie would laugh and reply that Ionists needed the sun's rays to reflect off the iron filings and make their paintings live.

The sun was doing that now, as Charlie scattered tiny shards of filings across the white canvas sheet she had spread over the floor. They were coloured in subtle shades of yellow and green, their shapes different and many of them angled or concave so as to diffuse the light at different angles. At first it seemed that she threw the filings randomly but after a while it became apparent that there was a method. The colours took on an order and the shaped pieces were placed deliberately rather than scattered without thought.

She was completely absorbed in the process, sometimes stretching to ease her back or to pause to listen to a passage of music that softly filtered through the surround sound hidden in the high, beamed roof of the turret room.

One of a pair of such rooms, it had been Charlie's home since she became serious about her art. Her father had disapproved of what he saw as a bourgeois occupation and had been callously critical of her work when he visited her in the games room on the ground floor of the family house in Rue Morillo, schooling her about working for the good and honour of France. Francesca hadn't been interested in the constant rows between father and daughter. She spent her days socialising, a leader of Parisian society with little time for her artist daughter. It had been Nina who'd rescued Charlie. Giving her the apartment in Montmartre on her eighteenth birthday. From the moment Charlie had moved in, she'd felt waves of relief as certainty dawned that there would be no clipped, cynical, undermining comment thrown over her shoulder every morning. Her father never mentioned her move and, gradually, she had transferred her favourite things to the apartment.

A small Steinway walnut boudoir piano stood by one edge of the studio window, a maple music chest nearby. Other furniture decorated with flower paintings lay close by the walls, leaving room for her bed, also painted, next to the wall opposite the window. Scattered next to the furniture were floral Chinese rugs, their pale colours complementing the delicate flower paintings. Along the wide balcony were garden tables and chairs, lamps hanging from the walls and pots of scarlet geraniums.

The large area left in the centre of the room was littered with tins of paint, plaster and metal filings. Canvasses were stacked along the window below the window seat and the walls were hung with huge, wild, glowing canvasses, changing colour and shapes as the sun slowly progressed across the wide, bowed, windowpanes. The contrast between the fantastic designs and primary colours of the canvasses and the delicate beauty of the impressionist furniture was extraordinary. No one had asked Charlie about the significance of the contrast and she had never volunteered an explanation.

*

Charlie stood back and walked around the scattered filings, which were now in a thick, oblong pile on the floor. She bent down now and then to move some or to add a particular colour. Then she picked up a tin of plaster powder and bent over a bucket, pouring some of the plaster into it. She walked across the room to an adjoining bathroom and filled a jug of water. Slowly she mixed the water with the plaster until it was a smooth paste. Then, taking a small plaster trowel she slapped the plaster onto a canvas, smoothing some parts and leaving ridges and whorls in others. She worked fast, moving her head from side to side to look at her work, pushing her hair out of her eyes as it swung across her face with the movement. Every now and again it would catch a smudge of plaster and she would stop to wipe it off, pulling the blonde strands through her long fingers.

She stood back again holding the trowel out, her eyes roving over the plaster. Satisfied, she picked up the canvas and placed it in a wooden frame to hold it over the filings on the floor. Tossing back her hair, she picked up two large electro magnets from the floor, carefully placed them over the back of the canvas and switched them on. Immediately the iron filings on the floor flew up to the canvas in a glittering stream to stick onto the plaster.

Charlie moved the magnets rapidly, trying to control the stream to match the patterns she had formed on the floor. In a few seconds the pile of filings had disappeared. She switched the magnets off and put them on the floor.

She put her hand on a corner of the frame and gently turned over the canvas. She smiled as she saw Nina's tea garden shimmering and glinting its yellows and greens in the sunlight of her Paris studio.

'You know, Charlie, I may not like your art, but you really are very talented.'

Charlie turned, startled.

'Albert, I didn't see you there.'

'You only see your paints and canvasses, I think, Charlie.' Albert smiled. 'How was Mauritius?'

She hesitated, embarrassed, leaned over to study the canvas.

'It's Nina's tea garden.'

Albert stepped nearer the canvas, his gold and onyx ring catching the light.

'Nina's tea garden?'

Charlie turned her head.

'I thought you'd seen it. The new one near the courtyard.'

'I wasn't there long.'

She picked at a loose piece of plaster.

'No.'

Albert looked at her sharply.

'Is anything wrong?'

She put the bit of plaster in a nearby wastebasket.

'No.'

Albert slowly walked over to the window, moved some canvasses and sat on the window seat, etched against the bright light.

'You're not happy, Charlie. I can feel it. Usually when you've finished a canvas you are bubbling.' He paused, looking at the work she had finished. 'And that is particularly fine. I have seen tea plantations in Sri Lanka and India and I can almost touch the bushes, see the girls plucking. It's brilliant.' He put his hands on his knees and leaned forward, a smile touching the corner of his mouth. 'But you are not bubbling.'

The corners of her mouth lifted in response.

'Do you really like it?'

Albert pulled a slim PC from his pocket, frowned a little as he sought some information.

'What are you doing the evening of twenty September?'

Charlie's nose screwed up in thought.

'Twenty September? That's three months away. I don't think I'm doing anything. Why?'

Albert leaned back against the window.

'Monsieur Thibault, the Curator of the Cluny Museum has asked if you will give an exhibition.'

Charlie looked up sharply, the sun catching a flash of green in her eyes as they widened.

'The Cluny? Monsieur Thibault? That's fantastic, but not even you could arrange that,' she hesitated, 'Ionist art?' she said slowly. 'You do mean Ionist, don't you?'

Albert nodded, his eyes watching her under the shadow.

'Monsieur Thibault would like to compare Ionism with the Medieval stained glass in his Museum. He thinks that Ionism is a similar renaissance. He thinks post modernism was a sort of dark ages.' The corners of his mouth turned up again. 'He wants to make the point to the Paris intelligentsia.'

'But the Cluny,' Charlie exclaimed, 'the whole world will visit the Cluny.'

'I think Monsieur Thibault is only interested in the views of the Parisians. To him intelligence in art ends at the Port Maillot.' He put his PC back in his pocket. 'But, yes, you are right, the whole world will visit the Cluny. The exhibition will last for fourteen days.'

'Fourteen days?' Charlie's face fell. 'I can't afford to put on an exhibition that big.'

'But I can,' said Albert.

She stared at him, shaking her head.

He held out his hands. 'Charlie, it gives me pleasure. I'm proud of your art. I'm also proud of your work in the Foreign Service.'

She walked over and took his hands in hers. 'That was a nice thing to say. My father . . .' she stopped. 'You're far too kind. It's another magnificent gift.'

He removed one hand from hers and put it over her other hand.

'Don't mention the job with Claud again. He didn't need any persuading from me. He knew you were right for the Foreign Service. He just needed reminding that's all.' He hesitated. 'There is a lot of time for me to make up, Charlie.'

Her eyes misted over.

'That's kind too. My father . . . he wasn't that bad. He just didn't understand, that's all. His upbringing was to blame, really.'

He squeezed her hand. 'Is that what was troubling you when I came in?'

She studied his face, saw the concern in his eyes.

'No, it was just something Nina said, that's all.'

'About your father,' he said, softly.

She drew in a breath. 'No. About you.'

Albert's eyebrows rose a fraction.

'About me? Something that troubled you about me?'

She took her hand away.

'It's stupid. I don't know why I'm telling you. She said Celik, the PKK Leader, was with you when you stayed.'

'Yes, he was,' replied Albert, smoothly.

'My God, Albert, he's a terrorist.'

'Rubbish. That's what the Turks say. He's nothing of the sort. He's a politician.'

'He's a terrorist, I tell you.'

Albert's lips tightened.

'How do you know?'

'I've seen the Intelligence reports.'

'Have you spoken to Gilbert about him?'

'Gilbert?'

Albert stood up.

'I suggest you speak to Gilbert. All I can tell you is that Celik was with me in Mauritius as a politician working with the French Government.'

'Nina said he was killed on her plantation,' she blurted out.

His eyes hardened.

'You know, Charlie, Nina is getting old, she imagines things.' He paused. 'Like your father.'

She looked away.

He walked over to the door.

'I've told you, Charlie, speak to Gilbert about it.' He reached for the door handle and turned to face her. 'You know, I may be Lebanese, but I don't kill people.' He looked at the painting, the colours rippling in the sunlight, and smiled. 'Don't look so worried, you silly girl. I didn't mean to criticise Nina. I know she means a lot to you. Taught you how to paint. But she can be difficult. Particularly about me.' He half raised his hand and looked directly at her. 'It's a bond that we two share, I think, to incur the displeasure of our relations.' He opened the door and quietly walked out of the room.

*

Charlie found Gilbert at his apartment on the Quai de Gesvres, overlooking the Seine with the twin towers of Notre Dame floating in the distance.

He took one look at her face, her plaster and paint spattered T shirt and jeans, her hair flying, and stood aside to let her in.

'What the hell's the matter, Charlie?'

She brushed past him and went straight into the living room, turning to face him as he followed her.

'Albert's just told me we were dealing with Celik.'

Gilbert blinked, his eyes creasing at the corners.

'What the hell are you talking about?' He looked at her, standing ramrod straight by the fireplace. 'Look, sit down, have a drink, tell me what this is all about.'

'It's about Celik. What was our Government doing dealing with him?'

He turned and walked to a dark wood bar in a corner of the room.

'Well if you're not having a drink, I am.'

'It's ten o'clock in the morning.'

'Good,' he said, 'it's a fine time to start.' He picked up a bottle. 'Brandy?'

She shook her head. 'If you go on like this, Gilbert, you'll kill yourself.'

He laughed. 'Come to my funeral. You won't come to me any other time, will you?'

She bit her lip. 'I'm very fond of you, Gilbert, but . . .'

'That's the word isn't it?' He waved the bottle in his hand. 'But.'

He turned to look at her. 'I could give you everything, Charlie. I could even give you peace.'

She looked startled. 'Peace?'

'Yes, peace. I could give you a job you could handle. No in fighting, no dirty deals to keep that bloody Minister of yours happy. I could give you a home, kids if you want,' he broke off, shrugged, 'if you want.'

She stared at him.

'It's what you want, isn't it?' she said, slowly. 'Peace. It's what you're looking for. What's going on, Gilbert? Is it this Celik business?'

He turned to pick up his drink. 'I don't know what the hell you're talking about. I don't know what Albert's told you about Celik but if you don't know you shouldn't ask.'

She clenched her fists. 'Is Albert blackmailing you?'

He swung round, the brandy slopping out of the glass, his eyes blazing.

'I don't fucking believe this, Charlie. You barge in here, like some wild thing on the run with some fucking idea about Celik and then some fucking mad accusation about Albert.' He started towards her. 'I think you ought to fucking apologise.'

She backed away, suddenly feeling a flood of fear. Gilbert never lost his temper, was never foul mouthed. He'd changed. Suddenly. Over the last few weeks.

He stopped as he saw her face.

'It's all right. I'm not going to harm you.' He laughed uncertainly. 'I'm sorry. It's the brandy, makes me bloody minded. I'd better give it up.'

Her eyes ran over him.

'Gilbert, there is trouble isn't there?'

The lines etched deeper alongside his mouth.

'Charlie, darling Charlie, you're my trouble. You don't think I'd be on the brandy for anything else do you?' The corners of his eyes creased. 'I'm forty five years old. I've never found anyone to . . . to love. I love you . . . and you don't love me. That's all there is to it. I'll get over it. But, in the meantime, I'll drown my sorrows.'

'That's not what you said to John Hammond. You said there were splits in the Government. Then Albert told me the Government was working with Celik. To me that spells trouble. And it's nothing to do with me.'

He took her hand.

'Sit down, Charlie.' He sat next to her on the dark leather sofa, putting his drink on the long wood block coffee table. 'What I told Hammond was true. There are splits. It's down to your Minister, Claud, he's against the EU Army idea and he's been trying to work against the President. But the President worked around him, made contact with Celik through the President's Intelligence Unit. The idea was to compensate the PKK for giving up the Kurdish homeland idea. In return, the Turks were to agree to stop pushing Kurds into Greece and the EU Territory. Albert was the banking go between. That is until Celik got killed in that boating accident.'

Charlie's teeth edged across her lower lip.

'You mean Albert was arranging to pay off Celik?'

'Yes.'

'For the President?'

Gilbert nodded.

Her jaw tightened.

'I have made a fool of myself.'

He nodded again.

Her eyes met his.

'Can you forgive me?'

'On one condition.'

She stood up, smiling.

'No.'

'You accused me of being blackmailed.'

Her eyes widened.

'Yes. I'm sorry. John Hammond told me. I didn't really believe him.'

He got up to stand beside her.

'I should bloody well hope not.' He paused. 'You know, Charlie, Hammond's the Director General of G8, but he's also British. You can't trust them. They always put their own interests first. So we fed him a little disinformation to throw him off track.'

'I'm really sorry, Gilbert.'

He picked up his drink and looked at her over the rim of the glass.

'Are you sure you don't want to come and live with me? Have some peace?'

She swallowed.

'I find all the peace I want in my art, Gilbert.'

He turned the corners of his mouth down.

'Your art looks like war to me.'

She laughed.

'So how could we live together.'

CHAPTER THIRTY-FOUR

Lev's face filled the plasma screen.

'What you are saying is that we are blind. Nothing new about Celik's death in Mauritius, no information about Banque Onde and Gilbert, and Abu Hamid has disappeared.'

Hammond didn't reply. Lev had made a summary, he wasn't asking a question.

Walt's face appeared on the screen alongside Lev's.

'Sorry I'm late. Budget meeting. Damn Senate Finance Committee wants to cut the US contribution to the G8 budget again.' He pursed his lips. 'I told 'em our HQ is a warehouse complex in Basingstoke. You know what they said? They said we seize so many criminal assets we need a warehouse complex to put them in and shouldn't need funding at all. How is Basingstoke anyway, John?'

Hammond looked around the meeting room where he was sitting, taking in the bare soundproofing tiles, the electric and communication cables, the steel table and chairs bolted to the uncarpeted floor.

'Could do with a makeover.' He smiled. 'Julia complained to me about it only the other day.'

Julia leaned forward.

'It's like being in a morgue.'

Lev looked at her lightly tanned face, the silver disc earrings on her ears, complementing the flecks in her Prada linen suit, took the cigarette from his mouth.

'Some corpse,' he said.

They laughed, the tension draining from Walt.

'So what's with Abu Hamid?'

'We don't know,' replied Julia.

'But G8SUR was watching him, wasn't it?'

Hammond put up his hand to stop Julia replying.

'My responsibility. I took G8SUR off Abu Hamid after the Antonov operation. I needed it to watch Turkish boat activity. The same as I told you about taking surveillance off Celik. Once the Antonov PKK arms shipment was destroyed, I assessed we should concentrate on the Turks. It is important for our work on the EU Army.'

Walt frowned. 'But wasn't Abu Hamid thought to be at risk after the Antonov attack?'

'It was a possibility. But G8SUR is stretched to its financial limit. I just haven't got the funds to chase every target.' He paused. 'Whatever the Senate Finance Committee may think.'

Lev crushed his cigarette in the china tray in front of him.

'And now?'

Hammond looked at Julia.

She leaned towards him. 'John has asked me to re-instate G8SUR on Abu Hamid. It's being re-calibrated now. We should pick him up in the next twenty four hours.'

'But it's a purely internal informant protection exercise.' Hammond added. 'The PKK were set back months, if not a year, by the Antonov interception. They haven't got the money or leadership to mount anything in the near future. So I'm not re-calibrating G8SUR to watch the PKK. It would be useful to know who's taken over, but not essential in the short term.'

'What made you change your mind?' said Lev. 'Last time we met, you thought we should find out more about Celik's death. It's one of the reasons you went to Mauritius. And what about the Kurdish riot in Paris?'

'I didn't think he should have gone to Mauritius,' Walt cut in. 'The PKK are spent. I thought so then and I think so now. That riot was Kurdish immigrants complaining about conditions in their slums in Paris. It wasn't the PKK. If it had been there would have been killings. And the computer analysis agrees with me,' he added.

Hammond looked from one to the other.

'I think Walt's right. We couldn't find anything in Mauritius.

The Coroner was as tight as a drum, but he was protecting the Government's interests. The Mauritians don't want trouble with some PKK hothead. Neither Keithley nor I could find anything suspicious about Celik's death. And there was absolutely no evidence linking PKK with the riot. It's not their style. A bomb, killings, yes. But not a riot with just a few broken heads.' He put his head on one side as Lev exhaled a cloud of smoke in a loud exasperated sigh. 'I know you have some sixth sense about this, Lev, but there's nothing to back it up. Nothing. And I think we should leave it.'

'So do I,' said Walt, quickly. 'We need to concentrate on this Turk Greek thing. Those bastards could destabilise the European Union and with it goes the Balkans, then the Middle East. We've got to get this EU Army thing going.' He brushed his hand over his crew cut. 'How come we've got nothing on Gilbert or that damn bank?'

Lev remained still for a moment. Then he shrugged, his massive shoulders rising to almost hide his neck.

'That is important. Okay, I agree. We lay off the PKK until this Army is established.' He opened a tin on his desktop and picked out a flat yellow cigarette and lit it. A look of horror spread across his face.

'You told me these were made from cured South African tobacco,' he said, slowly.

'They were,' smiled Hammond. 'They cured the nicotine.'

Lev's eyes disappeared beneath his brows.

'You mean they are lights, no nicotine?'

Hammond nodded.

Lev deliberately stubbed out the cigarette. 'Bastard,' he muttered.

Walt chuckled.

'They looked good, Lev.'

Lev ignored him. 'You let them do this to me, Julia?'

Her dark eyes sparkled. 'I don't want you as a corpse, Lev.'

'You're all against me,' he moaned. 'I have no other cigarettes.'

'Then we'd better get this over with quickly,' laughed Walt.

Hammond straightened his back.

'Banque Onde couldn't be penetrated with my equipment in Mauritius. It's completely firewalled. I've asked Julia to attack it from here.'

'It's going to be a long job I'm afraid,' Julia said. 'We've got to decrypt individual personal keys with one time thousand K encryption changing every twelve hours.'

'Which means Albert's got a lot more to hide than the confidential business transactions of his clients,' Walt said. 'Was there anything on him in Mauritius?'

'Nothing,' Hammond replied. 'The odd rumour that he's involved in moneylaundering, but that's par for the course in Mauritius.' His eyes strayed to the electric cables on the walls. 'I pushed his stepdaughter about him, but I got nowhere.'

Walt's head jerked up. 'Charlie? The girl in the safe room? How come she was in Mauritius?'

Lev slapped his hand on his desk and laughed out loud. 'Sounds like unaccompanied baggage, to me.'

'Lev,' warned Julia.

'Okay, okay,' Lev spluttered. 'But this Charlie keeps turning up in the most unexpected places.'

'She was on sick leave,' said Hammond, evenly, 'at her aunt's plantation recuperating from the riot.'

Lev shot up an eyebrow at Walt.

Hammond watched them exchange glances.

'I saw her for all of an hour. I told her I knew her stepfather was blackmailing Gilbert.'

Walt's smile vanished. 'That must have stopped her in her tracks.'

'It did. She let me know very clearly that she didn't believe me.'

'I'd have liked to have seen that,' murmured Lev, glancing at Walt again.

Hammond laughed shortly. 'I think, Lev, you would have interpreted it as an overreaction. I think she suspects there's something wrong about Albert but I don't think she knows anything. Anyway, I've put the thought into her head and I intend following it up. She's our best lead until the computer comes up with a penetration of Banque Onde.'

Walt nodded. 'And Gilbert?'

'Oh yes,' said Hammond, 'she's very defensive about Gilbert. I think she feels he's in some sort of trouble and wants to help. I'll be following that up as well.'

Lev opened up the tin of yellow cigarettes and looked at them. 'What about the French? Anything new on the negotiations?'

Hammond stretched the fingers of one of his hands.

'Tricot's still in hospital after the riot. But the Interior Ministry have backed off. The French will allow the EU Army to defend their vulnerable points. So that problem's gone away.'

'Good,' smiled Lev, 'so it's just a question of bringing in the Turks now.'

Hammond shook his head.

'I've just had a communication from Claud, the French Foreign Minister. He wants more detail on the impact on France's sovereignty if the Turks demand a command and control interest in the Army.'

'Hell'n'tarnation, more delay,' exploded Walt.

Hammond's nose twitched slightly. 'Not really. I'll tell him that of course the Turks will be given a command and control interest, but since the French will be in overall command they can override the Turks whenever they wish. I'm seeing him the day after tomorrow when I get back to Paris.'

Lev's eyes hardened.

'This overall French control. Are you sure about this?'

Hammond shook his head. 'It's as I told Genscher at our first meeting. The EU Army is about Special Forces work. Quick, in and out, based on G8 intelligence. They have their own line of command. The French general staff can posture and strut about, but by the time they've put a plan together the action will be over. Led by us and the Germans if the French Special Forces are ever reluctant, which I doubt. They're good people.'

Walt nodded. 'Sounds good. Is that all?'

Hammond stood up and stretched. 'It is for today.'

Lev and Walt disappeared as Julia switched off the screen.

'What about the ten hour flight from Mauritius,' she said.

Hammond looked puzzled. 'What d'you mean?'

'You told Walt and Lev you'd only been with Charlie for an hour.' She leaned across him to release the door security switch, her perfume lingering with her. 'I have to do the security check on your seating before take off.' She looked up at him. 'Remember?'

CHAPTER THIRTY-FIVE

'I thought I might find you here.' Hammond slid onto the black leather chair across the table from Charlie.

She looked up, astonished.

'What are you doing here? Find somewhere else.'

He looked amused.

'Come on Charlie. After being there for you on the 'plane, I thought we'd moved on.'

She swept a strand of blonde hair from her cheek.

'I'm frightened of flying that's all. You were just someone to hold on to.'

Hammond caught sight of a waiter in the dim light.

'Whisky on the rocks.' He looked at Charlie. 'Make that two.'

The waiter nodded and shuffled off, his head bent as he peered around the black topped tables to see if anyone else wanted serving.

Hammond turned to Charlie. 'You're fond of this place aren't you?'

'L'Imbecile? Yes, I suppose I am. I told you before, I come here to get away.' She stretched out her fingers and looked at her sky blue nail polish. 'That is unless you're here.'

Hammond leant forward to look at them.

'Disturb you, do I?'

She pulled her hands back.

'No. You make me angry. I told Gilbert what you said. About the blackmail. He was furious. Told me not to trust you. He was right.'

She stood up, her lower lip clenched between her teeth. Hammond caught her hand.

'I'm sorry. Gilbert's not what I came to talk to you about.'

She tried to pull away.

'It's important,' he said.

She stopped, arrested by something at the back of his eyes. She wasn't sure what it was. A hint of urgency, a glimpse of steel. It was so fleeting she could have imagined it. But something in her responded to it, compelled her to stop. She drew in her breath, then laughed at herself. It was the atmosphere. L'Imbecile had been cleverly designed to make people feel breathless. She studied his pale eyes, the thin lines alongside his mouth were inscrutable in the darkness, and she knew again, as she had known every time she had met him, that the atmosphere had nothing to do with how she felt. What was it Gilbert had said? He was British, you couldn't trust him. That certainly wasn't what she felt. When she'd flung herself at him on the aircraft when it took off from Mauritius she'd felt complete trust. But Gilbert was shrewd, read character better than anyone she knew, except perhaps Albert. So she'd have to be careful. Clamp down on her feelings. Keep Hammond at arms length.

'If it's business, I'll stay,' she said, tightly.

The look she'd seen earlier fleetingly returned, then vanished.

'It is,' he said, 'I need your help for my meeting with your boss.'

'Claud?' she sounded surprised.

He nodded. 'But I can't very well talk about it if you're standing up.'

She put her hand behind her to hold her short yellow silk skirt in place as she edged onto the chair.

He watched her. 'It's a pretty colour.'

'I thought we were going to talk business.'

'Can't I compliment you on how you look?'

Her chin went up. 'Not if we're talking business.'

He smiled.

'So I can tell you how beautiful you are another time?'

She looked down at the table.

'Tell me about this business you want to talk about.'

He sat back.

'Well, at least that wasn't a "no".'

Her head came up again.

'I want a private meeting with Claud,' he hurried on, 'you can be present, of course. But I think it's time we wrapped up our discussions on the EU Army and I don't want a bunch of bureaucrats getting in the way.'

The corners of her mouth widened, touched by a gleam of moisture either side.

'We haven't cleared up our sovereignty questions yet. There is still a long way to go.'

He moved his shoulder sideways to lean against the wall. What little light there was left his face altogether.

'When you lie to me, Charlie, don't wet your lips. It's a bad habit.' He suddenly shifted forwards. 'I want you to tell Claud that I have given him all the time he's going to get. We've spoken to the Benelux countries, the Poles, the Czechs and the Italians. The movers and shakers. They're on side. Either Claud and your Government sign up to the EU Army at my next meeting with him or we're going to the Greeks and Turks without you.' He paused as he watched her face. The shock, disbelief, seep into her. 'Take it or leave it.'

She took a deep breath, forcing her mind to concentrate.

'Our talks were confidential. You had no right to approach the others before we are ready.' She clenched her fist. 'We still have to talk about Turkish command and control.

Hammond watched the ice rattle in his glass.

'You know, Charlie, you're no good at this. You're too honest. If you really were concerned about Turkish control you wouldn't be sitting here. You'd have walked away. But your brief is to delay, so you think you have to drag things out, sit here and argue.' He moved into the dim light. 'Leave it to Claud. He knows all the tricks.' He deliberately looked at her clenched hand before saying slowly. 'Like Albert.'

'Salaud,' she breathed. Blindly, she shoved herself out of her chair. At the last moment, she grabbed the edge of the table and stopped, just avoiding a half hidden, half stooped waiter.

Hammond heard her swear. Burst into laughter.

'I must be having a good effect on you, Charlie.'

CHAPTER THIRTY-SIX

The two motorcycle outriders split up. One eased a red Volvo into the slow lane and the other accelerated ahead to a bunch of cars and a truck a couple of kilometres ahead. Hammond idly looked at the speedometer of the black Mercedes. It read just over 200 kph. It was a sensible speed. So often when he'd been ferried down the French freeways, the speeds had approached 250 or even 300 kph. A recipe for disaster he'd always thought. But he never complained. The G8 drivers were all the same. Intent on getting from A to B as quickly as possible. In their minds speed equalled security. And when their safety record had been fed into the G8 computer against the risk of attack, the analysis supported them.

Hammond smiled as the thought brought Nina and her Jaguar into focus. Then, uncomfortably, the thought was dislodged by the image of Charlie's face as she left him at their last meeting at L'Imbecile. She hadn't responded to his laughter as she nearly collided with the waiter. She'd thrown him a look which, with all his experience, he hadn't yet interpreted. At the time, he'd shrugged it off, thinking her petulant. But, on reflection later at his apartment, he realised that petulance was not one of her characteristics.

Now he tried to concentrate again on the image of her face. Romantics would no doubt have described it as haunted. But romantics didn't deal in reality, so the word meant nothing in his analysis of her feelings. Oppressed would be a better way to describe it, but it was more indefinable than that. She wasn't depressed and certainly didn't look weary. Both characteristics showed in those who were truly intimidated. Anyway he certainly didn't want her to feel oppressed in any way. He needed the combination of her spark and sympathy to work away at Gilbert.

He was sure that in Gilbert lay the pointer to French policy. The man was tormented.

His train of thought switched suddenly. His eyes narrowed to slits as he strove to reconstruct that look on Charlie's face. It was there now, deep behind the green eyes as L'Imbecile's dim light fleetingly caught them. It wasn't torment, that was too strong. What showed, in that millisecond, was something he feared deeply, and which probably explained his disinclination, his inability, to analyse it. Knowing he was making a mistake he would bitterly regret, Hammond dragged the explanation to the surface. Slowly and reluctantly he faced the truth. Charlie had been distressed. And she shouldn't have been, because her actions and words had displayed the anger he had deliberately pushed her into. But, in that final, departing glance, her eyes had betrayed her. The distress hadn't been at his attack on Claud or Albert, she was angry about that. The distress was about him. And it hit him that she was in love with him.

His mind froze, refusing to go down the next avenue. Almost guiltily, he looked around the car. Searching for any reaction to his thoughts. As if they had been spoken aloud.

No one moved.

Angrily he switched his mind to his meeting with Claud. What he'd told Charlie at their meeting was not an empty threat. Either the French agreed the EU Army concept now and moved on to discussions with the Greeks and Turks or they would be left out. Politically he was sure the French couldn't accept that. Their borders were inundated with refugees pouring in from Turkey via Greece. They might not want an EU Army but they had to stop being swamped. There was no way they could intervene with the Turks by themselves so the Army was the only viable option short of war. And war was too horrific to contemplate. If Greece attacked Turkey, the Muslim extremists would light a touchpaper that would explode the Balkans and the Middle East. Within days Pakistan would be drawn in, a flickering fuse for India and the inevitability of going nuclear. After that, even the G8 computers were unable to predict the outcome of the chaos.

'Two minutes, Sir.' The driver spoke without turning his head. The bodyguard sitting next to Hammond leaned over and tapped his colleague in the passenger seat twice on the shoulder. Both of them gripped the handles of their doors, one on each side of the car.

Hammond thought it was typical of Claud to insist on having the meeting in his Ministerial helicopter. He'd said he'd been worried about their security and Hammond had reluctantly agreed, seeing no need to pile another difficulty on top of the problem he already faced with Claud. But it was still a waste of time and money which could be better spent elsewhere.

*

The rendezvous was 60 kilometers south of Paris in a disused quarry just outside Orleans. Claud's helicopter was moving in for its final approach. As he sat in the jump seat, Louis, his bodyguard, adjusted the heat scanner, searching for the body heat of anything nearby. His combat uniform made him uncomfortably hot in the confines of the helicopter. He looked forward to getting out into the breeze, which he saw flickering the smaller branches of the trees below. He cast a quick glance at the Minister sitting in the rear seat of the helicopter, working on his papers. Satisfied he was safe for the landing, he swung his eyes to look out of the square window to his right and watched the lip of the hill as the helicopter swept up and over it, flying low, scattering a flock of sheep, sending them running in circles around the small field looking for a way out. He moved against the cabin wall as it tilted and a group of tall pines flashed by.

'One minute.' The co-pilot leaned around the cockpit divider, showing his finger to emphasise the message. It hadn't been necessary. Louis still had his earphones on. But it was no secret that the French Special Forces despised the Minister of Foreign Affairs as nothing more than a jumped up Marseilles wharf rat. The finger was for Claud.

Louis smiled and jumped up, pointing a finger at the far side of the door opening. His Sergeant, Rafael, moved to it, both of them ready to scan the landing point and secure it on touchdown. They braced themselves as the helicopter swept in a tight circle, their eyes scanning to and from the near and far perimeters of the quarry. There were four men and two women there, posted earlier to keep the area secure. Dead end job, Louis thought. Hours standing around in the bloody countryside with little to do. It was one of the reasons they hated Claud. There had been no terrorist attacks since Al Quaida had been put down. Claud liked the security just so as to fluff his own ego. It was a dead bore for Louis and the other Special Forces Units who would otherwise have been at base having a drink or on exercise doing something a lot more enjoyable than standing around trying to be alert.

Hammond's car came into Louis' vision just before they touched down. The outriders were peeling off either side, ready to take up their positions between the car and helicopter. Louis flung the door open and jumped the last six feet between the helicopter and the smooth rock of the quarry floor. Rafael ran to his left and watched the far side as the wheels touched down in their peculiar spongy movement. Louis watched Hammond's bodyguards as they threw open the big Mercedes' doors and ran to crouch in the lee of its wheels.

In the seconds it took for them to make one last scan of the bare rock rim of the quarry, Hammond had got out and was standing between the two open doors of the car. Louis started to beckon him, then cursed as he saw one of the perimeter guards emerge on the outcrop to his left. There was always one fucking idiot, he thought, who spoilt a perfect operation.

He drew in his breath to shout at him. Sucked for air. Nothing came. Feeling stupid he went to put his finger in his mouth. But his hand didn't respond. He heard a rattle and his eyes dropped to see his Glock machine pistol lying on the stone by his feet. A roar started in his ears. A red mist sweeping across his eyes. Rocking now he felt his knees jar as his body crunched its weight onto them, into the rock. Dimly his brain flashed up the figure of the perimeter guard again. Slimmer, smaller than anyone in his unit. For a second the shock cleared his brain. Long enough for him to see the pool of blood stretching away from him into a crevice. As he pitched forward he distinctly heard the voice of his old trainer. Telling him that time spent cursing is the difference between life and death.

Tansu watched Louis take her bullet in the neck. Sweeping round, she trained on Hammond. But he was still between the car doors. Frozen in safety. Dropping and rolling she fired a burst at the G8 guard by the rear wheel. Spurts of rock chips followed her as she scrabbled down the incline. Opening a shot to Hammond. Instinctively she fired. Hands over her head. Hearing the metallic strikes as the bullets smashed into the car doors. Then the scream of a bullet hitting home. More rock chips sprayed her from the right.

Rolling, she dived into the old metal gravel chute by the site of a long gone rock crusher. Careening, swinging, tumbling, she toppled downwards. Scrabbling to stop flying over the edge. Into the maelstrom of bullets that followed her from two of the perimeter guards. She was almost sobbing now. The blood spurting from her lip as a sharp turn jarred her teeth into it. The whine and ricochet of the bullets stopped suddenly. As the chute entered the trees and threw her twenty feet above the river. Where the breath was driven from her as she hit the water.

CHAPTER THIRTY-SEVEN

The room was empty except for the three of them. The President had requested no calls and no interruptions. Gilbert was aware of a tenseness, an expectation, a foreboding in the high ceilinged room which seemed to be emphasised by the late sun as it silently streaked faint lines on the dark blue carpet.

'I'm glad you're safe, Claud. Unharmed. Thank God.' The President held on to Claud's hand, emphasising his concern.

'Thank God for our Special Forces Unit, you mean.' Claud put his other hand over the President's. 'If it hadn't been for them I wouldn't be here now.'

'G8,' murmured Gilbert.

The President looked at him sharply. 'Yes, of course, and G8. Although they didn't lose anyone.' He pulled his hand away from Claud's grasp and walked quickly to his desk.

'Pity the killer didn't get that bastard Hammond.'

Gilbert drew in a breath.

The President waved his hand impatiently. 'Yes, yes, I know. But he has been a damn nuisance, you have to admit. He's moved the negotiations along far faster than I thought he could.' He paused. 'Than anyone else could,' he murmured.

Claud laughed uncertainly as he sat down facing the President. 'At least he had to postpone our meeting.'

One side of the President's mouth lifted slightly. 'That is a positive benefit.'

'I thought we were here to discuss the attack on Claud,' Gilbert cut in.

The President sat down and leaned over his desk to pick up a bottle of orange juice. He twisted off the cap and carefully poured the contents into a blue cut glass.

'You know, Gilbert, your continual opposition to my plans to stop this bloody EU Army thing is becoming intolerable.'

Gilbert's hands clenched as he shifted his position in his high backed chair. 'You've never been in combat, never had to write a letter to the family of one of your men who's been killed. I have. And what's important now is to find out how Louis was killed and why.'

Two spots of colour suddenly tinged the President's cheeks.

'Louis?' he spat. 'Louis? Who the hell could care about him? He didn't do his duty. He damn near had Claud killed.' He stopped abruptly, breathing heavily. 'I fucking misjudged you. All you care about are the little people. You haven't an ounce of wit about you for the politics, for the safety of France. You had it easy in Kosovo. Dealing with peasants. Well, I'm not a fucking peasant and nor is Claud. We are France, we are the Government. And what we say goes.' His voice rose. 'Do you understand.'

Gilbert jumped up, walked forward and, ignoring Claud's gesture to sit down, put his hands on the President's desk and leaned towards him.

'No, I don't. I don't understand why you want to push Greece to war with Turkey. I see a conflagration that will enflame every Muslim in the world and will end with Pakistan going nuclear. You're asking me, a soldier, to understand that?'

The President sat back, pressing his hands to his forehead, his eyes squeezed shut. He sat there for a moment then opened his eyes and put his fingertips on the desk.

'I'm sorry, Gilbert. I apologise, I forgot myself.' He paused. 'Look, sit down, Claud, sit down.' He made a waving motion with his hands, moving one of them to his glass to take a sip of orange.

'Have you seen the report on the riot in Strasbourg last night?' He went on without waiting for a reply. 'An estimated three and a half thousand Kurdish refugees living on our side of the border went on the rampage demanding the Germans release three hundred of their relatives into France.'

Gilbert nodded. 'Yes. The Germans have a holding centre on their side of the border. The Kurds on our side claimed the three hundred were relatives, had a right to come here. We persuaded the Germans to let them come in.'

'Did you also see that over a thousand North African migrants smashed out of our holding centre in Marseilles and tore the town centre apart? Two cities. Shops looted, pavements torn up, police beaten, citizens terrified. For what? To open up our borders and allow more of the bastards to pour in.' He put up his hand as Claud started to speak. 'No Claud, let me finish. Gilbert has got to understand.' He stabbed his forefinger on the desk. 'Who is going to stop them? Us? We can't. The Brits? They aren't affected. They won't. The Germans? They can't even control their own problem. The Bulgarians? Forget it, they're peasants and anyway the Turks pay them off.'

Gilbert leaned forward, urgent. 'An EU Army can stop it. Get the Turks into it and they'll join with us. Seal off the borders to stop the inflow. Control the Mediterranean.'

'And we lose our control of our nuclear weapons,' the President snapped. 'We kept them out of NATO, we kept control then. Why lose control now?'

'Because if we push Greece to war with Turkey there will be an inevitable Muslim reaction and Pakistan is bound to go nuclear. That's why.'

The President looked at Claud.

The Foreign Minister swallowed, shifted himself in his chair.

'If we keep control of our nuclear weapons Pakistan won't go nuclear.'

Gilbert looked at him scornfully. 'Can you guarantee that?'

'Yes,' said Claud softly. 'The Pakistanis, and Indians too for that matter, will be left under no illusion that we will pre-empt them as soon as our satellites pick up any impulses to activate their weapons.'

Shock whitened Gilbert's face. 'You didn't tell me any of this,' he whispered.

'You didn't need to know.' The President said, calmly.

'But I'm Minister of Defence,' Gilbert's voice took on a harsh note. 'I had a right to know.'

'Your record to date, Gilbert, is one of a soldier of peace,' Claud said smoothly. 'Hardly one to trust with the policy of a pre-emptive nuclear strike.'

'But now you've been told, I'm sure you see the strength in our policy.' The President looked at him over the rim of his glass. 'We've no need of an EU Army. Once Greece has secured the Turkish mainland border and the Kurds have Kurdistan, we won't have a migrant problem from there. Albert will see to that. We can then turn to North Africa and seal that off as well.'

'We've thought it all through,' the President urged. 'We just need your support that's all. For heaven's sake, man, can't you see it's for the best. It's the best for France? We can't lose control of our nuclear weapons.'

Gilbert sat staring at the picture of Napoleon at Austerlitz above the President's desk. In his mind he knew the safer alternative lay with the EU Army, tucking Greece and Turkey into bed together. But for France he had to admit that her independence lay in her nuclear weapons. His mind went back to the oath he took when he became an officer, in those days when soldiering was just training and fun. Then his eyes strayed to the picture again. Napoleon glowered down, astride his massive grey hose, Copenhagen. He had nearly lost the battle of Austerlitz and but for the loyalty and trust of his generals he would not have had time to complete the creation of the most democratic state in history. "La belle France" Napoleon had said when his generals spoke of their loyalty "La belle France is immortal, not me".

Gilbert dropped his eyes. 'I understand,' he said, simply.

'Good,' smiled the President, briskly. 'Now let's get this attack on Claud out of the way. There was only one attacker, so I assume it was a crank or something. Shouldn't take us long. Got an angry lover looking for you, Claud?'

Claud straightened his back. 'I think there's more to it than that.'

The President's face puffed out as he laughed. 'Yes, yes, I was only joking, Claud. I've asked my personal Intelligence people to come along. I've asked Albert as well.'

'I think . . .' Gilbert began.

'I know, Gilbert, you've got your own Special Forces Report. But that tells us about the details of the attack. It doesn't help us to identify the killer. With the problems we have at the moment, I want to keep this tight. I'm using my own people.' He looked deliberately at Gilbert. 'I can trust them.'

'Well, don't forget G8 will be crawling all over this. They won't let an attack involving their Director General go away lightly.'

The President's mouth tightened.

'That bastard Hammond. I suppose we're going to have to smooth his damn feathers somehow.'

There was a knock on the blue panelled door.

'Come,' the President said.

Gilbert looked around and, for the first time, realised why no one else had been in the room. No personal private secretary, no note taker. He caught the gleam of amusement in the President's eyes.

'Just between us three, eh, Gilbert?'

He had no time to reply before the spectacles of the Director of the President's Intelligence Unit eased into the room, followed by his brown jacketed Deputy and Albert.

The President motioned for them to sit at the ornate conference table on the far side of the room and stood up to join them. He crossed over the rich piled Aubusson carpet and sat in the cherry wood and ebony Napoleon chair at the head of the table.

'Thank you for coming, Albert.'

The steel rimmed spectacles made a nodding gesture, acknowledging a welcome even if it had been unspoken. The President looked at them.

'Tell us what you can.'

'The killer is medium height, thin, angular. Almost certainly a woman.'

'There are plenty of thin, angular men,' Gilbert said.

The spectacles didn't waver from facing the President.

'Comments would be appreciated after I've finished.'

The President raised his eyebrows slightly at Gilbert.

The spectacles caught a flash of blue as they moved to study the blue double doors.

'One of the female perimeter guards was garrotted. She would never have been caught off guard by a man. A smaller, vulnerable looking woman would have appeared non threatening.' He coughed, as if to criticise a stupid lack of common sense. 'The killer hid the body in an old metal water duct. The heat hid the body temperature. She,' he stopped, the spectacles reflecting their faces as they made a slow review of his audience, 'she then moved up the slope and shot Louis.' He cleared his throat. 'Louis was clearly unprepared. Witnesses say he looked at the killer for fully two seconds before he was killed. She then turned her fire on to the Mercedes.'

'To take out the G8 bodyguards, we know that. What about Claud?' The President bristled.

The spectacles lifted as the nose wrinkled.

'The shooting has nothing to do with the Foreign Minister.'

There was a silence.

'But my bodyguard. He was shot. I was the target. I had to be. I'm a Minister.' Claud blurted.

'Louis was shot because he would have been behind the killer when she went for her real target, the Director General of G8. All the bullet strikes except the one which killed Louis were taken by the Mercedes and one in the calf of a G8 bodyguard. The killer didn't wait to be sure of her target. She went in fast and went out by her escape route within seconds.'

Gilbert frowned. 'You mean she didn't wait to make sure she had killed Hammond?'

The spectacles glinted as they nodded. 'She knew her target but didn't unduly risk her life to ensure a kill.'

'A threat more like,' said the President. 'A personal thing, like that Turkish Ambassador in London.'

'No. She was too operational for that. Clever, elusive, flexible. She's done this sort of thing any number of times.'

'Terrorist?' asked Claud.

'Could be. Could be organised crime.'

'Of course,' said Gilbert, 'G8. Take out the Director General. Send a message. Even if he isn't killed, the message is clear.'

The spectacles remained still.

'Which is why I've asked Albert to join us,' said the President, breaking the silence.

Gilbert looked up, sharply. The President had known about this all along. He was pulling the strings, just as he'd pulled them in the argument about the EU Army.

Albert was speaking.

'The President has asked me if I will speak to my contacts to see if any light can be shed on this attack.'

'Contacts?' Claud blinked.

'Claud, I am sure you do not wish to be impolite to our colleague,' the President said quietly. 'He is not obliged to tell us who they are. In fact, if he did so he would be endangering his own life. Suffice to say, at the level he conducts business he is more likely than anyone else to find out who is responsible.'

'And stop another attack,' Gilbert put in quickly.

'What?' said the President. 'Oh, er, yes, of course.' He cast a glance at the spectacles, catching the glint in them.

'Hammond must be warned,' added Gilbert.

The spectacles swung towards him.

'G8 will have come to the same conclusion. There is no need to warn him. It may look as though we accept responsibility.'

'I think he should be warned.' The President fiddled with a bottle of Perrier water. 'But at a low level. Better not to make too much of it. I can speak to the British Prime Minister, concern, sympathy, that sort of thing. But warnings, that leaves us open to criticism for negligence if something was to happen to Hammond. No, better do that at bureaucrat level.'

'If I may,' said Albert evenly, 'I would like to suggest my stepdaughter, Charlie Dedain. You all know her. She is in Claud's department.' He paused, flicking open his cigarette case. 'And she knows Hammond very well, if you understand my meaning.'

CHAPTER THIRTY-EIGHT

The bees hummed lazily in the pine forest that lay as a green backdrop for the white art deco house overlooking the sapphire velvet of the Mediterranean Sea, gently lapping the coast at Anamur in southern Turkey. Albert slowly turned a page of his book, a smile flickering on his lips as he came across 'In Phaeacia'. Flecker was the only English poet who truly understood the eastern Mediterranean and captured its colour, smell, history. No one knew he read Flecker, just as no one knew of his collection of paintings by the German idealists Hoffman and Exter. The luminous blues, greens and reds threw out their iridescence in the softly lit vault hidden two stories below the ground floor of his house. His favourites, the Wave and The Three Grecian Girls were still on the top twenty list of missing art. But it was not for that that they remained hidden. He could easily have paid a price no one could refuse. He kept them hidden, as he kept his Flecker hidden, because the brash, the uninitiated, the people he mostly dealt with, would confuse them with Romanticism. The elegiac mood of both paint and words would be misunderstood. Those who really knew Flecker, Exter, Hoffman understood the difficult construction of complete harmony that lay behind their work. Hiding the exquisite detachment of a fine iron willed drive to achieve. And Albert had no desire to appear soft to the brash or iron willed to the discerning. Unless he chose to do so in his own time.

He had shown a glimpse to Tansu when he had read her some Flecker, in part to educate her, in part to keep up the appearance of wooing her. But now, as he lay on a lounger on the white marble terrace, looking across the pines and cypresses, the orange groves and gardens, the sea and wooden boats and waves that Exter and

Hoffman and Flecker sculpted so finely and so purely, Albert knew she had fallen into the trap and thought him soft.

When he learned of the attack on Hammond at the meeting with the President, Gilbert and Claud, Albert had known immediately who the killer was. The description fitted Tansu and her mode of operation was unmistakeable. A fast display of mayhem without undue concern that the primary target wasn't eliminated. It was a tactic she had developed in Turkey. Debilitating attacks, sometimes hitting an official or officer but more often spraying the civilians nearby. Causing unease, a distancing between State and people. If Celik hadn't been so weak and rejected most of her operations, Turkey would have been in chaos by now. But Albert had told her specifically that there were to be no more operations until the Limnos attack. He didn't want to risk losing fighting men and women. And he certainly didn't want to risk losing her just before the crucial corner of his carefully built edifice to become President of Kurdistan was slotted into place.

He had been so angry, that he had come up here to his house above the town of Anamur to calm down. He had bought time with his suggestion to talk to his contacts, but he still hadn't worked out what to tell the French President when, inevitably, he was called on to report. And he still wasn't sure whether he was more angry because Tansu had thought him soft or because she was stupid enough to try and hit Hammond.

G8 was the one organisation that Albert respected. Hammond, Leviatski and Walt Sable made a trio who understood the harmony of chaos and who had formidable computing power to calculate risk and to unravel the maze of complexity, obstruction and disorder.

Albert knew Hammond had been to Mauritius under the cover of Keithley. He also knew Hammond had found nothing. But the telltale signs on the Banque Onde's external computer links had told him that G8 had launched an attack on his internal systems. Albert had paid many millions of dollars to a number of firewall experts to obtain the maximum protection for his communications from hacking. None of them had been conscious to the others and, like the builders of the pyramids, they had been quietly disposed of when their work had finished. So Albert was not worried that human intelligence was available to G8.

There were, of course, the employees in the bank but they didn't learn about any of the transactions. Those remained hidden within the computers obeying Albert's encrypted commands without question. There was always the vulnerability of G8 tracing the external communications. But there were so many cut-outs, false trails, encryption changes, that their computers would be running flat out for weeks before any rewards were forthcoming. By which time Banque Onde would be the least of their problems.

His business in Mauritius was in the clear. And if there was any doubt about that, Charlie would have told him after she'd seen Gilbert. She would have asked him about Celik again. She hadn't. In fact, she'd put her arms around him and asked him to forgive her for being so silly and told him again how much she loved him for setting up the Cluny Exhibition.

Now Tansu had put all that at risk. She had focussed a spotlight on the area of greatest weakness. The activities of the PKK.

Albert sighed and shut the slim volume of Flecker. He walked slowly across the terrace, breathing in the syrupy smell of the pines, relaxing his limbs. He stepped over the wide French window lintel onto the cypress plank floor. A different smell now as the cypress still exuded its musky scent seventy years after the house had been built. He carefully moved around the angular cherry wood table which carried the glass Daphne and Chloe lamp. Behind it was a pillar. He looked closely at the rose petal wall light and it swung out as it recognised his iris imprint. He put the copy of Flecker in the recess and flicked the light back into position.

He turned, seeing the room as he'd seen it all his life. Nothing had changed since his memory of it when his parents used it as a holiday villa, travelling there from Beirut by boat. They had been happy days, laughter, games, time, precious time, with his father and mother. He had come here after they had been killed by the French. The housekeeper and her husband had brought him up and then looked after him, selling the produce from the land and the wine in the cellars to provide a meagre sustenance. He had slipped into Anamur as a five year old and stolen fruit, bread, anything he could to contribute to their survival. Until, when he was seven, the local tobacco smuggler picked him up to watch the beaches.

'Albert, I missed you.'

Startled, he turned. Tansu stood in the terrace doorway. The light streaming around her, emphasising the whippy steel of her body.

'Hello, Tansu,' he said.

As she moved out of the light towards him he saw that her hands were bandaged.

'So they took a piece out of you after all.'

Something in his tone made her stop.

'You know it was me?'

'Who else?' he said dryly.

She started towards him again, holding out her hands.

'You're not angry, are you. I thought . . .'

'You didn't think at all,' his voice cut across her like a whip.

She stopped, hesitated then made to move against him.

'I came here because I thought you wanted me.'

He stepped back, his eyes dead.

'When I want someone, I want an intellectual equal, not an obsessive who thinks like a backstreet tart.'

Two smudges of white appeared either side of her nose.

'What do you know about how I think, you arrogant shit. You know nothing about how it feels when you . . . you have to do things to survive as a kid in Turkey. If I'm a backstreet tart, the Turks made me that. If I'm an obsessive, they made me that too when they killed my mother. It's all they understand. Kill them and they're frightened. If I kill enough of them they'll be so frightened they'll give me what I want.' She stopped, her eyes wide, the whites showing clearly around the black iris, her breath coming in short gasps, her voice rising. 'And I'm going to go on killing them. And you're not going to stop me.'

Albert looked over her shoulder through the door, across the marble balustrade on the edge of the terrace towards the distant, broken hills above the bay.

'I'm not interested in your sad little life story. I've heard it all before. In a thousand different rooms with a thousand different women.'

She stormed towards him. Albert didn't move. Kept his gaze on the hills.

'Hammond isn't a Turk,' he said, calmly.

She checked, putting a bandaged hand to the hair by her temple.

'Is that what all this about? I thought it was about me continuing to be operational instead of acting out your pasty faced politician.'

He drew his gaze away and felt for his cigarette case, moving towards the square white leather sofa in front of the black and white marble surround fireplace.

'"Acting out" is the right expression, Tansu. If you had learned what I have been trying to teach you, you would know that I have no objection to your killing Turks when it is convenient.' He took out an oval cigarette and lit it, sitting down as he slid the lighter into his trouser pocket.

'What I object to is your ignorance, pig headedness if you like, in attacking G8 at the most sensitive time before we attack Limnos.' He turned his eyes on her, deeper in his face now behind the tight lines down either side of his nose. 'That was a cheap whore thinking, not the leader I took you for.'

'They put a fucking informant, a fucking spy into my organis- ation. Abu Hamid smashed the Antonov, broke up the arms shipment. Hammond was responsible. What else do you think I'm going to do. Put out a fucking welcome mat?'

His lips tightened as he turned his head towards the fireplace.

'You haven't learnt, have you Tansu? Yes, you've put on the clothes, the chic of a politician, but you still have the temper and language of a street fighter.' He shook his head slowly. 'I wonder if I did the right thing in choosing you to head the PKK.'

Tansu caught the inflection, looked around her uneasily.

'What do you mean?'

Albert shook his head again. 'That's all you can think of, isn't it? Violent means to achieve your ends. No, Tansu, my men aren't going to come in and remove you. If the Turks haven't changed you by violence I certainly shan't. If I can make you understand that, there's still hope for you and for the Kurds.'

She turned her head, sharply.

'There's hope for us anyway.'

He leaned forward, gently putting one of his hands under hers, leaving it just touching.

'That is where you're wrong, Tansu. Killing Hammond is

necessary. But it's the timing of it that's important. It was the wrong time. G8 will put all their energy into finding, identifying the attacker. Identifying you. I need you free to plan the Limnos attack, bring it off. I need you by my side to bring the Kurds to power, to end the Turkish rule. I need you when I become President.'

He leaned his face closer to hers, his breath fanning her lips, his voice a murmur. 'The fulfilment of hope doesn't depend on actions, Tansu, it depends on the finite moment the actions are taken. I've seen this all my life. Great struggles have been lost because there was no political touch, no feeling for time, only impatience, unsophistication and the ultimate evaporation of hope, through the spiral of failure.'

Her eyes dropped from his to his lips. Slowly, she moved forward a fraction to kiss him, feeling the frenzy fire through her as he responded.

*

It was dark when they spoke again about the attack on Hammond. They sat at the wrought iron table on the terrace, the flames of black candlesticks flickering momentarily as warm breaths of air climbed up the hill and lost themselves in the pine trees. In that light Albert almost thought Tansu attractive, the gold necklace and bracelet throwing her dark hair and black dress into relief, but he knew it was an illusion. What attracted him was her mental toughness, her ability to battle through setbacks, her response to his teaching.

'It wasn't just revenge,' she spoke through a mouthful of lobster. 'I had to show my people I wasn't just a mouthpiece, I could kill with the best of them.' She paused to pick up a glass of Riesling near her elbow. 'There was talk, you know, after I revealed Abu Hamid to them. Talk about a woman not being strong enough, being weak and allowing a spy next to her.' She swallowed the wine. 'I had to show them I could take on the most difficult target of all.'

He watched her pile a mound of lobster on her fork and wondered how such a thin frame contained such a huge appetite.

'But, in fact, you succumbed to them. They still look to you as a leader through violence. They need to trust your judgement if they are to accept you as their master. There is a difference, you know. A leader is useful for as long as there is success. Look at Celik, for instance. Few remember him now, let alone regret his passing. But a master, a master is revered, respected and, above all, feared. If you were a master you would not have been s . . .' he stopped dabbing his lips with his napkin. 'You would have seen no need to pander to their petty jealousies.' He saw her mouth tighten slightly and hurried on. 'They are only jealous, you know. That is all. You have nothing to fear from them. So no more heroics. From now on you are their master. You say and they do. And when you feel the urge to kill, ask yourself if the timing is right.'

'And if it is?'

'Then go ahead.' He smiled. 'I only ask that you take care of yourself for me.'

'You do mean that don't you,' she said quickly.

His teeth glinted white between his lips.

'You know I do.'

He waited as she drank some more wine, sliding the glass back onto the table to rattle the cutlery.

'What about Limnos,' he said. 'The arms shipment, the troops. Are they on schedule?'

'Yes,' her eyes sparkled, 'Romin is a brilliant organiser. The arms are to be shipped in four days. There is a Moosar taskforce in charge of it. Eight men and four women. Two of them the train guards, the others passengers. No one will know they are connected with the shipment. They will make sure there's no interference, disembark with the shipment at Balikesir, and meet up with our group there.'

'The Export licence?'

'Already with one of the train guards.'

'Good. And after arrival at Balikesir?'

'The crates will be loaded on lorries and go by road through Balikesir to Edremit on the coast.'

'Won't that be suspicious? Agricultural goods going to the coast?'

'The Export licence is genuine. The rail staff won't question it at

Balikesir. All they'll see is the stuff being loaded onto the lorries, then they'll be off to the bar. They won't care where it's going.'

Albert nodded. 'How many troops?'

'You haven't told me what to do with the arms flying in from Moosar to Bandirma.'

'You don't need to know about that yet. What about the troops?'

She pursed her lips and hesitated. She saw the look on his face and changed her mind. 'Two hundred, including thirty-four women.'

'Thirty-four women? They'll never pass for Turkish combat troops.'

'No. But they won't be recognised and I need them.'

His eyelids drooped slightly to cover his annoyance.

'And if they're killed or captured, it will take the Turks ten seconds to convince the Greeks they're not involved. The finger will point at the PKK and you will be eliminated.'

The sound of crickets broke the silence.

'I need them,' she repeated.

'You don't,' he said quietly.

She bit her lip.

'I'm sorry. I'm just used to using women the same as men.' She brushed the tips of her bandaged fingers through her hair. 'They're often better. Of course, it's different this time. I'll replace them.'

'Don't dwell on it, you only need telling once.' He paused. 'Did I ever tell you how good a politician you're going to make?'

She laughed. 'That's not what you said earlier.'

'My prerogative,' he smiled. 'Where are the uniforms? How are you going to hide the men?'

'We've got four sixty foot diesel cruisers harboured in the marina over there.' She pointed towards the lights of Anamur. Tomorrow they'll move out at intervals and move in four positions off the coast at Edremit. The men will filter in to the countryside around Edremit over the next three days staying at campsites. The fourth night they'll rendezvous with the four cruisers, board and make their separate ways to Limnos.'

'Separate ways?'

'Yes, I'm sure that G8 will be watching shipping movements

after the Samos attack last month. They will suspect a group of boats approaching a Greek island from Turkey.'

'And the weapons, uniforms?'

'Ferried on board on the fourth night.'

'Your troops, are they prepared to stay on Limnos, fight it out, until the Greeks retaliate?'

She nodded.

He leaned forward to adjust one of the black candles.

'It may take a little time. The UN will try to get involved. We've got France on side to press for war, but they won't go public. I don't think the Greeks will hesitate. But we might need a few hours.'

'I understand. The positions we will take up will be defensible for that long.'

He rubbed the fingers of his left hand together.

'Not "we", Tansu. You will be with me, in Ankara, with the rest of your troops taking over the Turkish Government.'

She compressed her lips. 'I can't. I must be with the troops in Limnos. They'll be on foreign soil. They need me.'

'They're expendable.' Albert said harshly. 'Get used to it. The most important part of this is to take over Ankara for long enough to get the Greek Army in to Turkey. Only you can do that. So don't let loyalty cloud your judgement. When they die on Limnos, they liberate Kurdistan.'

'They're my friends. I've been with them most of my life.'

He looked out across the pine trees. 'You can't have friends any more Tansu. A lover, yes. But not friends.'

CHAPTER THIRTY-NINE

Gilbert poured himself another brandy, gripped the glass and tilted his head back. He no longer felt its fire and warmth. It was the distancing effect of the liquor that he welcomed. He saw the morass he was sliding into but somehow it wasn't happening to him. The person who was consenting to war, who was helping open the door to a French pre-emptive nuclear strike was a shadow. An amorphous being, sliding in and out of a fog where loyalty and duty stood stark one minute then disappeared into indefinability the next. All Gilbert knew for sure was that the brandy kept him away from that nightmare, kept him safe and sane.

The telephone call he'd just received from the President had brought that nightmare into sharp reality again and Gilbert watched his hands shake as he poured more of the brandy into the empty glass. Anything to keep away from the exhausted phantom who was being swallowed in a mire he dimly recognised as conscience.

When he'd heard the President's clipped voice telling him that Albert had identified the PKK as being responsible for the attack on Hammond, the fog had lifted and Gilbert found himself saying that he would inform Hammond immediately.

But then the President's voice had brought in the first tendril of mist when he said that alerting G8 to the resurgence of the PKK at this moment would jeopardise the PKK attack on Limnos. Stumbling, Gilbert had found some firm ground and replied that obviously the PKK attack had already jeopardised the whole French operation and that was a good reason for abandoning the scheme. Getting more confident, he heard himself saying that the attack on Hammond showed the PKK was out of control, which was another good reason for calling a halt.

There had been a silence and Gilbert had felt his heart beat faster as he saw the mist recede, falling away before the strength of his argument.

Then Gilbert had heard the low monotonous tones of the Director with the steel spectacles. An examining Judge had approved a warrant for his arrest on the charge of espionage and treason against the State for his activities in Kosovo based on Albert's evidence. Whether that warrant was served or not depended on Gilbert. If he did as agreed at the last meeting with the President and approached Charlie Dedain with a low key general warning for her to give Hammond, there would be no unpleasantness. But any attempt at any time to go public on any of the issues would be met with immediate arrest and a very public trial with only one outcome. The fog then closed in so completely that he hardly heard the President saying that he was pleased that Gilbert would speak to M'mselle Dedain as agreed. Gilbert was about to put down the phone when, echoing out of the darkness, he heard the President's voice again, murmuring that he was also pleased to say that the PKK had given a firm assurance that no such attack on Hammond would be made in the future.

Gilbert knew with the certainty of a clear horizon that the assurance meant nothing, altered nothing. But the other person, the phantom deep within him who took responsibility for navigating through the dense weather, seized on it like a star sighting in a stormy night.

*

The knock on his apartment door came two hours later. He put down the book he'd been staring at blankly and started for the door. Catching sight of himself in the mirror, he checked, did up his shirt buttons, smoothed back his hair to try and straighten it, rubbed his eyes with his fingers but it did nothing to hide the yellow red moisture there. Shaking his head slightly, he grasped the handle and pulled the door open.

Charlie stood in the hallway, the electric light catching the gold in her hair. Her lips were parted, her eyes clouded, a tenseness about her that Gilbert had not seen before.

He beckoned her in, not trusting himself to speak. She brushed past him, taking in the litter of papers, dirty plates and cups, the open brandy bottle on the tray, the half full tumbler on the side table by the rumpled chair. Turning, she looked at him, catching him unawares. The red rimmed, yellow streaked eyes stared bleakly out of black rimmed, hollowed sockets. His hair had visibly whitened, and strayed across his head in greasy tendrils. His clothes were creased and egg yoke stained his shirt.

She caught a wave of sympathy welling up inside her.

'Gilbert, you've got to tell me what's going on.'

He felt the softness of her voice reach into him, feeling for the man he used to be. Everything he needed lay in those words, in the way they were spoken. By telling her everything it would release him, would bind him to her, would bind her to him. He felt the desperate weariness start to drain away as he grasped the moment.

'It's about our involvement with the PKK, Hammond, the weapons . . .'

'John?' she exclaimed. 'You mean it was the PKK which tried to kill him.' She stepped forward, gripping his arms, the tenseness in her now tangible.

Hammond, he thought. It was always Hammond. A sense of jealous hopelessness brought the weariness surging back to overwhelm him. He drew in a shuddering breath and turned to reach for the tumbler of brandy.

'Yes,' he said, starkly, 'they tried to kill him. But they won't try again.'

'I read the report,' she murmured. 'The attack on him, but it didn't say . . .' she broke off. 'The PKK? How do you know?'

He stared at her, the tumbler halfway to his lips.

'You don't know?'

She backed away as she saw the expression in his eyes. There was a distance in them that almost frightened her.

'No. How should I? I don't see the Intelligence reports, only those I'm sent.'

'No one told you?'

'No. Why should they? I mean, who would?'

He shrugged his shoulders.

'No one,' he muttered. 'Anyway, that's it. Your boyfriend was targeted by the PKK and got lucky.'

'He's not my boyfriend,' she said angrily.

He sank into the chair, still clutching his glass.

'Okay, Charlie, whatever you say. Anyway, the President wants you to tell him that the PKK have taken him off their target list. The attack was a mistake. That's why I asked you to come.'

'The President? Why me?'

'You're close to Hammond.'

She shook her head.

'There's got to be another reason. The President could go through Claud.'

'It's embarrassing. The President wants it kept low key.'

She was silent for a moment.

'How d'you know the attack was a mistake? They tell me you haven't been to the office for days.'

'I still get the reports. Our source in the PKK says that the attack wasn't approved. It was carried out by one of their members whose brother was arrested last year on a G8 warrant. She waited until the right moment.' He shrugged. 'It won't happen again.'

'How can you guarantee that?'

'She was disciplined.'

There was a silence.

'What did you mean about our involvement with the PKK, the weapons?' she said, slowly.

'Nothing,' he replied, sharply.

She looked at him for a moment.

'I care for you, Gilbert. I hate to see you like this. There's something wrong and you won't tell me.'

His eyes creased at the corners, his head moving slowly from side to side as if desperate to hold back whatever trouble was inside him.

She knelt beside the arm of the chair.

'You can't go on like this, Gilbert, I've told you before. What's it about? The PKK? The Army? The President?'

'It's too much, Charlie,' he whispered. 'I don't know where to begin.'

She put her hand out to touch his.

'Just tell me.'

'What can you do, if I do tell you?'

'It depends.' She paused. 'It depends on what it's about.' She frowned. 'I can talk to Albert about it. He knows everyone. Can fix anything.' She smiled. 'You know that.'

The words seared through him, scrubbing out the brandy fumes, unscrambling the haze in his head. He pushed himself to his feet.

'That's a good idea, Charlie. But not now. I can't talk now.' He returned her smile. 'I'm fine. Now I've got to get to the office.' He looked down at his clothes. 'Have a shower and change first.' He paused. 'You wouldn't like to stay and help me would you?'

Without a word, she got up, went to the door and walked out.

He watched her go. Glad to fall back into the chair and into the mist that had, for a moment, frighteningly cleared.

CHAPTER FORTY

The goods yard at the railhead in Guryev in Kazakhstan where the Ural River reached the Caspian Sea was freezing. Beams of yellow light fed out from the high towered lights, faintly picking out the shapes of massive diesel locomotives and trucks resting on the maze of rails that somehow went through a series of crazy patterns until they formed two orderly twin tracks east towards Oktabrsk and west towards Astrakhan.

Heavily clothed figures moved in and out of the shadows, treading carefully to avoid obstacles hidden in the blackness where the feeble lights couldn't penetrate. Every now and again they stopped at a brazier rubbing their hands over the hot coals winking out of the holes made by pickaxes in empty oil drums. The stillness of the cold night air was punctuated by the clatter of trolley wheels and the clunk of boxes being dropped onto the wagons. Every now and again a fit of coughing underlined the smog of diesel fumes and coal smoke which filtered up towards the lights, creating a filmy haze that hung over the whole yard.

Tansu wasn't out of place there. Other women, Kazakhs, Uzbekis, Russians, toiled amongst the men, lifting the crates and driving the forklift trucks. She wore the standard uniform of dirty blue overalls, her thin frame almost lost in the baggy material which covered her padded clothing underneath. She even helped lift some of the long metal banded boxes which had shifted out of line on their pallets, grunting with the strain and joining with the others in the shouted instructions and yelled warnings as the heavy crates of weapons were moved from the warehouse onto the closed wagons.

'Who's in charge here?' the voice cut through the noise made by the loaders like a chain saw.

Tansu turned, dimly saw the official serge uniform, the large epaulets emphasising the huge girth of the woman wearing it.

'Come on, I haven't all night to waste, who's in charge?'

'I am.' Romin, the weapons salesman from Moosar, stepped out of the shadows. 'Who wants to know?'

'Customs.'

'I didn't say what, I said who.'

She stiffened, her jowels bulging into her collar.

'Don't you take that tone with me. Where are the papers for this consignment? It's export isn't it?'

Romin let his shoulders make a little bow.

'I'm sorry. I'm a bit tired. Haven't eaten since breakfast. The papers are with the guard. They've already been inspected.'

'Not by me, they haven't.'

'You'd better speak to Ozbay in the Customs Office. He cleared it.'

She shifted her bulk from one foot to the other.

'That's why I'm here. That shit Ozbay's been clearing too much for too long. I'm here to sort him out. Get me the papers.'

Romin shrugged.

'But it's Government stuff. Agricultural machinery for the Turks. I've got to get it off in the next ten minutes. Otherwise I'll miss the schedule.'

She stood there, a brazier wavering her massive shadow onto the side of the wagon. Then slowly she kicked one of the boxes with the toe of her boot.

'Open it.'

Romin spat on the rail.

'You fucking open it.' He turned to Tansu. 'Get this fucking lot on the train. I'm not wasting any more time.'

Tansu bent down, started to shift the box.

The woman brought her fist down on Tansu's back. 'I said open it, you little tart.'

Tansu gripped her wrist and straightened. They heard the woman's arm snap before Tansu bent back and, swinging, slung her into the gap between the two wagons. The woman's mouth opened to scream but her back hit the buffers, breaking in two, before her wide open eyes glazed over and she slumped onto the rail.

For a moment, nobody moved. Then one of the loaders stepped over the rail to pick her up.

'Leave her there,' Tansu rasped. 'Just take her uniform off. They'll find what's left of her after the train's moved. Just another accident.'

The man stepped back.

'Bloody lighting here,' he said. 'There's always accidents at night.'

Ten minutes later the last of the doors slammed shut and the low moan of the diesels ground into a roar. Tansu watched from beside the rails as Romin and his Moosar guards climbed into the last wagon.

The pale light shimmered indistinctly on the wagons carrying the weapons she'd meet in Balikesir in three days' time. She stood there as the wagons rumbled by, stood there until the red light on the last wagon became part of the orange glow in the distance.

Tansu didn't bother to look at the body of the Customs' Inspector on the rail. By the time the last of the ninety wagons had rolled over it, it was unrecognisable.

But she carefully folded up the woman's uniform and hid it under her overalls. It would be careless to let that be found.

CHAPTER FORTY-ONE

'I'm just going onto the roof to feed the tomatoes,' Rosie said.

Hammond looked at the bottle of Tomorite in her hand.

'You don't mean to tell me you brought that with you from London. You can get that stuff here.'

She put a hand up and shifted her dust cap more firmly on her head.

'You can't trust what these Frenchies put into their fertiliser.' She drew down the corners of her mouth. 'The stories I've heard, I can tell you. No. Tomorite's what my old man used to use, so it's good enough for me. Remember BSE,' she said darkly.

He thought of contradicting her, but changed his mind. Rosie had an answer for everything. 'I'll be in the cabin,' he said.

'Don't forget the alarm. I won't hear the front door up there.' She hitched her apron and walked towards the roof garden stairs at the end of the room.

Hammond opened the cabin and slid inside, closing the door behind him. He leaned forward and switched on the plasma screen and the front door alarm.

Julia's face appeared on the screen framed by her chestnut hair and a chocolate brown top, with a high collar.

'Good to see you still alive John,' she smiled.

'You nearly got your promotion, so don't be glad,' he laughed.

'I can wait a couple of years.'

'Thanks,' he said, dryly. 'What news?'

'We can definitely say the attacker was a woman. Other than that we've still nothing to go on.' She paused. 'Except we're pretty certain the attack was on you, not Claud. The computer has analysed that Claud was deliberately kept safe. Otherwise the attacker would have taken out the helicopter after lift off, killed you both.'

'Someone who doesn't want the French on their backs?'
She nodded. 'Could be.'
He frowned slightly.
'Then it's political. Organised crime wouldn't bother about that.'
She waited, letting him think. The computers had followed the same analysis but had got no further. Nor had any of the G8 team working on the problem. It could be one of a dozen political terrorist groups. Each with their own reasons to make a statement and kill the head of G8. Or it might be a lone woman, disgruntled.
His frown deepened.
'Have we re-established surveillance on Abu Hamid?'
'Yes. About half an hour ago. He's in Diyarbakir.'
'Have you tried to contact him?'
She shook her head. 'No. I wanted to speak to you first.'
'Right,' he broke off as he saw the door alarm blinking. 'I've got to go. But send someone to contact Abu Hamid personally. Don't speak to him on the mobile.'
She leaned forward, her face almost filling the screen.
'Have you some reason for this?'
'Sorry, Julia, I've got to go. But do it right away.' He put his hand out to switch off the screen, saw the concern on her face. 'I don't think I should have switched G8SUR off him. It's probably all right, but I want to be sure. And I want someone to talk personally to him.'
He just caught her puzzled look before the screen shut down. He wasn't sure why he'd suddenly felt anxious about Abu Hamid either. But lurking at the back of his mind was a picture of Abu Hamid being sent back early from his holiday to sabotage the PKK arms shipment on the Antonov and then nothing else. Silence. Even when Celik had been killed in the accident, Abu Hamid had remained silent. He'd been told to keep low but he wasn't the sort of person to pass up the dollar bonus he'd get if he had a report to make on Celik's successor. And Abu Hamid was close enough to the PKK centre circles to find out, in fact the only G8 informant close enough to find out.
'It's all right, I'll get it.' Rosie bustled across the room to go downstairs to the front door.
Hammond watched the television screen slide across to hide the

cabin before sitting down on a sofa and picking up a copy of Paris
Match. He was leafing through it when Rosie arrived breathing
heavily after her climb up the stairs.

'Miss Dedain to see you,' she said, 'or I should say "Madamey-
sel Dedain", seeing as how she's French.' She looked at Hammond
from under her eyebrows.

Hammond stood up.

'Don't take any notice of Rosie, Charlie. I'm firing her.' He
looked at Rosie. 'Insubordination.'

Rosie puffed out her cheeks.

'I'll tell you what, Miss, it's him as needs firing. I don't know
what you see in him. I'll get you a nice cup of tea.' She threw a
dark glance at Hammond. 'Or do we drink this French coffee now.'

Charlie laughed as Rosie closed the door.

'What does she mean about what I see in you?'

'Never mind Rosie,' he said, curtly. 'What have you come to see
me about?'

Charlie's chin went up.

'Well, if you're just going to be bad tempered, I'll go.'

He put his hand out.

'No. I'm sorry, Charlie. Rosie winds me up sometimes, that's all.'

Charlie looked at him speculatively.

'So she does mean something. Have you been talking to her
about me?'

'Talking to . . . No. Of course not. Why . . .'

'Here's your tea, love.' Rosie shuffled over and put the tray down
on the sycamore desk. 'I'm really glad to meet you. Mr Hammond's
told me so much about you.' She lifted her eyebrows slightly at
Hammond before turning round and heading for the kitchen.

Charlie went into an uncontrollable peal of laughter as the door
closed.

Hammond grimaced. 'I don't see anything to laugh at.'

'You wouldn't. She has me married to you already.' She went
off into another peal of laughter.

'What's so bad about that?' he snapped.

'She wiped her eyes. 'Why? Are you asking me?'

'No, I'm not.' Exasperated he swung round, collided with the
desk, knocked a teacup off the tray.

Charlie darted forward to stop it rolling off the desk just as Hammond leant over to do the same thing, overbalanced trying to hold onto the cup. They went down with a crash.

'Merde,' gasped Charlie as Hammond's weight crushed her into the floor.

The kitchen door swung open and Rosie stood there surveying them. Without a word she marched over, took the teacup from Hammond's raised hand and inspected it.

'I'll remind you that's the best china, Mr Hammond.' She paused to look down at Charlie. 'You all right? I'll get you a clean cup, love.'

Charlie sat up, rubbing her arm as she watched Rosie go.

'She is a treasure, John.'

'She's an interfering menace,' he retorted.

'But you talk to her about me.' She turned her head to look at him, her lips parted a little.

Irresistibly drawn, he leaned forward and kissed her.

Surprised, she drew back, drawing her hand across the blonde hair at the back of her neck. 'You didn't mean that, did you?'

He grasped the top of the desk, pulled himself up, put out a hand to her.

She didn't move.

'Did you?' she insisted.

'No,' he said, blankly. 'I'm sorry. I shouldn't have done it.'

The green eyes clouded. 'Then why did you?' she asked.

'Why did you come here?' he said, tersely.

Her eyes narrowed briefly. 'I asked you a question.'

His lips tightened. 'Well, what man wouldn't,' he said, boorishly. 'You're pretty enough, aren't you?'

He saw her face whiten. Quickly she got to her feet, turned and for the second time that day, walked wordlessly out of a room.

'That wasn't nice, Mr Hammond.'

He turned to see Rosie standing in the kitchen doorway. 'Nor is it nice for you to go telling those fibs.'

*

Rosie turned and stepped back into the kitchen, the door slamming behind her. Hammond had never known her to be angry. But then she thought of Charlie as the pretty girl in her match making scheme. She had no idea that Charlie was a G8 target. Someone to be played, not pampered. Charlie was in love with him and she had to be strung out until she lost control of her emotions. Only then, when her mind started its spiral into the blur of incompleteness, would she be prepared to tell him about Gilbert. And when he knew about Gilbert, he'd know about the French objectives.

His gaze drifted to Kahn's painting of the Corkscrew Swamp and suddenly he realised that Charlie had never told him why she'd come to see him. He started for the door, only to realise immediately that he was too late. Charlie had gone. Fighting a rising feeling of emptiness, he opened the cabin again, forced his mind to recognise that he'd missed a trick. Charlie may have come to talk to him at last about Gilbert and he'd been so intent on the operational text book that he'd missed an opportunity to soften and let her talk. Savagely, he shut the door and brought the screen to life.

CHAPTER FORTY-TWO

'The whole building's empty,' said Julia.

Gunter's dark brown eyes blinked as he reached for his laptop and settled it more firmly on the lumpy hotel bed. The last time Julia had spoken to him about the building had been in Ankara in another hotel. He'd had to adjust his laptop on the lumpy bed there, too. Listening as she'd told him that G8SUR had found Abu Hamid in the building near the gold bazaar at the market in Diyarbakir. Now, after a very unpleasant journey in a hired Beech-craft, during which he'd been thoroughly sick as the plane had lurched and corkscrewed through blinding rain and stomach churning lightening, it appeared that Abu Hamid was not in the building. Was not here in Diyarbakir at all.

'You mean Hamid's gone?' he asked, sourly.

Julia smiled what Hammond called her nursery smile.

'You archaeologists are so literal, Gunter. Don't worry, your awful journey hasn't been wasted. Hamid is still there. He hasn't moved.'

'He's been there at least six hours. Do you think he's asleep?'

'Yes, probably. He's made some small movements, so we know he's alive.'

'That's comforting.' Gunter breathed in, as if he was trying to catch a drift of her perfume. Something to make her more tangible than the flat, brown haired, brown eyed, red lipsticked image on the screen.

Julia caught the note in his voice. She'd always been fond of Gunter since the day she'd recruited him sitting in those hard, upright pews of the little church in Garmisch. But Gunter was an operational agent and any feelings beyond fondness were verboten, out of order, forbidden.

She drew back.

'The building's been empty since G8SUR started tracking it. Abu Hamid must have been using it as a safe house. The sooner you go in, the better. If he leaves, you may not be able to approach him. So get going right away.'

Gunter blinked again. He just wished she wasn't so cold. Just wished she . . .

'What about back up?' he said.

'We won't have any human surveillance. It's too risky. By yourself, you can meander through the vegetable market, speaking Kurdish, buying stuff. If we have people following you in that market they may create patterns, attract attention. We'll have you on G8SUR and we'll be able to detect any known PKK members near you. They'll show up on the computer records.'

It was going to be very lonely, he thought. No back up. No rescue. Just a harsh warning through the chip implanted in his left ear if PKK were spotted by a remote satellite a hundred miles up in the sky.

'And what about unknown PKK members?' he asked.

A tiny frown appeared between her eyebrows.

'G8SUR will pick up any surveillance on you, you know that. Just get going.'

'Yes,' he said. He didn't ask what would happen if he got into the building and it was suddenly surrounded by PKK. It wasn't a question that could be answered. And he didn't want Julia to think he couldn't hack it operationally. The building was empty. It was Abu Hamid's safe house. Approach it with caution and there wouldn't be a problem.

'I'll go now. It's seven and the market will be busy. The lights aren't very good there either so that will help.'

He looked at Julia and flicked the control switch. He thought her face softened in the last second before it disappeared from the screen and he almost switched the laptop back on. But he stopped, telling himself it had probably been a trick of the light.

He carefully put the laptop into the bottom of the battered cardboard box he'd carried into the hotel with his cheap plastic holdall. The laptop was hidden under another piece of folded brown cardboard and covered with pots of honey. Deliberately,

244 DAVID BICKFORD

Gunter broke the paper seal on one of the pots and dribbled the honey over the other pots, leaving a sticky oozing mess. He put the plastic bag on top, making sure the broken pot was tipped under one of the bag's plastic feet. No casual snooper would touch it and someone with more intent would have to be extremely efficient to want to. It was as good a hiding place as any in a room bare of furniture except a wooden slatted bed and a melamine covered single cupboard.

He had thought of wearing a djellabah to go out. But he wasn't armed and had nothing to hide. So he left his room wearing the same sandals and dark loose top and trousers he'd worn when he'd signed the stained, well thumbed hotel register an hour earlier.

The hall was empty, silent except for a couple of drowsy flies buzzing near the hookah by the soiled and chipped wooden chair and table that served as the reception desk. He crossed the filthy blue tiled floor and let himself out into the narrow alley.

The stench of rotting rubbish littering the fetid water in the open drain hit his stomach. Already weakened by the flight, he gagged and put his hand to his mouth, gulping to get control of himself.

An old woman came up. Put her arm out to steady him.

'Are you not well?' she asked.

He saw her eyes glittering in the light through the open doorway. The rest of her face was hidden by her black chador.

'Yes, I am well, mother,' he answered picking up her Kurdish dialect. 'Thank you.'

He retched again.

'You need to rest,' she said, starting to lead him through the door.

'No, no, I am well,' he gasped, pulling away, alarmed.

'Here,' she called to a small man squatting by another doorway. 'Help me, this man is ill.'

The man slowly got up, dusting his hands against his dirty cotton jacket. He coughed, a rasping rattle that came from deep inside his chest. He spat into the drain and walked towards them.

'What's wrong?'

'Nothing,' Gunter rasped urgently. 'Tell her I'm well, there's nothing wrong.'

The man peered up into his face and coughed again.

Gunter took the full force of the man's sour breath. Gasping, he bent double and heaved over the open drain.

'I said he was not well,' the old woman nodded to the man. 'Help me get him inside from where he came.'

Gunter was past caring. Heaving and retching every time he smelt the man's breath he allowed himself to stumble and be half carried to the chair by the hookah in the hotel hallway.

The old woman looked around.

'Ulku,' she shouted. 'Ulku.' Her hidden face turned to Gunter.

'Another person he's poisoned with his filthy food.' She prodded the hookah. 'Look at this, not cleaned in months. The mouthpiece not changed either.' Her head came up, her body rigid with disgust. 'Ulku, you poisoner, come here.' Her shrill voice echoed around the hall.

Gunter shook his head, desperate now. 'Please, don't complain mother, it was not the fault of Ulku. I have not eaten here.'

'No matter,' she replied, almost hissing now in her mounting anger. 'You were probably poisoned by your bedclothes. The dirt on this floor shows what your room must be like.' She looked sharply at him. 'Where is your room?'

Gunter bit his lip. Just shook his head.

'I am going,' the man said.

'Yes, go.' She nodded. 'I shall find Ulku.'

Gunter saw his chance. Gathered his shredded stomach muscles and sat upright. A wave of nausea swept over him. He clenched his teeth and dug his nails into his palms.

'I am alright now. The sickness has passed,' he said, starting for the door.

He watched her eyes squint at him.

'You do look a little better,' she said slowly. 'Perhaps . . .' She looked around. 'I don't know where Ulku is. Perhaps I shall speak to him later. If you do feel better, that is.'

Gunter nodded. 'Yes, yes. It was very good of . . .'

'Ulku,' she shrieked, 'you are a lazy man, your dirty hotel has poisoned this man.'

Gunter looked across the hall, saw Ulku shift his bulk through the doorway, hesitant, a hand to his unshaven chin, a half grin on his face.

'You're not staying here old woman. What business is it of yours?'

'When I have to help this man out of the gutter because of his sickness, it is my business.' She put her hands on her hips. 'And it will be the authorities' business in the morning.'

Ulku shifted uneasily. He paid off the police, that was only natural. But the authorities were a different matter. He only vaguely knew who they were. And he knew they were not even vaguely aware of who he was. He shut the door, looked at Gunter.

'Are you ill?' he asked.

Gunter forced a smile still pushing his way towards the door. 'I had a little sickness. But I am well now.' He saw Ulku frown and rushed on. 'But I assure you I had it before I came to stay at your esteemed house.' Gunter carefully avoided the word "hotel".

Ulku's face lit up. 'You see, old woman?'

'He needs to be in his room,' she said stubbornly. 'I helped him from the street.' She glanced at Gunter, her voice rising again. 'Ungrateful man.'

Gunter saw Ulku's expression darken again. He couldn't afford a scene. Hamid would have to wait.

'You are both very kind,' he managed a weak smile. 'I will go.'

'Well, help him,' the old woman shouted.

With Ulku holding his arm and the old woman behind him, Gunter slowly walked up the wooden stairs, stumbling every now and again as the stair rail shifted under his weight.

At intervals, another shriek from the old woman reverberated off the walls as she found yet another deficiency in Ulku's standards of repair and cleanliness.

Woodworm, damp, peeling plaster, worn paint, stains, dust, cobwebs and cockroaches were all prodded and inspected with increasing incredulity and volume.

With every step, Gunter's mind focussed more sharply on the spilt, sticky mess of honey under the plastic bag in his room. He knew, with a clarity which scythed through his aching head, that this old harridan would pounce on that oozing, treacly cardboard with another agonising shriek. This time of surprise as the laptop tumbled out of the box that no ordinary person would have touched.

He stopped outside his door. Stepped away from Ulku.

'Thank you, both,' he said.

Ulku grunted and turned to go.

The old woman pushed him.

'Help him inside. I want to see this goats' pen you have given him for a room.'

Gunter's mind whirled. Desperately he backed up against the door.

He saw the old woman's eyes narrow. Suspicious. Wary.

'My undergarments,' he blurted. 'You understand.'

She didn't move, her eyes hard. Then suddenly she cackled.

'I've seen enough of them in my lifetime, but if you wish I'll return when you are in bed. Bang on the floor.' She turned to follow Ulku. 'I'll look at the kitchen.'

She picked her way down the stairs, her high pitched whine following Ulku all the way.

Gunter slid into his room. Went straight to the cardboard box, lifted out the jars and grabbed the laptop.

Five minutes later she was back and he watched from his bed as the old woman brought curses on Ulku's head for the state of the bedroom which, unbelievably, was an even stickier mess than the kitchen. It wasn't difficult for Gunter to feign the stillness of the sick. Any movement reminded him of the honey splashed all over him in his urgency to get the laptop underneath his loose top and secured by his belt.

Gunter spent an agonising hour lying in the sticky mess before he silently got up. Before he left he sent a message to Julia telling her he was late and that he was keeping his laptop secure on his body so that G8SUR could be programmed to know where it was.

Immediately afterwards he cautiously left his room, crept down the stairs. The hall was empty now. He slipped out into the night. This time he was prepared for the stench in the alley and saw no one there. The journey to the vegetable market was easy. Straight down the alleyway, giving him plenty of time to smell out any surveillance there.

He was impatient now, his mind taut, hoping that Hamid hadn't left the building. He should have checked with Julia, but opening the video link was risky with that old woman nosing around. Just taking the time to send Julia the message had sent his pulse racing. He had no desire to make things more difficult.

The alley suddenly opened into a small square and a babble of voices. Stalls and carpets laid on the ground were piled high with vegetables and fruit of all kinds. Gas and oil lamps hung from the wooden stall canopies, flickering in the shadows thrown by the throng of men and women, pushing past each other or suddenly stopping to inspect the wares. The atmosphere was gay, with bursts of laughter or a babble of good natured bartering. The languages were a mix of Turkish and Kurdish in their various dialects. This part of Diyarbakir was for the slum dwellers, many of them in rickety wooden structures that served instead of the stone and basalt of the other buildings in the neighbourhood.

Here were ripe candidates for the Seventh, Eighth and Ninth circles of the PKK. The bombers and killers, the supporters, and their families. And here were informers and ripe candidates for informers. Turks who would sell out their parents or sisters or brothers to the secret police for the price of a meal. Here Gunter had to tread with the utmost care. If he gave any indication that he had a purpose other than an evening's shopping for his supper, he would attract attention.

He merged with the crowd without stopping, moved in behind a large woman waving her arms, her chador flapping, as she talked to her companion. After a few steps Gunter stopped suddenly in front of a stall littered with green and red peppers. He picked up a couple and sniffed them, pressing his thumb into the crowns. He put one down and picked up another, sniffed, put his head on one side and nodded. Dipped his hand in his pocket, counted out three coins to the stallholder, grinned sheepishly as the stallholder rubbed his fingers together, scowling at the stickiness on them.

Moving on, he turned, as if looking for another stall. Cast a quick glance around, covering the upper stories of the overlooking houses. Making the same gesture with his head he turned back and slowly pushed his way towards the alley on the far side of the square. Despite his urgency he forced himself to stop and buy onions and tomatoes, gathering a plastic bag from the onion seller and having a spirited couple of rounds with the tomato man, arguing and complaining about the price just enough to blend in with the other buyers.

Trying to move more quickly he shifted into the alley and poked around in the lock up shops there, his breath catching on the pungent smell of spices and the sweetness of dried fruits. It was hard work, pushing and prodding his way, stopping to check behind, leaning to check in front, bargaining and bluffing to buy rice and currants and pine nuts and cinnamon and oregano to convince any unseen follower that he was building up to cook a slow, steamy bowl of stuffed peppers, which was what any sensible person would do for themselves if they had to stay overnight in the squalor that Ulku called an hotel.

The edge of the basalt building where Hamid was being watched by G8SUR came into sight.

The chip inside his ear told him in Julia's voice that he had twenty yards to go before the entrance to the building.

He let go of one of the plastic handles of his bag and stopped suddenly as it sagged, threatening to throw his supper out onto the filthy grime encrusted cobbles. Struggling with the bag, he slid inside the narrow yard at the entrance to the building. Fumbling with the vegetables and packages, he let the people immediately nearest him go by. Slowly, he stopped the fumbling and gradually slid into the shadow, his black loose clothes hiding his shape as he put the bag behind him. He inched round the corner until he was completely hidden from the alley.

The man didn't give him a chance. Flashing his knife at Gunter's stomach in the same movement he made to shift out of the shadows.

Sweat streaked through Gunter's pores, soaking his armpits and back. His heart pounded, choking his breath. He tried to step back.

'No,' the man whispered. 'Here, to me.'

Gunter moved on to the knife, feeling it jab the laptop strapped there under his belt buckle.

'What's this?' The man lifted the knife to jab it under Gunter's chin and thrust his hand under his jacket to grab the laptop. He pulled, ripping the jacket. Held the laptop up to the film of light that trickled from the alley.

'What's this?' the man repeated, jabbing the knife into Gunter's chin.

Gunter lifted his head, tried to draw some spit into his mouth to moisten it.

'Paints,' he breathed. 'Paints. I paint.'

Anything to gain time, to get the knife moved, to give him room, just a split second.

'Money.' The knife jerked up again. 'Money.'

The laptop dropped to the cobbles.

Gunter almost sobbed with relief. Money. He dropped his hands, put them in his pockets, pulled out the notes and coins, held them out.

'Money,' he whispered. 'All I have.'

The knife made a quick slashing movement, laying open his chin. He fell to his knees as the pain sliced into his head then down through his body. He felt the notes snatched from his hand, watched the coins jingle and roll into the crevices of the cobbles. Then he was alone. Watching the blood drip steadily onto his trousers.

'He's gone. You can get up now.'

Julia's voice. G8SUR hadn't seen the knife cut into him. She was urging him on. Getting the operation finished.

He shook his head. Fighting the pain firing across his chin, churning his stomach. Another bout of nausea. He dragged his head up, looked into the archway and saw the heavy wooden door. Stretching up, he grabbed the handle. Hauled himself up.

'The laptop.'

Her voice again.

Hanging on to the handle he picked up the laptop. Leant against the archway, his lungs quivering to find oxygen in the dark, clammy night air. He shoved the laptop inside his trousers, secured it with his belt.

He turned to the door to inspect the lock. He needn't have bothered. The wood was splintered and the door hung open. Only an inch, but it was open.

Gunter's breathing almost stopped. This was Hamid's safe house. The door should be locked. He stepped back. He couldn't ask Julia for instructions. This was a voice guided operation only. It was too dangerous for him to have a voice response chip. Any movement of his lips in that hostile territory would have been noticed and reported. He was mute.

'The building's empty.' Julia was pushing again. Relying on G8SUR. But Gunter knew G8SUR had been fooled in the past, had failed to spot a body's electric impulses where a concentration of electricity existed, like a fuse box or cable.

He breathed in, sweat drenching him again, as he tried to block out the pain. He pushed the door, gently, so gently, feeling it gradually swing.

Closing his eyes, he counted to ten. Opened them, peered into the gloom. Put a foot across the threshold.

Silence.

Another step, then another.

Silence.

The stairs were in front of him.

'Up the stairs. First floor. Second door on your right. Hamid's in the far corner.' Her voice was clipped, giving him no quarter.

He felt his legs tremble. Terrified of failing, he launched himself forward taking the stairs two at a time. The stone taking his weight without a sound. He paused at the top.

Listening. Straining his ears. Wiping the blood from his chin.

Silence.

Making up his mind, he walked straight to the second door on his right. He was too far in now to escape.

He pushed the door open.

The room was completely black. He could see absolutely nothing.

Swallowing, he whispered.

'Abu Hamid, Hamid.'

From the far left corner he heard a gurgle.

Putting his hands in front of him, Gunter moved towards the sound. The room was empty. No furniture.

'Hamid. Are you OK?'

Again he heard the gurgle.

Wetting his lips he put his hand inside his belt and pulled out the laptop. Opening it, he switched it on.

The light in the plasma screen threw out a glow, picking out the black blinds at the windows, picking out Hamid squatting on a chair in the corner. Instead of his ears, there were two bloody stumps.

A chill rocketed straight down Gunter's spine into his stomach.

Desperately, he reached out to get Hamid to his feet.

In the glow he saw Hamid's eyes flare wide, his head violently shake from side to side, his mouth open to shout.

But he had no tongue.

Gunter began to shake.

The thought of running streaked through his mind. But he couldn't. Couldn't leave this wreck behind.

'Quick, Hamid. You have to get up. They'll be coming.

Again that tortured face, the frantic shaking head, the wild eyes.

Gunter leant down. Physically dragged Hamid from the chair.

Heard the click of the detonator.

And in that final, infinitesimal fraction of life before death, the brightest yellow seized his brain, flashing red, with Julia's face smiling out, leaving him with a last thought of that subtle perfume.

*

Julia saw the explosion through the eyes of G8SUR. It lifted from Hamid's room and spread in rapid mushrooms the whole length and breadth of the basalt stone building. It shot through the alleyways, burning and blasting the fruit vendors and the vegetable sellers and the buyers and the bargainers. It smashed the children and the old women, the stone chips scything them like grape shot from a cannon. It rippled flame into the square and into the wooden slum dwellings. Flinging the screaming, burning dwellers onto the cobbles to sprawl in smouldering heaps.

In the stunned, shattered moments of the sudden still aftermath, all Julia could think of was the laptop. No risk it would be discovered now.

CHAPTER FORTY-THREE

The President's face was livid. A vein bulged pulsing his left temple, twitching the eye, which was almost hidden by the fleshy, screwed up cheeks.

'Get me Intelligence,' he exploded.

His secretary looked up from his desk, startled.

'Intelligence, Mr President?'

'Yes, bloody Intelligence, woman. Are you deaf? Get him. Now.'

Frightened, she'd never seen him like this, she fumbled with the intercom. Her voice quavered.

'Jean, he wants Intelligence.' She paused. 'I don't know who.' She gulped, as she listened. 'He said "get him".'

She looked at the President as she waited, sitting with his back to her, intent on the television. She closed the switch, gripped her hands together.

'He's coming now, Mr President.'

There was no reply. Curious, she half rose to see the television screen, but it was blocked by the President's bulk, as he sat hunched forward, his shoulders bulging with tension into the folds of his neck.

The blue panelled door slid open, and she became riveted on a pair of steel rimmed spectacles. They fascinated her, held her, so she saw nothing else.

'Get out.' The President had turned to face her, the vein throbbing now, the eyes just slits above the gash of his mouth.

She sat, suspended in disbelief.

'Get out,' he yelled.

Terrified, she threw herself out of the chair, half ran, half stumbled through the door, almost sobbing with relief as it closed behind her.

In fury the President turned on the spectacles.

'What's this?' He pointed to the television. 'What the bloody hell is this?'

The spectacles turned towards him.

'I don't know what you mean, Mr President.'

The President was almost screaming now. 'What do you mean you don't know, you should bloody know. You're Intelligence. The whole bloody world knows. And you stand there, like a bloody idiot.'

The spectacles glinted as they took in the television pictures, started to mist as the reporter's words made sense of them.

'Diyarbakir? Two hundred dead? It's not . . .'

'It's bloody happened,' the President screamed. 'Look at it, it's bloody horrific and your bloody PKK did it.'

The man took off the spectacles and polished away the mist, surreptitiously wiping the sweat from under his eyes with his fingers.

'They're not my PKK,' he muttered.

The President swung round, his voice low, trembling with rage.

'The last time you were in this office, you told me that the PKK had not targeted Hammond deliberately, that you had assurances from that little shit Albert that such a thing would not happen again . . .'

'But . . .'

'Shut up and listen to me.' The President was jabbing his thick fingers now, his lips wet with spittle. 'You told me that the PKK would lie low until they attacked Limnos. You knew we didn't want a searchlight on them at all. So you tell me what the hell is happening there.' The finger jabbed at the television. 'It's bloody monstrous, it's torn all our plans apart.'

The spectacles shifted from hand to hand, sweaty fingerprints blurring the glass.

'I . . . I don't know. I'll . . . I'll find out.'

The President's breath rasped. 'No you bloody won't. Get me that bastard Albert. I want him here now.' His breath rasped again. 'Now. D'you hear? And get me Claud and that other bastard Gilbert you think you have under control.'

The intercom buzzed. The secretary's voice was almost inaudible.

'G8 are calling.'

The President clenched a hand and slammed it into the other palm.

'That bastard Hammond.' He glared at the spectacles, back on the face now, trying to appear intelligent. 'You deal with him. Tell him we're in the dark, have no information. But get the others here first.'

The blue panelled door closed, leaving the President watching the CNN pictures, the smouldering debris, the blood, the gut wrenching sight of the inevitable child, mewing quietly as a white coated figure wiped its sightless, stone chip embedded face.

He didn't move for an hour. And no one approached him. Until the secretary, still trembling, opened the door to admit Albert, Claud and Gilbert.

By the time they arrived the President had been so saturated with news coverage that his horror was completely dissipated by repetition. But his rage was still there, fanned by the stupidity of the PKK.

Wordlessly, he walked to his desk, picked up a bottle of orange juice and flung the top onto his blotter.

'As there is no explanation for this crass attack, I want to outline our future tactics.' He looked straight at Albert. 'You are to cease all activity with the PKK. You will leave Paris immediately for Mauritius where you will stay. You will not enter France again. Is that understood?'

Albert's face didn't move as he slid out his silver case and selected a cigarette.

'Your explanation for this, Mr President?'

The President's cheeks puffed out, almost hiding his lips.

'You ask me that? After Diyarbakir.'

Albert moved a Louis Seize chair by the desk and sat down, crossing his legs.

'The attitude you display explains exactly why I did not tell you about Diyarbakir.'

In the dead silence, Claud's face registered shock. No one treated the President this way. No one spoke to him like that.

Gilbert coughed, the smell of stale brandy wrinkling Claud's nose.

'Can someone tell me what this is about?' His speech was thick, like liquid cement.

Claud looked at him contemptuously. 'Haven't you seen the news? What the hell's happening to you?'

Gilbert shrugged, his crumpled jacket sliding up to reveal a loose shirt tail.

'The PKK blew up a safe house in Diyarbakir an hour ago,' Albert filled in.

'And killed at least two hundred people in the process,' Claud said viciously.

'Including an informant,' Albert added.

Gilbert swayed slightly, rubbed his bloodshot eyes and sat down, dazedly stretching through his mind for a safety net, needing time to be able to find it.

'I thought they were getting ready to attack Limnos.'

'So did we.' Claud addressed the President sharply, trying to shift the stupefied expression Albert's words had fixed on his face.

Albert caught the interchange.

'They are,' he cut in, 'they'll attack Limnos just as we planned.'

The President slammed his hand on the desktop.

'They're not. G8, the whole world, will be watching. They'll have every Intelligence agent they've got digging, and what about the Turks. Nobody will be able to move, let alone shift the weapons and personnel needed to attack Limnos. They'll be seized the moment they poke their heads out.'

'Exactly,' agreed Albert.

'What the fuck do you mean?' snarled the President.

Claud blinked. He'd never heard the President use that word before.

'I mean,' answered Albert smoothly, 'that there are over a quarter of a million Kurds in the first nine circles of the PKK and over ten million in the fringes, the tenth circle. Neither G8, nor the Turks, nor the whole combined police forces in Europe have a hundredth of the manpower needed to pick them up. They won't need it, of course, because we've arranged for at least twelve hundred activists to be available for arrest over the next twenty four hours.'

Gilbert shook his head. 'What are you talking about? It doesn't make sense.'

They watched Albert settle back slightly, a magnetism seeming to emerge from the movement, which drew them to his hooded eyes as if he'd thrown out a net, like a primeval tribesman to snare his prey.

Gilbert listened as Albert told them. And in his utter belief of what he heard, he knew that a word of protest, a glimmer of dissent would find him Albert's victim. So he sat and let the words etch themselves into the swirling mists of his brain that had been swirling there so long.

'It is simple,' said Albert. 'Tansu has to get two hundred male fighters into four positions on the Turkish coast to take off for Limnos. At the same time she has to move the weapons shipment from Kazakhstan into those four positions the night of the attack. Any of those movements may attract the attention of G8 or the Turks.'

The President thrust his head forward.

'What do you mean, "may"? Is she already moving them?'

Albert put up his hand. A tiny gesture that was magnified by their expectancy of his reply.

'At the same time, Tansu has to work eighty fighters into Ankara to take over the Presidential palace and the Parliament building.'

'Eighty?' blurted Claud. 'How can you take over the Government with eighty men?'

'We have had sleepers in the Palace and Parliament for at least a year now. The eighty will merely consolidate their work.'

'Work?' ejaculated the President.

Albert's lower lip shrugged.

'Assassinations, executions. What you will. The point is that the Turkish Government will have no effect, no meaning, two hours after the attack opens on Limnos.'

Albert stopped. 'I am a little dry,' he murmured. 'Perhaps a drink?'

They were so absorbed, so mesmerised, that Claud got up and silently poured brandy into three glasses. The fourth, a glass of Riesling, he handed to Albert.

'But what about this senseless attack in Diyarbakir?'

Albert sipped his wine, looked for somewhere to put the glass, shuffled the photograph of the President's wife onto one side and put the wine in its place.

'The fighters were in place in their safe houses by the coast yesterday. They are clean. None of them are on any register for violent activity or even political activity.' He raised his eyebrows at their unspoken question. 'We've checked.'

The President clenched his fist. 'But if that's so, why Diyarbakir?'

Albert let his eyes dwell on theirs for a moment, each in turn. His nostrils flared slightly as he gave a small sigh.

'Tomorrow evening the arms will arrive at Balikesir from Kazakhstan and will be transported by lorry to boats already in place near the safe houses. Tomorrow night the fighters will leave in the boats for Limnos. Then, at the same time as the attack on Limnos, the other fighters will emerge from tunnels and sewers in Ankara. The twelve hundred PKK who have agreed to be arrested will focus the Turkish authorities at Ankara on Diyarbakir and the south. The information those arrested will give, are expected to give, will make sure of that. The Turks will be so busy with the south they'll forget the north, and Limnos.'

'But two hundred dead. That was needless.' The President spread his thick hands.

Albert shook his head slightly.

'But don't you understand? Two hundred dead shows that the PKK will stop at nothing once the President's Palace and Parliament building are taken. The populace will be cowed, not knowing who will be next. I can then step in as interim President of Kurdistan supported by the PKK and restore calm. At least until we can negotiate with the Greeks and stop the fighting. After that it won't matter, we will have a Kurdish homeland in the south. The Turks can have the rest willingly. If the Greeks let them.'

Gilbert wanted to shout about the Muslim reaction in Iraq, Iran, Pakistan. But the words wouldn't come. It was too late. He could only show support and dimly hope that he could live with that afterwards.

'It makes sense,' he said, thickly. 'Militarily the casualties will be high on a Greek Turkish fighting front, particularly when the Greeks storm into Istanbul. The two hundred killed in Diyarbakir will soon be forgotten. And Albert's right. The Turkish authorities will be looking the wrong way. Limnos and Ankara will be much easier to take.'

The President's head jerked up.

'You approve?'

'Of course I approve. I approved the attack on Limnos didn't I? This is a sound military proposition. We should be thanking Albert.'

Gilbert wondered if his last sentence had gone too far. But the President was nodding.

'Claud, what d'you think?'

Claud mentally sniffed the air. The President's colour was back to normal, the huge pulsing vein no longer visible.

'Gilbert's right. It's brilliant.' He looked at Albert. 'You go, tomorrow?'

Albert looked at them over the rim of his glass and nodded.

'Good,' said the President. 'France will not forget you, Albert.' He glanced at Claud. 'Send in my secretary, Claud, will you. I must draft a letter of condolence to the Turkish President.'

CHAPTER FORTY-FOUR

'Are you sure Julia Simmonds is up to the job?' The Prime Minister carefully turned over a page of the G8 Report Hammond had given him a few minutes earlier.

Hammond focussed on the picture of the Queen above the fireplace.

'I've given her forty eight hours' leave. She needs a rest.'

'That doesn't answer my question.'

Hammond moved his gaze to the Prime Minister's eyes.

'I was hoping you were merely being conversational. If she wasn't up to the job I wouldn't be giving her leave.' He rubbed his jaw with a finger. 'I'd be giving her the boot.'

The Prime Minister half smiled.

'So what went wrong?'

Hammond's lips tightened.

'I did. I removed surveillance on PKK when I should have increased it. I put Celik's death down to an accident when I should have realised he'd been assassinated. I thought the PKK had been neutralised by the Antonov arms loss. In fact there's been a leadership change which has put them on course for more violence. I now think that the Paris riot was more than just unrest. It was planned by whoever is now leading the PKK.'

The PM shifted in his leather chair.

'But you must know who's taken over.'

'Not yet. Abu Hamid was our inner circle informant. We didn't activate anyone else in case it alerted PKK.'

'But they were alerted. They were waiting for your man.'

Hammond looked out of the window, onto the Horse Guards Parade Square behind the Prime Minister's Office, saw a group of soldiers in full dress exercising their glossy horses.

'They were waiting for more than that,' he said slowly.

The PM stopped shuffling the papers, lifted his eyes, waited.

Hammond got up, walked around the Sheraton table with the vase of flowers on it and went to the window, watching the soldiers and their horses showcasing on the gravel parade ground.

'We've studied G8SUR's digital images. The explosion occurred at the moment Gunter lifted Hamid from the chair. Hamid was the detonator. As long as he sat on that chair the circuit remained broken. As soon as he stood up it was closed and . . .' his voice trailed off.

'How long was he sitting there?'

Hammond kept staring out of the window.

'We don't know. It could have been days.'

The Prime Minister picked up a pencil, tensed it between his hands. 'I suppose . . .'

'Yes.' Hammond's voice was harsh. 'They would have tortured him just to get any information they could. He would have been in terrible pain for every moment, unable to move.'

The Prime Minister blinked suddenly.

'My God. I think I would have stood up just to finish it.'

Hammond turned. 'Which means the PKK told Hamid exactly what would happen if he did. He waited for us. Hoping we'd be smart enough to realise what was happening. Hoping I'd be smart enough to realise what was happening.'

The PM shook his head.

'Julia . . .'

'It was nothing to do with her. I allowed myself to be needled by the French, by their slackness in guarding me at the meet with Claud. I didn't stop to think. Just ordered Julia to get someone out to meet Hamid as soon as possible. She had no reason to believe the PKK were active again.'

The PM slowly stood up, walked around the desk, pushed the yellow curtain to one side to join Hammond by the window.

'She's that good?'

Hammond nodded.

'Then we need her back to work now. I've had the Turkish President on the secure link. He wants all available help right away.'

Hammond was silent.

The PM put a hand on his arm.

'I can't lessen the blow, John, but there's no one I would rather have leading G8 than you. You know that. And so do the Americans and Russians. Both Presidents have been on to me, making sure you'll not resign. Fighting terrorism is no different to fighting any other war. We take our hits, learn, get up and push on, until we take another hit. Then we do it all over again. Until the terrorists are worn out and their politicians have had some sense knocked into them.'

Hammond's mouth formed a half smile.

'And our politicians have had some sense knocked into them.'

The PM laughed.

'The bloody French being the prime candidates, you mean.' He turned and moved back to his desk. 'Well, I've had some good news then. That bastard Claud has emailed his Government's consent to an EU Army to include Turkey and proposes a meeting of all officials in a week's time.' He picked up a paper and thrust it towards Hammond. 'You've done well. I knew you would. We've got the bastards cornered at last.' He watched Hammond read the text. 'You can concentrate on the bloody PKK now. Dealing with the Greeks and Turks will be child's play after the bloody French.'

Hammond handed back the paper.

'They'll still need watching though, particularly that banker Albert. There's something,' he paused, 'something wrong in his relationship with the Defence Minister, Gilbert. It might just be corruption, but Albert has connections stretching from Beirut through Russia and Eastern Europe. That attack on me happened just after I'd been investigating him in Mauritius.' He stopped. 'I'm sorry, I'm rambling. I need to analyse it more. But I want to put you on notice that the French don't want this Army and I think they will still work to undermine our efforts.' He pointed to the desk. 'Despite this email.'

The PM slowly sat down, picking up the email.

'I was afraid you'd say something like that. You know, John, if we don't get that Army in place, I can see Europe going up like a tinderbox. The Germans are putting huge pressure on the Greeks and Bulgarians to tighten their borders with Turkey. If the Turks won't stop pushing Kurds and who knows what across their borders, and they won't unless they get more troops to help them, I am desperately afraid the Greeks will try and sort out the Turks themselves. And you know what that means.' The PM shook the email at Hammond. 'What the hell are the French up to? If they don't agree the Army, what do they possibly think they can gain?'

Hammond leaned forward on the desk.

'It's not what they can gain. It's what they won't lose. Their independent nuclear capability.' He stood up sharply. Exasperated. 'Whoever gave them the means . . .' He stopped. Shrugged. 'They won't let go of it. However much trouble it causes. They've always protected their interests, however selfish. And they've always had other people to come and get them out of trouble. That's the enigma.'

'Bastards,' murmured the PM.

'I'll second that,' nodded Hammond.

*

Two hours later Hammond was clambering down an aisle of the spectator's area at the Queen's Skating Club in West London. He felt a chill stab from the ice through his summer lightweight suit. He looked up at the restaurant with its wide windows overlooking the arena and hesitated.

A couple were executing a complicated step dance down the ice to a disjointed cacophony of sound, which included at least a dozen drums and another dozen guitars. Walking down two more steps he tapped Julia on the shoulder and pointed to the restaurant. Her eyes widened a little. Then she nodded, holding up three fingers.

Hammond was relieved there were only three minutes more of that jarring music. If the couple fell over, he hoped, it might be finished quicker still.

He strode back up the stairs and walked past a couple of giggling girls putting their skates on.

'I thought it was finishing with that lot,' he pointed to the ice.

One of the girls looked up, a pair of deeply blue eye shadowed eyes looked up over a deeply red lipsticked mouth.

'No, there are three more of us pairs.'

He shook his head. 'How old are you?'

'Ten,' she said, going back to fiddle with her skates.

'You surprise me,' he answered, shifting towards the restaurant again.

'I'm the youngest in the Junior Nationals,' she shouted after him.

'That's not what I meant,' he replied. But she didn't hear him.

The amplified music in the restaurant was even louder than it was in the arena. This time a large girl was being swung around by a thin, spotty boy who lowered her until her head was an inch from the ice. A group of kids by the window applauded, shrieking and hugging each other.

Hammond shuddered and walked to the bar. He ordered a large scotch and ice and took it to an empty table where he could see Julia at work.

She was in a box with the other five judges. Motionless except for her head, which followed the dancers around the rink. She seemed impervious to the din, not even tapping her foot to the beat, taking no notice of the yells of approval from various sections of the audience when their favourites performed a complex manoeuvre without coming to grief. Once there was a groan as the slight blonde girl with the blue eye shadow and red lipstick fell out of her partner's grasp and slid across the ice. Undaunted she scrambled to her feet and sped back to him, her red lips in a forced smile, her eyes slicing into him like a blade into ice.

She's got guts, thought Hammond, and determination. No wonder he saw those qualities in Julia. She had skated since she could walk.

The noise stopped suddenly and Julia raised a placard with the number 4.9 on it. It was lower than the other numbers held up by the judges. She put it down, turned to look up at the restaurant and got to her feet.

Shortly after, she was sitting opposite him, nursing a Bombay martini, her dark hair and eyes set off by her sharp, black suit, probably made by one of the new London designers. 'I need this,' she said, taking a gulp. 'Those kids, they're so, so fast. You can hardly keep up with them.'

'Well, you weren't on the ice,' he remarked dryly.

'That's not the point,' she laughed, 'you've got to keep an eye on their footwork all the time, their body positions, line, form. They're so fast. Miles ahead of my day.'

'Slowing down?' he quizzed.

She stopped laughing.

'If you mean . . .'

He lifted his hand.

'Don't be so defensive. I'm only joking.'

She swirled the olive in her martini.

'There's not much to joke about.'

He looked up swiftly. 'That's not like you.'

'Oh I'm not blaming myself for Gunter's death. I've analysed that, so have the computers. There was no indication . . . No, it's just that I recruited Gunter. Remember when I met him, at an organ recital in Garmisch, quite romantic really, the music, the church, the mountains.' She stopped.

'I didn't know,' he murmured.

Her head went back as she laughed.

'Good heavens, it wasn't anything like that. You couldn't love Gunter. He was like . . . well . . . like a mascot. You needed him. You know, for assurance, stability. But you were wary of him too. In case . . . I suppose in case you lost him.'

'And now that we have?'

She finished her drink.

'We get on with it. Just like down there.' She pointed to the rink. 'If you fall, you get up and go on. Tend to your bruises in private.'

He looked at the ice.

'In that case, you were a bit hard on that little blonde girl. She got up.'

She stared at her empty glass.

'You don't win points for getting up. Anyway her technique was flaky.'

'I thought she was very gutsy, determined.'

'That's why the other judges marked her up.' She swept her dark hair from her eyes. 'But gutsy skating, if you don't have perfect technique, lands you on your . . .'

'Dignity,' he suggested, laughing.

'Conscience,' she said, surprising him. 'It's easy to be gutsy and determined. But real determination is working and slogging to hone the technique. That's what's hard.'

'And why you can live with what happened to Gunter and Hamid, and the others?'

She nodded, lifted her chin.

'Unless you say different.'

'I didn't to the PM just now.' He leant back, searching her face. 'You are the best. Don't question it.'

She let her eyes rest on his.

'And the catch?'

'You're to go back to work immediately. I underestimated what's going on in the PKK. Something's building. First Celik's killing. Then the Paris riot. Now the Diyarbakir atrocity. The whole tempo's quickening, the scale mounting.'

'Two other things,' she cut in. 'The secrecy about the new leadership and the attack on you.'

His eyes narrowed. 'Are you linking them together?'

She bit her lower lip for a moment, the teeth white against the dark brown lipstick.

'Your attacker was a woman.'

A shriek of laughter from a group of girls split the pause.

'Are you saying the PKK's been taken over by a woman?'

'Why else keep it secret. In normal circumstances the Kurds would never accept a woman to lead them. If she'd killed Celik, the inner Council would be shattered. Then they'd try and sort out a successor. When I left the office, G8SUR hadn't picked up Celik's three advisors. Either it hadn't swept over their present positions or they're dead.'

His eyes flickered briefly.

'They're dead. Everything you've said makes sense. The escalating violence. She's showing that she can deliver.'

Julia stretched out her fingers on the table.

'But even after Diyarbakir she's not announced herself.'

'Which means there's something even more spectacular in the pipeline.' He pushed his glass away and stood up. 'I'm going back to Paris. I've got to prepare for an officials' meeting on the EU Army.'

'Not another,' she said angrily. 'It's just a waste . . .'

'Not this time,' he interrupted. 'The French have agreed. We're all meeting with the Turks.'

'Allelujah,' she mocked.

He grinned. 'I know, watch the French. But I also want to speak to Charlie. I'm sure she knows what Gilbert's up to. And if we know that, we'll know what the French are up to.' He stopped as she climbed out from the table. 'In the meantime, feed your analysis about a female PKK Leader into the computer.'

'I did. Before I left.'

'Good. Then there should be a result when you get back to Basingstoke. And I want every contact in Turkey seen and debriefed. I don't care about cost or manpower. Whatever's out there has got to be stopped.'

She walked with him towards the exit, passing the girl with the blue eye shadow and red lipstick. The girl's lips tightened. Julia walked past ignoring her, waiting a little before she said, 'There you are, she's blaming me already. A born loser.' She turned back and moved towards the judge's box.

'And why you haven't blamed me.' Hammond murmured.

CHAPTER FORTY-FIVE

Charlie walked slowly across the dimly lit, heavy wooden planked floor of the Cluny Museum, listening to the echo of her footsteps, the serene beauty of the twelfth century tapestries and wood-carving touching in her a tinge of envy for the amount of time their creators had in which to fashion each piece. Time paid for in plenty by the medieval monks and princes avid for the sublime in a rough and brutish existence. How hard it was to find any patron these days, she thought, whose objective was beauty not profit.

She knew Albert was financing her exhibition here in the Cluny for whatever profit he might find in keeping her sweet. Information she might let slip about the French Government perhaps, or a whisper from the EU, a rumour from the UN. She knew he watched her closely, set up little probing conversations, usually leading on from her art, always leading to some political issue. In a way she felt uneasy about the exhibition, but the chance was too big, too certain never to be repeated.

The thought of becoming a full time artist, no longer doing her duty as a player in the Foreign Ministry's game of constant duplicity, was irresistible.

She walked through a stone doorway into a dark space, the gloom only broken by narrow beams of light reflecting the whole spectrum. The depth of colour and the simplicity of the medieval stained glass brought a catch to her throat. A thousand years ago the craftsmen had found ways to mix pigment in hues of such intensity that splendour took on a whole new life. And it was of such longevity that it never dimmed and lived here in the Cluny as it had done centuries before in cathedrals and churches throughout Europe.

'You are wondering why we have only these fragments?'

She jumped, turning to find the Curator at her shoulder.

'Monsieur Thibault, I didn't see you there.' She turned back to the stained glass. 'No, I understand the reason for that. What I don't understand is our stupidity in destroying all this beauty throughout the ages with wars and persecution.'

'So that artists like you can inspire us with fresh thoughts, a new appreciation, the excitement of treasure in our own age.'

She flushed slightly. 'Thank you. But you flatter me. Ionism is not to be compared to what we see here.'

Thibault put his hand on her arm.

'M'mselle, do not mistake your mother's donation to my Museum as having swayed my judgement of your art. Monsieur Albert . . .'

'Was more persuasive,' Charlie supplied.

Thibault looked hurt. 'I assure you M'mselle . . .'

'If we are going to put on my exhibition together, I think you should call me Charlie.' She smiled.

'I saw the Ionist exhibition in Montmartre,' he said stiffly. 'I saw the floor, the coloured filings flowing under the glass.' The stiffness vanished. 'The light flashing off them, then the pictures on the walls, sparkling with intensity, the whole . . . the whole reminded me of this room, this stained glass. A thousand years, I thought, a thousand years and nothing has been seen like it, until now. M'mselle . . . Charlie . . . I implore you, do not think this is your Mama or Monsieur Albert's doing. It is mine. I, Thibault, Curator of the Cluny, have the honour to present to the world the greatest transformation of natural light since . . . these,' he waved his hand majestically towards the glass panels.

Charlie swiftly bent over and kissed him on the cheek.

'Thank you.' She stood back from him. 'Can I really have an Ionism floor here?'

Thibault gulped audibly.

'Of course, Charlie. What would the exhibition be without the floor?'

Charlie's eyes sparkled. 'And can I interlace my paintings with the windows?'

Thibault wrung his hands.

'Of course, Charlie. What a wonderful idea. I can't wait to see it.'

'And can I . . .'

'Charlie, you're here, thank God.'

Gilbert stood by the door, his hand clutching the stone doorpost to steady himself. 'I've got to see you.'

Thibauld's eyes wavered from Gilbert's ragged, raw edged face to Charlie's look of concern. He coughed.

'I must get back to my office.' He coughed again. 'Work you know.' He took Charlie's hand. 'Come and see me when you've looked around. Tell me your ideas.' He backed from her nervously, edging around Gilbert in the doorway, before his shoes made a castanet clicking noise as he walked rapidly away.

Gilbert watched him go.

'He's Albert's man,' he muttered, 'what are you talking to him for?'

She frowned. 'My exhibition. What did you think?'

'Oh. I didn't know you had an exhibition, they just told me where to find you.' He shivered, drawing his loose coat around him. 'It's cold in here.'

The lighting behind the stained glass made the room warmer than most in the Museum. She started to contradict him, then she saw the thinness of his frame, the way his clothes hung from it.

'What are you doing here? You should be at home.'

Gilbert stayed silent.

'Come over here,' she said resignedly. 'It's warmer in this corner.'

Hesitantly he walked over to her, pointed to the gothic printed sign on an ornately carved oak bench, "Thirteenth century, from the crypt of Rheims Cathedral".

'Does that mean I can't sit on it?'

She laughed, sweeping her hair from behind her neck.

'Men have been sitting, praying on it for eight hundred years, I don't think one more will hurt it.'

He stood by the bench, slightly stooped.

'Is that what I need? Prayers?'

'Go home Gilbert. What you need is a good meal and some rest,' she said, practically.

He shook his head, sank down on the bench.

'That won't do me any good now.' His head sank on his chest. 'It's far too late.'

She hung back, finding his dejection confusing. She'd never seen a man give in to despair. Her father had been the traditionalist: never cry, never complain, life wasn't fair so don't expect it to be. Even the artists she knew, who ranged from hyperactive to manic depressive, had shown some spirit, some sense of fighting on.

He raised his eyes, bloodshot and puffy against the background of deep purple and grey that tinged his face.

'Sorry. I need a drink, that's all.' He reached into his pocket and fumbled out a flat bottle of brandy.

She watched him tilt his head back and tremble as the liquor hit his stomach.

'What the hell is going on, Gilbert? You've got to tell me.'

He laughed. Almost hysterically.

'I tried to tell you last time. But all you wanted was to talk about Hammond. If you'd listened to me . . .' his voice trailed off.

She began to feel angry.

'What do you mean if I'd listened to you? I did. You told me about John, the attack on him.'

He waved the bottle at her.

'John, John, it's always bloody John.' He stopped, trying to focus on her face. 'You could have stopped it, if you'd listened.' His head dropped down on to his chest again. 'Bloody Hammond,' he mumbled, 'always bloody John.' His head suddenly jerked up. 'I love you, you know that.'

She kept silent, knowing whatever she said would have no effect. She stood there sensing a gathering sadness that her love of John Hammond had somehow transformed itself into the ugly weapon which was destroying this man who had held her admiration and affection for so long.

'You bloody stupid cow,' he suddenly shouted.

Shocked, she felt her mouth go dry. Uncertain she looked towards the doorway.

He pushed himself to his feet. 'You just don't understand do you? You drift about in your job, your head in this bloody art, not seeing what's going on. And you think it's Hammond I'm worrying about.'

He put up his head as she started to speak. 'Don't. Don't say a word. I saw your face. It was written there. Feeling sorry for me that Hammond's taken you, wondering why I'm so . . . so bloody about it.'

'He hasn't. Gilbert go home, this isn't getting us anywhere.'

Gilbert clenched his fists. 'That's what I mean. All you can think of is him, you can't think about what's happening, what Claud's doing, what that bastard Albert's doing, what happened in Diyarbakir . . .'

'Diyarbakir?' she cut in. 'What's that got to do with anything? The PKK . . .'

'Who is the PKK?' he shouted, the veins standing out from his neck. 'D'you know? D'you care?'

'Of course I care,' she shouted back angrily. 'I saw the pictures too, you know.' Her voice altered, quietened. 'What did you mean about Albert?'

His breath came in short rasping gasps. A prism of light picking out beads of sweat shimmering on his forehead. He passed a hand across it, rubbing his fingers down his face, then let it drop limply to his side.

'He ordered it.'

She suddenly felt her legs buckle, put a hand behind her to hold onto the wooden safety rail protecting the stained glass.

'Ordered it?'

Her reaction scythed into Gilbert. He'd known she wasn't ready for what he had to tell her, but he had to tell someone. And in all honour she was the only person he could tell. She was French. She was a civil servant. She wasn't G8 or English or Hammond. He could never betray his Government to them. Deliberately, he opened the bottle, sucked down its contents.

'Albert is the banker for the PKK.' He coughed, wiping a dribble of alcohol from his chin. 'He is responsible for the killings in Diyarbakir.'

She saw it in his eyes then. He was telling her the truth. She was facing it, she could no longer push it away, no longer hold

Albert's dimly perceived menace at arms length. Now she had to listen and nothing, not even the mention of John Hammond, would deflect the flow of horror that Gilbert now unleashed.

In a voice that sometimes dropped to a whisper, Gilbert told her about Albert and Tansu, he told her Tansu was Albert's mistress, he told her that Albert had used her aunt Nina's house in Mauritius to cover the killing of Celik and he told her of the other killings as Tansu took over as leader of the PKK and, as the glow of light from the images of saints past filtered on to the wreckage of his once fine face, he told her about Albert's involvement in the murder of the two hundred people in Diyarbakir.

Long before he had finished, her unshed tears had given way to the mounting nausea in the pit of her stomach. Forcing herself to speak, she asked him why he hadn't told her these things earlier.

'I tried to tell you. After Hammond was attacked. Before the killings in Diyarbakir,' he replied quietly.

'When I asked if it was about John?'

He nodded.

She brushed the hair away from her face as if to brush away the guilt.

'It's too late now, isn't it?'

'Not for you.'

She looked at him sharply, trying to read his expression. He shook his head.

'I'm not important now. It's what you can do that's important. Vital.' He hesitated. 'You've got to speak to Hammond.'

'But why? After Diyarbakir he knows the PKK must be targeting him. We can keep this to ourselves. Speak to Claud. The President. They'll stamp on Albert. We can't let our Government down. Have fingers pointed at France for harbouring that bastard.' Briefly she saw a picture of her mother. Wondered if she knew about Tansu.

He looked at her, vaguely wondering if she was capable of accepting the magnitude of what he was about to say. In the mists of his brain he knew he had to tell her, and wished that, for once, the fog which passed for his mind would clear, leaving him lucid, urgent, urgent enough to be able to persuade her. Illogically at the back of his mind, he remembered something about St Jude, the patron saint of lost causes. He almost laughed. It was all this weird light and coloured windows and their martyrs and saints. He could almost smell the incense.

'Charlie, listen to me very carefully. I think I can only say this once.' His lower lip trembled. 'I don't feel very well. So listen. Please.'

Frozen by his tone she nodded.

He took in a shuddering breath, his whole body stiffening in the effort of concentration.

'The President, Claud, the President's Intelligence Unit are working with Albert for the PKK to take over the Turkish Government. The plan is for the PKK to attack Greece disguised as Turkish troops. The Greeks will retaliate and attack Turkey. In the chaos, the PKK will take over key points in Ankara and arrest or kill the Turkish Government Ministers there. They will then approach the Greeks for a negotiated settlement. They want the Kurds to have a homeland in the south of Turkey. The Greeks can then do whatever deal they want with the Turks.' He stopped, breathing heavily and wiping the saliva from his mouth.

Charlie tried to make sense of it.

'But why? Why is the President involved?'

'Because it will end the Turkish oppression of the Kurds, stop the Turks shoving them across the border into Greece and then into France.'

She shook her head. 'But the EU Army's going to stop that.'

He was gasping now, sweat sliding down his face to drip on his shirt, leaving a widening patch.

'The President's not going to have an EU Army. He's not going to lose his grip on our nuclear weapons. You have to believe me.'

'But weapons. The PKK haven't got the weapons for an attack on Greece.'

He looked as if he was going to be sick. His top teeth clamped down on his lower lip, a trickle of blood oozing down his chin to darken the patch on his shirt.

'I arranged the documentation for an arms shipment from Kazakhstan.' He stopped. For a moment she thought he'd passed out. His eyes were glazed and his chest had stopped heaving. She bent over him, feeling for his pulse. Suddenly he reached out, grabbing her wrist.

'The shipment arrives in Balikesir tomorrow afternoon. It's covered by Kazakh documentation for an agricultural machinery shipment to the Turkish Government.' His body shuddered as he made one last, supreme effort.

'You've got to tell Hammond. He'll know what to do. Tell him ... tell him to try and keep some ... honour for us French. He'll ... he'll understand that I think.' He slumped back, his body folding on one side to slide off the bench.

For a moment she knelt there, torn between calling an ambulance and shouting for Thibault. But something held her back, some instinct that Thibault was, as Gilbert had said, in Albert's pocket. She felt for Gilbert's pulse. Felt the uneven pressure as his straining heart struggled to keep him alive.

Then, quietly, she got up, took off her shoes and walked barefoot across the wooden boards towards the door.

'I thought you'd come here to discuss your exhibition with Monsieur Thibault.'

She looked up. Standing there was Albert.

CHAPTER FORTY-SIX

Charlie clenched her hands, pressing her nails into the palms, battling the panic which choked her throat.

Albert looked over her shoulder, squinting into the darkness.

'I think Gilbert needs some help, don't you?'

She couldn't speak, could only think of trying to push past him, through the doorway into the open hall beyond. He stood aside to let her go. From behind the walls on either side of the door two casually dressed men moved quietly in front of her, blocking her in.

'That was very rude of you, Charlie,' Albert said, as he crossed the room to look down at Gilbert. 'So he did pass out? I wondered why he stopped talking.' He nudged the prone body with his toe. 'I'm surprised he's not dead, the amount of brandy he's been drinking.'

He nodded to one of the men.

'Bring him with us.'

The other man gripped Charlie's arm. The pressure jolted her beyond panic, into the zone of hopelessness, her voice barely audible.

'You can't take me.'

He stood watching her, picking his cigarette case out of his pocket and carefully lighting up.

'I can do what I like, Charlie. Espionage is a dirty word. As for him,' he pointed his cigarette towards Gilbert, 'he will be treated like the dirt he is. But you . . .' He paused, drawing in smoke and exhaling it in a thin stream. 'Francesca will not want a scandal.'

His words thrust an image of her father into Charlie's mind. Suddenly she felt angry.

'She won't care after she knows about you and that terrorist woman.'

His eyes narrowed.

'Gilbert told you about that. It wasn't very wise of him,' he murmured. 'The other things, well, I could have coped with him telling you those. I only need you out of the way for a few days. But Tansu.' He drew on the cigarette again. 'Tansu is different.' He walked over and took Charlie's cheek between his thumb and forefinger, pinching it. 'I wouldn't like Francesca to know about that. I need her.'

Charlie gasped, pulled her face away.

'D'you think she'll stay with you after she knows what happened?'

He laughed. 'How like you, Charlie, to stumble onto the only reason I'd have for getting rid of you. Nobody would have believed your mad ramblings about a ploy by the President to help the PKK attack Greece.'

He saw her eyes flicker towards Gilbert. 'No one would have believed him either. His espionage was in Kosovo, nothing to do with this. He could have said nothing in public.' He shrugged. 'But you, you have to threaten me with telling Francesca about Tansu. The most stupid, unnecessary thing you could do.'

Charlie dug deep for some courage. 'You said she wouldn't like the scandal.'

'Not the scandal you were thinking of Charlie. The other scandal, you being the lover of that,' he pointed towards Gilbert, 'a traitor, selling our secrets to the Serbs in Kosovo.' He turned back. 'You don't really think you could have got anyone to listen to the rubbish that man was telling you about me and the President do you? No, you little fool. The only thing that threatens me is Francesca believing that Tansu is my mistress. And she will because she knew Tansu was with me in Mauritius.'

He threw the cigarette on the floor and ground it with his foot. 'I'm sorry, Charlie. I like you. I like your art.' He gestured towards the stained glass. 'I genuinely wanted to see your exhibition. It's not often that life really lives in art. But you captured it. The zest, the excitement.' He spread his arms out. 'I'm sorry.'

He nodded to the man by Gilbert's body. 'The plan's changed.'

He poked a foot towards Gilbert. 'You go back to his apartment. Take her with you. Don't be seen going in. You know what to do next. He'd been drinking and they had a scene. Make . . .'

'Who's been smoking here? Who's been smoking?' Thibault's sharp voice echoed from the far end of the hall, his footsteps quickening as his nose led him to the cigarette fumes.

Albert stepped between Charlie and the Curator, nudging the man holding her so he slid them both around the doorpost out of sight. 'You must blame me, Mr Thibault. I must apologise. I forgot myself.'

Thibault looked at him uncertainly. It was unforgivable to smoke in this Museum. But the man was haughty and had apologised and had donated five million francs and was paying for Charlie's exhibition. Thibault shook his head, made a clicking noise with his tongue.

'You are a disgrace, Monsieur Albert.' He smiled suddenly. 'But are always welcome as long as you don't burn the place down.' He took Albert's hand and shook it. 'Did I see Charlie with you?'

Charlie heard him, tried to bite the hand that was clamped over her mouth. The man winced, pulled his hand tighter.

'I think she must have left,' Albert said smoothly, 'tell me, have you a preliminary costing for the exhibition, perhaps in your office?'

Thibault's eyes lit up. 'You know when you first told me about your desire to fund this exhibition of Charlie's work I was torn. I must be honest, I didn't know much about Ionism, I thought it was the usual post modernist street trash, but we need the publicity.'

'And the cash,' added Albert dryly.

Thibault's head made a little sideways dance.

'Really, Monsieur Albert. No, it was when I saw the exhibition in Montmartre. I suddenly stepped into the future, like a space fantasy. The spectrum dazzling before me, under my feet, surrounding me, suffusing . . .'

'Yes, yes, I understand.' Albert impatiently poked him with his finger. 'But I need to talk about the cost. Not here. In your office.' He started to move away, his mind searching for a topic. 'Do you want a glass floor for instance?'

Thibault threw up his hands. 'Oh thank you, the most expensive item. But the most essential, the very essence of Ionism, casting a prism . . .' He stopped, his face rapt. 'Come let me show you.'

Albert bit his lip. It wasn't often he made a mistake, but he knew he'd made one now as he watched Thibault start to walk excitedly towards the door to the stained glass room.

Charlie started to struggle, but was no match for the man who bodily lifted her off her feet and took her to the end of the room behind one of the false walls holding three of the stained glass exhibits.

Thibault stopped as soon as he walked into the room.

'What's this?' He stooped and peered at Gilbert. 'What's he doing here? Where did he come from?' He sniffed. 'He's been drinking.'

Albert stepped up to grasp Thibault's elbow.

'I was hoping you wouldn't have to see this,' he muttered, trying to pull him away.

'It's the Minister,' exclaimed Thibault. 'Colonel Gilbert. I . . . I don't understand. He was with Charlie.'

Albert physically pulled Thibault upright, his face inches from Thibault's.

'It's why I'm here. Colonel Gilbert's been under a lot of strain. These riots everywhere, the immigrants.' He gave a knowing nod. 'You know.'

Thibault's throat jerked as he swallowed. 'The Interior Ministry, he was there I heard.'

Albert's mouth turned down.

'You see what I mean. A great strain.' His eyes held Thibault's. 'Not something he would wish talked about.' He paused. 'Not something the President would wish talked about.'

Thibault felt mesmerised. Nodded, fumbling for the handkerchief in his top pocket, wiping it across his brow.

'Yes, I understand. But . . .'

'I brought my chauffeur.'

Thibault jumped as the man quietly emerged, the light from the hall playing on his flat facial features.

'But how did you . . .'

'Never mind that. I think we should get the Minister out of here, don't you?' Albert's forefinger moved momentarily. The man

stepped forward. Hefted Gilbert over his shoulder. Albert patted
Thibault's arm. 'There. No harm done. He'll soon sleep it off. I
hope you'll forgive me if I don't stay. But if you'll show me the
back way out . . .'

'Yes, yes, of course. A disturbing business, but,' he looked slyly
at Albert, 'not something we're unfamiliar with, eh?'

They turned and followed the chauffeur. Thibault discreetly
keeping his eyes averted from the swinging shape of Gilbert lolling
across the broad shoulder.

Charlie heard them go. Terrified, she slammed herself forward
towards the black panel. The man holding her was expecting it.
Gripping her mouth, he swung his other fist into the pit of her
stomach. With a cough, she slumped forward. The man shoved a
foot forward to steady himself, caught it in her high heeled sling-
backs, tripped and crashed through the panel.

'What's that?' Thibault shouted, turning and running back into
the darkness.

'Charlie,' he gasped, 'what . . .' He saw the man. 'What the
hell . . .'

The man dropped Charlie, crunched over the panel and
stretched his arms out.

'No.' Albert's voice whipped out, echoing down the hall.

Thibault's eyes flickered white in the sparks from the broken
wiring in the panel.

'This is terrible . . . I can't think . . . Charlie . . . Charlie?' He bent
towards her. 'She's dead.' His voice cracked. 'She's dead.'

Albert pushed the man to one side, felt her pulse. 'She's nothing
of the sort,' he said, matter of factly. He looked at the man.

'You, you bloody fool, stop those damn wires arcing.' He stood
up, ran a hand through his hair. 'I don't think I can apologise, Mr
Thibault. I can only ask for your indulgence.'

Thibault stayed bent over the panel, stretching his hands to
touch the stained glass, gently feeling it as though searching for
broken bones in a child.

'It's not damaged,' he breathed, 'it's not damaged.' Slowly he
got to his feet, then his whole body started to tremble with rage,
his cheeks suffused in the red light thrown by the scarlet glass robe
of St Peter in the window beside him.

'There is no apology you can find for this. It is sacrilege. You will leave here immediately.'

Albert moved towards Charlie. Thibault put up a hand. 'Without M'mselle Dedain. Charlie stays here until she explains herself to me personally.' He turned to the man. 'Get out. Now.'

The man started to slink away.

'Stay there,' Albert ordered.

'I'm adamant, Monsieur Albert,' Thibault shouted.

'Then I shall speak to the Minister of Culture,' Albert said, evenly. 'I'm sure another Curator can be found quickly enough to secure Charlie's exhibition.'

Thibault was silent.

Albert pressed his advantage.

'Look, Thibault, if you can't see what's been going on I can't help you.'

Thibault blinked nervously.

'I'm only interested in this,' he waved his hand around the room, 'the Museum. That's all,' he muttered. 'Charlie must explain.'

'She and Colonel Gilbert had a row,' Albert said crisply. 'He can be violent. Particularly when he's been drinking. She phoned me, begging me to come. I sent my chauffeur and bodyguard here straight away.'

Thibault clasped his hands together. 'But why didn't she come to me? I was in my office.'

'And cause a scandal? Why do you think I didn't tell you?'

Thibault's nose twitched.

'You're right. She'd better leave.' He looked at her. 'Tell her not to bring her friends here in future. Disgraceful. Disgraceful behaviour.'

Albert raised a finger at the man. 'Gently now.'

The man picked her up, joined the chauffeur in the hall, waiting patiently with Gilbert, still motionless over his shoulder.

Following Thibault, they made their way through the side passageways to the side door. The chauffeur went to get the car.

'Are you sure we shouldn't get a doctor,' said Thibault after a while.

'He's dead drunk,' snorted Albert. 'What good's a doctor for him?'

'But Charlie, she's still unconscious.' Thibault bent over her, lying still in the man's arms.

'No marks on her,' observed Albert, 'she's just fainted. Much better to get her home.'

The chauffeur re-appeared.

'Take them home,' Albert said. 'I'll get a cab.'

The men put Gilbert and Charlie in the back of the Citroen and started to get in themselves.

'Not you,' Albert pointed to his bodyguard. 'You stay with me.' He leaned through the driver's window. 'You know what to do?'

The chauffeur nodded, moved the shift and glided away over the cobbles.

'Now, if you feel up to it, Mr Thibault, we'll talk about the costs of Charlie's exhibition.' Albert smiled as he put a hand on Thibault's shoulder. 'And the repairs to the stained glass, of course.'

Thibault shook his head.

'There are no words to express your kindness, Monsieur Albert. Charlie is a lucky girl indeed to have such a stepfather.'

CHAPTER FORTY-SEVEN

The train rumbled over another set of points, jerking Romin's head to hit the side of the wagon yet again. He didn't swear. He'd sworn the first dozen times it had happened, but he'd soon become used to it. He hadn't got used to the stink of the fertilizer in the paper bags that were stacked around his hideout though. He'd managed to get the door open during the long nights as the train rumbled and whined its way through the desolate miles of scrub and woodland mixed with pasture and grain fields, the noise altering to a hollow clacking as they crossed the iron bridges spanning rivers and streams, but it had made little difference. The smell had seeped through his clothes, through his skin and into his bones.

So far there had been no real trouble. The Kazakh Government documents had magicked the weapons through Astrakhan, Makhachkala and Baku, although the Customs man in Baku had wanted to inspect the crates. Probably because it was a port town and there were more opportunities for sweeteners. A hundred US dollars had sent him on his way. Cheap at the price, but three months' cost of living for him.

Romin had made a mental note for Moosar to have a permanent contact there.

His mobile trembled in his pocket. He pressed it to his ear trying to hear over the racket as the wagon wheels clattered and juddered their way along the rails.

'Where are you?' He just heard Tansu's voice.

'Speak louder. We're coming up to Kirovakan, the Turkish border,' he shouted.

'Are you spread out?'

'I've got the men in the last, middle and front wagons where the weapons are.'

'Any trouble?'

Romin didn't think the man in Baku was worth mentioning.

'No.'

'Tell me when you've reached Kutahya.'

Kutahya was about a hundred and twenty kilometres from Balikesir.

'Yes.' He looked at his watch. 'We're eighty minutes behind schedule.'

'That's OK. We've got four of our men driving the train from Erzurum. They'll catch up.'

'I hope they do. Otherwise it's going to be very tight.'

But she had already switched off.

Sighing, he shook out a Lucky Strike. It was the only comfort he had in this foul, suffocating job.

CHAPTER FORTY-EIGHT

The Citroen screeched to a halt, tipping Charlie and Gilbert to the floor. The chauffeur started to mouth off at the idiot who'd hurtled his scooter the wrong way out of Rue Serpente, then thought of the two in the back seat. He leaned over, saw the sprawled bodies, put his hand on his door handle to get out. Behind him a car hooted, then another, prompting a cacophony. He hesitated. The man in the car behind moved up, touched the Citroen's fender, made a rude gesture with his finger. The chauffeur swore, replied in kind, shoved the gear into drive and lurched forward, turning the volume of the radio up.

Charlie felt the pain in her ankle as it caught under the passenger seat. She opened her eyes, felt a wave of pain surge through her stomach, tried to draw her legs up to ease it. She wondered where she was. Confused by the sound of traffic and the darkness in the well between the seats.

With a start she remembered. Could almost feel that fist thudding into her, see the cruelty of Albert's expression as he spoke to her. Then the car moved sharply to the right and she felt a weight drop onto her shoulder. Sliding herself from under it she managed to turn and saw Gilbert, his mouth hanging slackly open, a sliver of spittle running from it. Her whole body tensed as the image burned its meaning into her. Gilbert and she, bundled like cattle into the bottom of the car. It could only mean one thing.

Cautiously she looked up, almost crying out as the movement stretched her stomach, bringing back a knifing pain. For a moment all she could see were the upper stories of tall windowed, iron balconied, brown buildings, dusk beginning to hide them. She could have been anywhere in Paris. Gritting her teeth, she leant on Gilbert's shoulder and raised her head a little further. She saw then that the car was on the Boulevard Saint Michel going north towards the Seine. Going very slowly as the evening rush hour snarled up the main central artery across the river.

Without thinking, she pulled on the door handle, ready to push herself out. It was locked.

Beads of sweat burst out of her face as another bout of pain gripped her. Gasping, she slid back over Gilbert's body.

Gilbert. The thought cut into her mind. What he'd told her, about Albert, her mother. She wrapped her arms around herself, trying to dull the pain in her chest, knowing there was something else he'd said. Something about Albert ... She remembered then, remembered the PKK, the attack on Greece.

North, she suddenly thought, the car was going north. It could mean only one thing. They were going to Quai de Gesvres. Gilbert's place. Albert would never send her to her home in Montmartre now or to her mother's house. Not after what he'd seen and said.

She looked at the chauffeur. He had his window down, having a surreptitious smoke. The traffic noise of a Paris rush hour dinned into the car to join the thumping bass of the music coming from the car radio. The buzz of scooters mixed with the blitz of the big motorbikes and rumble of bus engines. All punctuated regularly by bursts of impatient horns and lorry klaxons.

Charlie pinched Gilbert's arm. Nothing happened. She squeezed both thumbs and forefingers through his jacket into his flesh. The stertorous breathing just continued. Desperate, she looked around for something sharp to jab into him, to wake him. She had to wake him. The alternative was just minutes away. In his apartment. When ... she stopped. She couldn't think about it. She looked up. The Place des Arts was sliding into view. They'd be on the Pont St Michel in no time. A clear run then to Quai de Gesvres.

She looked at Gilbert, lying there with his mouth stupidly open. Anger started to burn in her. This useless lump had brought her to this. He hadn't the guts to stop Albert and the President, just muttered about honour and France, then left it all to her. In fury she battered his face with her fists, tears of rage splashing down her cheeks.

A tremor ran right through his body. He choked, then threw his head from side to side, his eyes blinking rapidly. She flung her hands over his mouth, shaking her head, the blonde hair whipping across his eyes. She felt his hand grip it, pulling her head back, his eyes wide.

She took her hands away, pulled at his wrist, trying to release her hair. He let go, swallowed, tried to speak. Swiftly she bent over his ear.

'Shut up,' she whispered. 'Listen.'

She looked up again, trying to see the chauffeur. The cigarette smoke curled up towards the upholstered roof, the music from the radio at full blast now. She bent down again.

'We're in Albert's car. Do you understand?'

His eyes focussed. Slowly he nodded.

'Albert heard us talking. His chauffeur's taking us to your place. You know what that means?'

He lifted his chest, trying to get her off. She slid to one side leaving him room to move. He lifted his hand to the door handle. She shook her head.

'I've tried,' she mouthed.

The car juddered as it shifted on to the Pont St Michel, nosing its way past the sombre building of the Prefecture de Police, the deep tinted car windows reflecting the street lights and the gendarmes under them, and denying their casual glances any view inside.

Gilbert beckoned her and she put her ear to his mouth.

'I'm not sure I'm going to be able to help, I'm weak as a kitten. Let me sit up a minute.'

Her heart pounding with despair, she helped prop his back against the door.

Gilbert sat there with his eyes closed, his mouth open, his chest rapidly rising and falling as he forced air into his lungs, tried to clear his aching head.

The car stopped under the traffic lights at the junction with Quai d'Horloge. Opposite waited the Pont au Change over the river and a quick turn into Quai de Gesvres. There was no time left.

Charlie fell back. She could never take on the chauffeur by herself. It was hopeless. Numbly she prepared herself for what was to come, praying it would be quick. She felt her whole body quiver with shock as the car accelerated rapidly across the road to take the bridge.

Gilbert screamed. A blood curdling, heart stopping scream that came from the depths of his lungs.

The chauffeur jerked his head backwards, his foot hitting the accelerator as Gilbert clawed his way up the seat and grabbed the chauffeur's head, bringing his arms together to lock them across his eyes. The Citroen rocketed across the road, smashed into the corner lamp post and ricocheted onto the bridge side kerb. The passenger door sprung open, broken away from the top hinge to throw a line of sparks as it struck the cobbles.

The chauffeur brought up his hands, wrenched Gilbert's fingers from his eyes, brought a hand back to the wheel, dragged it to stop the car's slide to the edge of the bridge.

Wildly spinning, the Citroen jumped the opposite kerb, whipping the wheels up and into the bridge buttress, hurling lumps of stone outwards to arc into the water below.

'Get out,' yelled Gilbert. 'Get out, Charlie. Get to Hammond.'

Terrified, she looked at him, the wild eyes, the manic frenzy of his face.

'What about you?' she yelled back.

'Get out,' he screamed.

She moved then. Flung herself over the passenger seat, fought the chauffeur's hand as it reached for her, bending the fingers back in frantic panic.

The car shifted sideways, shoving more stone from the buttress, the front wheel already plunging towards the water.

The chauffeur grabbed Charlie and hauled himself towards the open door.

'It's going,' he shouted.

Gilbert made one last effort, pushing on his legs, he brought his body over the seat, pinning the chauffeur there, seeing the fear pump into his eyes.

'Get off,' the man yelled. 'It's going. You bastard.' He began twisting and shoving to fling Gilbert off. But Gilbert hung on, his eyes shut tight to summon the last ounce of strength to hold him back so Charlie could get away.

Charlie tried to pull herself towards the space where the passenger door had been, sobbing as her energy waned. She felt the car lurch again as the rear wheels drove it through the gap in the bridge.

The chauffeur screamed as the car tilted into the hole, the water below plainly visible now.

In a final, desperate reflex, Gilbert kicked out, shoving Charlie through the door, and down twenty feet into the swirling depths. Then in a grinding, grating, engine screaming roar the car burst through the last of the stone buttress holding it, toppling, to smash into the dark river, drifting for a moment under the bridge before it sank.

CHAPTER FORTY-NINE

For a moment Hammond couldn't understand the news flash he was watching.

Gilbert and Charlie had died in an horrific rush hour accident when their car had smashed through the Pont au Change and dived into the Seine. The bodies of Gilbert and the chauffeur had been found in the wreck. Divers were searching for Charlie's body, believed to have been swept down river.

His pulse rate rising, he watched the written text repeat the flash. There was no mistake. Charlie was dead.

Shaking, Hammond poured himself a scotch. Charlie dead. It wasn't possible. Only yesterday, was it yesterday? He'd tried to tell her, then couldn't . . . because he wasn't allowed to . . . wouldn't allow himself to. Now he couldn't tell her even if he wanted to. He hadn't expected love, not that depth of love anyway, but now, in the aftermath of that newsflash . . .

He put the glass down, the scotch tasted bitter. Blindly he went to the phone. Dialled Francesca's number.

'Hello.' It was Albert. Hammond wasn't prepared for him.

'I . . . I'm sorry, I wanted Francesca.'

'Mr Hammond,' Albert's voice was expressionless. 'You rang about Charlie I suppose.'

'Yes. I'm . . .' Hammond stopped, trying to control himself.

'We are devastated, Mr Hammond,' that same flat tone. 'Francesca is in her room. Under sedation.'

Hammond couldn't speak.

Albert finally said. 'I'll tell her you rang.'

'Yes. I'm . . . tell her I'm sorry.'

' "Sorry" is not a word I would have used in the circumstances,

Mr Hammond. But then the English are,' he paused, 'understated, are they not?'

The receiver clicked as the connection was terminated.

Hammond flushed as the barb struck home. He stood and stared at the phone. Albert was right. Saying sorry was like a schoolboy trying to escape some minor punishment. He felt a coldness creep over him. The last time he'd seen her, Charlie had offered herself to him, not just a fleeting offer, Charlie wasn't like that, but an offer of a lasting love. He'd flung it back at her. Sorry wasn't the word to excuse that. There was no escape from it. He tried to blank it off, force his mind forwards.

There was also no escape from the fact that the two people most likely to tell him what was going on in the French Government were dead. Now that the French had agreed to the EU Army and the negotiations with the Turks were to begin, that might not matter so much. But having no possibility of seeing into the French mind was daunting.

He shook himself slightly, conscious that his mind had to switch to work. For now, Charlie had to be a number in his calculations, nothing else.

Feeling the shock hit him, he reached for the whisky bottle again. Then stopped. Charlie was gone. She was the past. He had work to do that was the future and the future was all that was left to obliterate the past. He tried to concentrate. He had to talk to Lev and Walt. Try and re group his tactics with the French.

Turning off the television, he operated the switch to open up the G8 communications cabinet.

The doorbell rang. A sudden, harsh sound. He left Rosie to answer it, but then realised she was at the Gare du Nord catching her train to London. He walked to the security screen, resenting the intrusion. By the front door was a figure in a loose raincoat and beret, head down, slightly bent. Typical down and out, beggar. There were hundreds of them in Paris, migrants mostly. He dismissed it, walking back towards the cabinet. But the bell kept ringing, insistent, demanding. He walked impatiently to the security screen, flipped the intercom on. 'Buzz off,' he shouted, flicking it off. He turned back, before spinning round to flick on the screen again. He hadn't been mistaken. Under the beret a lank strand of blonde hair had been jerked loose by the raincoat collar.

'Who are you?' he shouted.

The beret moved backwards and he found himself looking with disbelief into Charlie's face. Both her eyes were black and a dark bruise ran the length of her jaw.

Hammond raced down the stairs, slammed open the door and picked Charlie up in his arms, carrying her inside and shoving the door shut with his foot.

He took her upstairs, anxiously looking at her white face and closed eyes. Laying her gently on the sofa, he went to the table and poured a brandy.

'Drink this,' he didn't trust himself to say more.

The glass rattled against her teeth as she swallowed some of the liquid. Coughing, she opened her eyes and tugged the beret off, her soaking wet hair dropping in long tendrils down her neck and over her ears. He took it and threw it on the floor, helped her out of the coat, feeling her sodden clothing underneath. She tried to speak.

'Don't try and talk. You've got to get out of those clothes,' he rasped. 'Stay there.'

He crossed the room rapidly and went through his bedroom to the shower. Switched it on, testing the heat with one hand. Opening a cupboard he found a towelling dressing gown. Hung it over the bath. Walking back to her, he helped her to her feet, pointing to the bathroom.

'Go in there. Take a hot shower. Call me when you're ready.'

Shivering violently, she nodded and shut the door.

Hammond put his hand on the doorpost to steady himself, letting the giddiness he suddenly felt pass. Then, taking a deep breath, he went into the kitchen and lifted down the box Rosie had marked with the word "Soup". It was divided into two. "English" and "French". With an insane urge to laugh out loud he picked out the only one in the French section. It was a bouillon, dedicated to getting another dose of brandy into Charlie without her knowing it.

CHAPTER FIFTY

The Prime Minister pursed his lips, the gesture magnified by the size of his image on the plasma screen.

'Are you sure, John, that this, er,' he looked down at the notepad in front of him, 'Mademoiselle Dedain is, well, you know, rational. I mean, well, she is an artist.'

Hammond shifted restlessly on his chair in the cramped cabinet.

'She's here if you really want to speak to her, but I wouldn't have called you if I had any doubts. It all ties in. Gilbert's behaviour recently, the French suddenly agreeing to talks with the Turks. I'm certain that what Gilbert told Charlie is true. Once that train gets to Balikesir the weapons on it will be out of our control. We can stop the attack on Limnos. We can warn the Turks but unless we do it right away the PKK will have the arms.' He paused. 'You know what that means.'

The PM gazed out of the screen, focussing on nothing in particular. Hammond waited.

'I'll call the French President right away.' The PM was crisp, back to business. 'And the Turks. They'll put a stop to it.'

'No,' said Hammond sharply. 'Not the French. They'll deny it, contact Albert and the weapons will disappear before they ever reach Balikesir.'

'I just can't believe it, the French President . . .' the PM's voice tailed off, then suddenly strengthened. 'In fact, I won't believe it. It's too fantastic. We've only got the word of some Ionist or whatever, who hates her stepfather. I'm sorry, John, I'm not doing it.'

'If you don't and it's true?'

The PM was silent.

Hammond dropped his eyes.

'Remember the Turkish Ambassador murdered outside the Foreign Office?'

The PM's eyes narrowed.

'You told me the Greeks killed him. To retaliate against the Turks for their attack on Samos. You told me your agent, Abu Hamid, had seen the attack.'

'I was wrong. It wasn't the Greeks at all. It's been the PKK all along. Directed by the French through Albert. Gilbert told Charlie the French want the Greeks to take on Turkey. Drive them from the mainland, secure the border, stop the Turks pushing the Kurds into Greece and on into France.'

The PM shook his head.

'But all they had to do was agree the EU Army. Then we could help the Turks sort out the Kurds, stop the forced migration.'

'But the French didn't want it.' Hammond tapped his fingers on the desktop. 'And for good reason. Gilbert told Charlie the French President wasn't going to give up his control of their nuclear deterrent.'

'I still can't believe it,' the PM muttered.

Hammond knew the PM in this mood. Michael Harris would hide himself in his northern stubbornness, dig his heels in.

'Then let me talk to the Turks as the Director of G8. Warn them that we have intelligence that the PKK are shipping arms to Balikesir.'

The PM ran his fingers across his mouth.

'I won't tell them about the French,' Hammond said quickly, 'or Albert.'

'There'll be no comeback on me if the whole story turns out to be rubbish?'

'No.' Hammond looked at his watch. 'Look I'll take the responsibility. Whatever. But we're losing time. If I'm right, you can talk to the French afterwards. If not . . .'

'If you're right I won't just be talking to them, rest assured of that,' the PM cut in.

'So I can go ahead?'

The PM picked up a black Parker pen, ran it through his fingers several times.

'Yes.'

He dropped the pen into the silver inkwell on the edge of his desk.

'And I'll pray you're wrong.'

*

Walt needed no persuading.

'Hell'n'tarnation those damn Frenchies, they haven't changed since Iraq. Why you Brits didn't sort them out years ago I'll never know. If you don't tell 'em, I will.'

Lev brushed some ash from his sleeve. 'But John's right. If the French are told, they will make sure Albert warns the PKK. We'll lose the weapons.'

Walt's nose expanded. 'You can be sure my President will take out the French the minute the weapons are detained.'

Hammond shook his head.

'We've got a problem.'

Lev laughed, smoke venting to hide his face in a wreathing cloud.

'You kill me, John. We have the biggest crisis since Al Quaida and you call it a problem.'

Hammond's mouth twitched.

'The Turks don't want to take out the train.'

'What?' Walt exploded.

'They say that if the PKK see them out in force along the rail line to Balikesir, they'll offload the weapons and abandon the attack on Limnos. Live to fight another day.'

Julia broke the silence. 'We've analysed it. They're right. The Turks can't possibly guard hundreds of miles of track. If the PKK sense any danger, they'll hide the weapons.'

Hammond's plasma screen suddenly hummed in the silence. He tapped it with his hand.

'Must get this fixed,' he muttered.

Walt grinned. 'If the PKK get those weapons you won't have to bother, you're top of their target list.'

'Thanks, Walt,' Hammond said dryly.

'You want Byelov, don't you?' Lev's voice sounded loud.

'He can do it,' Julia cut in quickly. 'Maxim is the only Team Leader who can get to Turkey in time.'

Lev looked at Julia over his cigarette, the craggy face lined in scepticism.

'Just how can Maxim do it, as you say, Julia? How can he possibly get enough men there in time? We don't even know what train to target.'

'It left Guryev in Kazakhstan three days ago,' Julia answered.

Lev squinted at her. 'How do you know?'

'Maxim told me.'

'You've already spoken to him?' Lev said sharply.

She didn't reply, her brown eyes squaring up to his on the screen.

'And I suppose Maxim has also told you how he'll get a hundred warriors and their weapons to attack this train within the next ten hours?'

'No. Just six.'

'Six,' Walt ejaculated. 'You haven't approved this, John, have you?'

'Not before you and Lev have approved it,' Hammond replied quietly.

'Which means you have darn well approved it,' Walt muttered.

Lev kept his eyes on Julia.

'Tell me,' he said, almost inaudibly.

'The team's got to be small,' she began, 'the Turks are right. Any movement of a large body of men is bound to be sussed by the PKK. A small team can take them by surprise. The same as we did on the Antonov attack.'

'And rescuing Hamid?' Walt rasped.

Julia flinched.

Hammond's face darkened. 'That was . . .'

'No, John. I can handle this.' Julia flicked her hair back. 'Hamid's not relevant. We sent Gunter to meet him. We had no idea he had been captured, so there was no operation mounted to rescue him.'

'She's right, Walt,' said Lev, stubbing out his cigarette.

Walt nodded slowly. 'Sorry, Julia, I must be getting sour in my old age.'

'It's good to be full of vinegar,' she smiled.

They laughed.

Lev pointed a yellow stained finger at her. 'What if the PKK have more men than the Team? Can't be contained?'

'The Team will follow operation annihilation procedures.'

Walt frowned. 'You can't use gas on a train. It'll disperse.'

She shook her head, blinking as a strand of hair caught her eye.

'West of Kutahya there's a three hundred meter bridge over the river. The trains normally run at sixty kph at that point. The bridge is high enough that if it is blown under the lead diesels, the wagons will follow them into the water. The Team will eliminate any survivors who surface.'

Walt's eyes flickered. 'That includes civilians, non PKK?'

She nodded. 'The risk of our Team being liquidated and the PKK retrieving the arms demands it.'

'And if all the wagons don't fall into the river?' Lev blew out more smoke.

'A two man LGR Team will incinerate them.'

'Can you transport enough laser guided rockets for that purpose?' Walt asked.

'Each member of the Team can take two, plus their other weapons and ammunition.'

Hammond's plasma screen hummed again in the silence.

'And your risk assessment of this operation?' murmured Lev.

She stared at him. 'High, the highest.'

Walt rubbed the side of his nose with his finger. 'Maxim should have more men.'

Lev looked at Hammond, raised his eyebrows questioningly.

Hammond sat very still.

'Julia's explained the balance of risk. More men equals the PKK discovering our intentions, less men equals our operation failing. As Walt said earlier, I've made my decision. Now I want to hear yours.'

The plasma screen hummed on.

'Maxim's for this?' Lev asked quietly.

Julia answered him with her eyes.

'Thank you, Julia,' said Walt. 'You're right. It's the only way to go.' He looked at Lev. 'I'm only sorry it has to be Maxim.'

'He's not dead yet,' said Lev 'He'll survive,' Julia said harshly. She looked at Hammond. 'Which is more than can be said for Charlie if Albert finds out she's alive.'

CHAPTER FIFTY-ONE

Standing by the track at the Kutahya rail sidings, Romin stretched as he watched the diesel drone its way up the line, leaving a single diesel in front of the red signal getting ready to haul the remaining wagons from Kutahya to Balikesir. Only twenty two wagons were left silently linked together, the others having been decoupled and dropped off by sweating, swearing railyard workers at various sidings as they reached their destinations on the long, slow, mind numbing, journey from Guryev.

Romin started as a drop of rain fell on his head. He looked up. The dark clouds he'd seen on the horizon as they drew into Kutahya were now boiling in towards him, flashing momentarily as beads of lightning split through them. He looked at his watch, ducked into the fertiliser wagon, coughing as his lungs took in the stench. Taking out his mobile, he speed dialled Tansu's number. There was no reply. Cursing, he shoved the mobile back in his shirt pocket. There was a three hour wait in Kutahya and it was going to be a very long one with no one to talk to. He couldn't speak to the men in the other wagons, the contact might be intercepted and look suspicious. There was no need for an innocent conversation to be held on a mobile link on a freight train with only two passenger carriages. He would only contact the men in an emergency.

The mobile vibrated in his pocket. It was a text message. Shielding the window with his hand, he scrolled it through, tensing as he saw it was in code. He searched through his memory, piecing the letters and numbers together. His teeth snapped together as he learnt there had been trouble in Paris, then his jaw relaxed as he grasped that there was no indication that the weapons movement had been compromised. Finally, he smiled as Tansu's message decoded the welcome news that as a precaution he would be joined by ten more fighters at eleven that night when the train would stop at the river bridge west of Kutahya. The drivers had already been told.

CHAPTER FIFTY-TWO

The rain was horizontal, sprayed against the bridge by the wind as if it had been driven out of a hosepipe. Maxim Byelov hung horizontally onto a girder with both hands and feet. He shook his head, drops flying out of his cap like a shower from a dog after a swim. He let go the iron girder with one hand and started to place the explosive in the joint where an upright reached skywards. A heavy gust hit his body, swinging it away from the girder. He slapped his hand back, gripping the iron, feeling the jerk on his body as the explosive fell and tugged on its safety line.

He ran his teeth over his lower lip, wondered how the other three were getting on. They'd been out on the bridge for forty minutes fighting the rain and howling wind, scrabbling for handholds on the slippery paint chipped iron, trying to place the explosives in the vulnerable joints. He envied the LGR team, hidden in a rock outcrop just above the rail signal mast two hundred meters up track. They might not be able to smoke a cigarette, how he ached for one, but they'd be comfortable up there, sheltered.

Drawing in a deep breath through his nose, he carefully hauled up the explosive, tightening the grip on his knees against the sharp ridge of the girder, clamping himself there against the wind. The explosives slid into place and he switched on the electromagnet to hold it there. He snatched his hand away and clutched the girder again, almost sighing with relief as the pain in his knees subsided. He hung on for a few more seconds, swinging with the wind, licking the rain from his lips and swallowing it.

Dreading to move, but knowing he had no choice, he stretched his hands along the iron ridge. Hand over hand, knee alongside knee, foot past foot, he inched backwards, blinking, eyelids squeezing the rain away so he could see. There was no way a PKK terrorist could do this, he thought. They could never have the training, day after day, month after month, until the pain merged with the pain of exhaustion and beyond, into a limbo where the nerve ends took over and drove the body on, far beyond the limits of normal comprehension. Maxim smiled to himself, he hadn't even got to the point of exhaustion yet.

It was the smile that did it. The fractional loss of concentration just as a violent gust slammed off the central pillar and hit Maxim from the opposite direction. He fell without a sound. The wind twisting his body like a leaf.

He gasped as his safety harness jerked tight on the line attached to the girder. A shadow loomed up and his teeth bit into his lip as his shoulder hit the central pillar, spinning him off, to slam into it again as the wind tossed him around. He tried to grip a stanchion but yelped as his fingers buckled against the concrete. He felt himself twisting again, peered into the dark to prepare himself for the next contact, drawing his legs up to take the impact with his feet.

It came with a sudden rush, jarring pain all the way up his legs into the base of his back. The pillar sweeping by with no hope of grasping it. He knew then that he couldn't avoid being smashed into that pillar every time his body made another wild swing. It was only a question of time before he was killed or battered into unconsciousness.

The face of his trainer flashed into his mind, solid, calm, never a shout. "You're not done, 'til you're done", he'd say. Over and over and over again.

Three meters. That was the length of the safety line. Three meters. Nine short hauls to the top on a good day.

Maxim waited until his body smashed into the pillar again. Then put a hand up the line. Hauled. His gloved hand slid down then held. He put his other hand up. Hauled. Slid down. Held.

The pain from his hip lanced through him as it drove into one of the bolts embedded in the pillar. He felt his body jerk again as it fell back onto the end of the safety line.

Gasping for breath he put a hand up the line. Hauled. Then again. Hauled. Felt the wind tug at him again. Brought his knees up to his chest into a ball. Coughed as his back and lungs took the impact, hanging on, clawing for breath. Pushed his arm up, gripped the line. Felt his muscles burn as he hauled. Spun as he whipped towards the pillar again. Shutting his eyes tight to take the hit, to try and lessen the pain. But it didn't come. The line was too short now. Drenched with sweat he hauled again. But nothing happened. His whole arm felt on fire. The muscles wouldn't respond. He couldn't go higher.

He hung there, the fire crisping into him as he kept his hands locked onto the line. Blood trickled down his chin as his lip slid under his teeth. The wind snatched at him again, drawing the fire into his chest and stomach, all consuming, drenching him in sweat, snatching away his oxygen, drumming his brain.

As he entered into the black zone where consciousness starts to drift, he hauled once more. Nothing happened. He flung another contraction into his muscles. His elbow shifted upwards. Suddenly the burn left him. Leaving him bathed in cold sweat. His arms slowly, mechanically, winching himself up. Until he felt the ridge of the girder, clamped his hands then his feet onto its length.

He clung there, his breath coming in great rasps. His old trainer had been right, he thought.

It took a strong mental effort to take his hand off the girder and reach for the explosive. To do it he squeezed his eyes shut and blotted out the sounds of the wind, moving as soon as the noise was blanked off. It came back immediately, but by then he was committed. The job was easy after that.

Sliding over the girder onto the rail track he walked across the other side of the bridge to see how the others were getting on. They only had one charge each and were waiting for him, huddled by an upright, sheltering.

'You place it, OK?' he asked.

They nodded. 'Wind was a bit nasty,' said one. 'I dropped my charge twice before I could fix it.'

'Yeah, me too, once,' said another. 'Bloody awful night.'

'Ready to move?' said Maxim.

They nodded again.

Maxim took in a deep breath and started to walk down the track towards the riverbank. When he reached it he pointed at two of the men to stay either side of the bridge. They bent down, swiftly disappearing into the rain, as they dropped into their positions. Maxim walked on another hundred meters before pointing the other man to a faintly rising piece of ground with the outline of bushes growing in it. Maxim walked away in the opposite direction, climbing up the opposite bank before dropping behind the large rock halfway up.

He picked up the small laptop he'd left there an hour earlier, switched on, his face an eerie green in the dull glow.

On screen was the picture of a train. Below, words were scrolling like teletext. Maxim read for a moment.

G8SUR had been locked onto the train, telling him that it had left Kutahya and was twelve minutes from the bridge. G8SUR told him that the rear wagon held one unidentified man and the four central wagons held another seven. Two drivers were in charge of the diesel. G8SUR also told him that there were two passenger carriages just behind the diesel. There were fourteen passengers.

Maxim studied the shadows of the unidentified men in the rear and central wagons. These were PKK. He was certain of it. The men in the central wagons weren't relevant. They would certainly go into the river with the wagons when the bridge blew. It was the man in the rear wagon who Maxim concentrated on. He might survive if the last wagon didn't roll on over the smashed bridge into the water. It could be useful if he was captured.

He typed out a rapid command to the LGR team to hold their fire until his order and warned the man opposite him what he intended.

Maxim didn't pay any attention to the passenger wagons. They were as irrelevant as the central wagons.

He took out the radio control device. Switched to test. Grunted as the blue confirmation light flicked on.

Satisfied, he sat back to wait, watching the green signal light by the rails flicker as sheets of rain partially obscured it.

His cooling body brought back the pain in his legs and arms and his mind went back to the bridge. Some people would have said he'd been lucky. But Maxim knew he hadn't. He'd struggled and cursed and shouted on his training courses. And he'd cursed his trainer the most, seeing no reason why the bastard pushed him so hard, gave him no respite, kicked him on when he had nothing left to give.

Now he knew. Without him he would still be out there, at the end of the safety line, dead or near it and, worst of all, jeopardising the operation.

He'd learnt there was another chance beyond the agonising burn, fleeting, but there to be taken. He'd taken it. And he had only his trainer to thank.

He lifted his head as he heard the faint echo of a train klaxon. Picking up his night vision binoculars, he looked up the track. A mile away the track wound round a rock outcrop, blocking his view. Faintly, above the noise of the wind, he caught the sound of a diesel. It faded then came back then disappeared as the klaxon sounded again.

Maxim picked up the night glasses again. This time he saw a beam of light, hazed by sheets of rain. It was quickly followed by the train as it emerged from behind the rock outcrop, the twin rails gleaming intermittently as the light lurched from side to side casting its beam onto them in a disorderly pattern. Maxim dropped the glasses, quickly picked out the beam, much smaller without the magnification. The noise of the diesel was louder now, driving the train on towards the bridge.

He took hold of the remote control detonator. He had to concentrate. Detonation at the right second was vital if those four central wagons were going into the river.

But something wasn't right. He lifted his head, like a dog sniffing the wind, searching for an explanation.

It was the noise of the diesel. It wasn't pulling any more. The engine was shutting down, slowing the train. He snatched up the glasses. He was right, the train was moving much slower. If it slowed any more, the central wagons might not get to the break in the bridge. There'd be no opportunity to take a prisoner now. He dropped the glasses. Out of the corner of his eye he saw the signal change to red, the colour carried clearly through the slackening rain. He heard the hiss of brakes as the diesel started to obey its command. It was too late now, the diesel wouldn't reach the bridge.

'Get to the diesel cab,' he shouted into his microphone. 'LGR stay where you are. Hold your fire.'

Maxim stood up and started down the slope. From the signal mast, in a hundred tiny flashes, a line of AK47s opened up on the man he'd posted opposite him. Maxim was stunned. The fire came from the ground. The train hadn't reached the signal mast yet. There were others out there, other PKK. Diving flat, he put his hand on his microphone.

'LGR. Take out Red by the signal mast. Red by the signal mast.'

He didn't wait to see the reaction. Shoving his hands forward, scrabbling through the long grass, small rocks and bushy scrub, he bellied his way down the slope. He hardly heard the dull crack followed by another. But he saw the flashes, lighting up the rain like search lights on a raid. The screams were lost as another two rockets smashed into the men by the signal mast.

Rodin didn't wait for the train to stop. He slammed open the wagon door and jumped out, hitting the ballast shingle in a rolling, sprawling, slide. In the fading moment of the last explosion he saw someone jump up from the side of the track and race towards the diesel. Gripping his AK47 he started to run towards the front of the train.

Maxim was running in a zigzag towards the diesel when the AK47 opened up. He heard the thump of the bullets as they went to one side. Diving to the ground, he rolled and fired the Glock. Without waiting, he jumped to his feet and ran five paces before diving down again. This time the AK47 fired wide to his left. The diesel was twenty paces away, the engine rumbling in neutral as it sat stalled at the signal.

Maxim spoke into his mike.

'Bridge, join me.'

The two men at the bridge broke cover, ran, crouched, towards him. To his right he heard the crash of wagon doors and watched as the seven men leapt out of the central wagons, their weapons flashing as they fired wildly up the line.

'Cover me. I'm going for the diesel.'

Behind him the Glocks opened up in short bursts. The men firing, diving for cover, firing as they slithered and dodged their way towards him. The PKK fire began to edge away up the embankment as the men drew it away from Maxim.

Judging his moment, he broke cover, crawled across the rail track and gripped the lower rung of the ladder leading to the diesel's door. Pulling himself up, he jerked the door open and thrust the Glock inside. The drivers' arms pumped upwards, their faces white in the reflected panel lights.

'Back up,' Maxim shouted in Turkish. The men didn't move.

'Back up,' he yelled in Kurdish.

The men looked at each other. Maxim daren't fire. He needed all the time he could get without being discovered. He drove his Glock into the nearest driver's teeth, blood spewing out of his mouth as he collapsed onto the panel.

'Now,' Maxim shouted.

The driver reached forward, pulled the gear lever, pushed the throttle. The engine screamed as it took the weight, started to shift the wagons backwards. A man's face appeared at the driver's window. Maxim shot it.

'Faster,' he yelled.

The diesel was yammering. Straining to gain momentum. Suddenly, through the rain, the noise of the explosion ripping into the cab. The diesel shuddered, then juddered to a halt. One of the men from the bridge crawled up the door ladder.

'LGR took out the last wagon. She won't move back.'

'Stay there,' shouted Maxim. He turned to the driver.

'You. Forward.'

The driver slammed the gear. Pushed gently on the throttle. Maxim grabbed his hand, thrust it right forward.

The engine screamed, driving the wheels to skid on the soaking rails.

The driver tried to pull the throttle back. 'It won't ... it won't ...'

Maxim slammed him against the window, gripping his hand even harder.

An AK47 broke out on the right, the bullets clanging on the diesel's metalwork. The man from the bridge grunted, fired with his Glock, fell forward and out, to scream briefly as the wheels cut over his body.

The diesel started to move, the wheels gripping the rails, driving the huge weight forwards, smoke belching from the exhausts. A line of stars burst on the armoured windscreen. Maxim ducked, firing out of the door towards the winking flashes. Two more stuttering flashes appeared. The bullets whining off the front of the cab. Maxim dropped to his knees, his hand still on the throttle.

A blinding flash lit up the cab. The last rocket laying the ground on the right to waste, leaving the rails glittering in the light, free to the bridge.

The diesel was moving faster now. More than walking pace. The bridge less than a hundred meters away.

Rodin knew what was going to happen. Desperate, he ran alongside the wagons, overtaking one after the other, his breath coming in sobbing gasps as he flung himself on towards the diesel. They were going to blow the bridge, he knew they were going to blow the bridge. The attack was too precise, too expert, to be the Turks. It had to be G8. He was cold with fear as he pounded on. He had to save the weapons. He had to get to the cab. His heart felt as if it would burst as he lunged for the ladder to the cab, his arm almost torn from its socket as the diesel's momentum dragged him off his feet.

Swinging both legs, he gained the bottom step, unhooked the pistol from his belt and fired up into the cab.

Maxim felt the tug of the bullets as they scorched his jacket on their way into the roof.

He swung the Glock and fired. The pin clicked. He watched as Rodin's face came over the footplate, his hand levelling the pistol.

Maxim kicked out, felt the bullet sear through his calf, before he threw himself on to Rodin's head, his hand scrabbling to hold the pistol. Rodin snatched his hand to one side, pressed the muzzle against Maxim's head. Pulled the trigger. The report smashed into Maxim's ear as the bullet ploughed down his cheek to ricochet. Spinning into Rodin's eye. Screaming, Rodin let go, screaming again as the wheels severed his legs.

The driver slammed on the brakes, the diesel's wheels shrieking as they sparked along the rails.

Maxim knelt on all fours, blood pouring down his cheek, a wave of darkness sweeping over him, choking the breath out of him. Dimly he felt the diesel slow, summoned up the depths his trainer had told him would be there, hauled himself up, ripped the throttle forward.

'No you don't, you bastard.' He gasped.

The wheels rumbled hollowly onto the bridge. He waited as the first span went by, then the second.

'You can stop now,' he said calmly.

Pulling out the remote control, he pressed the switch. His legs collapsed and he crumpled down, to sit with his back against the cab wall.

The explosions were quite small. Simply removing the critical sites which held up the first two spans of the bridge. The central wagons carrying the weapons neatly fell, together with the span they were on, to hit the water flat, throwing up a spume of spray which rattled on the rest of the bridge, before sinking rapidly to the bottom of the water.

The diesel, with the two passenger carriages, lurched alarmingly off the rails but didn't follow.

Maxim gestured to the driver. 'Had enough excitement for one day?' he asked.

CHAPTER FIFTY-THREE

Charlie got up from the sofa under Wolf Kahn's Magenta Background and pulled the belt tighter around the cotton dress she was wearing.

'No John, I can't stay any longer. I've been here two days.' She looked down at the floral patterns on the fabric and laughed. 'Anyway, just look at this dress, I can't wear it another minute.'

Hammond looked puzzled.

'What's wrong with it?'

She looked amazed.

'What's wrong with it? Green lemons and blue oranges on red and white stripes.'

'Rosie likes bright colours.'

'Yes, well, it was very kind of her to bring it for me but I really do have to go.' She pinched her lips together, then brought her hand up to feel the bruise on her jaw.

'That hurt,' she said ruefully.

'That's the point,' said Hammond, 'you're not ready to go anywhere yet. And when you do, it'll have to be arranged very carefully. We can't risk it getting out that you're alive. You know that and I intend to keep you safe Charlie, I'm not going through all this again.'

She looked away. Picked up a copy of Le Monde from the coffee table and tapped the front page with her finger.

'You got the train, destroyed the weapons. I'm safe now.'

He took the newspaper from her, tossed it back on the table.

'But we haven't got Albert, or that woman Tansu. You'll be safe only as long as they think you're dead. While you're here they can't find out, and I can protect you.'

Her eyes widened, the pale green irises clearly visible.

'But I can't stay here indefinitely. It's ridiculous. I've got to get back to work.'

'We'll get you away, soon, but not yet. You can't go back to work until this business has blown over. Anyway,' he added as an afterthought, 'you're not really suited to the Foreign Ministry.'

Her eyes blazed.

'Just because some people are corrupt, not all of us are.'

'Come on, Charlie, you know that's not what I meant. Ever since I've known you, you've been out of your depth in the Ministry. You're special, creative, you're an artist, not a diplomat. Why not admit it?'

'You two aren't arguing again?' Rosie put a tray with a coffee pot and cups on top of the copy of Le Monde.

'Rosie,' exclaimed Charlie. 'I wish you wouldn't creep in like that.' She paused. 'How long have you been listening?'

'Long enough to know you don't like my choice of dress for you, Miss,' Rosie said grimly. 'I got that special from Alf Green's.'

Hammond looked at Charlie mischievously.

'That explains it.'

Rosie sniffed. 'I'll not have you making fun of Alf Green, Mr Hammond. My old man bought all his presents for me from Alf.' She wiped her hands on her bright green and yellow squared apron. 'And what my old man thought was good enough for me is good enough for any Frenchy.' She peered at Charlie. 'Not but what I think of you as a Frenchy, Miss, for you ain't,' she said confusingly. 'Not in my mind anyways.'

Charlie laughed.

'Thank you, Rosie. I take that as a compliment. But I didn't mean to offend you when you've been so kind.'

'That's all right dearie, I know you haven't been yourself.'

'Can you tell Charlie she needs to stay here,' demanded Hammond impatiently.

'Telling her she's no good at her job is no way to persuade her, Mr Hammond.'

'Well said, Rosie.' Charlie smiled. 'There is no reason to stay here.'

There was a slight pause. The distant roar of the Paris traffic drifted through the open window. Someone shouted on the balcony opposite.

Rosie picked up the coffee pot and began pouring it.

'That's not what I meant,' she said mysteriously.

'Well, what do you mean,' asked Hammond, beginning to sound irritated.

Rosie stirred some sugar into Hammond's cup and gave it to him.

'Do what my old man did for me.'

A frown creased Hammond's face.

'I didn't know he'd put you in a safe house when he was operational.'

'Ooh Mr Hammond,' said Rosie exasperated. 'You're so slow sometimes I wonder you can do your job. Marry Charlie. That's what my old man did for me.'

There was a dead silence. A maze of emotions wrote themselves across Hammond's face. Suddenly he laughed.

'You're right, Rosie. You're a treasure. Of course.' He turned to Charlie. 'Will you marry me?'

Charlie reddened, looked at Rosie, saw her smile and nod.

'How typical,' she fumed. 'You can't even propose by yourself. You are . . . you are . . .' She looked into his laughing eyes. 'Oh of course I will.'

'There you are Mr Hammond,' said Rosie as she walked round their embrace and headed for the door. 'That wasn't so difficult, was it?'

CHAPTER FIFTY-FOUR

'I am outraged by such an allegation.' The French President's eyes bulged, his face and neck bright red, straining at his collar.

'I didn't come here to Paris to exchange diplomatic pleasantries, Mr President,' the PM's Manchester accent was very broad, 'I came to tell you I know what you're at . . . what you've been doing,' he corrected.

'G8 seize a train load of PKK weapons and you tell me that I . . . I, the President of France . . . conspired to sell them to these terrorists. It's preposterous. What evidence do you have?'

The PM leaned across the President's desk, his mouth a tight line, his finger jabbing on the inlaid marquetry.

'I'm not telling you my source. If I had evidence I could publish, I'd be in New York now, in the UN Security Council, slinging you off it, and not before time.' He sat back. 'No. I don't need evidence. I've caught you trading with terrorists and you know it.'

The President stood up.

'This meeting is at an end. I shall tolerate it no longer.'

The Prime Minister looked up at him.

'When the Turks capture Albert, do you think they'll sit around drinking coffee and asking him polite questions?'

The President took his hand away from the intercom buzzer.

'Albert? He is a banker, not a terrorist. You are absurd.'

'Is that what Albert'll tell them when they clip the electrodes onto him?'

A trickle of sweat dribbled past the President's left ear.

The PM folded his hands in his lap.

'Of course, you can try and find Albert first. But there's no guarantee of that. The only guarantee you have is that as soon as I leave here I shall travel to Ankara, speak to the Turkish Prime Minister.'

The President blinked.

'You mean you haven't spoken to the Turks?'

'Not about Albert's and your involvement, no.'

'I wasn't involved.'

'Of course you weren't.' The PM waited a few seconds. 'But you believe Albert may have been?'

The President slowly sat down, opened a bottle of orange juice, rattled it against a glass as he poured out the contents.

'Albert is a man of many parts, access to vast wealth. No President can safeguard against members of his Government, civil service, being corrupted.'

The PM smiled. 'The attack on Greenpeace in New Zealand for instance?'

The President shot him a look of loathing.

'If, by some chance, Albert arranged for these weapons to be shipped through French Government intervention, I shall personally see to it that the persons involved receive the maximum punishment.'

'Quite,' said the PM.

The President sipped his juice in silence.

'There is more?' he said eventually.

The PM coughed.

'Yes. When I see the Turkish President, I shall not refer to this conversation but to the fact that you entirely agree with the establishment of the EU Army and you welcome the Turkish partnership. As a sign of your good faith, you have offered to fund forty percent of the running costs.'

'But . . .'

'There are no buts.'

The President gripped the edge of his desk.

'Very well.' He leaned sideways to flick the intercom.

'I haven't finished yet,' the PM said crisply.

The President's head seemed to sink into his shoulders.

'I might find it a better alternative to let the Turks find Albert.'

The PM's face remained blank.

'You will freeze all Albert's assets in Paris and Mauritius. Deny him access.'

The President sat up straight.

'On what grounds?'

'You'll find some,' the PM grated.

'But I can't tell Mauritius what to do.'

'The French have been telling Mauritius what to do for centuries.' The PM stood up. 'Right, that's my shopping list.'

The President flicked the intercom. 'The Prime Minister is leaving now.'

He leaned back, his eyes slits in a grey face.

'You British, with your pretence of high morals, what have you done to stem the tide of migrants into Europe, into France?'

'Well, at least we don't protect our interests by wasting other people's lives.'

'Meaning?'

But he was talking to the blue panelled door on the far side of his office.

CHAPTER FIFTY-FIVE

Tansu looked bleakly out across the arid plain towards Syria. She had raced back to the house in Mardin as soon as she'd heard that the train had been sabotaged. She could trust the Kurds in Mardin, the home of her bodyguards. She had already received messages from some cell leaders asking her what had happened, demanding instructions, couched in language that was suspicious, wary. She knew the disaster had undermined her authority, threatened to undo all the good the explosion at Diyarbakir had created. And as she stared out of the window, she had no idea how she could claw her way out of the mess.

What made it worse was sporadic news that the Turks were retaliating against the Kurdish population in Kutahya and Eskisehir, the nearest city. There was a news blackout on the media, but she'd had text messages talking of an indiscriminate round up of all Kurds and at least two shooting incidents. The cell leaders had enough weapons to make a bloody protest if she wished but the loss of the weapons in the Antonov and now the train had left her powerless to mount a sustained coup. Isolated protests, with the element of surprise lost, would only result in more casualties and her position being eroded even further.

She swore softly. Whoever betrayed them was dead. She'd find them eventually and she would make sure they took so long to die one video tape would be far too short. And the videos would be flashed across the Internet and circulated in the cafes and bars so everyone would see and know.

She was still clenching her fists when a bodyguard tapped her on the shoulder. She turned. Sulan and Yenev, the cell leaders that were to have attacked Limnos, stood by the long dark cedar wood table that served as her desk next to the bare stone block wall. One of the guards next to them carried a tray with glass cups and a tall embossed brass coffee pot, a trickle of steam drifting from the spout. A friendly gesture she'd ordered before the cell leaders arrived. She needed to give a little to be assured of their support now.

She didn't smile as she looked at them. She needed to be grave, but not concerned. To admit that she had no plan to fall back on was to invite swift annihilation. She had to play for time.

'Thank you for coming,' she said, 'sit down.'

She felt herself relax a little as they obeyed her. She waited as the guard poured out the coffee, handed the cups around then stood back for instructions. She signalled to all her bodyguards to leave. They hesitated, then walked across the stone slab floor through the doors to leave her alone with the cell leaders. She caught the quick exchange of glances between them, relaxed even more as she saw them settle back in their chairs.

'Are your men still in the camps by Edremit?' she asked.

They nodded.

'It's still quiet up there,' Sulan said. 'But I came through Uzak and the Turks had checkpoints everywhere, they were hauling Kurds to one side, putting them in lorries.'

'What happened to them?'

He shrugged.

Yenev put a hand on the table. 'I heard they're processing them, putting some into holding centres, giving the rest a curfew order, limiting their movements.'

Tansu frowned. 'I haven't seen anything on CNN or FOX about this.'

'I think it's localised at the moment, just around Kutahya,' Yenev said.

Tansu drank some coffee, slowly, waiting for one of them to speak.

Yenev put his cup down, the thick coffee sliding over the rim to make a small pool on the table.

'What happened, Tansu? How did the Turks find out? We lost six men there.'

'And the others,' added Sulan. 'Whoever they were.'

'They belonged to the people supplying the weapons,' said Tansu, 'the men on the train were guarding them.'

'How . . .' Sulan stopped as she lifted her head, her dark eyes like coals.

'There is to be an Inquiry,' she said coldly. 'The operation was perfectly alright when the train was in Kutahya. It went wrong when the relief team went in at the bridge. They were careless, the Turks spotted them. It's just as well the team leader's dead. I would have executed him myself.' Her eyes bored into Sulan. 'I will not tolerate sloppy leadership.'

Yenev coughed nervously. 'I heard the two bodies our survivors found weren't Turks.'

'What do you mean by that?' she said sharply.

'Well . . . nothing . . . they thought . . . well they thought someone else had attacked them.'

'Who,' she rapped out.

He looked down at the tabletop.

'G8,' he muttered.

'So that's it,' she ground out, 'they excuse their incompetence, their getting taken by a bunch of fucking Turks, by saying G8 attacked them. And, you,' she stopped. 'Look at me when I'm talking to you. You spread the story, like some girl who's afraid of the dark.'

He flushed. 'I'm . . .'

'You're in danger of losing your command,' she hissed. 'How dare you come in here trying to find excuses for them. They let us down, they let the weapons go, we have to fall back on our secondary plan, all because they were badly trained and badly led.'

Sulan leaned forward.

'Tansu, what . . .'

She turned on him, her lips stretched back over her teeth.

'Don't you protect him.'

He wet his lips. 'I only wanted to ask what the secondary plan was. What I am to do.'

She glanced at Yenev.

'I'll tell you what we're going to do when this spineless piece of shit has pulled himself together.' She got up, tugging down the hem of her short, tight black skirt. 'Now get out and wait for my instruction.'

She resisted the temptation to call in her guards. And was rewarded as Sulan and Yenev slunk out, wordless.

She let out her breath in a long sigh. She'd held them off for the moment. Time enough for something to turn up or for her to get out, to use her air ticket to Paris.

'Excellent, my dear, you're learning.'

She swung round. Albert was standing by the other door, his hand holding to one side the gold tapestry carpet which hid it.

'Albert,' she gasped. 'Albert. I didn't expect you 'til tomorrow.'

He stroked her hair as she came into his arms, his hand cradling the back of her neck. What a bore she was. Still skinny, ugly, violent. He smothered a sigh.

'What will you do when I'm not around?' he murmured.

She hugged him tighter. 'Don't say that, don't ever say that.' Standing back she took his hand, silently led him back through the curtained door to her bedroom.

He thought of Francesca.

Albert reached for his cigarette case, tapped the flat cigarette on the lid, carefully lit it with his lighter and lay back on the pillow.

'Your performance in there,' he pointed towards the locked door with the tip of his cigarette, 'was very convincing. You have won yourself time. But why did you think it necessary to do so?'

She tensed. 'I thought it was what you'd want,' she said, 'we've lost the weapons, what the hell else could I do until we'd spoken?'

'If you had spent less time thinking, seething, about who betrayed us you would have had more time to create our strategy,' he said coolly. 'Countering disaster comes first, dealing with betrayal comes second. Not that we've had a disaster,' he added.

She turned onto her elbow.'

'What d'you mean? Of course, we've had a disaster. Losing those weapons was a fucking disaster.'

'You see? You're so full of anger you're still not thinking straight.' He pushed himself against the pillow to sit up straight, his back leaning against the headboard. 'What about the second shipment by air to Bandirma?'

She sat bolt upright.

'The second . . .'

'While you have been pacing about here, terrified of your cell leaders, I have been in Bandirma with Moosar. The second shipment is safely stowed in the cattle pens of my farm there. Such a waste to have paid for it and not make use of it, don't you think.'

For a moment she was speechless. Then she flung her legs over the side of the bed and sat there.

'I'd forgotten. How could I?'

'Because I told you to forget it,' Albert said simply. 'I didn't want you to remember. The last thing I wanted was for you to tell anyone. It was the rail shipment that I wanted all eyes focussed on.'

She turned to him.

'But why?'

'In case something went wrong with the first shipment. I didn't trust the French.' He paused. 'I was right.'

'Gilbert?' she ground the name out between her teeth.

He nodded. 'I thought he might break. All that French honour and military gentleman rubbish. He was too much the hero. When he began drinking I prepared a fallback plan.'

'The second shipment?'

He nodded.

'But how's it going to help? The Turks are fully alert. We can't get them to Edremit. There's no way we can attack Limnos now. There are roadblocks being set up around Kutahya. You heard Sulan and Yenev. Kurds in that area are being picked up on sight.'

He watched her wrap a short silk dressing gown around her thin body, its blackness making her skin more sallow.

'You've come a long way since we first met, Tansu.'

She looked at him searchingly.

'That doesn't answer my question.'

'If you had come as far in your political thinking as you have in,' he paused, 'other directions, you wouldn't have to ask.'

The line of her mouth tightened.

'Why do you always have to be such a bastard?'

'Because you won't always have me. You have to understand that.'

'I don't care about our age difference. I love you.'

'It's not love I'm talking about,' he snapped, 'it's about my legacy, what I'll be remembered for. A Kurdish homeland. Kurdistan. A place for me to rest. A country of my own.' He stopped. Breathing rapidly. 'You and I have that in common. Both of us orphaned. Both without a country. I can give us one. But I won't always be around and you will take over.' His eyes held hers. 'You will have to know how to run Kurdistan, how I will run it. Otherwise you will lose it. And I shall be nothing.'

Silently, she walked over, took his hand. 'I'm ready,' she said.

*

The shadows deepened over the escarpment as the sun fell rapidly to the horizon, painting the sky scarlet. The stone walls behind Tansu's cedar table desk glowed pink in the reflected light from the windows. The only sound was the Toyota Landcruiser's diesel as it ground up the hill, carrying the two Turkish bankers away from Mardin to meet their helicopter, which would fly them back to Ankara. Albert had seen them by himself. They would have been nervous if they had met Tansu. Not because of her chic sophistication but because she had the smell of death about her.

Now, after the guard had lit the oil lamp on the table and laid it for supper, Albert told Tansu what had been in his mind.

'I had a call from my friend in the French President's Intelligence Unit,' he said, watching the lamplight flicker on the silver cutlery. 'He told me that the French Government were about to freeze my assets in Paris and Mauritius.'

Tansu's face whitened. 'You mean they've confiscated your property, our money?'

'No. That's what I mean about forward planning, Tansu. Of course, they didn't find anything. I have long had a laundering pattern to drain my accounts in Paris and Mauritius. The money and other assets are now with those bankers in Ankara. They are liquidating all the property and bond holdings. We need cash now.'

She waited, not prepared to ask a question and show her ignorance.

'The bankers will distribute the cash to seventy two collecting points throughout Turkey.'

'Can't that be traced?'

THE FACE OF TOMORROW

'No. The bankers are using Hawala money dealers. No money will change hands. The Hawala dealers will make it available to our PKK leaders in each city or town against the bankers' verbal guarantee that a similar total sum will be available to the dealers when they require it.'

She knew that it wasn't the time to press for more information on the Hawala system. The question now was what the money in those towns and cities was going to be used for.

Albert waited while the guard put plates of smoked salmon in front of them.

'I suppose I will have to get used to Kurdish fare sometime,' he smiled.

'But not their wine,' she laughed, as the guard poured some Riesling into their tall blue glasses.

'God is good,' he said in Kurdish.

She repeated the words. 'You see the accent is on the first word.' Her eyes blinked in the lamplight. 'But you are improving.'

He swallowed a piece of salmon, followed it with a sip of wine.

'There are ten million Kurds in south eastern Turkey,' he said slowly. 'We are going to move them west, to flood the main cities of Turkey. Bring the place to a standstill. Then we'll move a mass of them into Greece.'

'Move them? All of them?'

'No. Of course not,' he said impatiently. 'But we can shift at least a couple of million of them. Possibly more.'

She looked at him, incredulity fighting with the fear of contradicting him. She compromised. 'Why?'

He picked up his knife, sliced a piece of salmon.

'Why were we going to attack Limnos? To get the Greeks to think the Turks were attacking them and to retaliate by marching into Turkey. In the chaos, we were going to stage a coup and force the Turks to give us our homeland.'

'Yes I know all that,' she said edgily.

'The background's important. It's a constant, it's our objective.' He put down the knife and fork, the salmon uneaten. 'We can no longer simply attack Limnos because the Turks will publicise the arms find and will easily be able to persuade the Greeks that any attack was PKK and not them.' He swirled the Riesling inside the glass for a moment. 'So we use surprise. Our PKK leaders in southern Turkey will persuade, and if necessary pay, as many Kurds as possible that the time has come for protest. We will get them on the move, hundreds of thousands of them, flooding through Turkey into the cities, Diyarbakir, Ankara, Istanbul. The Turks will try and stop them, try to return them back to the south. But there'll be too many of them, and our PKK fighters will fight their way through the Turkish checkpoints. Then we move thousands of our people north, over the Greek border and keep them going. The Greeks will be forced to march into Turkey to stop them. When that happens we go back to our earlier plan. A coup in Ankara, using the weapons in Bandirma. We no longer attack Limnos but we use those fighters in Ankara.

He forked the salmon into his mouth and chomped on it.

Tansu looked stunned. For a moment she didn't speak, then she leant forward.

'But how are you going to get so many of our people moving?'

'The money. Our PKK helpers from the eighth circle will go among the millions of tenth circle Kurds and persuade them to get moving in a huge peaceful protest first to Ankara then Istanbul. They'll pay them, with a promise of more money when they reach their destinations. It will be a huge, silent protest. Can you see it?' The ring on his little finger glittered as he swept his hand across the table. 'Hundreds of thousands of Kurds marching across the whole of Turkey, advancing on Ankara, Istanbul, walking, crammed on trains, buses, lorries, cars, carts, anything that moves.'

He took a drink of the wine, wiped his mouth with his napkin. 'The Turks won't be able to stop it. Then they'll start to arrest people, put them in camps. Still the Kurds will come on. And you know the Turks. They'll start to use force. They'll kill people, wound them. Women, children.' He stopped, his eyes resting on the tapestry carpet curtain covering the door. 'And still the Kurds will come. Think of it. Two million people on the move.'

Tansu reached out to him. 'Our people will be massacred. They'll turn back.'

His nose flared.

'No. They won't. Their blood will be up. They'll keep coming. Like a tidal wave. And after a few days those Kurds who are in

Istanbul will push over the border into Greece. At the same time, we'll send hundreds out by boat, every boat we can lay our hands on. All heading towards Greece. The Greeks won't be able to cope. They'll start to fight back. They'll have to march into Turkey.'

He was breathing fast now, a faint line of sweat under his jet black hairline. 'Then we attack the Turkish Government in Ankara. We use everything, the weapons, the migrants, everything. And we call for support. We call on the Iraqi Kurds, their Muslim brothers, anywhere and anyhow. We pour oil on the flames until we get what we want. A free Kurdistan.'

She was silent for a moment.

'If we inflame the Muslims to the south of us it could spread. The Middle East. Pakistan. India.'

He dabbed his mouth with his napkin, poured a small measure of Riesling into his glass.

'What's the most important thing in your life, Tansu?'

Slowly, she nodded.

'Kurdistan and us.'

CHAPTER FIFTY-SIX

Charlie climbed out of the closed van and breathed in, letting the scent of the frangipani bushes drift into her, relieved they had arrived. The flight in the G8 Hercules had been uncomfortable, noisy and dirty. She was wearing some thick jeans and top and a hideous pair of dark sunglasses, which Rosie had bought her in Paris, and she yearned for a bath and a change. The secrecy thrust on her during the move from John's apartment had exasperated her.

Standing on the driveway in front of Nina's faded apricot and white plantation house, looking at the unchanging peaks of the Rapilles in the distance, gave her the first sense of a firm footing since that day in the Cluny Museum. She drew in another breath.

Even John's proposal had seemed to be another blow at the foundations she had built since she was a child. She hadn't expected it. She had wanted it, wanted it from almost the first moment she'd met him, but he'd always seemed so remote, as if she was a kite and he was far down below manipulating the strings to make her fly in one direction, then another. She had wondered if she'd fallen in love with a father figure, to suffer the same distant control, the slights and put downs, and she'd been ready to erect the same barrier she'd used against him and run.

But the two days with John in his apartment had soon put an end to those thoughts. She had watched him at work, the icy calculator, and then she'd had him to herself, sensitively exploring her world of art and music, laughing a great deal and between them creating an indefinable bond. She'd tried to analyse it, but couldn't. It just reminded her of a fragment from an old Kafiristan love poem:

We'll work and play together

And laugh together at things
Which would not amuse our neighbours.

And she was satisfied then that here was no father figure but the man who would love and protect her for the rest of her life. It was then that the danger she was in hit her. For the first time in her life she was really happy, with the prospect of that happiness being unlimited. Except it could be cut short in one short stroke if her survival was made public.

'Come on darling, I can't walk down the steps to come and get you.' Nina stood on the veranda, the slash of her red lipstick violently clashing with the orange silk scarf which wound round her green straw hat and rested on the collar of her yellow flowing Kaftan. Charlie didn't dare look at her shoes.

'Hello aunt,' she said and turned abruptly as she felt tears prick the back of her eyes. 'John, come on, Nina can't wait to see you.'

'The love of my life,' laughed Nina. 'What have you been doing with my niece, you naughty man.'

Hammond took her hand and kissed her on both cheeks.

'Making an honest woman of her. At least I will be when we all get back to London.'

Nina looked at the faded bruises on Charlie's face.

'Did you have to torture her into saying yes?'

'It's a long story, aunt,' Charlie smiled. 'First I need a bath and a change of clothes.'

'Thank goodness for that,' said Nina going into the reception room. 'I wasn't going to say anything, dear, but,' she shuddered, 'those frightful clothes. I'm so glad they aren't some new fashion from Paris. By the way,' she added without pausing, 'your staff arrived last night.' She unwrapped the scarf and took her hat off, shaking her red hair and combing it with her fingers. 'I must say I do approve, particularly the butler, he's a fine figure of a man.'

'Nina,' Hammond said warningly.

'Just my little joke,' her pale blue eyes full of mischief.

Hammond looked at her. 'I'm not so sure,' he laughed.

'Go on, you two,' Nina smiled. 'You're in Charlie's room. Your,' she paused, 'butler has searched it thoroughly at least three times today to my knowledge. Bath, rest, then come and talk to me at dinner. I shall go for a walk.'

Hammond stopped and turned. 'I wouldn't advise that, yet.'

She stared at him for a moment.

'No, I suppose not,' she said eventually. 'I'll paint instead. Is that all right?'

He nodded gravely, putting out his hand to touch her arm before following Charlie down the picture strewn passage.

'Did you mean that, about Nina not going for a walk?' asked Charlie as they got to her room.

He closed the door.

'Yes. The exfiltration from my apartment went fine. But by now Albert will have had time to think about how the weapons on the train were blown. At first he'll think it was Gilbert but from what you told me it was obvious that Gilbert had spoken to no one else when he collared you at the Cluny. If Albert thinks about it long enough he may reach the same conclusion. It's only a short step from that to asking himself whether you actually survived. We've given him every cause to believe you're dead so far. He knows you're close to Nina so he may well think about coming here. The last thing I want is Nina being taken by his people. Hostage or worse.'

She reminded Hammond of her aunt as she ran her hand through her hair, the blonde bright in the light streaming through the half shuttered windows.

'I'm selfish aren't I, insisting we came here.' She hesitated, looking at him. 'It's been . . . very sudden. Not my being in love with you but . . . but you're being in love with me.'

He walked towards her.

Her hand moved in a slight arc. 'I wanted to share this. All this. The beauty. The colours. It's . . . it's where I've been happiest. I wanted us to start here.'

He put his arms round her, saying quietly, 'I know.'

CHAPTER FIFTY-SEVEN

The dining room was made to seem even smaller than it was by a clever use of blue embossed silk wall coverings from floor to ceiling. The wall chandeliers hung low to give an air of intimacy and the glowing matching mahogany furniture reflected the soft light to give an air of warmth, which was enhanced by the deep blue plain carpet.

The French President sat in the fine carver at the head of the oblong table under Van Gogh's picture of the Church at Auvers, which he'd loaned from the Musee d'Orsay. The President saw Albert's eyes stray to it.

'Not your sort of thing, Albert, is it? Church?'

'What makes you think I am a Christian?' Albert murmured.

The President shot a glance at Claud.

Albert delicately sipped his coffee.

'I was thinking how long it takes for genius to be recognised,' he said.

Claud threw his coffee spoon onto the saucer.

'If you hadn't let those weapons . . .'

'No, Claud,' the President cut in, 'that's not what he meant, is it, Albert.'

Albert's shoulders imperceptibly shrugged.

'I don't wish to apportion blame, Mr President, although Gilbert's condition was, shall we say, apparent for some time. No, you're right, the loss of the weapons is regrettable, but not the end of the story.'

Claud leant forwards, pushing his brandy glass away.

'I thought this was a farewell dinner.'

Albert kept his eyes on the President.

'If you want an EU Army, if you want to lose your nuclear independence, yes, it is.'

The President returned his stare. 'What makes you think the end of the story might be different. You've lost two weapons shipments. What makes you think our paying for you to arrange another will be any different?'

'We won't use weapons this time. At least not in the quantity we previously planned for. So we don't need to rely on third parties.' Albert glanced at Claud. 'Unreliable third parties. This time we will have a peaceful protest. We will march two million Kurds through Turkey so it comes to a standstill. Then we march them over the border into Greece. The Greeks will have to react.'

Claud's mouth turned down.

'That's nonsense. It's fantastic. How can you get that many Kurds to march to your tune?'

'Simple,' replied Albert, fishing in his jacket pocket for his cigarette case. 'Money.'

'You've got money alright,' grunted the President. 'We let you get it out.'

Albert's lighter snapped shut.

'I never had much money personally,' he replied. 'And my clients' money is theirs.'

'How do we know?' rasped Claud rudely.

Albert raised his eyebrows. 'Because the law says my clients' money is theirs.'

Claud's teeth ground.

'No. Not that. How do we know that you haven't much money?'

'Because I'm telling you so,' said Albert quietly. 'If you don't believe me then let us end this conversation.' He glanced at his watch. 'I have to go soon anyway.'

'No. Wait a minute,' the President said quickly. He sat back, rolling his cigar in his pudgy fingers. 'How much money and how do you think you can persuade these people, these Kurds, to march through Turkey?'

'Fifty million US dollars will buy sufficient Kurds to get them moving. The rest can be promised cash later. As long as they see some Kurds getting cash they'll believe our promises.' Albert narrowed one eye as smoke curled into it. 'Many will come just because they want a homeland. They want a Kurdistan. Those will believe us because we are PKK and have fought for them.'

'No weapons?' Claud asked.

'Here and there, to provoke the Turks. The more they retaliate the more we can whip up the Kurds. We need them in a frenzy when we storm the Greek border.'

'No attack on Limnos.' Claud pressed.

'No. We haven't the weapons for that,' Albert said evenly.

The President wet his lips with his tongue. 'Why didn't you think of this earlier?'

'There was nothing to provoke the Turks. The weapons seizure has done that now. They're retaliating. Locking up Kurds, brutalising them. The situation's changed.'

Claud looked at the President.

'We can support a Greek occupation of Turkey in the EU, the UN. Get the border sealed.' He paused. 'It's a better option than the last plan.'

*

Albert walked the last kilometre to his house on Rue Morillo. He wanted to relax, to think how he was going to transfer the fifty million dollars to his bankers in Ankara without the President's Intelligence Unit, particularly that slimy bastard in the steel rimmed spectacles, finding out. The Hawala dealers in Turkey were already stretched dealing with his own funds. Although fifty million was a small sum compared to that, he didn't want to overload them. The thought came into his mind that he could take his time too. He didn't need the money. He just felt the French should pay. After all, they were going to benefit. He smiled to himself. In that case he'd just transfer the money to a couple of shell trading companies in Istanbul. Then take out a series of cash withdrawals and trade them for narcotics from northern Afghanistan. He'd make a good profit that way. And he had any number of offshore shell companies to keep the books straight for the Istanbul end. The French would never trace it. And certainly wouldn't bother once the Greek border with Turkey was sealed and the Kurds had stopped siphoning out.

He put his hand in his pocket and reached for his latchkey. He always felt a faint annoyance when he let himself into the house. He'd have preferred it to be his own rather than Francesca's. But he needed her, and she wouldn't move.

He stopped as he reached the hall, holding the front door open. Francesca was on the phone in the sitting room. He couldn't see her through the open door but the tone of her voice held him arrested. She was almost hysterical.

'But, darling, where are you, what happened?'

'No, tell me now.'

'What do you mean "don't tell Albert"?'

'Charlie? Charlie?'

Albert froze, his eyes slits. It couldn't be true. Charlie was at the bottom of the river. He tried to grapple with what he'd heard, then in the back of his mind he heard Francesca clicking the receiver trying to reconnect the broken line. Instantly alert, he backed through the open door and closed it, walked up the street and waited by the corner, trying to gather his thoughts. Steady his mind.

Ten minutes later he let himself into the hallway again.

'Hello Francesca,' he shouted. 'I'm home.'

She came out into the hall, her face white.

'Hello Albert,' she said quietly, a tremble in her voice.

Albert took her hands. 'Why, Francesca, is something wrong?'

'No. No. I have a slight headache, that's all, darling. I'm just on my way to bed.'

She started for the stairs. 'It's nice to see you home early,' she said, over her shoulder.

CHAPTER FIFTY-EIGHT

The Turkish checkpoint in Van was choked with shouting, jostling Kurds, struggling to keep their places in the vast sea of people that spread out to both sides of the street and disappeared around the corner half a kilometre away. Men cursed and swore as they staggered under the weight of the crowd, trying to protect the women who screamed at their children who were in danger of becoming lost among the trampling legs of the milling, resentful mob.

Yelling to make themselves heard, the Turkish police and soldiers prodded, pushed, hit, to separate the crowd and herd people into the inspection boxes.

Grinding their gears, klaxons blaring, fenders tangling, a jumble of buses, lorries, cars and tractors fought to drop off their passengers and get through the vehicle checkpoint to pick them up the other side.

Bags, sacks, suitcases, pushcarts were heaped in side alleys, where more Turkish police searched them, spilling a trail of clothes, tinned food, trinkets and ornaments onto the cobbles and into the open drains. Watching them, the owners screamed or wailed or just stood in dumb silence as their privacy was ripped open and their meagre belongings wrecked.

Tansu was exhilarated. Standing at the window of the front room of a seedy top floor apartment overlooking the street, she watched the police gradually being swallowed up by the crowd as it surged and swayed obeying a stream of conflicting commands. She was controlling the PKK organisers who were moving surreptitiously among the crowd, directing it on the ground.

Beside her was a girl in her early twenties who was speaking into her mobile. To the Turks she was a hotel receptionist, hard

working and respected. To the PKK she was an eighth circle
supporter who for years had passed on information gleaned from
the Turkish civil servants and military who had stayed at her hotel.

Three women hovered in the middle of the paint peeling room,
all PKK, holding their mobile phones to their chests as if they were
rifles. They were there to help Tansu relay her orders.

Tansu leant out of the window and looked up and down the
street. The crowd heaved and rippled as far as she could see. She
turned to the girl, the receptionist, standing next to her.

'Tell the organisers to spread the people out,' Tansu ordered
sharply. 'Get them into the side streets and start bypassing the
checkpoint.'

The receptionist put her fingers to her mouth.

'There are soldiers in the alleyways. They're blocking them off.'

Tansu left the window, pushing a low, plastic table out of her
way. Turned on her.

'Are they going to open fire?'

The girl drew in a sharp breath.

'Yes . . . no . . . I don't know.'

Tansu let her eyes stray over the other women.

'What do you think?'

They stood stock still, their breathing shallow, overpowered by
the raw menace.

'If you don't understand this is war,' Tansu ground out, 'you
will end up in the hands of that Turkish filth out there.' She
paused. 'And you know what that means.'

The girl swallowed, her eyes fixed on Tansu.

'How can we win?' she whispered.

One of the women made a choking sound, put a hand on the
wooden bench behind her and sat down, hugging herself, slowly
moving back and forth.

Tansu's eyes blazed as she opened the palm of her hand to slap
her. Then, suddenly, she stopped. Put the hand on the woman's
shoulder instead.

'I'm sorry,' she murmured. 'I forget sometimes. I have no family.
Nothing to lose. You make the greater sacrifice.' She bent, holding
the woman for a moment.

Then she straightened.

'I want you to see something.' Going to the old portable TV on the pitted melamine shelf screwed into the wall, she switched it on.

Puzzled, they watched her, the woman on the chair bent forwards to see around the others.

The picture flickered on. An announcer sat at a white wood desk with a blue background and logo behind her. She spoke rapidly in Turkish. Tansu let her talk for a moment then switched channels. This time two CNN reporters were speaking in English, cut in and out of an anchorwoman. The news text and news flashes ran in a continuous ribbon of text below them. Tansu flicked the remote control. Fox News came on. The same format. The same scroll of news text under the changing picture. Tansu went on flicking the channels, pausing to watch them until the Turkish programme came on again.

She tossed the remote onto the shelf.

'What did you see?' she asked them.

The three women fixed their eyes on the receptionist. She hesitated, trying to find the right answer.

'Well?' Tansu prompted, like a teacher with a dim pupil.

'The news,' the receptionist started uncertainly, 'then a feature on Sardinia, er . . . an American soap . . .'

'Exactly,' Tansu slapped the top of the television. 'Now what didn't you see?'

They looked at each other, bewildered, the receptionist staring at the television, as if to conjure the answer out of its blank screen.

Two white patches appeared either side of Tansu's nose as she watched them.

'Look,' she almost shouted, picking up the remote, flashed CNN up again. 'That's what you didn't see,' she banged the remote on the screen. 'Us. The Kurds. Being herded around by the Turks. Our possessions trashed, being shoved into detention centres. This is CNN. If they aren't filming us, making us news, who is? No one.' The last words echoed around the sparsely furnished room.

Tansu saw them flinch, thought of Albert, and took the violence out of her voice.

'Sit down.'

They looked around for somewhere to sit, the receptionist choosing the plastic table, keeping her arms tight to her sides and her knees pressed together.

Tansu nodded towards her. 'You knew Bora and Demir didn't you?'

Fear touched the receptionist's eyes.

'I didn't . . .'

'That's the answer you give the Turks, not me,' said Tansu dryly. She turned to the others.

'Bora and Demir were our brothers. They came from here in Van. It was their home. They ran a small garage. You may remember them. Years ago the Turks forced them out and they had to live in Diyarbakir, miles from their family, their friends.' She paused for effect. 'Not long ago they were killed when the Turks blew them up with the aircraft they were trying to salvage for us.'

The receptionist shifted slightly on the table.

'Yes,' said Tansu, 'you remember, don't you? You remember the sacrifice they made. They gave their lives trying to get weapons to us.' She looked at the girl. 'Bora was your cousin, wasn't he?'

Wordless, she nodded.

Tansu drew the mobile out of her pocket.

'The only way we can get CNN to take notice of us, to put us on their news across the world, is to make sacrifices.' She shook the mobile at them to emphasise her words. 'We must get our brothers and sisters through to Istanbul, then across the borders into Greece. These people,' she pointed her finger at the window, 'are the first. We are going to get a million, two million, to follow. If these get stopped here in Van we have no hope for the future. Bora and Demir will be dust on the empty plains.'

She waited, letting her words sink in as the noise of the crowd echoed around the walls of the room. Silently, the woman on the chair got up and dialled a number on her mobile.

'Move them into the alleys,' she said quietly, 'move them around the checkpoint.' She listened for a moment. 'Yes I know the soldiers are there. Drive on through them.' She looked across at Tansu. 'And if they fire on us, kill them.' She listened, shook her head as her voice took on a note of desperation. 'I don't care, as long as we get through.'

Tansu's mobile buzzed. It was Albert. She put her hand on the back of her neck.

'How are things going?' he asked.

'We're on our way,' she replied. 'We had a small hold up, but the goods will be moving on in the next few minutes. You can release the goods from areas B.C.D, 1 and 2 now.'

'Excellent.' He paused. 'Have you time to do something for me?'

'Not really, unless it's important.'

'You remember the three people I played bridge with,' he said cautiously.

'Bridge?' she exclaimed.

'Yes. Bridge. In Paris. You remember?'

'Oh, bridge,' she said, 'yes, of course.'

'Well I had unexpected news. The woman's turned up again.'

Tansu's body went rigid. 'Then . . .'

'Yes,' Albert cut in. 'You're quite right.'

Tansu felt her chest pounding.

'I'll look forward to meeting up with her.'

'I thought you'd find the time.' The connection went dead as Albert switched off.

CHAPTER FIFTY-NINE

Hammond walked through the now familiar yellow silk wallpapered hall of 10 Downing Street hardly glancing at the oil paintings, smiled at the APS as he continued through the outer room and went straight into the Prime Minister's office.

The PM was standing by the square table between the two tall windows, talking to someone seated on the leather sofa to the left of his desk. He glanced over as he heard the door open, came over and took Hammond's hand.

'John, good of you to come at such short notice. I'm sorry to drag you back from Mauritius.' He turned to the person on the sofa. 'You know the Greek Ambassador. But you haven't met the new Turkish Ambassador, he arrived three days ago.'

The Ambassador stood up, as tall as Hammond but much broader, with a hawk like face and dark black hair brushed back in a wave.

'It's a pleasure, Mr Hammond. We are much in debt to G8 for seizing the weapons at Kutahya.

Hammond shook his outstretched hand.

'I am sorry that some of your nationals were hurt.'

'No one seriously, I assure you. It was a miracle. I have spoken personally to Lev Leviatski about the bravery of Maxim Byelov. He will be remembered by my Government.'

'Maxim's healing nicely,' smiled Hammond. 'As for Lev, well, a supply of Turkish cigarettes will be more welcome to him than a medal.'

The Ambassador laughed. From the side pocket of his worsted suit he took out a flat, yellow box.

'It will be arranged.' He offered a cigarette to Hammond. 'Would you like one?'

'Don't tempt him,' the PM said, 'he's given up and I don't want to go through the agony of him having to give up all over again. It was hell.' He broke off. 'Oh, good, Keithley.'

Hammond and the Ambassador turned as Keithley came into the room.

'Prime Minister, Ambassadors,' he said. He patted Hammond on the shoulder, murmuring, 'I didn't think wild horses would drag you back from Mauritius.'

'They wouldn't have,' Hammond replied in an undertone, 'but Charlie's joining me, she's just stopping off in Paris to collect some things for our wedding.'

The PM went to stand by the fireplace, a brass fireguard protecting the empty grate.

'Right, Ambassador,' the PM's Manchester accent made the lack of formal address to the Turkish Ambassador sound friendly. 'You'd best tell them what you told me. You needn't wrap it up.'

The Turkish Ambassador sat down, watching Hammond as he leant on the edge of the square table.

'Your last communication to my Government gave us to believe that the French Government were to agree the formation of an EU Army to include my country. And that the French had agreed to forty per cent of the funding and the immediate establishment of a chain of command to allow elements of the Army to be deployed within days.

Hammond nodded. 'Yes, that's right. The French have given their guarantees.' He glanced at the PM. 'The French President confirmed it with the Prime Minister.'

The APS quietly walked in carrying a tray of coffee. He put it down on a mahogany stand opposite the windows. The PM frowned, waved him away with his fingertips.

The Turkish Ambassador waited until the door was shut with the APS on the other side.

'Our Foreign Minister received a telephone call from the French Foreign Minister yesterday morning informing him that the French Government were reconsidering their funding for the EU Army and that no decision could be made for at least a month.'

Hammond opened his mouth to speak. But the Ambassador cut him short.

'We don't have a month, Mr Hammond, I doubt we have a week.'

'Tell him what you mean, Ambassador,' the PM said testily. 'He's been in Mauritius,' he shot a glance at Hammond. 'And his mind wasn't on Turkey.'

'We are facing a rising tide of Kurds moving from their south eastern heartland towards the north west. At first there were a few thousand. We held them at Van. But at least another fifteen thousand suddenly appeared there and they broke through to Erzurum in the north and Diyarbakir in the south.' He licked his lips. 'You remember Diyarbakir?'

Hammond nodded silently.

The Ambassador looked at the PM.

'As soon as they broke through Van another mass of Kurds, at least sixty or seventy thousand this time, headed for Adana in the middle west and Sivas to the north. Police and troops tried to stop them at Gaziantep and Malatya. The same thing happened, they surged around the checkpoints. Up 'til then we had adopted a policy of containment and arrest. But at Malatya we ordered the troops to open fire. The Kurds simply overwhelmed them.'

'Did the Kurds fire back?' Hammond asked.

'Only in isolated incidents. The checkpoints were either crushed in huge rushes by the crowd or just bypassed in the alleys with our soldiers swamped by the mass of people.'

Keithley leaned forward. 'So where are you going to contain them?'

'If it was just that number we would deploy the troops and police to do so,' the Ambassador replied, 'but at 4.00 am this morning my Ministry telephoned to say that swarms more people are converging on Diyarbakir, Malatya and Gaziantep, there are too many to count.' He paused.

'Excuse me a moment,' Hammond said, picking up his laptop and putting it on the table.

'Julia,' he said. 'What's G8SUR picked up on southern Turkey?'

'Sixty eight identified PKK have moved overnight to Kayseri, Eregli and Sivas.'

Hammond tapped the keys to bring up a map of Turkey. 'That's on a north/south line in central Turkey isn't it?'

'Yes.'

Hammond moved the map into the corner of his screen.

'What about these large movements of people, have you been monitoring those?'

'We've concentrated on the PKK members themselves. Their latest movement is consistent with other movements to Van, Erzurum and Diyarbakir in recent days. But no weapons have been shifted. We've watched the crowd movements but can't make them out. There's another huge movement of at least a hundred thousand gathering in the south at the moment. Have a look.'

The PM, the Ambassadors and Keithley crowded around Hammond's laptop screen.

The first thing they saw were clouds of dust, sand coloured plumes steadily rising upwards and outwards. The scale on the screen showed them to be three kilometres long and half a kilometre wide. The name Gaziantep scrolled across the bottom of the screen. Suddenly the focus altered and into view came tens of thousands of people walking determinedly in huge groups, spread out, mixed in with vehicles of every type.

The picture altered to Diyarbakir. It started with a metalled road then panned along until it picked out a line of buses, two abreast, trundling along the highway. Behind the buses came dozens of open lorries interspersed with cars. The line went on for four kilometres. Behind that, spread across the road into the scrub, were thousands upon thousands of men, women and children. Suddenly, the speakers on the laptop picked up a hum that loudened until it filled the room.

Then the picture flickered off and Julia's face replaced it. 'It's the same going towards Malatya,' she said. 'The computers calculate about sixty thousand people going there.'

'Thank you Julia. Keep me informed.' Hammond shut the laptop with a snap.

They looked at the Turkish Ambassador as he walked back to his seat, ashen faced.

'It's well organised,' said Hammond, looking searchingly at the PM.

The PM shook his head.

'Have you any ideas, Ambassador?'

'This is PKK. No doubt. They are inciting the Kurds. We have heard talk of a woman. After Celik's death, there were whispers that a woman had taken over the leadership.' He wiped his mouth. 'It makes sense. There were plenty of rumours before that about Celik's operational planner being a woman. But we never identified her.'

Hammond cast another glance at the PM. But again the PM shook his head.

'We can't hold them,' the Ambassador suddenly burst out. 'Not if they keep coming like that. We've got to get help.'

'It's not that bad, surely,' said Keithley, 'there can't be that many of them.'

The Ambassador's eyes dilated. 'There are ten million of them.'

'My God,' Keithley muttered.

'You see, that's why we want this Army. We need the troops. If we had an EU Army we'd have the troops, we could stop them. The French say a month. If the Kurds keep coming like this, Turkey will come to a standstill, we'll be finished in a week, a fortnight at most. Our only alternative is to push them across our borders, get rid of them.'

'Into Greece?' The Greek Ambassador rapped out.

'If necessary.'

The Greek Ambassador half rose out of his seat.

'If you don't contain these Kurds within your borders we'll do it for you.'

The Turkish Ambassador reddened. 'How? Invade?'

'Yes. Give these bloody Kurds their homeland. If these hordes,' he pointed at Hammond's laptop, 'threaten us, believe me we'll march into Turkey and give them Kurdistan.'

The Turkish Ambassador was white with fury.

'We'll never give up our southern heartland for the PKK, for a bunch of dissident Kurds.'

The Greek Ambassador got up.

'Then there'll be war.'

The PM half rose from his chair. 'Gentlemen, please. This isn't getting us anywhere. The solution lies in the EU Army and deploying it into Turkey. I will speak to the French President right away, try to find out what changed his mind. If he insists on delay, I will speak to my colleagues in Europe. Try to get military support for Turkey.' He pushed himself upright, turned to the Greek Ambassador. 'We need time. We need a European solution. And the UN.' His chin came up. 'War is not an option.'

The Turkish Ambassador got to his feet.

'You saw that mob. If it grows, we won't have time to approach each European country for military aid. We have to have the French behind us now.'

The Greek Ambassador took a step towards him. 'Or give the Kurds what they want.'

The Turkish Ambassador glared at him. 'We'll fight before we do that.'

'They'll do it, too,' said the PM after the Ambassadors had left. He took up his customary position by the fireplace.

'Sorry, John, I couldn't let you tell them about Albert and that Tansu woman. They would have learnt about the French. It would smash any hope of getting an EU Army. So your job, and Keithley's here, is clear.'

'Find Albert and Tansu,' said Hammond simply.

The PM nodded, putting his arm on the mantelpiece. 'Get them and this whole Kurd thing will fizzle out. But get them before the Greeks are involved. We won't be able to stop a war after that.'

*

In the hallway Keithley put a hand on Hammond's arm.

'John, we need to talk about Charlie's safety. While Albert and Tansu are loose, she's at maximum risk. She shouldn't be in Paris at all.'

Hammond waited for the porter to open the door.

'As far as they're concerned she's dead. And I've got two G8 minders with her, Lionel, so she's perfectly all right, thanks. Anyway, as soon as she's in London she'll be with me.'

He walked out into Downing Street.

CHAPTER SIXTY

The butler, as Nina had christened Charlie's large, very correct, G8 bodyguard checked his rear view mirror before getting out of the Citreon van and looking up at the tall studio windows of Charlie's apartment in Montmartre. The maid, as the robust G8 female bodyguard had inevitably been called, stayed with Charlie in the closed back of the van.

The butler, dressed in green overalls with a logo that identified him as an electrician, pressed the doorbell. Standing in the shadow, he quickly inserted Charlie's key, pushed the door open and started an imaginary conversation with an imaginary person who'd opened the door.

He was inside very quickly and disappeared as the door shut. A few moments later, the maid's eyes shut as she listened to her ear microphone.

'All clear,' she said, 'come on. But make it snappy.'

Charlie breathed a sigh of relief as she walked into her studio. The canvasses were just where she'd left them. Stacked under the window, hung from the walls, light glittering and spraying off them in myriad colours.

'Blimey,' exclaimed the maid. 'I thought your aunt's were bright enough. I need sunglasses for this lot.'

Charlie laughed.

'Well, you won't need them because I'll leave them here.' She went over to her walk in clothes closet. 'Help me pack will you.' She went to pull the door handle.

'No,' shouted the maid, 'wait. Let me check.'

'I've checked,' said the butler, 'no wires, no one there.'

The maid pulled the door open, checked inside, rattling the coat hangers as she pushed the clothes one way then another.

'Yep. That's OK,' she said. 'You can take what you want from here.'

'Get me that large case will you,' she asked the butler, pointing to a high shelf.

He looked around.

'There's a chair over there,' she pointed.

He walked over and picked it up, manoeuvring through the doorway and standing under the shelf. He stood on it, testing momentarily, and reached up for the case.

'Hang on,' he muttered, 'I'd better check it.' Feeling in his pocket he drew out a small flat instrument and started to run it around the locks. He stopped suddenly, grunted. 'Hang on,' he drew in a breath, gave a violent sneeze. 'Sorry about that.'

He continued his test, put the instrument in his pocket and lifted the case up, heard the slight rattle inside, dropped it, jumped off the chair.

'Mothballs,' Charlie choked.

He glared at her then laughed uncertainly.

'Bloody 'ell.'

'Come on, hurry up,' said the maid.

Charlie finished packing, snapped the case shut, picked up her make up and perfume and put them in an overnight bag.

She looked around, feeling a little lost. The apartment had been part of her life for a dozen years and had been the forge where she had cast the iron filings which had started Ionism. She wished she could have shared it with John.

Her eyes caught the painting she'd done of Nina's tea garden in Mauritius. She had to admit it was her best work to date and shivered slightly as she recalled Albert's compliments. She almost went to pick it up. But something stopped her.

'I'm ready,' she said.

The butler nodded, went ahead, down the stairs, and opened the front door. He looked up and down the street and across at the buildings opposite. Nodded at the maid.

'We can go,' said the maid, picking up the case and starting down the stairs.

Charlie cast one last farewell look backwards, saw the tea garden painting again, gave a little sigh and ran back to pick it up.

It didn't come away from the other paintings immediately and she gave it a tug. She almost fell over as it came away suddenly, the other frames falling over in quick succession.

The maid dropped the case and jumped back up the stairs.

'What . . .' She got no further.

'I'm keeping it whatever you say,' Charlie's mouth was set.

'Okay, okay, bring it, but hurry up.' The maid ran to the stairs, bent to pick up the case again and joined the butler by the front steps.

They stood to one side to let Charlie into the van, then heaving in the case, they climbed in. The butler started the engine.

'Wait,' shouted Charlie. 'That's Francesca,' she pointed to an elegant blonde haired woman dressed in a pale fawn check tweed coat climbing out of a car. 'She didn't wait for my call. She must have come to see if I was here. Stop. Please, stop.'

The butler put the handbrake back on.

'OK, but just for a minute, and through the window. I won't let you get out.'

Charlie leaned out of the window and waved as Francesca walked towards the front of the Citroen.

'Mama.' She shouted louder, 'Mama.'

'It doesn't smell right,' hissed the maid. She pointed to a figure coming out of a house further down the road. 'What's he doing? What's he's carrying?'

The butler looked intently down the street. 'RPG.'

He slammed the gear into reverse, revved the engine and screamed the car backwards.

'Cover Charlie,' he yelled.

The maid grabbed Charlie, threw her in the back and spread her limbs in a shield over Charlie's body.

The heat of the explosion seared through the windows and metal of the car, the shock waves from the grenade rocking it on its springs. The butler threw the wheel over and rammed on the handbrake, slewing the car around to face the opposite direction, feeding power through the gears, driving the car forwards and away from the blast.

Charlie screamed and thrust herself upwards. Out of the rear window, she caught a glimpse of a blackened shape that had no resemblance to a human being.

Francesca didn't exist.

CHAPTER SIXTY-ONE

Tansu waited for Albert at Enez, a small town just on the Turkish side of the border with Greece. It had been an ancient Aegean sea port but relentless silting had now placed it three kilometres inland and of no importance except as a tourist curiosity. A little further down the coast was the Greek fishing town of Alexandropoulis, which was also of no account except for its lighthouse, which made a useful backdrop for holiday snapshots.

Tansu had chosen Enez for her headquarters not only because it was so uninteresting, but also because she could direct the hundred thousand Kurds to the north of her. The whole of Turkey was awash with nearly a million and a half Kurds milling throughout the towns and cities. Tens of thousands had pushed their way in ferries across the sea from the Turkish mainland to Gelibolu and the land bordering Greece and were now spread out either side of the highway hidden from her by the rolling, dry brown hills.

Further north, thousands had stormed through Istanbul and reached the town of Edirne next to the Greek border and were holding there until her order to move, camping out in the narrow alleys, caravanserais and green fields of the old town, which had once been the capital of the Ottoman Empire.

Thousands of other Kurds were spread along the border between the two towns, sleeping in the open in the hilly landscape, which was dotted here and there with trees and white painted concrete houses.

Tansu knew that she was in a critical phase now. Until a few days ago, the Turks had defended checkpoints, put up barricades, infiltrated the army into the back streets to try and stop the huge, mad, onrush of the Kurds. But now the Turks had turned. Reports had come in that large groups of Kurds were now being hounded north towards the Greek border. Other reports coming in from the coast down to Izmir and beyond, as far south as Megiste, confirmed the new Turkish tactic of driving the Kurds out towards Greece.

Thousands of Kurds had already left the Turkish coast and were travelling west towards the Greek islands. They sailed in ferry-boats, fishing boats, sailing boats and rowboats. Anything that could float had been commandeered by the seething, howling mobs that had streamed through the port towns all along the coast, driven on by the Turkish soldiers and police in a frenzy maddened to uncontrollable hysteria. Hundreds of Kurds had been shot, they littered the streets, squares, alleyways and harbour walls, their blood spilling into the drains and water as they moaned for help or simply bled to death.

Tansu, her lieutenants and support staff watched the pictures on her satellite TV in the small farmhouse that served as her communications centre. CNN helicopters had circled the towns, cities and ports, their long range cameras devouring the drama.

'Poor people,' whispered one of the men transfixed in front of the screen.

'Get back to your work,' snapped Tansu. 'It's what we want. Enough pictures like that and we get the sympathy we need from the rest of the world.'

She looked up as she heard a helicopter approaching.

'That'll be Albert.'

She walked out into the harsh sunlight, blinking as the helicopter threw up a cloud of dust in the farmyard.

Albert climbed out, his linen jacket and trousers crumpled.

'I've got ten minutes, Tansu. The Turks have restricted private flying. We've come in under their radar but they're tracking us, so I need to get to Ankara as soon as possible. Is everything set?'

Tansu nodded.

'Come in, you look as though you need a change of clothes.'

He followed her into the operations room. The men and women there watched him furtively, not daring to speak. They had heard of Albert, the banker, Albert their President in waiting, but he was the man who gave Tansu orders. And the man who could do that and succeed was a man to be feared, even above the Turks.

Tansu took him through to her bedroom. The frightened maid fled. Tansu shut the door and slowly walked towards him.

He looked at the combat trousers and military jacket. 'Later,' he said abruptly. Surprised, she glared at him as he went on. 'I saw CNN on the flight here. It's going well. When do you push the others into Greece.'

Pulling herself together she looked at her watch.

'Departure in an hour. We can't wait longer. The Turks are bringing up heavy stuff, tanks. We've blocked the main roads but we've got reports they're manoeuvring across country.'

Albert stripped off his jacket. 'That'll make good television. What about the Greeks?'

'They've been moving up troops, flying some in to Alexandro-poulis and Edirne. But they've mainly demanded that the Turks deal with the situation. The BBC World Service reported an hour ago that the EU Defence Ministers are meeting and the UN Security Council will meet later today.'

'Too late.' Albert pulled out a suit from the case on the chair by Tansu's bed and started putting on the trousers.

'You're sure all the weapons have got to Ankara?'

'Yes. Every single one. It was easy in all the chaos.'

Albert put on a fresh shirt, lifted his neck to fix his tie.

'And our fighters in Ankara? Are there enough people to support them when they attack the Parliament building?'

Tansu leaned over and straightened his collar.

'You'll have no problems. There are two hundred and thirty fighters including those under cover in the Parliament building. Then we've got a hundred and eighty thousand of our people massed in Ankara already. Another three hundred thousand are on their way. It's unstoppable. More and more are joining in. You'll get the Parliament building. It's just the Greeks we need to worry about now. Making sure they march into Turkey.'

Albert picked up a brush and ran it through his hair.

'Well, there don't seem to be a lot of them on alert at the moment. If they don't march in we'll be in trouble. We can't hold the Turkish military for long once they get organised.'

'Leave that to me,' Tansu touched his lips with hers. 'Now get to Ankara.' She stood back. 'You look like a President now,' she said, fleetingly wondering why he'd pulled away.

She walked with him to the helicopter.

He put his mouth to her ear. 'Make sure some of our people get in the way of those Turkish tanks. We need the pictures.'

Just as he was about to climb on board, he shouted. 'I almost forgot. Have you killed that bitch Charlie yet?'

Tansu stopped abruptly. 'I thought you knew. Our team tried to get her early this morning. She was going to her apartment in Paris. Her bodyguard got her out. We missed.' She hesitated, not knowing how to tell the rest of it.

Albert read the pause, saw the flicker of fear in her eyes.

'And?'

'Francesca was killed,' she said baldy.

He went rigid, then quite suddenly put his hand on the doorframe.

'That saves me doing it.' He turned and looked her squarely in the face. 'But don't fail. I want the bitch dead.'

He climbed in and closed the door.

She stood and watched the helicopter until it was out of sight.

A short man in khaki denims and a loose jacket came up to her. 'Message from Ankara.'

She nodded, but her mind was half on Albert. By tomorrow night if all went well, he would be the President of the newly born Kurdish homeland. Kurdistan. She ran the word around her mind. But if the Greeks didn't attack the Turks as he'd anticipated, then tomorrow night might see him dead. It was the first time she'd thought of failure and she shivered slightly.

'Are you alright, Tansu?' the man asked, pulling his jacket tighter in a nervous tug.

She blinked. 'Yes. Of course. What's the message?'

'The teams are ready to attack the Parliament building.'

She imagined them, doing as she had done on her operations. Waiting in safe houses. Nervously inspecting and re-inspecting their weapons. Or half submerged in sewage in the tunnels deep underground. Or sweating in the cabs of lorry loads of explosive ready to slink out of a garage and drive to a target. Or, on this occasion, to drive at speed behind blocking cars to break through the Turkish barricades. To allow the lorries to reach their targets. The drivers knowing they had seconds in which to jump out and to save themselves.

She ran her hand across her forehead. 'Have we really got as much cover in Ankara as we hoped?'

'Reports are coming in from all over the city. Our people are there in thousands and thousands. Every checkpoint is covered. Roads and squares where the military are out in force are surrounded by us. Our people are ready to move when you give the order.'

'And the other cities?'

'The same.'

Tansu looked out across the hills and the sunburnt grasslands looking an even deeper brown in the setting sun.

'Give the orders to get the crowds moving onto the checkpoints and military secure areas. Now. It'll be fully dark in thirty minutes. The police and soldiers will be fully occupied with crowd control by then. In one hour give the order to the teams to move in on the Parliament and other buildings.'

He looked puzzled.

'But you'll give the orders yourself, won't you?'

She gave him a faraway look.

'No. I've decided to lead us across the border into Alexandropoulis personally. We can't afford to fail there. We've got to get the Greeks to retaliate.'

He swallowed.

'This isn't wise, Tansu.'

'Do as you're told,' she snapped icily. 'And get me that truck.' She pointed to a green Toyota pickup by the farmyard gate.

*

Tansu focussed her binoculars on the Turkish Customs Post. It hadn't been strengthened. Thirty or forty soldiers hovered in front of it, some smoking, others leaning on their weapons. It was just a token force. The Turks wanted them to get across the border. Beyond, at the Greek border post, a large number of soldiers were drawn up, in a formal display of strength, at least a hundred and fifty. They looked efficient and ready for action. They could deal a blow which could bring the whole exodus to a shuddering halt.

Sweating slightly, she reviewed her strategy. It was difficult to manoeuvre the mass of the Kurds in a flanking movement, so the main body had to make a frontal assault. She could lead or she could drive. And she'd decided to drive. A few PKK fighters would lead the charge and she would follow behind the crowd with the other fighters. They were more frightened of her than the Greeks and would keep the mob going when they stalled if the Greeks opened fire.

She nodded to her bodyguards and they slowly drove up to the rear of the buzzing, humming crowd. She wore a chador, choosing that to identify with the main body of women who sat, uncertain, in groups on the ground.

Picking up a microphone she shouted into it.

'People of Kurdistan, the Turks are coming in their tanks, with their machine guns. We must run. Run.'

Electrified, the crowd shimmered as people started to move, women getting up, children screaming in alarm as the adults suddenly overshadowed them.

'Run,' screamed Tansu.

The stampede broke. Shrieking, yelling, pushing, shoving they started running. Stamping over figures who'd stumbled and fallen.

The Turkish soldiers heard the howl far too late. Looking up, they saw the head of the mob already streaking towards them. Unable to run, they rammed home the bolts on their weapons and fired off a ragged volley.

A dozen Kurds fell, screaming in pain or flopping down as the bullets struck home. The PKK team fired on the run, ripping into the soldiers, then the mob was on them, surrounding each of them in circular groups, arms and legs pumping as the crowd became individuals letting their terror explode into rage.

Tansu's bodyguard held out his mobile.

'HQ reports we're breaking through all the way down the line. We've crossed the Tunca and Meric rivers in Edirne and we've breached the border on a three kilometre front.

Ahead, Tansu heard the rattle of organised gunfire.

'What's happening up there?'

Another bodyguard touched her shoulder.

'The Greeks have stopped us. They've lined the road and fired over our heads.'

Tansu suddenly felt weak. She should have been up there, leading them. Another minute and the mob would turn back.

She speed dialled her mobile, trying to get the team leader up front.

The bodyguard saw the number she dialled.

'It's no good,' he yelled, 'he's dead.'

'Get me his number two.'

The bodyguard dialled, gave her the mobile.

'This is Tansu. You've got ten seconds to get going, d'you hear? Open fire and charge for the Greeks. Get that fucking crowd going. Ten seconds.'

She turned to the bodyguards, pointed to the slowing mob in front of her.

'Fire over their heads.'

The rattle of gunfire galvanised the horde, jumping them into a running, screaming rabble pushing into the people in front of them.

'The Turks are coming,' yelled Tansu through the microphone. 'They're right behind us.'

A wave rippled forward, driving them on towards the Greek customs post.

Suddenly two Greek soldiers fell, blood oozing over their uniforms. The Greek Commander watched as the crowd saw it, howled savagely and started down the road towards him.

'Pick your targets. Fire,' he yelled.

The automatic weapons scythed into the crowd. The front line disappeared under the feet of those behind them, berserk now, intent only on killing the Greek soldiers in front to save them from the Turks behind. The noise crescendoed to an unearthly bellow as the whole ten thousand Kurds took off as one and ran, shaking the ground, down the road towards the Greeks.

'The Greeks have fired into us,' the bodyguard said calmly.

Tansu nodded. There was nothing she could do now. Only wait.

The bodyguard answered his mobile. 'The Greeks have opened fire west of Edirne, we've had many casualties.'

'Thank you,' she said.

The firing suddenly died away, the howl of the mob breaking down to the keening of the women tending the dead and wounded.

The bodyguard listened to his mobile, then a broad grin lit his face. 'The Greeks have abandoned the post. They're regrouping a kilometre up the road. Do you want us to go on?'

She shook her head.

'No. Not straight into them. Spread out north and bypass them. Join up with the others. We've got to help our people in Edirne. Tell the crowd behind us to move up. Get the message to Istanbul. Every available Kurd is to push on.'

She banged on the roof of the truck. 'Move on.'

The bodyguard's mobile buzzed again. He listened.

'They've broken through,' he shouted.

'Who has, where,' she said coldly. 'Report properly.'

He swallowed. 'At Edirne. We're well into Greece there now.'

'There's news coming from Ankara,' another guard said. 'There's fighting throughout the city. Heavy casualties on both sides. But a huge mass of our people are entering the city from all...' he broke off, 'wait a minute.' He listened, a wide smile creasing his face. He threw his arm up. 'We're attacking the Parliament building.'

'I hope they kill all the fucking Turkish politicians in it,' spat Tansu.

CHAPTER SIXTY-TWO

Hammond stared at Lev speaking from the plasma screen which dominated the Emergency Response Communications Centre buried five stories under the Prime Minister's office in Downing Street. The deep shadows under Lev's eyes emphasised the starkness of his message.

'G8SUR now estimates there to be three hundred and fifty thousand Kurds in Ankara, one hundred and thirty thousand moving west deeper into Greece, and over one million spread through Turkey heading generally towards Istanbul. There are huge new movements of them around the Turkish/Iraq border beginning to shift in the direction of central Turkey.'

The PM looked round the room as if to find an answer in the faces of the people assembled there, the Defence Secretary, the Foreign Secretary, the Chief of Staff, the aides, the advisers, but they remained silent, as if numbed by the speed and size of the mass movement of people.

One of the security doors hissed open to let through an aide who walked briskly up to the Foreign Secretary. He took a note from the woman's hand and read it. He leant over and handed it to the PM.

'The UN Security Council is deadlocked. The French won't support a resolution to send UN troops in.'

Hammond's lips tightened. 'What a surprise.'

The PM watched the security door close behind the woman, then gave a short bark of laughter.

'A few months ago she told me the PKK was finished, the Kurds would never swamp Turkey. And I believed her.'

Hammond felt Julia move against him as she suddenly leant

towards her computer. 'You'll want to see this,' she said flatly, 'I'll put it on the screen.'

The faces of the people in the room suddenly whitened in the glare of the neon ceiling lights as they looked up at the plasma screen.

A CNN reporter was lifting up his microphone.

'I am speaking to the President of the new Kurdish homeland, Kurdistan.' He turned to face Albert. 'You claim to be President of Kurdistan. But it doesn't exist.'

Albert smiled into the camera, calm, polite, persuasive.

'Kurdistan was the ancient homeland of the Kurds,' he said. 'For centuries we have been oppressed and fought over. Now our people have had enough and our inner circle have elected me to be President of Kurdistan. I intend to bring Turkey to a standstill economically and politically until our homeland becomes a recognised legal entity.'

'So how can you be President of a country that doesn't exist?'

Albert looked at him contemptuously.

'The Turkish Government, their military and police force have killed three thousand, four hundred Kurds in the last few days. They have driven over one hundred and sixty thousand of us out of Turkey by land and sea into Greece. There are ten million of us.' He paused. 'How many more Kurds will the world allow the Turks to kill and expel before Kurdistan becomes a reality?'

Hammond flicked off the bulletin.

'That bastard,' breathed the PM.

A smartly dressed woman hurried up to the Defence Secretary, whispered in his ear. The Defence Secretary nodded and turned to the PM.

' "That bastard", as you call him, has persuaded the French to call off agreement to the EU Army. The G8 representative at the EU Defence Ministry has just reported deadlock. The Belgians are now supporting the French. The Greeks are now threatening to take action themselves.'

The PM suddenly looked old. His face was grey and a tic worked under his left eye.

'If Greece go into Turkey the whole war can spread. The Turks will fight and that could bring in the Kurds from Iraq and then the Muslims from the Middle East.'

The Chief of Staff grunted. 'And on to Pakistan. This whole thing can set off Kashmir again. And, if so, India will retaliate.' He stopped.

A computer keyboard chattered in the corner, a secretary bent over the console.

The Defence Minister cleared his throat.

'Perhaps we should . . .'

The PM put his hand up to stop him as a green phone rang by his elbow. He picked up the receiver.

'Yes.'

'Yes.'

'I see. Surely you . . .'

He looked surprised.

'The line's gone dead,' he shouted over his shoulder. The technician sitting in front of the communications bank shook his head. 'The caller cut off,' he said.

The PM stood up, as if unable to bear the tension any longer.

'That was the Turkish Ambassador. The PKK have seized the Parliament building. They're holding a number of Government Ministers hostage.' His voice grated. 'The Turkish Army Generals have taken over the government of Turkey.'

The chatter of the keyboard stopped.

The Chief of Staff looked stunned. 'They'll never give in to the Kurds.'

The Foreign Secretary's voice took on a pleading note. 'Surely there are enough Ministers still functioning to run the Government.'

Lev's voice cut into the room from the plasma screen.

'We've had an updated report that seven members of the Turkish Government were killed when the PKK stormed the Parliament building.'

'Then Turkey's going to war.' The PM rubbed a hand across his forehead. 'Unless,' he looked at Hammond, 'unless G8 can eliminate that bastard Albert and the PKK Leader, what's her name?'

'Tansu,' supplied Julia.

The Foreign Secretary tugged at his tie.

'What good will that do?'

'The PM's right,' said Hammond. 'The PKK were a spent force until Celik's death. Albert arranged that and the Tansu woman's been brilliant, she's completely turned the PKK around. Diyarbakir, now this. Two million Kurds on the move. More to come. And where did the weapons come from to arm the PKK for the attacks in Ankara? If we can take Albert and Tansu out, the PKK won't survive. We have a chance of giving the Turks time to regroup. We've already got teams in Turkey searching for them. If we get them we might just gain enough time to stop the Greeks marching in.'

'Won't the Turks do it?' the Chief of Staff said crisply.

'I don't care who does it,' the PM leaned forward. 'It's the only option on the table.' He jutted his chin towards the Chief of Staff. 'Or can you bring off something spectacular in the EU Defence Ministers' meeting? Persuade the French to help out perhaps.'

The Chief of Staff shifted in his chair, looked at the Defence Minister.

Julia's computer buzzed.

'G8SUR has an urgent update,' she said. 'The pictures are on screen,' she paused, 'now.'

At first it was difficult to discern what G8SUR was relaying to them. Then the pictures cleared and they were watching two lines of tanks stretching for kilometre after kilometre, travelling fast, a fine spume of dust over them.

The Chief of Staff looked at Julia. 'Those are Greek tanks. Where are they?'

She typed a command into the computer.

'Near the Greek border with Edirne and Enez,' she replied.

'That's where the Kurds made their overland crossing into Greece isn't it?' the PM asked.

She nodded.

Relief flooded his face. 'So the Greeks are going to sort them out. Send them back. Thank God.'

Hammond stiffened as another picture flashed onto the screen.

'What are those bridges?'

Again Julia typed in a command to the computers.

She looked at Hammond disbelievingly.

'They're the bridges over the Tunca and Meric rivers. The tanks are driving on into Turkey.'

'Shit,' the Commander in Chief exploded.

But no one heard him.

'Quick, have a look at Enez,' Hammond said.

They sat wordless as they watched a line of tanks stream through Enez, heading towards Istanbul.

One of the PM's telephones rang.

'The Greeks can't be so stupid can they,' said Julia, the paleness of her face accentuated by her dark hair.

The Prime Minister stared at the telephone receiver in his hand, then looked up, his eyes haunted, his voice was so low they could hardly hear him.

'That was the Greek Ambassador. He's informed me that Greece considers the expulsions of Kurds into its territory as an act of aggression by Turkey. As of now they are at war.'

He looked around the communications centre and took in a deep breath.

'Get me the American and Russian Presidents. Get an update from the UN and EU. And get me the Presidents of Iraq, Syria, Iran, Israel and Pakistan. I'll take them in my office. Then I'm getting some sleep.' He looked at Hammond and the Chief of Staff. 'Keep me up to date.' He started to walk away, then turned, anger reddening his gaunt face. 'I can see no reason at all why those fucking Turk and Greek bastards won't continue killing each other. No reason at all.'

The killing started in earnest half an hour later when the first line of Greek tanks met up with the Turkish tanks moving north out of Istanbul. G8SUR gave them a grandstand view in the Communications Centre. The battle had been short. The small unit of Turkish tanks overwhelmed by the mass of Greek armour. The G8SUR pictures showed the burning hulks stuck in the hilly country which had given them no room for defensive manoeuvre.

Julia fed CNN onto the screen in a segment in the left hand corner, the shouting, excited reporters contrasting with the computer monotone commentary of the G8SUR reports.

As the night wore on, they watched Greek naval vessels shelling Izmir and air attacks going in against Turkish air bases at Istanbul and Ankara. The surprise and speed of the Greek attack gave the Turks little time to respond. Then later the Turks had thrown in air attacks against the Greek bases at Thessalonika and Volos.

General fighting broke out in the Turkish sector north of Istanbul, the outskirts rapidly becoming a shambles as the Greek tanks drove on, shelling the Turkish strong points. Several times the Turks rallied, driving the Greek infantry back.

Then the picture began to change. Turkey was in complete chaos. The country had almost come to a halt as Kurds blocked highways, railways and cities. The Turkish military rapidly began to shoot anyone on sight, desperate to manoeuvre troops towards Istanbul.

The scene was terrifying.

The Communications Centre was continually alive with movement as more reports came in. The UN remained deadlocked. The French refusing to join the Draft Resolution, which deplored the situation and called for UN intervention.

'Typical UN,' snorted the Commander in Chief. 'Only they could call the killing of a hundred people an hour deplorable.'

Without a UN Resolution the US, UK and Russia refused to intervene. Instead imposing immediate sanctions and calling on the Greeks and Turks to agree a ceasefire.

The EU, the Foreign Minister said, was irrelevant at that stage.

At seven in the morning, the Greeks crossed the bridges into Istanbul and began fanning out.

As they came on, the Kurds changed tack. The milling, chanting mobs that had slowed and halted the Turks suddenly cleared the roads for the Greeks, cheering and waving as they went by.

At eight o'clock, CNN flashed a video of Albert, filmed by the PKK in a secret hideout and released only to CNN.

Albert, still immaculate, still smiling, still calm, announced that another half million Kurds were just assembling to march into the west of Turkey. At that moment, he said, eleven Turkish airfields were occupied by tens of thousands of Kurds blocking in the aircraft there and choking the roads. Military bases had been swamped by more thousands, by sheer force of numbers. Turkey, he announced, was at a standstill.

At ten that morning, reports were coming in of electricity pylons, gas, water and fuel supplies being sabotaged by PKK and Kurdish elements.

The atmosphere in the Communications Centre was foul as the

air conditioning struggled to cope with the constant movement of people and their stale breath and sweat as they urgently tried to keep up with the speed of the Turkish collapse.

It came at three thirty in the afternoon with the Greeks still a hundred kilometres from Ankara.

In an electrifying broadcast, the exhausted Turkish Defence Minister spoke to the world on Turkish Television.

Haltingly, prompted by his written text, he announced a cease-fire with the Greeks. A Kurdish homeland was to be established as a sovereign nation with Diyarbakir as its capital. The Kurds would return home. The details were to be supervised by the UN.

An hour later another video was released by the PKK. The camera zoomed in and the Communications Centre was filled with Albert's presence.

'As President of the new State of Kurdistan, I welcome the negotiations under UN supervision to determine our future as the newest member of the international community.'

The camera panned away to look out across the mosques, stone houses and basalt walls of Diyarbakir.

'Diyarbakir. The capital of Kurdistan.' He paused. 'I show you the face of tomorrow.'

*

An hour later Hammond and Julia were summoned to the PM's private office.

The PM had changed. The look of helplessness had been replaced by a new energy.

'Thanks for coming,' he said briskly. 'The ceasefire's holding, I take it?'

Hammond nodded. 'For the moment.'

The hunted look flashed fleetingly into the PM's face.

'What do you mean, "for the moment"?'

Hammond felt tired. 'I mean that while the Kurds can negotiate at the UN, can actually establish a new state and run it, the ceasefire will hold.'

The PM's brow cleared.

'Well that's obvious,' he said with newfound confidence.

Hammond tried again.

'If Albert and the PKK Leader, Tansu, are eliminated, who will hold the PKK, the Kurds, together?'

'There must be others.'

'But no one with their credentials.'

The PM stared at him.

'They tried to kill you.'

'They'll try again,' Hammond gave a small shrug. 'Once those people set a target they never stop. I can live with that, but it's not the point. The point is, that if Kurdistan works then we have a real chance of peace spreading out into the Middle East and beyond. Albert and Tansu can give peace the best chance it's got.'

Slowly the PM walked to the mantelpiece, putting his foot on the brass fender.

'You're right, of course,' he murmured. 'Albert and Tansu must survive, must be protected.' He paused. 'But it's a hell of a sacrifice John'

'I've got Charlie,' Hammond smiled. 'It's no sacrifice at all.'

*

'By the way,' Julia said as they left the PM's office. 'Charlie's flight from Paris landed at Heathrow thirty minutes ago. She's now on the G8 helicopter coming into Battersea. I forgot to tell you.'

She saw the spark of anger reach his eyes.

'But I did phone, Rosie. Got her to put the champagne out.' She laughed. 'She says she's put that hideous picture up.'

'That's Aunt Nina's rose garden. Charlie'll be very upset if it's called hideous.'

'Actually, Rosie . . .' Julia started with a straight face.

Hammond shook his head. 'Don't tell me.' They both laughed.

'I must go.' He looked at her. 'Get some sleep, Julia. You've been up all night.'

'I wish I was meeting Gunter,' she murmured.

'I'm sorry. I know that hurt you very much.' He put his hand on her shoulder.

'I've still got my work,' she said, lifting her laptop briefly. She looked at his worried face. 'Get going, I'm fine. Keep in touch.'

CHAPTER SIXTY-THREE

Hammond's driver parked the car on the Thames side of Battersea Heliport near the edge of the pontoons holding the helipads. Hammond looked at the river racing past, picking out the silver and gold glints as the sunlight caught the wind ruffled water. Just like Charlie, he thought, full of colour, never still, always bubbling, excited by the future.

Albert was wrong. Charlie was the face of tomorrow.

The lights of the helicopter drifted in past the huge towers of Battersea power station, its spotlight joining the sunlight to dance on the river water before settling on the deserted landing circle.

Hammond jumped out of the car and ran to the door, helping to pull it open.

'Charlie,' he shouted over the rattle of the settling rotors.

'She's not coming, John.' Keithley climbed down the steps.

'What do you mean "she's not coming"? She was perfectly alright when I spoke to her yesterday.'

'That was before Albert became President of Kurdistan.'

'What's that got to do with it?'

The rotors had stopped now.

'You know very well,' Keithley said quietly. 'You and Charlie are both on his list, Tansu's hit list.'

'But I'm protected. She'll be safe with me.'

'But you are not perfectly safe whilst she's with you.' Keithley took his arm. 'She told me to tell you.' He hesitated. 'She loves you too much to live with you. Thinking all the time they might kill you because you were looking after her.'

Hammond shook himself away.

'Then I'll talk to her myself.'

'You can't see her. She's already in witness protection,' Keithley said harshly.

'But I must see her,' Hammond said desperately.

'You know you can't, John.' Keithley's voice softened. 'She's doing this for you. You have to accept that.'

Hammond's jaw tightened.

Keithley measured him with his eyes. 'Have you thought about her? She's already survived two PKK attacks. How long do you think she'll live if she's with you. How long do you give yourself?'

The sound of the river suddenly pounded into Hammond's mind, churning and spinning an image of gunfire and Charlie fading into the mist.

Without a word he turned and, half seeing his bodyguards move in to protect him, he walked back to the car and the world Albert had created.